FIC Modes

Modesitt, L.
Imager's challenger.

OCT 2 1 2009

(3593/ke   )

Imager's Challenge

Tor Books by L. E. Modesitt, Jr.

The Imager Portfolio
Imager
Imager's Challenge

The Corean Chronicles
Legacies
Darknesses
Scepters
Alector's Choice
Cadmian's Choice
Soarer's Choice
The Lord-Protector's Daughter

The Saga of Recluce
The Magic of Recluce
The Towers of the Sunset
The Magic Engineer
The Order War
The Death of Chaos
Scion of Cyador
Fall of Angels
The Chaos Balance
The White Order
Colors of Chaos
Magi'i of Cyador
Wellspring of Chaos
Ordermaster
Natural Ordermage
Mage-Guard of Hamor
Arms-Commander (forthcoming)

The Spellsong Cycle
The Soprano Sorceress
The Spellsong War
Darksong Rising
The Shadow Sorceress
Shadowsinger

The Ecolitan Matter
Empire & Ecolitan
(comprising The Ecolitan Operation
and The Ecologic Secession)
Ecolitan Prime
(comprising The Ecologic Envoy
and The Ecolitan Enigma)
The Forever Hero
(comprising Dawn for a Distant
Earth, The Silent Warrior, and
In Endless Twilight)

Timegod's World
(comprising Timediver's Dawn
and The Timegod)

The Ghost Books
Of Tangible Ghosts
The Ghost of the Revelator
Ghost of the White Nights
Ghost of Columbia
(comprising Of Tangible Ghosts
and The Ghost of the Revelator)

The Hammer of Darkness
The Green Progression
The Parafaith War
Adiamante
Gravity Dreams
Octagonal Raven
Archform: Beauty
The Ethos Effect
Flash
The Eternity Artifact
The Elysium Commission
Viewpoints Critical
Haze

Imager's Challenge

The Second Book of the
Imager Portfolio

L. E. MODESITT, JR.

A TOM DOHERTY ASSOCIATES BOOK

NEW YORK

This is a work of fiction. All of the characters, organizations, and events portrayed in this novel are either products of the author's imagination or are used fictitiously.

IMAGER'S CHALLENGE: THE SECOND BOOK OF THE IMAGER PORTFOLIO

Copyright © 2009 by L. E. Modesitt, Jr.

All rights reserved.

Map by Jackie Aher

A Tor Book
Published by Tom Doherty Associates, LLC
175 Fifth Avenue
New York, NY 10010

www.tor-forge.com

Tor® is a registered trademark of Tom Doherty Associates, LLC.

Library of Congress Cataloging-in-Publication Data

Modesitt, L. E.
    Imager's challenge : the second book of the Imager portfolio /
L.E. Modesitt, Jr.
        p. cm. — (Imager portfolio ; 2)
    "A Tom Doherty Associates book."
    ISBN 978-0-7653-2126-8
    I. Title.
    PS3563.O264I44 2009
    813'.54—dc22

                                                2009019454

First Edition: October 2009

Printed in the United States of America

0 9 8 7 6 5 4 3 2 1

For David and Carol Ann Nyman

CHARACTERS

CIVIC PATROL

Artois	Commander of Patrollers
Cydarth	Subcommander of Patrollers
Harraf	Captain, Third District
Warydt	Lieutenant, Third District
Mardoyt	Lieutenant, Headquarters

HIGH HOLDERS

Ryel D'Alte
  Irenya D'Ryel [Wife]
  Johanyr D'Imager [Disinherited Son]
  Dulyk D'Ryel [Son and Heir]
  Iryela D'Ryel [Daughter]
  Alynat D'Ryel [Nephew]
Suyrien D'Alte [Chief Councilor]
  Kandryl D'Suyrien-Alte [Younger son]

IMAGERS

Poincaryt	Maitre D'Esprit [Head of Collegium]
Dichartyn	Maitre D'Esprit [Head of Collegium Security]
Dhelyn	Maitre D'Structure [Head of Westisle Collegium]
Dyana	Maitre D'Structure
Jhulian	Maitre D'Structure [Justice]
Rholyn	Maitre D'Structure [Advocate/Councilor from the Collegium]
Schorzat	Maitre D'Structure [Head of Field Operations]
Ferlyn	Maitre D'Aspect

Chassendri	Maitre D'Aspect
Ghaend	Maitre D'Aspect
Draffyd	Maitre D'Aspect [Doctor]
Heisbyl	Maitre D'Aspect
Quaelyn	Maitre D'Aspect [Master of Patterns]
Rhennthyl	Maitre D'Aspect [Collegium Liaison to Civic Patrol]
Isola	Chorister

EXECUTIVE COUNCIL OF SOLIDAR
Suyrien D'Alte
Caartyl D'Artisan
Glendyl D'Factorius

FACTORS
Chenkyr D'Factorius [Rhennthyl's Father]
Rousel D'Factorius [Rhennthyl's Brother]
    Remaya D'Rousel [Rousel's Wife]
Veblynt D'Factorius [Paper Factor]
Ferdinand D'Factorius [Stone/Brick Factor]

Honor is all too often an excuse to abuse power.

Belief does not make an image, but can destroy one.

The philosophers assume that the rules of the world do not change;

that is a false truth.

What is unseen cannot be separated from what one images.

Do not trust those who will not follow their own tenets.

Guilt cannot be imaged, but it can destroy an imager.

The thought is the deed.

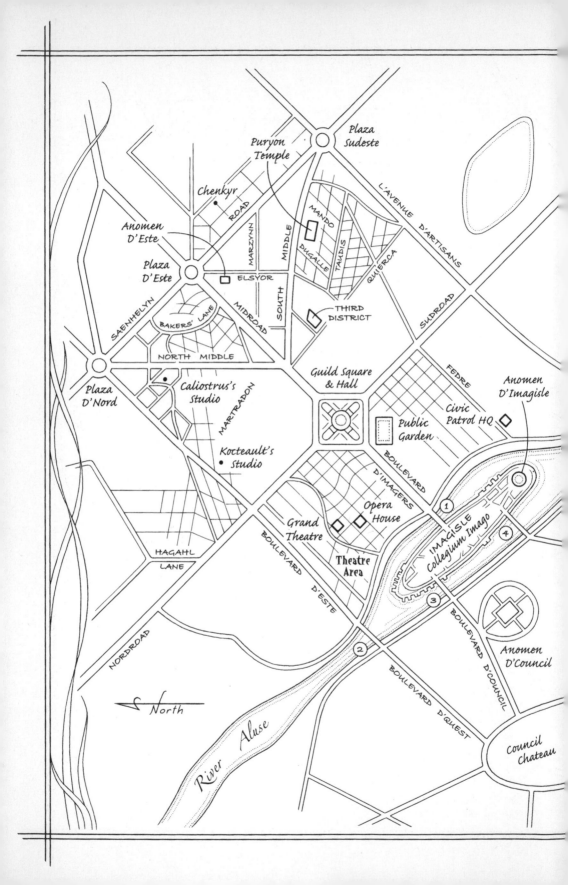

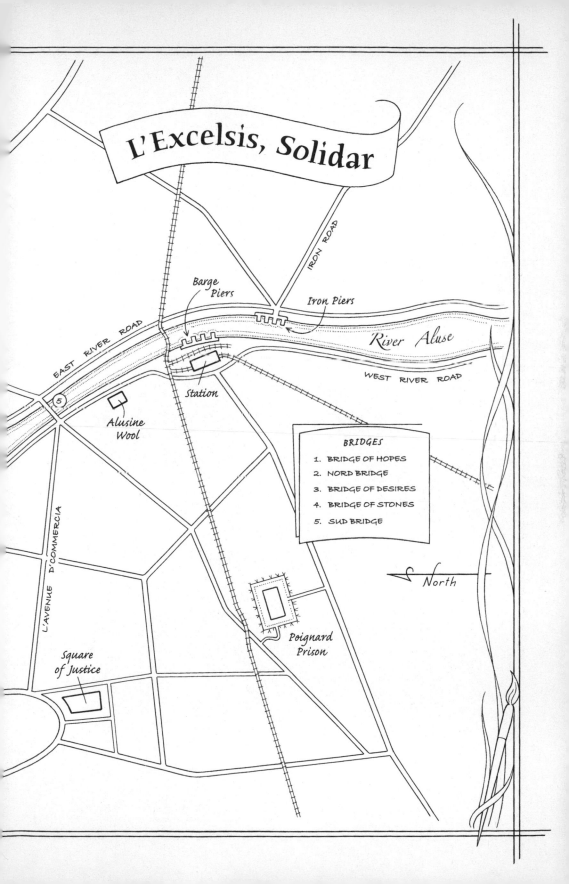

L'Excelsis, Solidar

IRON ROAD

Barge
Piers

Iron Piers

River Aluse

EAST RIVER ROAD

WEST RIVER ROAD

Station

⑤

Alusine
Wool

L'AVENUE D'COMMERCIA

BRIDGES

1. BRIDGE OF HOPES
2. NORD BRIDGE
3. BRIDGE OF DESIRES
4. BRIDGE OF STONES
5. SUD BRIDGE

North

Poignard
Prison

Square
of Justice

Imager's Challenge

On Vendrei, the twentieth of Erntyn, just before the bells rang out the seventh glass of the morning, I hurried across the quadrangle of the Collegium to the administration building to meet with Master Dichartyn—imager Maitre D'Esprit, the director of all security operations for the imagers of Solidar, the second-most senior imager of the Collegium Imago, and my immediate superior. The faint mist that had hovered above the grass earlier had lifted, and the morning was cooler than usual, perhaps foreshadowing the end of harvest and the coming chill of fall. Both moons were high in the morning sky, with Artiema full and Erion waning, although they were easy to miss in the white sunlight angling over L'Excelsis, sunlight that tended to turn the granite buildings of Imagisle a whitish gray.

As I reached the open door to Master Dichartyn's first-floor study, the first bell rang out from the tower of Anomen Imagisle.

"Come in, Rhennthyl."

I entered the small room with its single desk and bookcase, and but two chairs. Master Dichartyn stood beside the narrow window with its louvered leaded glass panes cranked full open. He turned and nodded for me to close the door. His dark brown hair was shot with gray, more than even a few months before, it seemed to me, but the circles under his eyes did not seem quite so dark, and his narrow face was not quite so haggard. A faint smile rested on his lips.

I closed the door, but did not sit.

"How are you feeling, Rhenn?"

"Most of the soreness in my ribs is gone, and Master Draffyd feels that I'm ready. He did suggest that I wear the rib brace for another two weeks as a precautionary measure."

"Given your . . . tendencies, that's doubtless wise." He gestured toward the writing desk, on which rested a silver pin—the four-pointed star of the Collegium, encircled by a thin band of silver. "You've seen those, haven't you?"

"Only on Master Poincaryt, sir. I wondered if he wore it because he was the head of the Collegium."

Master Dichartyn shook his head. "You know we don't wear images of rank . . . not precisely. The pin merely signifies that you are a master imager, but not what class of master. We've found that it reduces misunderstandings for those imagers who have to work outside the Collegium. You wouldn't be wearing it except for your assignment as Collegium liaison to the Civic Patrol of L'Excelsis." He paused. "Go on. Put it on."

I picked up the pin and fastened it onto my gray waistcoat—the same cut and style as worn by all imagers—at the same spot where Master Poincaryt had worn his, just below the point of the left collar of my pale gray shirt.

"Good. That's where it belongs. Now . . . take it off. You only wear it while you're away from the Collegium and on duty with the Patrol—or going to or returning from such duty."

"Yes, sir."

"You'll report to Commander Artois at eighth glass on Lundi. After that, I imagine you'll have to be there at seventh glass. Do you know where the Patrol headquarters are?"

"They're a block or so up Fedre from East River Road, aren't they?"

"That's right. Now . . ." Master Dichartyn fingered his clean-shaven chin, not that any imager was bearded, as he often did when he was considering how to word something precisely. "Commander Artois is a solid, sometimes brilliant man. He doesn't like the Collegium, but he does like imagers like you—too brave for your own good. He knows that you've taken out the Ferran and three other assassins." Master Dichartyn smiled wryly. "He also doesn't like facts being kept from him, but he's not terribly fond of surmises or other ideas that aren't backed with solid evidence. This could present a certain problem for you."

I could see that, because I often felt how things might go long before I could prove it. While I was usually right, I certainly wasn't infallible, and that could prove difficult.

"Oh . . . you might be interested to know that while you were recovering, the First Minister of Ferrum recalled their delegation to Ferrial for consultations and a proper period of mourning for the death of Envoy Vhillar."

"Did Master Poincaryt have to suggest anything?" I wanted to know if the head of the Collegium had been required to use the threat of revealing that Vhillar had been a renegade imager.

"Apparently not." There was a glint in Master Dichartyn's eyes before he added, "The letter of sympathy for the unfortunate accident did mention that

Master Poincaryt also sent his regrets for the loss of such an able envoy with talents that were far beyond his portfolio. That was sufficient, it appears."

I nodded.

"From time to time, you will continue to meet with Maitre Dyana, Rhenn-thyl. Your skills in indirection may be adequate for the civic patrollers, but they leave something to be desired for someone who will need to deal with High Holders in the future."

That was a veiled reminder and reprimand all in one. "Yes, sir."

"Now . . . so far as your new duties go . . . you've studied the procedures manual of the Civic Patrol closely, but remember that events on the street sel-dom accommodate themselves to written procedures. I'm certain that you've considered this, but wherever possible, let the patrollers have the credit for what happens. If matters go badly, and it is your fault, take the blame. Take all of it. Do you understand?"

"Yes, sir." What that meant was that matters had better not go badly where I was involved.

"Do you have any questions?"

"No, sir." I didn't know enough about my new duties to have questions, and as in so many events of the past year, I had the feeling that by the time I knew enough to ask questions, it would be too late.

"Unless you run into extreme difficulties, I'll see you here next Jeudi eve-ning at half past five."

"Next Jeudi at half past five."

He nodded, and I inclined my head in return, then opened the door to the small study, a chamber most modest for the second-most powerful im-ager in Solidar, and perhaps in the entire world of Terahnar.

As I walked across the quadrangle to return to my quarters and to con-tinue my studies of the procedures manual of the Civic Patrol, I couldn't help but wonder over the circumstances that had brought me from a journeyman portraiturist to an imager Maitre D'Aspect. While I certainly hadn't planned on being an imager, I knew that being an imager was far more palatable to my father than being an artist had been. As an imager, even as a low-level master, I had status, even a hint of power, and that was something my father the wool factor could appreciate, and now that I had a beautiful and accept-able young woman in Seliora interested in me, my mother was hopeful that, despite her Pharsi background, a marriage would be in the offing.

There were a few problems with being an imager that they did tend to gloss over, such as my having been wounded twice in the past year, and others that I hadn't mentioned in any detail to them, such as my unresolved difficulties with High Holder Ryel, who was absolutely certain, sooner or later, to try to destroy me in some fashion or another, or the fact that Seliora's family, while certainly wealthy, still possessed certain connections that were highly useful, but not necessarily totally legal.

Although Samedi was the first day of the weekend for most people in L'Excelsis, for me the weekend didn't begin until almost noon—at the earliest. I still had to rise just before dawn and hurry down to the exercise chambers. Because of the bruises and other injuries I'd suffered in dealing with the Ferran spy and his assassins after the Council's Harvest Ball, I couldn't do a number of the exercises, and my running was far slower than it had been. After the four-mille run, I just stood there on the west side of the quadrangle, catching my breath, panting, and sweating. My ribs ached, but not so badly as they had almost three weeks earlier.

Clovyl stepped over to me. "Not too bad for a cripple." Even though he was an imager tertius, he was in charge of conditioning and training for all imagers in the covert branch of the Collegium, and he knew exactly how much to press me. "You're improving."

Not too bad at all, considering I'd only been able to run for the past week or so, but then, I'd been in good shape before the explosion that had thrown me into the stone wall surrounding the Council Chateau, and my shields had taken the brunt of the impact, although Master Draffyd had pointed out that was also why I'd been bruised all over, because they had distributed the impact as much as cushioning it.

"We'll wait another few weeks before you get more training in hand-to-hand combat," he added. "Master Dichartyn thinks you'll need it sooner or later."

I just nodded. My suspicions were that Master Dichartyn felt I needed it more to keep me humble than for any other reason . . . but he'd been right most of the time. I just had to remember what Seliora's Pharsi grandmother had said—that while Master Dichartyn and the Collegium were not my enemies, neither were they my friends. The Collegium looked out for the best interests of imagers as a whole, not for individual imagers, and individuals often paid the price. That was why Claustyn—one of the friendliest imagers I'd known—had died in Caenen, the only reminder a stone plaque bearing his name on the memorial wall adjoining the dining hall. I didn't even know how or why he'd died.

"I'll let you know," Clovyl added before turning away and addressing Dartazn. "You're slowing down there."

"Late night last night, sir." Dartazn smiled apologetically.

I couldn't help grinning as I walked back toward my quarters in the building that housed single imagers tertius and a few single junior masters like me.

After showering and shaving, I dressed and headed for the dining hall. Once there, I still felt strange taking a seat at the masters' table, the smaller table at one end of the hall, set perpendicular to the two long tables, one for imagers primus, and the other for imagers secondus and tertius. My lack of ease came from the fact that I'd only been a master for a little over two weeks, and I was by far the youngest at the table. Ferlyn was the only master who was close to my age—the only officially revealed master, at least, because some of the field and covert operatives, such as Baratyn, who headed security at the Council Chateau, held the hidden rank and pay of Maitre D'Aspect. I sat next to Ferlyn, and we were joined by Isola who, although technically a tertius, was granted master privileges as the chorister of the Nameless at the Anomen D'Imagisle.

"Good morning, Rhenn, Ferlyn."

"Good morning," I replied. Isola was always cheerful, and while we were generally expected to attend services on Solayi evening, for me that had been no real problem, because her homilies were usually so good that it didn't bother me that I wasn't even sure whether I believed in the Nameless.

"Did either of you see *Veritum* this morning?" asked Ferlyn.

"I'm part of Clovyl's morning torture group. I usually don't get a chance to pick up the newsheets until after breakfast. What's happened now?"

"The Oligarch of Jariola claims that the Ferrans are massing forces on the border next to the coal mines, and Chief Councilor Suyrien has sent a communiqué to Ferrial suggesting that Solidar regards that as a hostile and provocative act."

"Is our southern fleet heading north from Caenen and Tiempre?" asked Isola as she passed the flatcakes and berry syrup to me.

"There's nothing in either *Tableta* or *Veritum*," Ferlyn replied. "The First Speaker of Tiempre issued another warning about our trade agreement with Caenen, though."

"Their implied surrender," I said dryly. "What did he say?"

"Something about now Solidar would pay deeply and in its heart for the treachery of its agreement with the demons of Caenen, that sort of thing." Ferlyn snorted.

"They're unhappy we didn't declare war on Caenen over their killings of our envoy's staff members," I suggested. "Then they could have had an excuse to invade and grab land."

"Submissive treaties are a less expensive way for the Council to get cheaper raw materials."

"The Abiertan Assembly is debating a declaration of neutrality, or they were last week," offered Isola. "If war breaks out, that would deny us use of the ports in the Abierto Isles for recoaling and resupply, wouldn't it?"

"If they pass such a measure," Ferlyn replied, "but I'd judge that they're stalling to keep Ferrum from declaring war on them, while they wait to see what we'll do."

That seemed more likely to me, but I concentrated on the corn flatcakes and sausage and syrup, along with the mug of hot tea that I'd poured.

"Does Ferrum have that large a navy?" asked Isola.

"Only ours is larger, and not by much, but our ships are newer and better. They have a larger army and more troop transports. If we didn't stop them on the high seas, they could certainly overrun the Isles."

I didn't pretend to understand the hostility of the Ferrans, especially since both Ferrum and Solidar tended to emphasize freedom of commerce, and neither was controlled by a hereditary ruler, despot, or oligarchy in the way lands like Jariola, Caenen, or Tiempre were. My own experiences with the late and less than honorable Klauzvol Vhillar suggested that they were every bit as ruthless as the Collegium was reputed to be.

I just listened as Isola and Ferlyn talked.

After breakfast, I hurried north along the west side of the quadrangle toward the large, oblong, gray granite building that held workrooms of various sizes, as well as some of the specialized manufacturing chambers—all lead-lined so that one imager's work didn't affect another's, the same reason why we all had separate quarters with lead-lined walls and leaded glass windows—because imagers' dreams and thoughtless desires could have most unfortunate consequences—as I well knew. After I'd become an imager tertius, Master Dichartyn had arranged for one of the smallest workrooms with northern light to be turned into a portraiture studio, and one of my additional duties, as possible, was to paint the portraits of senior imagers. I'd only just completed the first—that of Master Poincaryt—not only the head of the Collegium, but also a Maitre D'Esprit, one of but two, the other being Master Dichartyn. Master Poincaryt was supposed to come by the studio to see it sometime after eighth glass. He hadn't seen the finished version, and I was more than a bit nervous about showing it to him.

Because I reached my workroom-studio with a good quarter glass to spare, I spent the time sketching an alternative design for the portrait of Seliora. While the convention was to paint most portraits—especially of women—in a sitting position, I'd decided to do Seliora standing. I'd seen the miniature that Emanus had done of his unacknowledged daughter—Madame Juniae D'Shendael—and that had been done with her standing, and it had a power that a sitting portrait seldom possessed.

Absently, I still wondered exactly what the connection had been between Vhillar and Madame D'Shendael. They hadn't been lovers. Political allies, perhaps, since Vhillar had represented Ferrum—which opposed all blood-based hereditary nobility, such as the High Holders of Solidar or the Oligarchy of Jariola—and since Madame D'Shendael had been writing and pressing for a Council of Solidar with at least some councilors being directly elected, rather than being appointed by their guilds or associations or by a vote among High Holders.

Just as the first bells of eighth glass began to chime from the anomen tower, Master Poincaryt stepped through the open studio door. "Good morning, Rhennthyl."

"Good morning, sir."

Master Poincaryt frowned, ever so slightly, an expression that lent severity to a lined and squarish face softened but a touch by a chin that was slightly pointed and rounded. Under jet-black hair and heavy eyebrows, also jet-black, his pale gray eyes took in everything, as always. He wore exactly the same gray garb as did every imager, with the addition of a small silver four-pointed star circled in silver and worn high on the left breast of his waistcoat, seemingly identical to the one Master Dichartyn had given me the day before. "Do I want to see the final version of the portrait?"

"I would hope so, sir. But it's not framed, and that will improve the setting."

"Is it that unflattering?" His words were offered with a smile.

"No, sir, but since it's your portrait, in the end you're the one who has to judge."

He laughed. "You flatter me, Rhenn. In the end, the artist is always the judge, for the portrait always outlasts the person painted." He walked over to the easel and studied the image. "It's accurate, and not too unflattering. It's a good work." He paused. "You didn't sign it, Rhenn, not fully."

"According to the Portaiturist Guild, only paintings which are commissioned and sold through the guild can be signed. So I just used my initials— 'R D'I.' That seemed the best compromise. Since it's acceptable, I'll arrange with the cabinetmakers to get it framed."

Master Poincaryt nodded. "Whom do you think you should paint next?"

The person I really wanted to paint next was Seliora, but I'd have to work out how to pay for the paints and supplies for that, since the Collegium had equipped the studio fully, but I didn't want to bring that up with Master Dichartyn. Not yet, anyway. "I hadn't thought about that, sir, but shouldn't it be Master Dichartyn, Master Rholyn, or Master Jhulian?"

"Those would be good choices, but of the three I would suggest Master Rholyn . . . for a number of reasons. I will discuss it with others. Whoever it is will be here next Samedi."

After Master Poincaryt left, I worked more on the design for Seliora's portrait and then tried a rough sketch of Master Rholyn from memory, setting him in the Council chamber at the Chateau, standing below the upper dais where the High Council sat.

Ferlyn and I were the only masters at lunch, unsurprisingly on a sunny Samedi, since there were perhaps a score and a half of Maitres D'Aspect across all of Solidar, only a handful of Maitres D'Structure, and just two Maitres D'Esprit. At present, the Collegium had no Maitre D'Image, and there had been but a handful of imagers that accomplished in the entire history of the Collegium. Most of the masters were married, and seldom took meals in the dining hall, except the noon meal during the week or when they had duties that kept them near the quadrangle.

Afterward, I reread sections of the patroller procedures for a while in the study of my personal chambers. I had mixed feelings about the evening ahead. I knew I'd be glad to be with Seliora, but I couldn't say that I was totally looking forward to a dinner with my parents and two other couples who were their friends.

I walked across the Bridge of Hopes at just before fourth glass, glancing down at the lower than usual gray waters of the River Aluse. I was holding full imager shields, as I'd had to do for months now, although I had doubts that High Holder Ryel would resort to something as direct as assassination, not after he'd had Taudischef Artazt garroted for attempting to have me assassinated. Still, matters couldn't have gotten any better, either, not since the High Holder's daughter had asked me to dance at the Council's Harvest Ball, and flaunted the fact before her younger brother, the heir to his father.

Once across the bridge, I looked for a flower seller, but I didn't see one. Then, no one had taken the place of the woman who had been shot when the Ferran had tried to kill me. In a strange way, I missed her and her faded green and yellow umbrella.

Before I had stood at the corner of East River Road and the Boulevard

D'Imagers all that long, I saw the familiar brass-trimmed brown coach that belonged to my parents. Charlsyn spotted me at close to the same time and eased the coach over to the curb, just in front of the west end of the narrow gardens that flanked the boulevard—behind the low stone wall at the edge of the sidewalk.

"Master Rhennthyl." He nodded.

"Charlsyn, thank you for picking me up." Although Charlsyn had never said a word, I had the feeling that he was as pleased as my mother had been about my becoming an imager master.

"You're most welcome, sir. NordEste Design?"

I nodded, trying not to smile too broadly, then climbed into the coach. Normally, I'd have used a hack to pick up Seliora, but when Mother discovered that, she'd insisted that the family coachman pick both of us up, declaring that it was unseemly that a master imager arrive in a coach for hire. Unseemly, anyway, if certain guests might be there.

From the east side of the Bridge of Hopes, the drive took only about a third of a glass before Charlsyn brought the coach to a halt before the north entrance of NordEste Design on Hagahl Lane. That was the private family entrance, with gray stone steps up to a small square and pillared covered porch that shielded a stone archway, and a polished oak door. NordEste Design was manufactory/crafting hall/home, all in one, to Seliora's family. The yellow brick building with its gray cornerstones rose three stories. All the casements and wooden trim—even the wood of the loading docks at the south end—were stained with a brown oil.

I clambered out and looked up. "If you'd just wait, Charlsyn. She's usually ready."

"Yes, sir."

I continued to carry full shields all the way to the door, but I didn't have a chance to even lift the brass knocker before Bhenyt—Seliora's young cousin—opened the door.

"Master Rhennthyl." He grinned at me. "She's already waiting."

"Thank you, Bhenyt. Lead on."

I followed him up the stairs toward the second level, which held the more public rooms of the two living levels, the second and third levels of the building, since the ground-floor level was given over to workrooms and power loom spaces. The carved balustrades and shimmering brass fixtures emphasized the elegance of the staircase, which opened at the top into an entry more than eight yards wide and ten deep. The walls were paneled in light golden oak from carved baseboards to ceiling. Only a yard or so of the intricate parquet floor was visible, largely covered as it was by a deep maroon carpet, with a border of intertwined golden chains and brilliant green leafy vines. An assortment of various chairs and settees were upholstered in the fabric designs that I now knew had been largely designed by Seliora and her mother. A pianoforte dominated the far end of the hall.

Seliora stood at the front edge of the carpet, wearing a crimson dress, trimmed in black velvet, with a filmy and shimmering black jacket and a matching black scarf. With her black eyes and jet-black hair, the effect was stunning—and not just to me, I'd discovered over the past year. If I could somehow capture that in the portrait . . .

She smiled, and for a moment, all I could do was look. Then I stepped forward and embraced her . . . gently, not wanting to disarrange her, at least not before dealing with my parents and their guests. I did get a warm kiss.

"You look wonderful," I murmured. "As always."

"If you had the chance, you'd tell all the women that."

"Only if they looked so good as you, and that wouldn't ever happen."

Seliora shook her head.

I offered my arm, and we walked down the steps and outside toward the coach. I extended my shields to cover her. Charlsyn kept his eyes on Seliora from the time we walked out the door until I helped her into the coach. So did young Bhenyt, closing the door only after we were both settled into the coach.

Once the coach was moving, Seliora turned to me. "Are there other guests besides the Ferdinands and the Veblynts?"

"Not that I know." I grinned. "What did Grandmama Diestra find out about them?"

Seliora offered a sheepish grin. "Ferdinand not only has his own brick kilns, but he has arrangements with other brick and stone manufactories across Solidar. That wouldn't work except for the ironway, you know," she pointed out. "I was thinking about that when we toured the textile manufactories last summer . . . just how much things have changed in the last century."

Steam engines and turbines had changed the world—in some ways, but not in others.

"What did she find out about Veblynt?" I was interested to know, because Veblynt was a newer acquaintance of my father, newer meaning in the last ten years. "Father had mentioned that he'd started by buying lots of ruined cottons."

"First, he's the son of a former ruined High Holder, who killed himself with an antique dueling pistol or died deliberately in a race, depending on which story you believe, about twenty-five years ago. Grandmama said that

Town of Georgina (KESWICK) Public Library

was too good for him, and that he made High Holder Ryel look like Rholan the Unnamer. Veblynt used what remained of his share of the family fortune and perhaps his wife's dowry to build a paper mill that uses hemp and rags and some sort of clay, I think, and now he supplies most of the paper for the printers in L'Excelsis. Mother thinks he was also an illegitimate son." She looked at me. "What do you think of him?"

"I don't know. He's quite charming. He was, anyway, the last time I met him, but that has to have been a good seven or eight years back."

"You haven't seen him or his wife since then?"

I laughed. "You might recall that I spent most of my time with Master Caliostrus and that my father wasn't all that pleased with my artistic ambitions." I shrugged. "Now I'm more respectable."

"And feared." Seliora tilted her head slightly. "I'll be interested to meet this Factor Veblynt."

"Oh?"

"No one becomes a success in ten years without secrets, especially someone with his background. I'd like to see whether he hides or flaunts them."

"More farsight?"

"Maybe."

I didn't press on that, knowing she'd said what she would.

Charlsyn drove right under the portico of the two-story brick dwelling in the fashionable section of L'Excelsis to the east of the Plaza D'Este, a dwelling large enough to signify prosperity, but definitely not a chateau or a mansion.

We were the first to arrive, but not early enough for me to ask Father or Mother questions because a deep burgundy coach pulled up under the portico right after Charlsyn had let us off and driven toward the stable. So we just waited inside the formal parlor as the other couple made their way to the door and were escorted inside. I could tell it was Veblynt and his wife, because I recalled that he had been shorter and slighter than I even years ago, while Ferdinand was stocky and close to my father's height.

Father made the introductions. "Rhennthyl, you might recall Factorius Veblynt, and this is Madame Eliesa D'Veblynt."

Madame D'Veblynt could have been a cousin—or some other close relation to Dulyk D'Ryel's sister Iryela—as petite and blond as she was, an older version of Iryela in a way.

"I'm pleased to see you both," I offered.

Father looked back to Veblynt. "Rhennthyl is a master imager. Rousel, whom you met last year, handles the business in Kherseilles. He and Remaya had a son this past summer."

"A very junior master, I might add," I quickly interjected, all too aware that I wouldn't have held the rank, at least not openly, if it hadn't been required for my assignment as liaison to the Civic Patrol of L'Excelsis.

"And this is Mistress Seliora D'Shelim. Her family owns NordEste Design," Mother said quickly.

Veblynt was slender, slightly shorter than Seliora. When he smiled, he revealed perfect white teeth, but the corners of his eyes didn't crinkle. "Mistress Seliora . . . the crafting of NordEste is indeed well known, as is all that lies behind it."

Seliora inclined her head politely. "I'm certain that what lies behind your success with your paper mill is far more intriguing."

Mother's eyes flicked toward me, but I just maintained a polite smile.

"Hard work," declared Father abruptly. "That's what's behind anything of value. All the ideas and all the inspiration don't amount to anything without hard work."

"A most blunt and accurate summation, Chenkyr," offered Veblynt.

At that moment, Ferdinand and his wife appeared, and there was another round of introductions, this one matter-of-fact, and before long everyone was seated in the formal parlor, and Nellica was bringing around a tray with the wines everyone had requested. I'd chosen the Dhuensa, and so had Seliora.

"As I recall," Ferdinand said after a sip of his Cambrisio and a moment of silence, "you were once a portraiturist, were you not, Rhenn?"

"I was journeyman for Master Caliostrus. That was before I discovered I had imaging abilities. I even painted a few portraits, mostly of young women and their cats, but also of a factor or two."

"Oh?"

"Factorius Masgayl was the first."

"Ah . . . the rope and cable fellow. I'd imagine he'll be doing quite well with his new facility near the naval yards at Westisle. I heard he won the contracts for the new cruisers, for all the cabling, that is."

"And Rhenn did a marvelous one of Tomaz's niece," Mother added.

"Ah . . . the one of little Aeylana. She looks so alive in that. I'm her unnamed, you know?"

"I didn't know that," Father said, but then he didn't really believe in the old custom of a fallback unnamed guardian, supposedly known by name only to the parents and the chorister of the Nameless.

I merely smiled. I had liked that portrait.

"Does your background as a portraiturist help you as an imager?" asked Eliesa.

I would have appreciated the question more had I not seen the momentary look that had passed from Veblynt to his wife. "I suppose everything helps, but since I'm the first artist who's become an imager in some time, it's probably more a matter of personal inclination than a result of artistic training."

"Can you still paint?" asked Veblynt.

"I can paint. Anyone can paint. I just can't sell anything that I paint."

He merely nodded to my reply, and that suggested he knew more than he was saying.

"Are you painting anything right now?" pressed Eliesa.

"At the moment, madame, I'm engaged in imager business." I smiled. "Except, of course, at times like this, which are seldom enough." Before they could ask another question, I turned to Ferdinand. "With all the concerns about war, how is your business coming?"

The bluff and square-faced Ferdinand shrugged. "It doesn't change much here. If I were in Estisle or Westisle, there would be some more Navy contracts, but they wouldn't be for much. If war breaks out, things will get worse. Afterward, if we win, I might have more business."

"Do you think war will break out?" asked Seliora.

"You might ask Rhenn," Ferdinand said with a laugh.

"He always tells me that he's often the last to know," she replied.

"There will be war," said Father. "The only question is who'll be fighting. There's always someone fighting, and it's all Namer foolishness."

"Don't you get more business when we're involved?" asked Veblynt.

"We get a bit more in terms of yards of wool sold, but the higher quality wool doesn't sell as well. . . ."

Before long, Mother rose and ushered us all into the dining chamber, where Father stood at the head of the table, his hands on the back of the armed chair, and offered the blessing.

"For the grace and warmth from above, for the bounty of the earth below, for all the grace of the world and beyond, for your justice, and for your manifold and great mercies, we offer our thanks and gratitude, both now and evermore, in the spirit of that which cannot be named or imaged."

"In peace and harmony," everyone murmured.

Ferdinand sat to Father's left, and Madame Ferdinand to his right; the Veblynts in the middle of the table, with Eliesa to my right, Seliora across from me, and Mother at the foot of the table to my left.

As soon as everyone had wine, Father offered a simple toast. "To friends and family."

Then he carved the marinated and crisped lamb, and various dishes appeared, beginning with individual salads of wild greens. Then came rice fries, sliced and boiled new potatoes in butter and mint, asparagus under lemon cream, and, of course, dark spicy gravy. Nellica carried them all in with her usual dispatch.

I'd just finished handing the gravy boat to Mother when Eliesa turned to me. "Are there any High Holders at Imagisle?"

"Even the children of High Holders must go to Imagisle, dear," Veblynt said. "Is not that so, Rhenn?"

"Very much so."

"Are they . . . treated the same as others?" Eliesa asked.

"So far as I've seen, everyone is treated in the same fashion." That was true in terms of the way the Collegium operated, but not necessarily in terms of the way people reacted, as I'd discovered with Johanyr, the eldest and most spoiled son of High Holder Ryel, who had tried to maim me for life and whom I'd partly blinded—enough to ruin his imaging and set his father after me.

"Have you known any? Personally, that is?"

"Imagers generally don't talk about their backgrounds, but I've known two, and there certainly might be others."

"I would imagine that with their training they might do well."

"One is a Maitre D'Structure, and she is quite accomplished. The other had far too great an opinion of himself and did not like to work, and ended up partly blinded because of his arrogance."

"I had heard rumors about something like that," mused Veblynt. "That might make matters rather difficult for the Collegium were his father a powerful High Holder."

I smiled. "One runs that risk in doing anything of value, as I imagine you have discovered in building such a profitable enterprise."

"Building something is often the easy part, young Rhenn," replied Veblynt. "Holding it is what takes talent. That's one reason why High Holders are called that."

"Some of them have reputations for, shall we say, ruthlessness," I offered. "Do you think that such reputations are overstated or understated?"

"Both. It depends on the High Holder." Veblynt smiled. "What would you think about Councilor Suyrien?"

"I've only seen him at official occasions," I temporized, "but I'd be most hesitant to cross him without a very good reason."

"That is true . . . from what I know. Yet he is considered a man of honor and moderation compared to, say, those such as High Holder Lhoryn and High Holder Ryel . . . as you may know."

The last words suggested that Veblynt knew that I'd had some dealings with Ryel—and that bothered me, because I'd never told anyone in my family about my blinding his eldest son. Johanyr had been a total bastard, who'd used his position to abuse young women and torment younger imagers. He and his toady Diazt had tried to cripple me, and in self-defense, I'd partly blinded Johanyr so that he couldn't image any longer. The only ones I'd ever told about the depth of my problems with Ryel were Seliora's family—and that was because Grandmama Diestra had discovered them in investigating my suitability as a suitor for Seliora. One never knew, but I doubted that anyone in the Collegium had told Veblynt—and that suggested High Holder Ryel—or Dulyk or Iryela, his other children—had been the ones to spread the word.

"I can't say that I've had any personal dealings with either, with the possible exception of dancing one dance with High Holder Ryel's daughter."

"Rhenn . . . you didn't ever mention that," Mother said, her voice containing hints of wonder and worry.

"That was at the Council's Harvest Ball. She asked me, and my duty required me to dance with her."

"What was she like?"

"She is quite good-looking, much in the same way as Madame D'Veblynt is." I nodded to Eliesa. "In appearance, they might well be related."

Eliesa flushed. "You flatter me."

"I think not." I paused. "I did not mean to imply more than I said, yet you could have changed places with her, and few would have noticed the difference."

"I must confess to being slightly older than Iryela."

I managed a polite and warm smile. "Will you also confess to being distant cousins . . . or some such?"

"Alas, you have discovered one of my secrets, sir."

"You really are related?" asked Mother.

"In a very roundabout way, but I would appreciate it if you did not mention this. Explaining can be so troublesome."

If explaining was so troublesome, why had I been set up to reveal the relationship? To give Veblynt some advantage in dealing with Father? Or was it the first step in High Holder Ryel's campaign against me? Or something else entirely?

"Family ties—and unties—can be most tedious, and better not plumbed in depth," said Veblynt smoothly before turning to Ferdinand. "We will be building an addition to the mill shortly."

"You're looking for stone and brick, like before?" asked Ferdinand, his voice hearty.

"As always."

I glanced at Seliora, but she had already begun to speak. "Eliesa . . . are all the High Holder balls as stiff and formal as Rhenn has said?"

"They are most formal, and the slightest misstatement can lead to difficulties." Eliesa laughed, if with a slight brittleness behind the sound. "That is why so often so little is said, for all the words that are exchanged. You are very fortunate to have wealth without holdings."

"I am fortunate to be able to contribute through honest work to what we have," Seliora replied warmly. "I've found it most rewarding to help create things of beauty. I must say that I pity anyone who must scheme and plot just to hold on to what they have, especially when they create nothing of lasting beauty or substance. Even worse are those who seek to destroy others because they spoke the wrong words."

I managed to suppress a smile at Seliora's ability to say everything so warmly and apparently guilelessly.

"And you, Rhenn, what do you think?" asked Veblynt.

I shrugged. "I was an artist. Now I'm an imager. We all do what we can, but it seems to me that scheming and plotting leaves one with very little in the end."

Veblynt actually frowned thoughtfully. "There are certainly High Holders and even some factors who would disagree with that."

"I'm sure they would, but that's why they're what they are and why I'm what I am."

Ferdinand laughed, perhaps more loudly than necessary. "Well said, Rhenn." He turned to Veblynt. "You know, that's one of the things I like about bricks and stone. I'd almost forgotten."

Almost everyone at the table looked confused.

Following a moment of silence, Ferdinand went on. "Worked stone and well-fired bricks are what they are, and they stay what they are. They don't rot like wood, and they don't say things that they don't mean, like all too many folks do." Then he looked at Father. "Excellent lamb, Chenkyr. Crisped just right, and I can't say that I've had better new potatoes in a long time."

After that, conversation stayed limited to food, the weather, the harvest, and general observations about just how irrational the Caenenans were with their dualogic god. Dessert was a solid apple and raisin cobbler, followed by brandy.

When both the other couples had left, while we were waiting for Charlsyn to bring the coach, I turned to Father. "I know you've always been close to Ferdinand, but why did you decide to invite Veblynt? He's nice enough, but I didn't realize that you were that close."

Father stiffened, as he always did when I asked a question he didn't like. "I just did. Besides, he hasn't been buying the offcasts as much as he once was."

"Dear . . ." Mother interjected, "wasn't it Ferdinand's idea? Didn't he say that it had been too long . . . or something like that?"

"Oh . . . that. He also said something about the fact that Veblynt had contacts, and that they might be useful if the Council had to order more uniforms and cloth goods."

"That poor Eliesa," Mother said. "I feel for her."

I wasn't sure whether I did or not, not after my brief dance with Iryela at the Council's Harvest Ball. I also had the feeling she was far more closely related to Iryela than she was saying.

At that moment, Charlsyn pulled the coach under the portico, and I eased the front door fully open, taking Seliora's arm.

"Will we see you two next week?" asked Mother.

"No. We're having dinner with her family and friends next Samedi. I don't know about Solayi yet."

"Thank you so much," Seliora said. "The dinner was lovely, and you both have been so warm and kind."

"You're very good for Rhenn, dear," Mother said. "I've never seen him so happy."

"He's very good to me. Thank you for a charming evening."

The warmth of her words sent a chill up my spine that lasted until we were in the coach and headed back to NordEste Design. The glass windows chattered in their frames with a gust of wind that foreshadowed the coming cooler winds of fall.

"What did you think of Veblynt?" I asked Seliora.

"He's definitely the son of a ruined High Holder, and he won't forget it. He doesn't like Ryel. He'd be more than pleased if you did in Ryel, but then he'd try to have your throat cut."

"No . . . he'd use me, and find some way to have me vanish without a trace. He still thinks of himself as a High Holder."

"You're right." Seliora nodded. "She's not much better, either." She smiled once more in the dimness of the coach. "That was a nice touch with the comparison to Iryela. You scared her."

I hadn't seen that, but I trusted Seliora's feelings about such things. I didn't understand what role Ferdinand was playing, especially if he'd been the one to suggest that Father invite Veblynt, unless he had a grudge against the man . . . or unless the suggestion was a warning to Father, who tended not to accept words of warning from others. I'd have to see what Master Dichartyn had to say about Veblynt, if he had anything at all to offer. For the moment, there was little enough I could do, except enjoy the little time left with Seliora.

"Next Samedi?"

"Fourth glass." Seliora grinned. "You'll have to put up with my family and their form of maneuvering."

I had the feeling that would be far less stressful, but I didn't want to talk about it. Instead, I put my arms around Seliora for the rest of the coach ride to NordEste Design.

She didn't object. In fact, she had the same thought.

One of the drawbacks to becoming a master, which Master Dichartyn had not been slow to point out, was that I had to take my turn as the duty master for the Collegium every so often on a Solayi—and this Solayi morning was my first duty. Because it was, Master Draffyd, who had helped heal my injuries, would remain at his home in the family dwellings on the north end of Imagisle so that I could send a messenger if something for which I was not prepared did in fact occur. During the previous weeks I'd been briefed on the duties, and from what I could tell, the duty master's task was basically to be present in case of problems, and to handle those that he could and to refer those that he could not to those who could—basically to Maitres Poincaryt, Dichartyn, Jhulian, or Dyana. I could go anywhere in the Collegium, just so long as the prime at the granite duty desk knew exactly where I was. If necessary, in the case of an emergency involving an imager, I could even leave Imagisle, but I sincerely hoped I wouldn't have to do that. There was also a secondus on standby duty in a small room off the receiving hall.

I'd never had duty as either a prime or a second, because such duties generally didn't fall on those still in training, and because I'd come to the Collegium at a far older age than most imagers. My first duties had not occurred until I was a tertius at the Council Chateau.

Before breakfast, I walked the grounds—those around the quadrangle, and that was a pleasure compared to the exercise routine and running I had to do every other day of the week. Since I was supposed to spend a good portion of my duty time in or near the administration building, immediately after breakfast I'd taken my copy of the patroller procedures to the conference room where I'd first been questioned. I'd told Haensyl, the duty prime, when I returned, although he was less than twenty yards away, and there I sat, reviewing the procedures.

I'd just finished the section on apprehension and charges when Haensyl appeared, his youthful face showing a certain worry. "There's a young little sansespoir here, with his taudischef."

A slum child with what amounted to an area gang leader? I stood quickly.

"I'll be right there." After the problems with Diazt and his brother, who'd also been a taudischef, I wasn't all that eager to deal with one, but I didn't suppose anyone was.

Haensyl hurried out, and I followed.

Two figures stood waiting before the polished granite desk in the receiving hall, a chamber where walls, floors, and columns were all polished gray granite. I'd discovered all that gray did have an effect in sobering people. One of those waiting was a squarish, almost squat, man with limp black hair cut in the jagged fashion affected by some of the younger adult male taudisdwellers. He stood no more than to my nose, but there was a toughness about him. The other was a child, probably no more than ten, if that.

"This is Master Rhennthyl," Haensyl said.

The squat man studied me. "You don't look old enough to be a master."

"I am. Rhennthyl D'Imagisle, Maitre D'Aspect. You are?"

The man's posture changed, if slightly. "I beg your pardon, Master Rhennthyl. I'm Horazt."

"You're the taudischef where?" I asked politely.

"Estaudis off South Middle, west quarter. This is Shault here. He . . . he did . . . he created a copper . . . a very bad copper. . . ." He extended an oval piece of copper.

"Ma . . . she said that we didn't have no coins." Shault's look was both defiant and fearful.

I took the copper and studied it. It was either a badly imaged copper or a bad forgery, but I couldn't see why anyone would go to the trouble of forging something as small as a copper. "Shault . . . I'd like you to walk over to the front steps with me. The rest of you stay here."

Horazt frowned, but nodded to the boy.

The boy followed me tentatively. Once we were just outside the administration building, I took a good copper from my wallet and showed it to Shault. "This is a good coin. I'd like you to look at it closely and then see if you can image a better-looking copper."

"You won't hurt me ifn I do?"

"If you can, you can keep the good copper, but I want you to sit on the steps and see if you can image it onto the stone beside you."

Shault sat down. "You really mean it?"

I handed him the copper. "You can keep it if you can make another."

He looked at the copper for a long time, then set it on the stone step.

The second copper wasn't much better than the first, but he was definitely an imager.

"Good. I need the copy, but you can keep the one I gave you. You can stand up."

He wobbled as he stood, and I grasped his shoulder to steady him. "Is Horazt your father or brother?"

"Nah . . . he's Ma's cousin, but he's the taudischef for the west quarter."

What that meant was that the finder's fee would be double—a gold for Shault's mother and a gold for Horazt. "What's your mother's name?"

"Chelya."

"Just Chelya?"

"That's all. Da died when I was little. Ma said it was elveweed."

"You're going to stay here on Imagisle and be an imager, Shault."

"I can't go home?"

"It wouldn't be safe for you," I pointed out. "You know that. Here, you'll have your own room, and three meals a day, as much as you can eat. After a few weeks, your mother can come visit you, and after a longer time, if you want to, you can see her on end-days. You'll have to learn to read and write."

"I know my letters."

But little more, I suspected. "You'll also get paid a few coppers a week."

"Better'n getting beaten . . . I guess."

That was about all I'd get in concessions. "We need to tell Horazt." I stayed close to Shault as we walked back into the receiving hall.

"Well?" asked the taudischef.

"He has imaging ability."

"I knew it."

"Horazt, do you have a full name, an official one?"

"A'course I do. Horazt D'Estaudis."

I should have guessed. "As taudischef, you get a draft on the Banque D'Excelsis for two golds. One gold is for you, the other is for Chelya. You will make sure she gets all of it."

"Couldn't do otherwise, now, could I?"

I smiled. "I will find out if she doesn't get it, and I'll also find out if anything happens to her, and if either happens . . . the west quarter will have a new taudischef."

For a moment he studied me. Then he laughed, wryly. "You know Mama Diestra, don't you?"

I nodded. "I also work with the civic patrollers."

"She'll get her gold, Master Rhennthyl."

"I thought she would. You'll have to pick up the draft here tomorrow. I'll give you a promissory note for it now. If you don't want to go far, one of the duty imagers will escort you to the branch of the banque here, and you can cash the draft for the golds without leaving Imagisle."

"I have to wait till then?"

"The banques aren't open on end-days, and we don't leave golds out. Does anyone sensible?"

A sly smile flitted across his lips. "Some might."

"I'll be right back with the note for you, Horazt."

I was glad I'd checked over the duty desk earlier, and that Master Dichartyn had briefed me on the procedures for intaking. The forms for the notes were in the second drawer, and all I had to do was fill in dates and names and the amount, and the reason. I did have to wait a moment for the ink to dry before bringing it back to the taudischef.

Horazt took the promissory note. "You write good, Master Rhennthyl." He slipped it inside his shirt.

"I'd hope so. I was once an artist."

At that, he stiffened once more, and just slightly. "Things'll be quiet in the west quarter."

"I'm sure that Commander Artois will be pleased to know that."

"Yes, sir." Then Horazt bent slightly and looked at Shault. "Boy . . . you listen to Master Rhennthyl. You do what he says, and if you got problems, you tell him. You got a chance to be someone. Someone your mama'll be proud of. You understand?"

Shault nodded somberly.

Horazt stood and looked at me. I understood the look, and I nodded. "We'll do our best."

He looked at Shault again, then turned and walked out of the receiving hall.

"Haensyl . . . get Kuert Secondus. Shault needs something to eat before anything, and we need to get him set up with a room."

The younger primes still needed their own chambers, but that section of the east quarters was arranged so that all the younger primes were quartered close together.

Kuert arrived in moments, his gray eyes taking in the worried-looking Shault. Then the second looked to me.

"Kuert, this is Shault. He'll need to eat something right away. He's imaged several things, and he'll need a room. I'll have one checked while he's eating. After he eats bring him back here." That wasn't the strict procedure, but Shault was pale, and I doubted that he'd hear or remember much until he ate.

"Yes, sir."

After they left, I checked the available quarters and, thankfully, there were two rooms left in the section for the very young primes. Once we'd settled on a room, I asked Haensyl, "Is there anyone who you'd trust to take Shault under their wing?"

"There's Mayra. She just made second. She's good with the young ones, and she's here now. I saw her just a bit ago."

"If you'd see if she'd help settle young Shault."

"Yes, sir."

Haensyl hurried off, but it seemed like only moments before he returned with an angular and gawky girl—close to being a young woman.

"Master Rhennthyl." She inclined her head.

"The Collegium needs your skills with young Shault. He's a taudis-boy, and being here is going to be hard on him for the next few days. Could you show him around today?"

"Yes, sir."

"He's eating now."

"I can wait, sir."

"Thank you. Where are you from, originally?"

"Gheant . . . it's a village outside Extela."

"Do you miss the mountains?"

"No, sir. I broke my arm chasing goats in the rocks. . . ."

Before all that long, Kuert and Shault returned. Shault looked far more alert, and the paleness had vanished.

"Are you feeling better?"

"Yes, Master Rhennthyl."

I looked at Kuert and Mayra. "Mayra will accompany you two and spend a little more time with Shault. He'll be in room nine in the junior prime quarters. I'll need a few words with him first, though."

They both nodded, clearly familiar with that aspect of matters, probably more so than I was, I suspected.

"Shault . . . if you'd come with me."

We walked to the conference room without speaking, and he took the chair on the side of the table. He looked lost in the large chair.

"Shault . . ." I offered quietly. "You need to understand a few rules about Imagisle."

"Yes, sir."

"The first rule is that you are not to try any more imaging except when a master tells you to try. The reason for this is simple. Imaging certain things will kill you. Imaging other things in the wrong place will also kill you. You don't have to give up imaging, and you won't. You will learn how and where to image. . . ." From there I went through the preliminary advising, although I did change the way I offered certain things, based on what I'd learned about the way things were done in the taudis.

Then I walked him back to the two seconds, who escorted him out of the receiving hall.

Haensyl looked up from the granite desk at me. "Sir . . . do many of them from the taudis make it?"

"Some do, but it's harder for them. Shault's young enough that in some ways it will be easier, but he's going to be lonely."

Haensyl nodded.

I went back to the duty study, thinking. Concentrating on the patroller procedures was even more difficult, because I kept thinking of Shault. The remainder of the day was uneventful, except for the drizzle that began just before the evening meal.

When I got to the dining hall, I was pleased to see that Mayra had arranged for several of the younger primes to sit with Shault. From what I could tell, while he was subdued, he occasionally spoke, and not just in monosyllables.

After dinner, I did attend services at the Anomen Imagisle, on the south end of the granite isle that held the Collegium. I did have to stand on one side, in a spot reserved for the duty master. Except for the imagers emeritus, of course, everyone stood through the services.

A small choir of imagers offered the choral invocation, and they sang well, a talent I certainly did not possess, and after that Chorister Isola followed with the wordless end to the invocation. She still remained the only woman chorister of the Nameless that I'd ever seen, not that choristers were restricted to being men, since no one could know or presume whether the Nameless was male or female, or indeed both at once. After that, she opened the main part of the service.

"We are gathered here together this evening in the spirit of the Nameless and in affirmation of the quest for goodness and mercy in all that we do."

The opening hymn was "Without the Pride of Naming," and I sang it softly, for the benefit of those near me, but I did speak more loudly through the confession.

"We do not name You, for naming is a presumption, and we would not presume upon the creator of all that was, is, and will be. We do not pray to You, nor ask favors or recognition from You, for requesting such asks You to favor us over others who are also Your creations. Rather we confess that we always risk the sins of pride and presumption and that the very names we bear symbolize those sins, for we too often strive to arrogate our names and ourselves above others, to insist that our petty plans and arid achievements have meaning beyond those whom we love or over whom we have influence and power. Let us never forget that we are less than nothing against Your nameless magnificence and that all that we are is a gift to be cherished and treasured, and that we must also respect and cherish the gifts of others, in celebration of You who cannot be named or known, only respected and worshipped."

After the confession and offertory, Chorister Isola stepped to the pulpit for the homily. "Good evening."

"Good evening," came the reply.

"And it is a good evening, for under the Nameless, all evenings are good." She paused momentarily. "In this time of year, harvest is drawing to a close, and before long, the winds will turn chill. With that cold that will end the year, many of us will feel a loss, often an unnamed loss, as if a year passing is a year lost. Yet there are those who seize upon the year, the name of the year, as if it were a vintage. You will hear people say, '755 was a good year, better than 754 . . .'"

Certainly, the past year, 755 years after the founding of L'Excelsis, had been a year of profound change for me, and in that sense, it had been better.

". . . yet when we focus on the names, whether those names are those of years or of people, or of places, we cling to the names as if they were locks on doors or bars on windows that would protect us. Names are but a false security because they do not reflect all that is. The number of a year does not capture the events of that year, the warmth of loves found, the bitterness of loved ones and friends lost, or the satisfaction of accomplishments. . . . The greatness of Rholan the Unnamer lies not so much in his rejection of names, but in his affirmation of life beyond names and labels. . . . The very name of the place where we meet—the anomen—is a reminder that we should hold to what is and not to the names of such places, just as we should recall the experiences of the years we have lived and not merely their numbers. . . ."

I listened as she finished the homily, glad that she was a good chorister, and one who made me think, even as I doubted whether the Nameless did indeed exist.

For some reason, her homily triggered thoughts about my own losses, but mostly about Shault, who had just lost all that was familiar to him, humble though it might have been. I was glad to see that Mayra was with him. She towered a good fifteen digits over him, but she seemed patient, and occasionally whispered instructions to the taudis-boy. Twice Shault pointed to me and murmured to Mayra. I was surprised that he'd located me among the more than two hundred imagers in the anomen.

After services, I hurried to catch up to Mayra and the two boys with her. "Mayra?"

She stopped and turned. "Yes, Master Rhennthyl."

"Is Shault settled in?"

"As well as he can be until we can get him to the tailor tomorrow."

"Good . . . and thank you." I looked to Shault. "In the morning, you'll meet with Master Dichartyn. He can be very stern, but you should listen to him carefully."

As I hurried away from them back to the duty study, I caught a few words from behind me.

". . . must be strong . . ."

". . . young for a master, but he's very powerful . . ."

And still less experienced than I would have liked, something that having had to deal with young Shault had reminded me.

4

Needless to say, at quarter before sixth glass on Lundi morning, when I entered the receiving hall to close out the end-day duty, Master Dichartyn was the one who was there, rather than Master Schorzat or Master Jhulian.

Master Dichartyn smiled at me. It wasn't a wry smile, not exactly, but it held a trace of amusement. "I understand you took in a young imager yesterday afternoon. A taudis-child."

"Yes, sir." Had I done something wrong?

"You seem to have made quite an impression on him, Rhenn."

"I just followed the procedures."

"He said that you scared his taudischef, and no one ever scared Horazt. Exactly what did you say to him?"

"I just told Horazt my name and that if the second gold didn't go to the boy's mother, sooner or later I'd find out, and there would be a new west quarter taudischef."

"I thought as much." Master Dichartyn shook his head. "You know that young imagers from the taudis have much more trouble adjusting to the Collegium. You're really too young to mentor a young imager, but Shault respects you, and that's half the battle. Master Ghaend will handle his assignments and day-to-day work, but you need to talk to him twice a week, at least for a while, starting tonight, after dinner. You know why, don't you?"

"He needs another taudischef, and one approved by Horazt."

Master Dichartyn nodded. "You'd better get on your way, if you want to eat and get to Patrol headquarters on time."

After that, I hurried to the dining hall, early enough that most of the primes and seconds weren't there. Neither was Shault. I slipped into a seat next to the gray-haired Maitre Dyana, because any other seat I would have taken would have suggested I was avoiding her.

"Good morning," I offered.

"Next time, don't scan the table when you're close enough to have your eyes read." Her bright blue eyes pinned me in my seat. As always, she wore a colorful scarf above her imager grays, and this one was a brilliant green, with touches of an equally bright violet. Her unlined face suggested she was far younger than did her hair and experience.

I laughed, if apologetically. "Every time I see you, I learn something."

"Good. You might even learn enough to survive your abilities, young Rhenn. Commander Artois has a good brain encumbered by solid grasp of protocol and procedure. He might listen to you if you can avoid offending him. The easiest way to offend him is to flaunt protocol and ignore procedures." She handed me the platter of sausages and scrambled eggs. "You'd best eat. You don't have much time, not if you don't want to arrive sweating and flustered."

I took her advice and drank my tea and ate quickly, then set out for my first day at the Civic Patrol, adjusting the gray visored cap that imagers wore when on duty off Imagisle.

Although the headquarters of the Civic Patrol of L'Excelsis was slightly less than a mille from the south end of Imagisle, there wasn't a bridge there. Instead, I had to take the Bridge of Hopes across the River Aluse and then walk almost two milles along the East River Road, before turning east on Fedre and walking another half mille.

The two-story headquarters building was of undistinguished yellow brick, with brown wooden trim and doors. There were three doors spaced across the front. The left one clearly was for a working patroller station, because I could see patrollers in their pale blue uniforms hurrying in and out, the mark of a shift change. The right door looked disused, as if locked. So I took the middle door, or rather the right-hand door of the set of double doors in the square archway above two worn stone steps leading up from the sidewalk. The left-hand door was locked.

Inside was a table desk, with a graying patroller seated behind it. He took in my imager's uniform and the silver imager's pin. "You're here to see Commander Artois, sir?"

"Yes . . . if you'd direct me."

"Second floor, up those steps and to the right. You can't miss it."

"Thank you."

The wide steps weren't stone, but time-worn dark oak. I arrived just before eighth glass on the second floor of the anteroom that led to the commander's private study. There were two small writing desks in the anteroom facing the wall on each side of the door through which I'd entered. Each had a straight-backed chair behind it, and two backless oak benches were set against the wall, facing each desk. Between the desks was a door, presumably

to the commander's private study. At the left desk sat another graying patroller.

"Master Rhennthyl?"

"Yes. I'm here—"

"To see the commander. You can go in. He's expecting you."

I opened the door and stepped into the study, a space no more than four
yards deep and six wide. Artois had risen and stepped around an ancient walnut desk set at the end of the study closest to the river. To his right, on the in-
nermost wall, was a line of wooden cases. On the wall opposite the desk was
a tall and narrow bookcase, filled with volumes. Facing the desk were four
straight-backed chairs. Two wide windows, both open, were centered on the
outer wall and offered a view of the various buildings on the north side of
Fedre and some beyond, but not so far as the Boulevard D'Imagers. There
were no pictures or anything else hung on the walls, and only a pair of unlit
oil lamps in wall sconces flanking the desk.

Artois was three or four digits shorter than I was and wire-thin. Under
short-cut brown hair shot with gray, his brown eyes seemed flat, the kind that
showed little emotion.

"Our latest imager liaison." He nodded. "Young . . . doubtless powerful
and shielded, and with Namer-little understanding of the Civic Patrol."

"Yes, sir. That's an accurate summary."

"Are you being sarcastic, *Master* Rhennthyl?"

"No, sir. I've studied the procedures, but I've only worked briefly with
one patroller. I do think I can learn, and there are situations where I might be
helpful."

"Outside of being an imager, what do you know?"

"I was a journeyman artist for three years after a seven-year apprenticeship, and my family is in the wool business. So I know something about art
and the guilds, and about factoring and commerce. I've been trained to take
care of myself." I doubted that there was much else I could say that he didn't
know.

"Do you know accounting?"

"I used to do ledger entries."

"You've killed men in the line of duty. How many and under what circumstances?"

I had to think for a moment. Diazt, the first assassin, the Ferran, Vhillar,
and at least two others. "At least six, sir."

"At least? You don't remember?"

"When the Ferran envoy's assassins tried to attack, I blew up their wagon.

There were at least three people killed, but I got knocked unconscious. So I don't know if there were more."

"Let me put it another way. How many have you killed face-to-face at different times?"

"Three." That was counting Vhillar.

"You realize that many patrollers have never killed anyone. That's not our task."

"Many imagers have not, either, sir, but even more people would have died if I had not acted."

"How many did you attack first, before they did anything?"

"None, sir. One of them tried to kill me three times before I killed him."

"Three times?"

"Yes, sir."

"I doubt they were all reported."

"The first and last times were." I paused. "I don't know that. Patrollers were there the first and last times. I don't know what they reported."

Artois smiled faintly. "Don't you trust our finest?"

"It's not a question of trust, sir. I don't know what they did. I reported to Master Dichartyn. He was my superior."

Those words actually got a nod, a grudging one, I thought.

"Do you know why we agree to have imager liaisons, Rhennthyl?"

"I've been told why the Collegium wants me here; I haven't been told why you agree to it, and it would be only speculation on my part to say."

"Only speculation." Artois repeated my words, sardonically. "Would you care to speculate?"

"No, sir. I'd rather know than speculate."

"You are here because you are potentially a powerful imager. Powerful imagers can cause great problems if they do not understand how L'Excelsis works. The Civic Patrol is a key part of the city. We want you to understand how matters really work. Occasionally, you will be helpful. Until you have a better idea of how, just stand back, protect yourself, and watch."

"Yes, sir."

"You will actually report to Subcommander Cydarth, and he will rotate you through observing various patroller operations. When and if you finish your initial rotations, you will use the empty desk in the outer study here. That won't be for some time."

"Yes, sir."

"You need to meet the subcommander." Without another word, Commander Artois turned and walked past me, opening the door.

I followed him out through the anteroom and to the right to the next door, where we entered a slightly smaller anteroom arranged in a similar fashion to that of the one outside the commander's study, save that there was only one desk, and no one was seated there. Artois pushed open the study door, already ajar, and stepped inside.

Subcommander Cydarth was standing beside his desk, looking out the window. He turned. He was taller than the commander and had black hair and a swarthy complexion. Part of his upper right ear was missing.

"Cydarth, here's your liaison, Maitre D'Aspect Rhennthyl." Commander Artois nodded to me. "I'll leave you in the most capable hands of the subcommander." He left the study without a word.

"The commander can often be abrupt, but he's quite effective." Cydarth's voice was so low it actually rumbled. I'd read of voices that deep, but I'd never heard one before.

"That is what Master Dichartyn said."

"I doubt he said it quite that way." Cydarth's smile belied the sardonic tone of his words.

I waited.

"There's one thing I want to emphasize before we get you settled. Most patrollers will call you 'sir' or 'Master Rhennthyl.' That is a courtesy, in the sense that you are not their superior. You cannot order even the lowest patroller to do anything. Do you understand that?"

"Yes, sir. Master Dichartyn made that clear."

"He would have. He understands a bit of what we do."

I managed to keep a pleasant smile on my face, but I had no doubts that Master Dichartyn understood far more than either the commander or the subcommander realized.

"For the next few days, you'll be assigned to observe the charging desk here in headquarters. I want you to study every person charged, and then read whatever past records we have on them, not that there will be many." He looked at me. "Do you know why?"

"To note on their charging record, because those who have committed a single major offense will either be executed or will spend the rest of their life in a penal workhouse. Those who have more than three minor offenses will be spending years in the penal manufactories or on road or ironway maintenance."

"Exactly . . . except for one thing. Do you know what it is?"

I had no idea. "No, sir."

"What if they're of common appearance and have changed their names?"

"Aren't repeat offenders branded on their hip?"

"They are after a second offense, but there are minor offenders who move to another city after serving time for one offense and then change their names. You'll learn to recognize that type." He gestured toward the door. "Let's get you settled in with First Patroller Gulyart. He runs charging downstairs."

Again, I found myself following as Cydarth walked swiftly to a narrow staircase at the end of the hall and headed down it. At the bottom was a door with a heavy iron bolt, which he slid aside before opening the door and stepping into a ground-floor chamber a good eight yards long and four wide. While there were several benches, most of the space was without fixtures or furnishings, except for wall lamps. On one side of the room was a low dais, or the equivalent, on which rested a solid-front wide desk. There were two chairs behind it. One was occupied.

When the patroller behind the desk saw us, he stood immediately, if slightly awkwardly. On each shoulder of the upper sleeve of his pale blue shirt was a single chevron of a darker blue.

"Gulyart, this is Master Rhennthyl. He's the new imager liaison to the Patrol. He'll be spending the next two weeks with you." Cydarth turned to me. "For now, you're just to observe." Then he turned back toward the staircase.

I'd expected another far older patroller, but Gulyart looked to be somewhat less than ten years older than I was, with short blond hair and pale brown eyes. He offered the first genuine smile I'd seen since arriving at headquarters. "Master Rhennthyl, I'm glad to meet you." He gestured to the wide desk. "The other chair is for you. A bit crowded, but this is the only way you'll see how charging works."

I didn't even have a chance to sit down before someone called out, "Gulyart! They're bringing in the prisoners from last night."

"The charging desk is only open until midnight," Gulyart explained quickly. "After tenth glass, they just put them in the holding cells. Most are just troublemakers or drank too much . . . a few elvers, at times, but we don't get that many most nights." He squared himself in his chair and adjusted the ledger-like book in front of him.

I sat down quickly.

The first prisoner was a little man with a big head and unruly wavy blond hair that stuck out from his skull. His hands were manacled behind him. His eyes were bloodshot and had dark circles beneath them. The patroller escorting him looked from Gulyart to me and back to Gulyart.

"He claims his name is Guffryt. He was picked up on the Midroad just off the triad. The charge is drunkenness and attempted assault on the patrollers who apprehended him."

"I was just heading to my place to sleep, and they grabbed me," protested Guffryt.

"Where is your place?" asked Gulyart mildly. "Your home address, please?"

After a long moment, Guffryt looked down.

"Where do you live?"

Finally, Guffryt replied, "Where I can."

"You're charged with public disturbance, drunkenness, assaulting a pa-troller, and vagrancy." Gulyart looked to me and gestured toward a set of stacked cases against the wall behind us. "The files are there. The names are alphabetical. The stack of cases to the left has the live files, the one to the right the names of victims where no one was charged. If you wouldn't mind see-ing if there's any paper on this man?"

It took me several moments to find the case with the names beginning with "G" and a few more to get to the end. "There's no one listed under that name."

"Thank you." Gulyart turned to the patroller. "Just a moment."

I sat down, watching as he wrote out a charging sheet, with the same in-formation as he'd already entered in the charging ledger before him, then handed the sheet to the patroller. "He goes to the magistrate."

I did know that lesser offenses were handled by the magistrates, rather than by one of the full justices.

"Let's go, Guffryt. Count yourself lucky," said the patroller, a hefty man.

I wouldn't have called him lucky, because he was facing at least a year on a road gang or in one of the penal manufactories.

Before the next prisoner arrived, I pointed at the cases behind us. "Are those all the records?" How could there be that few files when there were close to two million people in L'Excelsis?

"Once someone's executed, their files go to the execution records in the cellar. If they go to a penal workhouse or permanent manufactory, the rec-ords go with them."

With that explanation, the smaller number of file cases made more sense.

Then yet another prisoner appeared, a scrawny dark-haired woman, more like a girl, I thought, until I saw the lines in her face.

"Her name is Arinetia," offered the patroller. "Battery with a broken wine bottle."

"He deserved worse than that. Ripped my clothes and wouldn't pay."

Gulyart looked at the patroller. "Do we have a patroller witness or a statement by the victim?"

"No, First Patroller."

"Nothing? I can't charge her with anything without a statement or a witness or a victim."

"Lieutenant Narkol had his men bring her in, sir." The escorting patroller looked helplessly at Gulyart.

"I'll have to release her."

At that point, the woman, even with her hands manacled, turned and lunged at her escort, trying to bite his arm.

Gulyart sighed. "I'll book her for battery against a patroller. Magistrate's court."

"Yes, sir."

I went to the file case, but there was nothing under the name Arinetia.

Right after the patroller hurried the woman out, Gulyart turned to me. "Odds are that the man she attacked was a taudischef, and if she's released, no one will ever see her again. Two to four months making brooms is far better for her."

"Did you get that from the lieutenant's action?"

"It's a guess, but his district has the south taudis-town, you know, the one east of Sudroad and south of D'Artisans." He turned to the next prisoner, not only manacled but gagged as well.

"This one's Skyldar. Jariolan, probably," explained the patroller. "He knifed a cabaret girl when she wouldn't go with him. She was dead when they got there. Here are the statements." He handed over a sheaf of papers.

While Gulyart wrote out the charging sheet, I went to the cabinet and was surprised to find a single sheet. "Gulyart, there's a sheet here on a Skyldar from Jariola. He served two months . . . just got out, it looks like, for roughing up a cabaret girl."

Gulyart shook his head. "Same girl, I'd bet, or one he thought was the same. Bring me the sheet, if you would, Master Rhennthyl."

At the mention of my name, the prisoner tried to jerk away from the patroller, who immediately clouted him with a short truncheon.

I handed the sheet to Gulyart.

"He's charged with murder, premeditated. Justice court."

I had the feeling that the morning would be long, very long.

After the initial surge of prisoners on Lundi, matters slowed down until midafternoon, when another group of prisoners—those arrested in the morning—arrived. In between the two busy periods, Gulyart filled out supplementary reports, checked the holding cells, and explained more about the charging duties. We also went across Fedre to a small bistro and ate quickly while a regular patroller took the charging desk. That meant he sat there, and if anything came up, he'd come and get Gulyart. The same pattern of activity followed on Mardi, Meredi, and Jeudi. On Meredi after dinner, I did stop young Shault and talk to him for a bit about his studies, as well as doing my best to encourage him. I didn't know how much it might help, but it couldn't hurt.

When I returned from my duties, such as they were, late on Jeudi afternoon, there was a message in my letter box, confirming that I was to meet with Master Dichartyn at half past fifth glass. I was glad for the reminder, but chagrined to realize I might well have forgotten without it. I immediately hurried back across the quadrangle.

The door to his study was open, and I knocked and stepped inside.

He was sitting behind the writing desk, fingering his chin. He gestured for me to sit down. I did.

"The good news is that Commander Artois has not sent me a message complaining about you. Other matters are not so sanguine, however, particularly given the invasion of Jariola by the Ferrans. That could easily lead to a similar invasion of Caenen by Tiempre, Stakanar, and other members of the Otelyrnan League."

"Because we'll have to deal with Jariola, Ferrum, and the Isles and because Caenen will be unsettled until a new High Priest is selected?"

"Our treaty with Caenen upset the Tiempran strategy, as it was meant to do. In reaction, the First Speaker of Tiempre has let it be known that great rewards will fall to those who strike at the enemies of equality." Master Dichartyn's words were dry. "Especially those who strike close to the heart. Keep that in mind."

Something else to keep in mind, as if there weren't too many things already.

"The Ferran government has stated that they have no issues with us and will respect our neutrality with regard to the unavoidable conflict with Jariola, but they suggest that we take special precautions to assure the safety of their envoy." Dichartyn looked at me.

"They think we'll side with the Oligarch, and they will immediately act if there's evidence of that. They also aren't pleased with what happened to Vhillar."

"Would you be?"

I didn't answer that. "Besides keeping my eyes open, what do you want me to do?"

"Report to me if you see anything unusual, even if you can't determine the cause."

"What about High Holder Ryel?"

"All actions have a cost, all choices a price. You should know that." His words were flat.

"You and the Collegium have made that very clear, sir."

"Can you imagine a land where any citizen believed he could do anything he wanted?"

"I can imagine it," I replied carefully. "I don't think it would last very long. Everything anyone does has an impact on others, in some way. Most people desire more than they can obtain through their own efforts, but if they felt that they could take what they could get away with taking, they would try. Before long, there would be chaos and no rule at all except by those who were very powerful in some fashion."

"The reason societies have laws, as well as unspoken rules and traditions, is to balance the costs and prices of the actions of individuals. In general, most individuals do not wish to pay the price of their actions, or not the full price."

I could see that. I could also see that the High Holders of Solidar were especially guilty.

"The Collegium's function in Solidar is very basic, and very simple. We are the price all imagers in Solidar pay for their comparative freedom and existence."

I wasn't so sure about that.

"Think of this, Rhenn. What is to keep you from putting on normal clothes and walking away from the Collegium?"

"Nothing . . . until you or Master Schorzat track me down," I replied dryly.

"Could we find you in a land of fifty million people? With what you know now?"

"But . . . other than becoming a laborer or a clerk or the like, there's little that I could do without being discovered. . . ." I paused. "Oh . . . in a way, that's part of the price. By the fact that you could track me down if I used imaging abilities, you restrict my use of them, which is what the Collegium does anyway."

"And if you took passage to another land, while you might be free of the Collegium, your use of your talents would still be limited by your need to survive."

"So . . . by abiding by the rules of the Collegium, paying that price, we obtain a better life than we could otherwise, and by paying the price of having and heeding the Collegium, Solidar also benefits."

"That's true, and obvious, so obvious that most imagers accept it without thinking deeply about it. The problem is that most outside of Imagisle neither understand nor accept that agreement between the Council and the Collegium. Any land has to decide, or at least agree to accept, who determines the public prices people must pay for their actions. In Solidar, at first we had warring rexdoms, but in all of them the rex was the one who made those decisions. Now we have the Council. In Jariola, the Oligarch and his council decide, in Caenen, the High Priest. What do they all have in common?"

"Property and golds?"

"And more. They all have power, position, and/or property at stake. Even in the Abierto Isles, where they have an elected parliament, the electors must have property. Is this important?"

Obviously, Dichartyn thought it was. "It must be."

He shook his head. "If those who decide the rules and the prices have nothing at stake, they will adopt rules and laws that will take from those who have and give to themselves, and they will pay little or no price at all. Our system of government is not perfect. No government can be, but it recognizes who has property, who has wealth, and who has power. No individual artisan has power, but artisans as a whole do, and our government structure recognizes that. Why do we not let those in the taudis have a Council representative?"

"Because they have little to offer and nothing material at stake?"

"Exactly. Government has a responsibility for their safety, for providing certain services, such as water and sewers, and for affording them access to public grammaires. The cost of those services is roughly in proportion to what those in the taudis offer to Solidar in terms of their labor and what they buy from others who pay taxes on what they sell. But . . . most of them don't think so. They feel oppressed and exploited."

"That's where agents and troublemakers will head, then."

He nodded. "Just keep watching."

"Sir . . . Master Poincaryt's portrait is framed."

"Have it delivered here. I'll have it hung in the receiving hall. That would seem most appropriate, don't you think?" He stood.

So did I. "Yes, sir." I inclined my head politely, then slipped out of his study and closed the door behind me, leaving him fingering his chin and standing at the window.

I still had a little time before dinner, but not much. So I walked across the quadrangle to the dining hall, picked up copies of both newsheets—*Veritum* and *Tableta*—and checked my letter box—the inscription now reading MA-RHE, short for Maitre D'Aspect Rhennthyl. Not so long ago, the inscription had been TF-RHE.

There was an envelope in my letter box, squarish, and of high-quality paper. The address on the outside was formal and written precisely in black ink.

> *Rhennthyl D'Imagisle*
> *Maitre D'Aspect*
> *Collegium Imago, Imagisle*

The address was written in an unfamiliar hand, neither that of Seliora nor my mother, nor my sister Khethila. I couldn't imagine who else might be writing. I finally opened the envelope.

Inside was a blank formal card. Glued to the card was a miniature knot tied in silver ribbon. There was no writing whatsoever.

I just looked at it for a long moment. It could only have been sent by or at the behest of High Holder Ryel, and I understood why he had waited long months. He wanted me to become a maitre so that I would lose more when he took his revenge for my partial blinding of his eldest son. To him, it didn't matter that his son and the brother of a taudischef had attacked me with the intent of maiming me and disabling me for life. To him, all that mattered was that I had dared to strike out against the scion of a High Holder—even if Johanyr had been an evil and lazy excuse for a student imager who had abused the sisters of junior imagers unbeknownst to the maitres. I paused. I hoped that abuse had been unknown.

Then, I shrugged. I couldn't change the past.

Master Dichartyn was at the dining hall for dinner. Usually, he ate at his dwelling on the north end of Imagisle with his family. I intercepted him before he could seat himself.

"Sir, I just thought you'd like to know I just received a formal card with a silver knot."

"That was to be expected, don't you think, once it became known you'd become a master? You're free to deal with it in any fashion that meets imager standards. If you'll excuse me, Rhenn . . . I see Maitre Jhulian."

I stepped back. While I hadn't exactly expected a reaction much different, his attitude still irritated and angered me. Part of the reason I was in trouble with Ryel was because Master Dichartyn hadn't understood just how evil Ryel's son Johanyr had been or how vicious the attack on me had been. And now it was all my problem? My problem alone? Seething within, I took a seat next to Maitre Dyana, the last chair on the left side. I could see Shault at the primes' table, talking to one of the other primes.

"I assume you told Dichartyn that you'd received notice from Ryel," she said calmly.

"Yes. You saw the card?"

"I saw a formal envelope, white. You just made master, and while it was not posted, word would have reached Ryel in a few days after you became Civic Patrol liaison . . . and you would not have spoken to Master Dichartyn here were the matter not of import."

I just wished I could have reached conclusions as quickly and as accurately as she did, but since she was the daughter of a High Holder, she did have some advantages in the matter at hand.

"What do you suggest, maitre . . . in general terms?"

"Protect yourself at all times, and arrange for accidents to occur to his agents."

"So Ryel can strike at me, and possibly at those around me, and the Collegium will do nothing unless it is so overt that the entire world would know?"

"Do not make it sound so dramatic, Rhennthyl. The Collegium does not ever become involved in individual disputes unless one of those involved has clearly and overtly broken the laws of Solidar, and often then only if such disputes threaten the Collegium. Ryel has merely sent you notice. Has he broken any law? Has he yet harmed you in any way that you can prove?"

The answer to that was unfortunately obvious. Still . . .

"So what can I expect from Ryel? Beside the fact that he will attempt to destroy me?"

"He will, indeed, attempt that."

"And I'm supposed to do nothing?"

"You are so impatient, Rhennthyl. He must strike first. You should know that. Then you can act as you will. So long as it does not involve the Collegium."

The unspoken code of the Collegium was never to strike first. But I didn't have to like it.

"High Holders can be most indirect. Such notice might just be a step to hasten you into rash and unwise action. In any case, I seriously doubt that any imager would wish the Collegium looking into his or her background and personal life. Once you are convinced by evidence, and not a mere card, that there is a danger, we should talk again."

That was both a warning and a threat. I nodded politely and changed the subject . . . slightly. "What can you tell me about High Holder Ryel?"

"He has extensive lands well north of L'Excelsis. He has the controlling interest in several banques. Like all successful High Holders, he is never to be trusted."

"Does he have a chateau here in L'Excelsis?"

"Did you not dance with his daughter at the Harvest Ball?" She raised an eyebrow.

"Perhaps I should have asked where it might be located, then."

"The majority of High Holders have what others would call estates near major cities, such as L'Excelsis, Nacliano, or Liantiago. They do occasionally like to see the theatre and opera, or hear a concert. I believe Ryel has a less than modest establishment several milles north of Martradon. There are a number of others in that general area."

"Does he have an extensive family?"

Maitre Dyana smiled wryly. "No High Holder survives an extensive family, and no extensive family survives a High Holder. Ryel had two sisters, one of whom died in childbirth, and the other of whom is married to a High Holder well to the west. I understand they do not speak. He had only one brother who died several years ago in a boating accident on the upper reaches of the Aluse. I believe there is one surviving nephew at this point."

"Could Johanyr ever inherit?"

"No. The Council Compact is quite firm on that. No one ever declared an imager may inherit property . . . from anyone. If you are fortunate enough to amass some golds, you can buy property and bequeath it—except to an offspring who is an imager. If you marry a High Holder's daughter, and she has property, none of that may pass to you, but it can pass to any offspring."

I hadn't realized that I'd never inherit anything from my family. I hadn't exactly expected to, but it was still strange to realize that I couldn't. "Do daughters of High Holders inherit?"

"Very seldom. Daughters are at best often regarded as markers in the equivalent of a High Holder's version of black-hand plaques."

"Wives are not all that well treated, either, I understand." I couldn't help but recall the one I'd had to execute—covertly—in learning certain imager abilities. Her husband had beaten her repeatedly, and she'd finally murdered him. She'd been convicted and sentenced to death.

"You'd best eat and get on with matters, Rhennthyl," Dyana added more gently. "As I told you when I first worked with you, technique is everything. Not power, but technique. That applies to covert actions and to High Holders."

I had the feeling that I needed to consider her words carefully and at some length.

Vendrei was no different from the rest of the week, starting with exercises, although I was still not participating in the hand-to-hand sparring, but doing solitary knife and truncheon routines, followed by cleaning up, eating, and a long walk to Civic Patrol headquarters, and another day at the charging desk. I did have to admit that the duty with Gulyart had given me a good indoctrination into the myriad forms of petty and mundane violence seldom seen by most citizens of L'Excelsis. But then, that was doubtless the point.

On Samedi, once more, I dragged myself up and to Clovyl's training and running session. By the time we finished the last of the exercises, it was pouring. We still had to run through the slop and puddles. For the first time ever, I beat Dartazn. Did that mean anything besides I ran better through water? I doubted it.

After a cold shower and shaving, I dressed and headed to the dining hall for breakfast, glad that I could at least use an umbrella crossing the quadrangle. I still hadn't figured out a practical way to use imaging shields against rain. Maybe there wasn't one. Master Dichartyn used an umbrella, I'd noticed.

There were no other masters present for breakfast, except for Ferlyn and Maitre Chassendri, both of whom were Maitres D'Aspect. Ferlyn and I sat on either side of her, since she was far senior to each of us. I still remembered the chemistry laboratory studies under her and how she insisted on perfection every bit as much as did Master Dichartyn.

I passed her the platter of egg toast, then the berry syrup. While she served herself, I poured some tea. "Would you like some?"

"Yes, please."

The egg toast was darker than I would have preferred, but not black-brown, and the sausages were perfect.

"You know, except for Maitre Dichartyn," Maitre Chassendri observed, "you're the youngest imager to become a maitre in centuries."

"I had the advantage of having him as a preceptor," I said, "and some fortune as well."

"Misfortune," she corrected. "Rapid advancement always comes from

Town of Georgina (KESWICK) Public Library

success in dealing with difficulties in hard times. We're looking at harder times, I fear."

"Because of the Ferran-Jariolan conflict?" asked Ferlyn.

"More than that," she replied. "The free-holders in the west are harvesting more produce than are the High Holders, and they're able to sell it for less. The same is true for timber holdings. Before long, the same may happen in the east, although the water control issues there make it harder."

"Why should that—" Ferlyn broke off his words as he looked at Chassendri.

"The free-holders are making more golds on their harvests," I said, "and the High Holders comparatively less. The only way the High Holders can compete is to impose stricter conditions on their lands. That will cause unrest, increase costs, and reduce their profits. If the High Holders sell land, the free-holders will buy it and use it to become wealthier—"

"All right, Rhenn . . . I see that."

"Fighting wars is expensive, and that means higher taxes," I pointed out. "The High Holders are pressing to support Jariola, and given the way the Ferrans have dealt with us, the Council doesn't have much choice."

"And tax levies are on land," Ferlyn finished. "So the High Holders are going to be squeezed two ways."

"Three," suggested Chassendri. "Conditions will get worse on some of the holdings, not all, because most of the High Holders actually manage their lands well, but workers on the poorly managed lands will leave. They'll either work for the free-holders or get conscripted. More High Holders will fall to debts, and their lands will be split between successful High Holders and free-holders, but in the end there will be more free-holders and fewer High Holders."

I could see that, but I didn't see it happening that quickly. "Won't that take time?"

"There are at least fifty High Holders who are so land-poor that were they businesses, they'd be close to bankruptcy," replied Chassendri.

"But they could sell their lands, or part of them, and besides," Ferlyn pointed out, "there are hundreds of High Holders."

"More than a thousand," said Chassendri cheerfully, "one thousand and forty-one High Holdings, to be precise."

Something . . . there was something. Then I had it, an obscure section of the compact that had created the Council. "The rebalancing provisions. The High Holders would lose a Council seat, probably to the factors, and the head of the Council would no longer be a High Holder."

"But . . . the High Holders could just split a few holdings up, couldn't they?" asked Ferlyn. "To keep the numbers above a thousand."

"They could," Chassendri pointed out.

Left unspoken was the point that few High Holders ever willingly let go of anything.

Those thoughts put a damper on matters, especially since we were close to being done with breakfast anyway, and I had another concern as well— Shault.

He looked so forlorn that as soon as I swallowed the last drops of my tea, I rose and walked over to the long table that held the primes and the seconds and said to him, "I'll need a few moments with you after you're done eating. I'll meet you by the doors."

"Yes, sir."

Then I just stood there for a moment and let my eyes run down the table, face by face, before I turned and walked away, slowly, listening.

". . . one you don't want to cross . . ."

I wondered about that, because I'd never done anything harsh to any of the primes or seconds, except for Diazt and Johanyr. I didn't have to wait long before Shault hurried out of the dining hall, his thin face pinched in worry.

"Sir?"

"I take it that there's a second who's giving everyone trouble, maybe from the taudis? More than likely, he's even suggesting to you that you need to do what he wants, or something will happen to you or someone else."

Shault's mouth started to drop open, but he closed it with a snap.

"Have you ever heard of Diazt or Artazt?" I asked.

"No, sir."

"Diazt was a second here. His brother Artazt was a taudischef in the hell-hole. They're both dead." I paused. "Right now, there are two things you need to know. First, no one will rescue you from being pushed around unless you study and work hard and unless you do your best to learn everything you can about imaging. Second, in time, things happen to bullies here at the Collegium." I paused. "Why do you think I'm telling you this?"

The poor prime shivered. I just waited.

"So I know it will get better? Sir . . . will it get better?"

I offered as gentle a smile as I could. "It will, but it won't be easy. You have more imaging ability than most primes and even some seconds, but you haven't had enough book education. Do you have someone helping you to read better?"

"Yes, sir. Mayra and Lieryns are helping me."

"Good. That's important." I paused. "One other thing. No student imager is allowed to harm another. That doesn't mean there won't be threats, or other nasty things. No one has actually hurt you physically, have they?"

"No, sir."

His response was firm enough and without hesitation that I believed him.

"Keep that in mind."

"Yes, sir."

"I'll talk to you later." As I left him, I wished I could do more for him, but that would only make matters worse. The way I'd approached him would certainly not have let the others think he was getting any favors. But Master Dichartyn had told me that I needed to talk to him at least twice a week, and he certainly had raw talent, more than I'd had at his age, and I couldn't help but hope that he'd be able to become at least a third in time. I was also pleased that Lieryns was helping. I'd always liked Lieryns.

At eighth glass I was in my studio, after trudging through a rain that showed little sign of dissipating. While I was waiting, I'd checked the small storeroom that held an assortment of unused items and found a fairly solid and flat crate that I hoped no one would mind my borrowing. At slightly past the hour, in walked Master Rholyn.

"I apologize for being late, Rhennthyl, but Master Poincaryt wasn't that precise in explaining where your studio was, especially for someone coming from the north quarters."

I'd assumed that Master Rholyn was married and living in one of the separate gray stone dwellings for senior imagers situated on the north end of Imagisle, but I hadn't known for certain. I smiled. "I barely knew whose portrait I'd be painting next. Master Poincaryt just indicated that I should be here."

"He can be terse to the point of being cryptic," replied Master Rholyn. "One reason Master Poincaryt decided you should paint my portrait is not only your present duty, but your past duty as well. Before we get into that, should I sit there?" He gestured to the chair.

"Not for a moment, sir. I'd like to ask a question. I didn't often observe the Council. When you speak to the entire Council or to the Executive Council, do you remain seated at your desk or do you stand?"

"In open discussion, councilors remain seated. To offer a motion, one stands."

"Then I will portray you standing." I carried the low crate over next to the chair. "If you'd put one foot . . . the one you'd use if you stood that way . . ."

"Rhennthyl . . . you know the chamber floor is flat."

"Yes, sir, but not if you were making a motion to the High Council." I paused. "I realize that's unlikely, but it's perhaps more politic."

He laughed. "Did Master Poincaryt suggest that?"

"No, sir, but if I didn't do it that way, he might."

Rholyn shook his head, then stepped forward and took the position.

"Look a touch to the right . . . please." I began to draw in the details on the design I'd already started.

After a time, I had him sit down for a bit while I worked on some of the angles, but I couldn't help asking, "Do you think the Council will actually declare war on Ferrum, sir?"

"No one really wants Solidar in a war, even the High Holders, but it's looking less and less likely that we can avoid it. Ferrum will use any pretext to try to obtain the iron and coal mines near the Jariolan border, and their army is large and well trained and equipped enough that any attempt to invade by us would be a bloodbath on both sides. Even if Jariola put all its efforts into attacking Ferrum, and we were able to blockade the Ferran ports, it could devastate both Ferrum and Jariola."

"So the strategy is likely to stall and negotiate and try to avoid all-out war until the covert field operatives can find a way to persuade Ferrum not to attack?"

Master Rholyn shook his head sadly. "Even if your assumptions were correct, accomplishing a change in Ferran policy would still be difficult, because all those who have power in Ferrum think alike, and the number of illnesses, accidents, and deaths necessary to change the collective political mind of the Ferran Assembly would be so noticeable that it would unite everyone against us."

That, unfortunately, made sense, and I had to wonder what the Collegium might be able to do against such a united opposition with a mere handful of talented covert field operatives.

By the time the anomen bells struck nine and Master Rholyn had left, I'd changed the design twice, but finally had one that would work while revealing—I hoped—something of the councilor's wit and temperament.

I thought about taking a hack out to see my parents before going to Seliora's, but with the rain splashing down everywhere, I decided against it. Instead, I stayed in the studio and set up the canvas. That took me far longer than I'd thought, and I worked through lunch.

What with one thing and another, and from changing from damp grays into better and drier ones, checking some aspects of the patroller procedures, and making sure that I had the "silver knot" card and envelope, it was after third glass when I set out. As always, I held full shields from the time I left my quarters. I allowed for extra time, but the rain had lightened into a drizzle, and the hack I took from the west side of the Bridge of Desires actually got me to the corner of Nordroad and Hagahl Lane well before fourth glass.

Seliora's cousin Odelia was the one to open the door. "You're early, Rhenn, but I don't think Seliora will keep you waiting."

"Can you tell me who's coming for dinner this evening?" I asked as we walked up the staircase to the second-level formal entry hall.

"I could."

"But you won't because that's Seliora's privilege."

"We don't infringe on each other." Odelia smiled. "I'll tell her you're here."

With so much of the extended family living together in the huge building that combined manufactory and lavish quarters, I could see that made good sense.

As I ambled around the entry hall, waiting for Seliora, I noticed a chair I hadn't seen before. It looked new, and I walked over to study it. The seat was upholstered in what I had earlier learned was a Jacquard-loomed needlepoint, a family crest of some sort. The design had to be Seliora's.

I'd barely walked away from it when I heard footsteps coming down the side staircase from the private quarters on the third level. I turned to wait for her. She was wearing blue and silver, flowing dark blue trousers and a matching blouse, with a pale silver jacket trimmed in the dark blue. I couldn't help smiling as we walked toward each other.

"You're early. I'm glad." She took my hands, then tilted her head and kissed my lips, gently but warmly. "You don't mind if we just sit here? I told Mama that we'd greet everyone."

"Who is 'everyone'? Odelia wouldn't tell me."

"Good." Seliora grinned, then turned and led me toward the settee closest to the archway at the top of the entry staircase. "She shouldn't have. Papa's sister Staelia and her husband, and Papa's cousin Duerl and his wife. Staelia has a bistro not that far from the river. Odelia and Aunt Aegina and Grandmama Diestra will join Mama and Papa and us . . . and Shomyr and Methyr. It's cool enough that you'll finally get to eat in the dining chamber."

We settled onto the settee.

"Is that a new chair?" I asked, gesturing to the one I'd looked over earlier.

"Unhappily."

"Oh? Done for a client, and they didn't like it?"

"High Holder Tierchyl. He did himself in with his favorite pistol last Mardi.

Your 'friend' Ryel managed it. I don't know the details, but Tierchyl was overextended. He arranged a huge timber harvest to pay the interest on his debts. Everything in the sawmill and in the drying barns, as well as the timber waiting to be stripped and milled, caught fire, including Tierchyl's mill itself. The Banque D'Rivages refused to extend any more credit or to even extend the term of the notes."

"But . . . a High Holder has to have tens of thousands of hectares."

"Most of them will have to be sold, Mama said. He had almost no cash at all remaining, and supposedly all his lands were security for the notes at ninety percent. There will be more than enough golds for a comfortable life for his widow and children, but nothing like what a High Holder requires." Seliora shrugged. "We're out the cost of the chair, as well as a hundred yards of special fabric. The wood isn't a problem, because most of it hadn't been even rough-shaped and can be used for other commissions in the future. It's still a loss of close to a hundred golds."

I winced. While I knew her family could afford it, the loss of more than I'd make in two years wasn't something to dismiss lightly. "Are you sure Ryel was involved?"

"Some of their lands adjoin, and Tierchyl had refused to sell certain properties to Ryel. That's the rumor anyway."

And Ryel had declared me his enemy. I glanced toward the chair. "It is beautiful."

"The design is unique. If we're lucky, we'll be able to use it as a model for someone else in the future."

"If not, it makes a lovely addition here."

"An expensive addition."

Within a few moments and before anyone thumped the big brass knocker on the main door, I heard another set of footsteps, slower but lighter, coming down the steps.

Without thinking I said, "That's your Grandmama Diestra. She wants a few moments with us before dinner."

Seliora looked at me, then at the archway, where Grandmama Diestra emerged, glancing at Seliora.

Seliora shook her head. "I don't care what your mother thinks. There has to be Pharsi in your background. You didn't even think about it, did you?"

"No," I admitted, somewhat sheepishly, before standing to welcome Seliora's grandmother. "Good afternoon."

Seliora rose and stood beside me.

"The same to you, Rhenn."

Seliora just said, "He knew you were coming before he saw you, and he knew what you had in mind. I hadn't said a word."

"You're surprised, granddaughter?" Grandmama Diestra chuckled.

I grinned, then gestured to the settee. While they settled themselves, I retrieved the chair I'd admired and set it down on the rich gold-green border of the magnificent maroon carpet that covered much of the parquet floor of the entry hall, then sat down facing them.

"Seliora tells me that you're working with the patrollers now. Which senior patrollers have you met?" asked Grandmama Diestra.

"Except in passing, just the commander and subcommander—and a first patroller named Gulyart."

"Do not trust Artois. He is not corrupt, but he would sacrifice his firstborn son to preserve the honor of the Patrol." She laughed softly. "Since it has no honor, there is no point in being sacrificed. Cydarth will do what he must, but there are rumors . . . I have heard nothing bad about Gulyart. Be most careful with Lieutenant Mardoyt or Captain Harraf. Neither is even honestly corrupt."

" 'Honestly corrupt'?"

"They don't stay bought," was her dry response. "What are you doing now?"

"I've been observing the charging desk. I'm supposed to do that for another week." Since she offered nothing else, I asked, "Do you know of a taudischef named Horazt?"

"He's one of the new ones, grandson of Chorazt." Diestra snorted. "I haven't heard anything bad about him. Why?"

"He brought a boy to the Collegium. The boy's named Shault. He's a beginning imager. I was wondering if there were any way to learn if the mother got the gold she was supposed to. Her name is . . . Chelya." I'd had to think a moment to call it up. "I think she's a cousin of Horazt's."

"Chelya . . . she's Mhyala's daughter, or one of them." She smiled, and a glint appeared in her eyes. "I'll find out, and I'll make sure that Horazt understands that you know. Might scare the little bastard. It won't hurt you." Her eyebrows lifted. "You have something else?"

I slipped the envelope I'd received on Jeudi out of the inside pocket of my gray wool imager's waistcoat and handed it to Seliora. "Open it . . . both of you should see it."

She deftly extracted the card. Both sets of black eyes—so alike were they—narrowed as they beheld the silver ribbon knot.

"Ryel . . ." murmured Seliora.

"As soon as he discovered I'd been made a master imager," I said.

"That way he loses no prestige among the other High Holders," added Grandmama Diestra. "Prestige is another form of power."

"A master imager of twenty-five is a worthy foe?" My words came out sardonically as I reclaimed the card and envelope and tucked them inside my waistcoat.

"There are far fewer master imagers than High Holders," Diestra said.

"There are far fewer total imagers." By that standard, poor scared Shault was a worthy opponent. I didn't like either of Ryel's sons, and from what I'd experienced, his daughter was just as cutthroat—all of which confirmed that they took after their father.

The knocker thumped loudly.

Both Seliora and I stood immediately, and she headed for the steps down to the entry. I let her lead the way.

Once on the street level, Seliora glanced out the side window. "It's Aunt Staelia and Uncle Clyenn." She opened the heavy polished oak door. "Do come in!" Her voice and posture were warm and welcoming.

"Every time I see you," replied Clyenn, stepping into the small foyer at the base of the steps, "you've gotten more beautiful." He turned to me. "You must be Rhennthyl. You're a most fortunate man."

"I am, indeed," I replied, keeping a smile on my face. I couldn't say that I disliked Clyenn on sight, but I would not have trusted him any farther than I had Johanyr. I didn't wonder that he had a scar that ran from below his left earlobe almost to the corner of his mouth.

Staelia was statuesque, more like Odelia and Aegina, but not so attractive, just tall, plain, and graying, but she had a radiant smile, bestowed primarily on Seliora.

"Aunt Staelia," Seliora said, "this is Rhenn. I didn't have a chance to tell you, but he's been made a master imager."

Staelia looked me over—our eyes were close to level—and smiled again, not quite so radiantly, but certainly warmly. "You two suit each other, I think."

Seliora led the way up to the main foyer.

Seliora's parents must have heard the knocker or the greetings, or been watching the lane from the third floor . . . or Bhenyt had told them. The possibilities were numerous, but Shelim and Betara moved to join us within moments of the time that Seliora and I had escorted Staelia and Clyenn up to the entry hall. In that short time, various servants had appeared, and a sideboard with wines had been opened. Shomyr—Seliora's older brother—brought out several bottles of wine. He was followed by Methyr, her younger brother.

"I see you've met Rhenn," said Betara, her voice and expressions so much like Seliora's that mother and daughter looked like sisters.

"We have indeed," boomed Clyenn. "Yes, indeed."

"Indeed," said Staelia. "Clyenn . . . if you wouldn't mind getting me a white Cambrisio."

"I can do that." He turned and started for the sideboard.

"You're one of the younger master imagers, I'd imagine," Staelia said.

"Yes, madame."

"Staelia, please." An amused smile appeared. "Save the 'madame' for Betara or Grandmama. Perhaps one of the youngest master imagers ever?"

"One of the younger ones," I admitted. "Not the youngest ever."

"Polite and modest, too. Dangerous, as well. I've seen that with the patrollers. The most deadly ones are the most courteous."

The instant assessments by Seliora's family—or by the women in the family—were both amusing as well as unsettling. I inclined my head. "And I believe no one is ever disorderly in your establishment."

Both Staelia and Betara laughed.

"A point to you. With Taelia and Sartan running it tonight, I hope it stays orderly." The last words combined dryness and worry.

Another series of thumps issued from below.

"That must be Duerl and Aesthya," offered Betara. "I'll greet them."

Shelim, who had said nothing, departed with his wife, leaving Seliora and me with Staelia.

"You must come and eat lunch or dinner at the bistro with us when you can."

"I'd like to, but it might be a while. I'm still learning my way around headquarters."

"It won't take you long," she predicted. "But don't order the baked pastry sausages. They're the one thing that Clyenn does that aren't that good—but people don't want them good. They want them soft and slathered with greasy white gravy." She shrugged. "So that's the way we fix them."

Betara and Shelim reappeared with another couple, guiding them toward us.

"Aesthya, Duerl, this is Rhenn."

"Ah, yes," offered the slightly plump but still sprightly Aesthya. "We have heard so much about you, and"—she looked to Seliora—"learned so little . . . other than you're a master imager."

"Very recently, I must confess," I replied. "I'm pleased to meet you both."

After that, there were goblets of wine in everyone's hands, and many pleasantries, and a few more questions about what I'd done. Before long, a set of chimes rang, and we all repaired to the dining chamber, through the recessed doors at the end of the foyer that the serving girls began to open as the sound of the chimes died away.

The dining chamber held a table set for eleven, but I could tell that the long cherry table could have taken leaves enough to seat twice that many, and the unused chairs set against the walls at the sides of the china cabinets and sideboards reinforced that impression. The chamber was illuminated by wall lamps set in polished bronze sconces with reflectors, as well as by three sets of candelabra on the table itself. The cutlery was all silver, and the porcelain chargers were gold rimmed with the NordEste design in the center.

Seliora offered the grace, and then we all took our seats. She and I had been placed in the middle of the table, with Shelim at one end and Betara at the other. I was flanked by Aesthya on my right, and Staelia on my left, with Seliora across the table—sort of, because with four on her side and five on mine, I was actually across from the space between her and Clyenn.

The meal began with a light red wine I didn't recognize and a cream of gourd soup with wild mushrooms, followed by sweet and bitter greens with vinegar and nuts, and then by what I could only have called a Pharsi ragout in flaky pastry.

The entire time the conversation varied from topic to topic, but never touched on any form of business.

". . . people fleeing here from everywhere . . . causes problems and unrest in taudis, especially in the hellhole."

". . . hasn't been this bad since the troubles years back . . ."

"Mama Diestra . . . she has fewer connections there . . . or in the south . . ."

"Capolito is bringing back the traditional Pharsi singers to sing . . ."

". . . won't draw diners . . . people want to eat and talk . . ."

". . . factors, maybe, they only talk about business anyway."

". . . wager it'll be less than three weeks before Stakanar and Tiempre are inside Caenen."

". . . couldn't believe that a high factor's wife would wear pink after the end of harvest . . ."

I ate sparingly, but I still took in more than I should have, and that was before dessert, which was a pastry tart with jelled and sweetened lime glaze over apples.

There was more conversation over dessert, and over the tiny goblets of warm brandy that followed, and it was approaching ninth glass before people began to drift away, although Grandmama Diestra had slipped out before dessert.

In the end, Seliora and I found ourselves sitting in the dim light of a single lamp, back on the same settee as where we had started, seemingly alone in the entry foyer.

"What did you think of the rest of the family?" asked Seliora.

"I like Duerl and Aesthya, and I really enjoyed meeting Staelia."

"Your feelings are much like everyone else's."

"What does Clyenn do?"

"You know Staelia runs a small bistro. It's only about two blocks from the Patrol headquarters. It's east of there and a half block off Fedre on Pousaint. Clyenn isn't too bad a cook, and he does exactly what Staelia tells him to. He's only strayed once."

"The scar?"

"The second one will be across his throat . . . not that anyone would find his body." Seliora's words were absolutely matter-of-fact.

"Pharsi treatment of infidelity?"

She shook her head. "Stealing of funds. You don't steal from family, ever. Infidelity can happen. It's frowned on, but people are people. Theft is deliberate. You have to think it out, and that's betrayal."

Put that way, I definitely understood. I also realized that I didn't understand Seliora's family quite so well as I'd thought I did. I smiled wryly.

"Why the smile?" Curiosity and worry lay behind her question.

"I was thinking of Rousel, and how it's a good thing he's operating a factorage for my family, rather than a spice brokerage for Remaya's family."

"They don't hold the Pharsi traditions as strongly," she said.

"I wouldn't know."

She smiled, slightly possessively, I thought. "I'm glad."

I thought about saying something about how she was so much more than Remaya, but decided against it, because the words would have implied the comparison, and comparisons are always odious, especially to a beautiful woman who loved me.

"You should stop by Staelia's. It's called Chaelia."

We talked a bit more, and I could see her yawning. "I should go."

Abruptly she straightened. "There's someone outside."

"We should go down and look."

Arm in arm, we did, and I looked through the small window to the left of the door casement. "I don't see anyone, but there's a hack there."

"Mother paid him to wait for you."

"I shouldn't keep him waiting, then. I'll be very careful." I raised my shields even before Seliora opened the door.

The muffled crack of a weapon and the impact against my shields were almost simultaneous, and I couldn't help but stagger back into Seliora.

"Namer-damned . . ." Who could have been shooting at me? Straight assassination wasn't what High Holder Ryel would have done. At least, I didn't think so.

In the distance, I could hear footsteps. Much as I was tempted to give chase, the shooter had too much of a head start, and it could also have been a trap.

"They've gone," Seliora said.

The hacker was looking around.

"I'll be right there!" I called.

I wasn't right there, because Seliora and I did need a little time to say good night and good-bye, but the hacker did wait. Betara had obviously paid him well, for which I was glad.

On the drive back to the Bridge of Hopes, I couldn't help but wonder if High Holder Ryel had changed his mind . . . or if I'd become someone else's enemy. But whose? I hadn't done anything to anyone at the Civic Patrol, and all the Ferrans had been taken care of . . . hadn't they?

Yet whoever it had been had known exactly where I'd be. I frowned. It couldn't be Ryel. He would have known I had shields. But who?

Tired as I was, I woke up on Solayi early enough to see both Artiema and Erion in a semidark sky before I trudged down to shower and shave. I took my time before heading off to the dining hall for breakfast. Even so, the only master there was Heisbyl, another senior and graying Maitre D'Aspect. Caliostrus had done a portrait of his daughter, and from what I recalled, the daughter did not look much like her father, except for the hazel eyes. Caliostrus had painted her eyes as warm, but Heisbyl's were flat. Given the tendency of my late portraiturist master to flatter his subjects, I would have wagered that her eyes were like her father's.

"Good morning, Rhenn." He shook his head. "To be young again, like you, and able to greet gray mornings early and cheerfully."

"Early," I replied. "Not always cheerfully."

"When you get to be my age, you'll look back on them and think they were cheerful."

That was a truly frightening thought, but I didn't say so. Instead, I just smiled and passed the teapot to him. "You have the duty today."

"Why else would I be here? And you?"

"I discovered I had a few things on my mind."

"Most of you who report to Dichartyn seem to. It's not something I'd wish to do. Running the armory workshops is far more to my taste."

"To each his own." I took a swallow of the tea before I started eating, but I couldn't see why supervising the armory production was any less disturbing than covert operations, except that we occasionally had to kill people directly, and what he did resulted in killing far greater numbers of people—just far less directly.

After breakfast I went to the library once more. I had another set of ideas I wanted to try out. Rather than look directly for High Holder Ryel or for books on High Holders, I decided to see what there was on laws dealing with land transfers, or anything on land holdings, or material on the original compact.

All in all, I spent more than two glasses tracking down one piece of information and then another. I did discover that a High Holder had to pass a minimum of four-fifths of his holdings on to his heir—unless the total of the lands to be received were greater in size than the average of all High Holdings, in which case the inheritance merely had to exceed the average. I supposed that meant a truly massive High Holding could actually be split among two or three heirs. The heir was first the oldest son, then other sons in birth order—but could be a nephew or a grandson. The only way a woman could inherit was if there were no male descendants, and no blood nephews, and her husband had to take the family name. That did create some interesting speculation about Junaie D'Shendael. If the four-fifths requirement could not be met from the estate itself, unless the putative heir could purchase or otherwise provide evidence of lands and assets sufficient to add to the inherited holding to meet that requirement, the High Holding was registered as dissolved.

The last point was that any High Holder had the right to override a purchase agreement for lands sold to a non–High Holder by registering such an override, but the High Holder undertaking the override had to pay fifteen percent above the original purchase price, and one-third of the fifteen percent went to whoever had contracted to buy the lands, and ten percent went to the seller, usually to the heirs who were no longer High Holders.

I did find out, through some obscure footnotes, the general location and extent of the holdings of the Ryel family—and the name passed with the lands to the heir, so that Dulyk would become High Holder Ryel with the death of his father. The Ryel familial lands lay some hundred odd milles almost due north of L'Excelsis and ran from the edge of Rivages to well beyond Cleville to the east. The holding had to be more than fifty milles east to west, but I couldn't determine how far north and south it ran. Ryel's colors were black and silver, and I knew I'd seen them somewhere, but couldn't remember when or where. Certainly, Iryela hadn't worn black, though I did recall silver.

As a result of my absorption in the library, I missed lunch, but that was not a burden, since I wasn't that hungry. Close to the first glass of the afternoon, I crossed the Bridge of Desires and hired a hack to take me to see Seliora. I hadn't said I was coming, but she was usually there on Solayi, and I wanted to see if she had any thoughts on who had shot at me on Samedi night.

Seliora was home. In fact, she was the one who answered the door. Once I was in the foyer, she did kiss me warmly before she escorted me up to the main entry hall. She wore simple dark blue trousers, a wide leather belt, a severe tan shirt, and a soft leather jacket.

"I'm glad you came now, rather than later. I wouldn't have been here."

"You have to go somewhere? Now?"

"In a half glass or so." She shook her head. "We don't usually work on So-layi, but one of our longtime clients has decided that his salon needs to be re-done before his daughter's wedding at the end of Feuillyt. That's only eight weeks from now, and we have to meet with him and his wife today because they're leaving for Nacliano on Lundi."

"I should have asked about coming today before I left last night, but I didn't think about it after what happened. Do you have any idea—"

"It can't be Ryel. High Holders don't operate that way."

"Unless he knows about my shields and is just having people shoot at me to wear me down and get me upset . . . or upset those close to me." I really didn't believe that, but I thought I should mention it.

Seliora frowned. "That could be, but I don't think so. When I get a mo-ment, I'll talk to Grandmama Diestra about it. She might have some ideas."

"I could use some."

"Rhenn . . . if you walk anywhere with other patrollers, you might con-sider . . ."

"Extending my shields to cover them? I've thought about it. It won't do me any good if every patroller around me gets shot." That would tax me even more, but the alternatives were worse. From what I knew about how High Holders handled revenge, Ryal was unlikely to have been behind it . . . but who else would have been? "You will see if anyone knows about any others like the Ferran?"

She nodded.

That was all I could ask. I grinned. "Did I behave acceptably last night?"

"Oh, Rhenn . . . you're always polite and charming . . . even when people don't deserve it."

I wasn't so sure about that, but it was nice to hear. "Do you think that we could go out to dinner next Samedi? Even at Terraza?"

"We could go to Azeyd's . . . if you'd like to try authentic Pharsi fare."

"I'd like that." I paused. "Is it owned by relatives?"

"Friends of Mother's. She'd be pleased."

Another set of chaperones, in a way, but just to be able to talk to her alone would be good, and the thought of Pharsi cuisine appealed to me. "Done. Fifth glass?"

Her smile was answer enough.

After that, we got to spend a few moments talking about nothing of great import, but before too long she had to go.

I spent more coins taking a hack from NordEste Design to my parents'. Because it was Solayi, and Nellica had the day off, Khethila was the one who answered the door.

"Rhenn!" She gave me a warm sisterly hug. Then we went to the family parlor where Khethila dropped into Father's chair. I took the one across from it.

"Rhenn, I finally got my copy of her book."

"Whose book?" I did grin as I said it.

"Madame D'Shendael's. You know that. I still can't believe you danced with her. You've never said any more about what she said, you know?"

"I can't, except that I did tell her that you had read all her books except for *On Art and Society*. She asked me twice if I made that up. I told her it was the truth."

I still wondered exactly what Juniae D'Shendael's connection had been with the late Ferran envoy, but I supposed I'd never know.

"She had to be polite, but what else was she like?"

"On guard. She's been pressing for a Council that has some councilors directly elected by the people, the way they do in the Abierto Isles. I heard that Councilor Caartyl invites her to every Council ball just to keep her in view of the other councilors."

"Would that vote include women? If it didn't, I don't see that it would make much difference in the way the Council worked." Her tone was dismissive.

"As far as the High Holders go, it would."

"Not that much."

"You might be right." I thought it would make a great difference, but I wasn't about to argue about it.

"You're being condescending, Rhenn."

I shrugged, then lowered my voice. "How are matters in Kherseilles?"

Khethila frowned, as if debating whether to pursue what she thought had been my condescension, then shook her head. "Someone bought the notes Rousel took out and demanded immediate payment. We arranged it, but it cost another twenty golds . . . and Father had to post a bond of another hundred with the Banque D'Kherseilles to keep the line of credit."

"So he lost nearly three hundred golds this season?" That amount of loss was hard for me to understand. Through bad judgment Rousel had lost in two months more than I'd make in six years, and the factorage in Kherseilles wasn't that large.

"Four hundred, if you count the bond," Khethila said quietly. "His receipts are down, too. I think someone has put out the word not to buy from him. We've even gotten orders here lately, asking us to ship to places like Mantes, and they used to take delivery from Rousel in Kherseilles."

"Do you know who bought the notes?"

"The Banque D'Rivages, but they wouldn't have done it except as an agent. Why would a banque nearly thirteen hundred milles from Kherseilles buy notes secured by the stock of a small factorage in Kherseilles?"

I had an idea, but at the moment I certainly had no way to prove it. Even if I did, what had been done was strictly legal. Ryel would have made certain that everything remained within the law, or at least within the appearance of the law.

"Someone's here . . ."

That was my mother's voice, coming from the hall.

"Rhenn! You didn't say you were coming." Accusation mixed with warmth in Mother's voice.

"I didn't know I was coming."

"That's probably because he'd planned to see Seliora, and she had other plans," suggested Khethila sweetly, a statement clearly offered as retaliation for what she thought had been condescension.

"I did see her, already, but it had to be brief because she had to work."

"On Solayi?" asked Mother.

"A large and urgent commission."

"Good for her," Father said bluffly. "She and her family know what's important. That's why they've been so successful."

The briefest of frowns crossed Khethila's brow.

"So long as they don't do it every Solayi," added Mother. "Didn't you have dinner with her family and some of their relatives last night? How was it?"

"They were all very nice. One of her aunts runs a bistro not all that far from Patrol headquarters. It's called Chaelia, I think."

"I haven't heard of it," Father replied.

"Is it in a good area?" asked Mother.

I laughed. "I don't know. I haven't been there, but it can't be too bad because it's only a few blocks from Civic Patrol headquarters, and that's only a half block off East River Road."

"If you eat there, dear, I do hope it's in a good area."

After that, we talked about, or rather I listened to Mother rhapsodize about Remaya and Rousel's son Rheityr.

I barely made it back to Imagisle in time to eat and then go to services. I stood where I could watch Shault. Lieryns was next to him, I thought, but I wasn't totally sure in the dim light, and I didn't want to get close enough that my observations would have been noted.

As often was the case, one part of Chorister Isola's homily resonated with me.

". . . Naming is as much about control as about labeling or identity. We tend to think that when we name something or someone we have gained control. The superior always uses a diminutive to an inferior. That, too, is part of the sin of naming. The man or woman who can act as though there were no names is far greater than one who insists on a hierarchy of names. . . . Is it any accident that those who most relish naming are those who are most loath to give up power, position, or control? . . ."

I had to admit that I really hadn't thought about the way names were used as a symptom of power and of how people used them in that fashion, but it certainly made a great deal of sense, and I made a mental reminder to try to watch for that in the days ahead.

Lundi was a very busy day at the Patrol charging desk. So was Mardi. Meredi morning didn't look to be that much better because, when I got to head-quarters, there were offenders waiting everywhere even before Gulyart and I started to register the charges. By tenth glass, when we had three-quarters of a glass off to eat lunch, we both were more than ready to leave the confines of the Patrol building. The rain had subsided to a comparative drizzle, not too uncomfortable for mid-fall, as we stepped outside.

"This week has been like most of them," Gulyart said. "There's no charg-ing done past Samedi at noon, and none on Solayi. So the holding cells are full by Lundi, and sometimes more than that, and it takes days before we get caught up. Last week was lighter than usual."

"I liked last week better," I said with a laugh. "You'd think some of them would learn."

Gulyart shook his head. "They only get one chance to learn, two at most, before they end up on penal work duties for life. Most who get caught aren't bright enough to see that."

That was obvious—once he'd pointed it out, but I hadn't thought of it that way. Some people just took longer to learn, but I could see the Civic Pa-trol's view. Why should law-abiding citizens have to pay because lawbreakers had a hard time learning?

We walked to the second closest bistro—Saliana's—because Gulyart said that he could only take so much of the heavy potato noodles at Fiendyl's, the bistro almost directly across Fedre from headquarters. Heavy noodles didn't bother me, just so long as they weren't greasy. Saliana was supposedly from Tilbora in the far northeast of Solidar, and her place offered more than a few goat dishes. I had a red-spice goat curry over rice, and I used every bit of the rice, flatbread, and lager to try to keep the food from burning my mouth.

"Hot, isn't it?" Gulyart grinned. "Brown-spice is as hot as I can take it. Captain Lheng won't go farther than yellow-brown."

"Next time, I'll have the yellow-brown." Even with the lager, flatbread, and rice I'd had with the meal, my mouth still felt like it was erupting in flame.

When we stepped out of Saliana's, something slammed into my shields. I couldn't help but stagger. A quick glance around revealed nothing other than people going about their business, and none of them even looked in my direction.

"You all right?" asked Gulyart.

"I slipped . . . tripped on something." I looked down as if trying to locate what it might be. I wanted the bullet—anything to give me a clue as to who was shooting at me—and yet I knew I didn't dare spend time searching. So I tried the idea of imaging it into my hand—and I had it in my palm. Except it was so hot that I almost dropped it and had to juggle it before slipping it into my waistcoat pocket. "I don't know what it was. Maybe I kicked it away." I shook my head. "I hate feeling clumsy like that."

I didn't want Gulyart, or any of the patrollers, to know that I was a target. That would just make learning about the Patrol even harder.

"Just be glad you weren't wearing riot gear," replied Gulyart. "Couple years back, more than that, I guess, because it was when I had just joined the Patrol, we had to go into the taudis below South Middle to put down a fight between two taudischefs and their enforcers. Some bastard threw hundreds of scrap bearings onto the street just as we charged them. Mualyt smashed his elbow so bad he got stipended out. That was the last time anyone talked about getting rid of the mounted riot squad. Most of them have other duties, though, these days."

There were three more prisoners waiting when we got back to the charging desk, and the rest of the afternoon wasn't much better, because they kept bringing in more prisoners.

As soon as I returned to the Collegium late in the day after finishing my observational duties, I made my way to Master Dichartyn's study, where I rapped on the door.

"Rhennthyl, sir. I need a few moments with you. Something's come up."

"I'll be with you in a moment."

A moment was close to a quarter glass, but that wasn't surprising once I saw Master Schorzat leaving, since he ran the covert field operative section of the Collegium and reported to Master Dichartyn.

As soon as I'd entered the study, Master Dichartyn looked up at me, almost wearily. "What have you to report?"

"On Samedi night, someone took a shot at me, and the same thing happened today at lunch, when Gulyart and I were walking back toward the headquarters building. I think the shot came from a window or the top of a building. I just told Gulyart I stumbled on something."

"Do you think he figured out what really happened?"

"He didn't press me or look at me strangely. If he did, he's not saying, not to me."

"If he is, I'll learn later," Master Dichartyn said. "Did you see anyone?"

"No. They were using a rifle, possibly a sniper rifle."

"Were they actually trying to hit you?"

"There was just one shot both times. Each hit my shields. Today, I managed to image the bullet into my hand." I slipped the flattened lead from my waistcoat pocket and handed it over to him.

"You imaged it into your hand?" His eyebrows went up.

"I couldn't very well go grubbing around for it. I thought it would either work or it wouldn't."

"How do you know you didn't just image a new bullet?"

"I don't, I suppose, except it was so hot it almost burned my hand, and it's flattened on one side."

"It's probably the one fired at you. Still . . ." Master Dichartyn studied it for a moment. "Definitely a sniper bullet. It could be Ferran or Jariolan, or even Solidaran. Might be Tiempran." He smiled faintly. "Have you offended any more envoys?"

"I haven't even met any more, sir."

"That doesn't mean you didn't offend them. It's likely that you didn't get all of those involved with the Ferran operation. Someone who was watching and identified you got away, and now has orders to remove you."

"Do the Ferrans even have a new envoy?"

"They do. He's been here a little over two days. One Stauffen Gregg. The Honorable Stauffen Gregg. He brought a staff of ten."

"I don't believe you mentioned that." I managed to maintain a pleasant smile. The "recall" of the previous staff now sounded like more of a return to a reprimand . . . or worse, not that my experiences had left me with any liking for the Ferrans.

"There was no reason to, until now. You aren't working Council security any longer."

There were times that Maitre Dichartyn could be condescendingly, obnoxiously infuriating. This was one of them. I kept smiling. "What do you suggest that I do about the sniper?"

"You'll need to get a good look at him if you want to deal with him. And it's probably best that you don't tell anyone on the Patrol."

Master Dichartyn's words were a veiled reminder that I wasn't to trouble the Collegium by leaving a would-be assassin alive. Nor was I to mix Collegium business with Patrol business. I didn't ask for more information. He didn't know any more or wasn't about to tell me, but I suspected the former.

"Is there anything else?" asked my superior. "I need to see Master Poincaryt."

"I've spent a little time on Samedi and yesterday evening with young Shault. I have to say that I worry about him."

"So do I, but your short visits are definitely having an effect. Ghaend reports that he is studying and making good progress, and Gherard says that the seconds have decided that if you're watching him, they'd best leave him alone."

I had my doubts that such forbearance would endure, but I could hope it would last long enough for Shault to gain understanding and confidence.

Master Dichartyn rose from behind his writing desk. "If that's all . . ."

"That's all for now, sir, but I thought you should know."

He just gestured toward the door. I left and headed back to my rooms.

Immediately after I entered my chambers, and the room that was study and salon, I walked to the writing desk, where I placed several objects on the left side of the writing desk—an oval ceramic paperweight, a copper pen nib, and a Solidaran silver crown. Then I covered them with a sheet of writing paper and stepped back four paces. I concentrated on imaging the pen nib onto the open palm of my right hand.

It appeared there, almost light as a feather.

I repeated the process with the coin and the paperweight. After looking closely at all three and seeing that they looked the same as they had before, I then set the three on the right side of the desk and lifted the paper on the left side. There was nothing underneath. To my way of thinking, I'd imaged the originals to my hand, rather than creating new objects by imaging. Either that, or I'd destroyed the originals and created copies, but that seemed most unlikely to me, since I didn't feel that tired, and imaging something from nothing or duplicating something through imaging took much more effort. Master Dichartyn had been skeptical of my ability to image the bullet that had been fired at me back to myself. Yet he'd seen me image items from one point to another before. Or was it that I'd been able to image something I hadn't seen or studied . . . and quickly?

I shrugged. I was hungry, and it was almost time for dinner. So I turned and headed out of my rooms, toward the staircase down to the quadrangle and then directly for the dining hall.

9

The rain and drizzle lifted on Meredi night, and the weather cooled so much that there was frost everywhere early on Jeudi. The grass and walkways were so slick that no one ran all that fast, and we finished in a ragged pack. I did wear my cold-weather cloak and gloves for the walk to Patrol headquarters, and with the wind, I was more than glad that I had. The building seemed empty when I hurried in off Fedre and made my way to the charging desk—also vacant, since I'd clearly arrived before Gulyart.

The glass was just ringing as Gulyart hurried in. He wasn't wearing a cloak, but a heavier blue wool uniform. "Good morning, Master Rhennthyl."

"Good morning, Gulyart. There's no one here."

"That's because there was trouble in the South Middle taudis last night, and the subcommander called in everyone he could, even some who had morning duty. We're going to be busy. We won't get a break for lunch, and we'll probably be working till sunset or beyond."

"What happened?"

Gulyart shrugged. "I don't know, except someone started street preaching one of those southern religions—"

"Not Caenen duology?"

"No. The Tiempran equality stuff."

I stiffened inside. Master Dichartyn had said something about the Tiempran First Speaker rewarding those who struck near the heart of their enemies. Was that the reason for the riot . . . or part of it? A year earlier, I wouldn't have known much more than the words he used, but the Collegium had been good for my education, if at the cost of a certain naïve tolerance.

The main faith in Tiempre was monotheistic, but the key tenet of their single powerful god was that all good qualities were present in all human beings. That in itself wasn't all that bad, to my way of thinking, but some of the corollaries were anything but good. If a trait wasn't present in all people, then it was suspect or evil. Because something like only one in a hundred thousand people had the talent for imaging, imagers were agents of the evil one. So were people who were excessively tall or short, and those who were what might be called village idiots were imprisoned in work plantations lest they contaminate others. Very intelligent people were looked on with skepticism, as were the deformed.

"It got out of hand," I suggested.

"Someone started preaching that the Council was following evil because it gave special privileges to the most evil of all—you imagers. He started in on the High Holders after that, screaming that they denied the goodness of equality and made it impossible for the people in the taudis ever to get good jobs, and then he finished up by inciting them to strike out against the Civic Patrol, because we're the agents of the evil oppressors of equality . . . something like that."

"And that started a riot?"

"It wasn't too bad." Gulyart snorted. "They've got almost a hundred waiting to be charged."

"Disturbing the peace and damaging property?"

"Mostly. Maybe twenty or so got caught assaulting someone, and a few attacked patrollers. They didn't get the street preacher, though. He'd better be hiding. Street preaching's a straight shot to life in a penal manufactory."

I could understand that. Any religion in Solidar had the right to assemble and worship—but only on private property and under a roof. It could be in a hovel or a barn or any structure, but street preaching or soliciting was banned. Soliciting was a misdemeanor the first time, but not street preaching. The possible connection to the Tiempran government was also disturbing, but how could one prove it?

"First Patroller Gulyart! The first prisoners are coming in."

A gaol patroller appeared with two men. "These two were part of the mob, disorderly. Nothing much else."

"What is your name?" Gulyart looked at a short, swarthy young man about my age.

After the slightest hesitation, the man looked blank.

"Appelio? Niomen? Habynah?" asked Gulyart.

"Adyon Khurnish."

"Adyon, son of Khurn," Gulyart murmured, "but put it down as he said it."

I checked the files for both versions of the name. "There's nothing here."

"If I hear him right, he's speaking what sounds like accented Tiempran. That means he's probably from Gyarl."

The prisoner had said nothing, but there had been a flicker of something when Gulyart had mentioned Gyarl—a comparatively small land, landlocked and sandwiched between Caenen and Tiempre with about half the people of Caenenan background and half of Tiempran. "He's from Gyarl, I'd wager,"

I offered, "but he doesn't want to let us know it." I had to wonder at that, because Solidar let in anyone who wanted to work as a laborer. It cost too much to post guards everywhere along something like eight thousand milles of coast—that was the area ships could approach enough to let down boats, anyway. Besides, unless someone spoke decent Solidaran, except it really was Bovarian, as it had adapted since Rex Regis had unified all of Solidar, he wasn't going to go anywhere but the fields or day labor. That wasn't exactly a threat to our peace and prosperity. Besides, how many could afford ocean passage?

"That's his problem, not ours," Gulyart said, hurriedly writing out the charging slip and filling out the line on the charging ledger, then looking at the other prisoner. "You? Habynah?"

"Isoloh Solonish."

I checked his name as well, but there was nothing. So I slipped back beside Gulyart and wrote out the ledger entry while he finished the charging slip.

"They're both charged with disorderly and disturbance."

As the two were marched out, I had the feeling that both had understood at least some of what we had said, but I didn't have time to say anything, because they were followed by another gaol patroller with three men, all in manacles.

"Hydrat, here," announced the burly patroller, "he was in for disorderly maybe a year back, far as I recall. Be under Hydrat D'Taudis. No father . . . half-Pharsi scum."

Hydrat's name was there, but the note was that the charges had been dropped.

"Charges were dropped against him," I told Gulyart.

"You're the fortunate one," Gulyart said.

"They'll drop these, too . . . officer. I wasn't doing anything."

"No, just being disorderly," added the gaol patroller, "throwing buckets of piss at the riot squad."

"I never touched a bucket."

Gulyart didn't say a thing, and I copied what he'd written on the charging slip, including the charges of disturbance, disorderly, and assault on a patroller.

"This one looks like all-Pharsi scum. Says his name is Chelam D'Whayan. He was one of the others throwing buckets of piss."

"That's not assault," claimed the scrawny and small black-haired figure, barely a man, if that. "Disorderly, not assault."

"You can tell the justice that. Is Chelam D'Whayan the right name?" asked Gulyart.

"Yeah. . . ."

The patroller yanked the manacles. "He's 'sir' or 'officer' to the likes of you."

"Yes . . . sir." The words were quiet, but Chelam's eyes flared.

There was no record on him, either.

The third was taller, with black hair and an olive skin. Pharsi-Caenenan heritage, I would have guessed. He gave only his name—Chardyn D'Steinyn.

The following prisoner was manacled and gagged. Welts covered the left side of his face, and a wound below his ear had been bandaged. Blood had soaked through part of the dressing.

"This one's major. Name is Fhalyn D'Sourkos. Disorderly, disturbance, and assault with a weapon. He used a pair of dirks against a mounted riot patroller. Horse had to be put down. He's gagged because he spits."

Gulyart didn't have the gag removed, but that name didn't have any record, either. Fhalyn did try to kick the gaol patroller on his way out. That type used the riot as an excuse, hoping he wouldn't get caught in all the chaos. I'd have wagered that as many as we'd end up charging, even more had escaped.

We must have charged close to twenty people before a woman patroller, wiry and tough-looking, appeared with two women who looked to be in their late twenties, but then . . . they might have been younger under all the smudged makeup.

"These two are charged with disturbance and street soliciting. They left their premises during the riot and solicited on the street."

Like street preaching, soliciting on public grounds and streets was an offense, a misdemeanor, but still a crime. Sexual favors could be solicited, but only if the solicitor stood inside a doorway or a window of property with the consent of the owner. Most of the time, I'd heard, patrollers allowed a little leeway.

"We didn't," said the brunette. "Aloust would have beaten us."

"Enough to bruise us where it really hurts," added the other, a thin, black-haired girl, who, upon closer inspection, probably wasn't any older than Khethila. "One of the rioters dragged me from the window. Then two patrollers grabbed me!"

"Your name?" asked Gulyart firmly.

"Alizara. That's it."

There were no Alizaras listed in the records, nor did the records show anything for the older woman, who had given her name as Beustila.

"Likely as not, neither name is real," muttered Gulyart.

"Aren't many of them false?"

"Not so many as you'd think, not when we can check for a hip brand, but there are plenty of false names. The girls change their names, or they use false ones for their work."

As Gulyart had predicted, we didn't finish until well after sixth glass. Because I knew I'd already missed dinner, I stopped and ate a sausage blanket and noodles at Fiendyl's. I only got a few glances, probably because everyone there had seen me more than a few times.

One man kept looking toward me until one of the servers stopped and murmured a few words to him, something like ". . . works over at the Civic Patrol . . . eats here a lot . . ."

I had a long walk back to Imagisle, and one that required carrying full imager shields the entire two milles plus. As I walked through the cool evening, glad for my winter cloak, with a brisk wind blowing out of the northeast, carrying a chill that must have come all the way from the Mountains D'Glace, I couldn't help thinking about all the people who had been charged and how almost none of them had any past record. There were never many, because the Patrol didn't like repeat offenders, but there had been one or two, sometimes three, out of every ten on the other days. Today, I only recalled two out of close to sixty. Maybe there had been three.

I was more than tired when I reached the quadrangle at close to eighth glass. Given the day, how late it was, and especially given Master Dichartyn's condescension of the afternoon before, I didn't see any necessity to report on what had happened at the charging desk. He would have been briefed on the riot, and a report was bound to be in both *Veritum* and *Tableta* as well.

I just washed up, undressed, and went to bed.

10

Vendrei wasn't all that much better than Jeudi at the Patrol headquarters charging desk, because we got another twenty prisoners who had been held at Third District station until we could work through those we'd already dealt with—and we still had to charge those brought in for the daily range of crimes and offenses.

The chargings slowed to a halt in the afternoon around fourth glass, and at that moment, a fresh-faced patroller, several years younger even than I was, appeared. "Master Rhennthyl, the subcommander would appreciate a few moments with you."

"I'm fine," Gulyart said. "Go while things are slow."

The young patroller led the way up the back stairs, and in moments I was in Subcommander Cydarth's study. Although Cydarth was standing by the window, looking out at a clear gray-blue sky, he turned to face me. He did not sit, nor motion for me to do so.

"Rhennthyl, how have you found the past two weeks on the charging desk?"

"Most instructive, sir."

"Oh, and in what fashion, might I ask?" As when I had talked to him before, his words were even, but still carried a sense of the sardonic.

"Certainly in more than any one fashion, sir. The volume of senseless and petty offenses cannot help but remind one of the need for law and patrollers. The few vicious crimes point out that there are always those who would hurt others, if not removed. The care with which the patrollers I have seen carry out their duties increases my respect for them."

"If you take only those thoughts back to the Collegium when you eventually return, the Patrol will be more than repaid."

I ignored the condescension and the implication that I would provide nothing to the Civic Patrol while assigned as liaison. "In time, I'm certain that I will learn more."

His face tightened for a moment. Then he shrugged. "You saw all those who were charged in the riot on Jeudi night, did you not? What did you think about them?"

I'd thought more than a little about it, but I was not about to share all those thoughts with the subcommander. "It seemed strange to me. The weather wasn't hot. There weren't any problems such as the time when that lace mill burned and they discovered that the women had been chained to their machines and burned alive. There wasn't a conscription team near. . . ."

"Exactly. You were here barely more than a week, and you can see that it shouldn't have happened . . . but it did." He paused. "You worked security at the Council Chateau, Master Dichartyn said. How closely did you observe the councilors and their visitors?"

"Most closely in the course of my duties. Otherwise, I never saw them."

"A few assassins ended up dead due to your efforts." He paused and looked at me. "Sometimes . . . one can determine where one stands by his enemies."

"That well may be, sir, but almost every councilor was a target of some assassin or another even in the time I was there. From what I observed of those charged here, there were a few more that looked to be of Ferran origin, but that may have been just what I saw."

"One of the men picked up in the riot spoke Tiempran and had a wallet with some Jariolan golds. How likely is it that a taudis-dweller who speaks Tiempran and Solidaran and has Jariolan golds in his wallet happens to be in a taudis riot in L'Excelsis by accident?"

"That would seem highly unlikely, sir."

"You might pass that on to Master Dichartyn."

"I'm certain he will appreciate that."

"As for you, Commander Artois has decided that you should spend the next week or so observing cases presented in the justice courts. That way, before you start accompanying patrollers, you'll have an idea of the process after someone is arrested and charged. You'll be observing and assisting Lieutenant Mardoyt. He's in charge of making sure that the prisoners and the officers involved in each case appear on time and with all the supporting evidence."

"Yes, sir." There was something behind Cydarth's words, and it didn't help that Grandmama Diestra had warned me against Mardoyt.

"Lieutenant Mardoyt has the study two doors down. He's expecting you." Cydarth turned and looked toward the window.

I didn't bother to say more, but stepped out of his study and walked through the empty anteroom and down the slightly dusty hallway. The second door was ajar. I rapped gently.

"Master Rhennthyl?" asked a smooth baritone voice.

"The same."

"Do come in."

As I entered, the man who rose from the small writing desk in a narrow room with a single window was blond, blue-eyed, and slender. Slightly shorter than I, he also offered a warm smile, and there was the slightest crinkle around his eyes when he smiled. "I'm very pleased to meet you. Subcommander Cydarth has been most favorable in his assessment of you, and I have to say that anyone who has demonstrated master qualities as both a portraiturist and an imager has my admiration."

I smiled as warmly as I could in response, even though I felt there was a calculating coldness behind the lieutenant's superficial warmth. "The subcommander was most admiring of your abilities, sir, and I hope that I'll be able to be of some assistance in addition to observing."

"I'm sure you will be." Another smile followed the words. "What we do— that's me, and now you, and four patroller clerks—what we do is to prepare the presentation of charges to the justices in the central judicial district here. Not for the minor cases that go to the magistrates; we just send them there with the charge sheets. There are six districts that serve L'Excelsis, and we handle all of the major charges from them. We have to make sure that the charging slip matches the prisoner, that a date and time is set for the case before the justice, and that we have an escort and a covered wagon to take each consignment of prisoners to the court building in the Square of Justice. We also have to make sure any patrollers involved in a case are present, and witnesses as well. Once the sentence is passed, we then make sure the papers are correct and complete before we turn the prisoner over to the penal guards."

"Is there an advocate for the ones who can't afford to pay for one?"

"There are two public advocates on duty every day at the court. They get half a glass, sometimes a little less, to meet with each prisoner before they go before the justice. But don't worry. You're mostly here to watch and ask questions. Just be here a bit before eighth glass on Lundi. Then we'll go over the prisoners and the schedule for the day, quickly, so that you can see what's involved. The clerks actually prepare the final schedule the afternoon before, but schedules are roughed out sometimes a week in advance. . . ."

The lieutenant went on for another quarter glass before he sent me back down to the charging desk. After that, we only charged two more offenders, both for trying to make off with hams from a butcher.

As we got ready to leave for the day, I turned to Gulyart. "Thank you. I appreciate your time and showing me how the charging desk works. On Lundi, I start to observe Lieutenant Mardoyt and the courts."

"I appreciated the help, especially this week." Gulyart grinned. "The lieutenant is very smooth, very polished. Watch him closely, and you'll learn a lot."

"I'm sure I will. I just might stop back here occasionally."

"You're always welcome, sir."

As I walked back toward Imagisle, I couldn't help but think that my own impressions, not to mention Gulyart's polite words, tended to confirm what Grandmama Diestra had said.

Once I got to the Collegium, I did have a little time to clean up before I headed to the dining hall. But when I did head in to dinner, I picked up a copy of *Veritum* because my eyes picked up the headline—"Ferran Fleet Alert." To one side was another story about the need for increased conscription.

I saw that the masters' table had only a handful of people there. Ferlyn was on the side away from me, seated with Ghaend and Draffyd. That reminded me that I had to see Maitre Draffyd at ninth glass on Samedi morning, right after the portrait session with Master Rholyn.

Closer to me were the two women maitres, and I stepped toward them.

"I see you've been perusing the scandal sheets," said Maitre Dyana from where she sat beside Maitre Chassendri. "Did you learn anything?" She flipped back the brilliant blue scarf, one of the many bright-colored ones she wore to complement her imager grays.

"Only that they don't seem to know much more than I do, and that's discouraging." I slipped into the chair beside her.

"That's the beginning of wisdom," added Chassendri, "when you realize that almost no one really knows much about anything and that the sum total of human knowledge can explain only a fraction of what we observe."

"Spoken like a true scientist." Maitre Dyana's words were both dry and cutting. "If we know so little, you might explain why we still don't live in caves."

"Given how intelligent so many seem to be," countered Chassendri, "why has it taken so long for us to learn how to build warm and comfortable dwellings, let alone steam engines and turbines, and ironway systems?"

"Politics," I suggested, "and the fact that there are far too many people who want more than they contribute. Or who would rather take from others than build or make it themselves."

"You're almost as cynical as Maitre Dyana," said Chassendri, "and you're far younger. I shudder to think of how misanthropic you'll be by the time you're her age."

"Young master Rhenn has lived longer beyond the walls of the Collegium than have most imagers his age," replied Dyana, her voice gentle, almost sweet. "He's been required to look at life from three very different perspectives. That sort of experience does tend to create a more realistic outlook than laboratory expertise."

"A lofty perspective, such as that of a High Holder who has to become an imager."

"Any High Holder's daughter would murder if she thought it would make her an imager, and bribe and suborn almost anyone to marry one . . . as you should know, dear Chassendri."

I froze, unable to say anything. Those were the most cutting words I'd ever heard from Maitre Dyana, as sweetly as they had been spoken.

After the briefest of pauses, Dyana went on in the same tone. "Rhenn has a far wider perspective than a High Holder, and that will make it harder for him to deal with such, but also will make him less understandable to them."

For the moment, listening to them, I felt more like a chemical substance or a creature on Master Draffyd's dissecting table. I still smiled, then asked, "What do you two think about the taudis riot?"

Chassendri shrugged. "They do riot at times. It comes with poverty and deprivation."

"You don't think it was that, do you?" Maitre Dyana looked at me.

"No. It's too soon after harvest. Food isn't dear, and it's neither that hot nor that cold, and the Council didn't announce increased conscription levels until after the riot, and the Patrol hasn't been harassing the elvers."

"What do you think?" inquired Dyana.

I grinned. "You have far more experience than I, despite your kind words. I was hoping you might offer an opinion based on your expertise." I poured some red Cambrisio into her goblet, and then into mine. I could use it after dealing with both Cydarth and Mardoyt.

Chassendri managed to hide a grin behind the platter of sliced Mantean beef.

Dyana chuckled. "Unlike my compatriot, I would so love to see you in twenty years."

I waited through that gambit while Dyana served herself the beef, the gravy, and the brown rice. Then I served myself.

Finally, she said, "The riot was most likely instigated by an outside source, but whoever did so will not have left any direct traces, but evidence leading to some other party."

"Couldn't it just be some of the High Holders who fear the factors and guilds getting more power in the Council?" asked Chassendri.

"It could be, or it could be the mercantilist factors who want to prove that the poor are that way because they deserve to be—that's the way the Ferrans operate. Or it could be someone in the taudis trying to get the Civic Patrol to crack down on the territory of a rival taudischef. Or it could be a foreign power with the aim of creating unrest and disruption here in L'Excelsis so that we would be less likely to become involved in war elsewhere. Or . . ." Dyana offered an enigmatic smile. "There are more than a few possibilities."

There were, and I didn't much care for any of them. I doubted that we even knew all of them . . . but I couldn't help wondering how much the words of the First Speaker of Tiempre had contributed to the riot . . . and whether it had just been his words.

11

When I walked along the edge of the quadrangle toward the exercise chambers on Samedi morning, I could see there was no frost on the grass or trees or walkways, but it didn't feel much warmer than earlier in the week because a stiff wind blew out of the northwest.

After the warm-up and conditioning exercises, and before I started the blade and truncheon routines, Clovyl drew me aside for a moment.

"Lundi, if Master Draffyd says it's all right, you'll start on a refresher in hand-to-hand combat, with some work on techniques that might prove useful on the streets with the patrollers."

"Good. These solitary routines get tedious after a while."

"They still might save your guts someday. You can't always image your way out of all the troubles you might face." He lowered his voice. "You're talented enough that you'll end up in more tight places than most could imagine. Master Dichartyn doesn't hesitate to use talent."

Or sacrifice it for a great gain for the Collegium. But I didn't say that.

Dartazn was back in running form, and I didn't finish the four-mille run within a hundred yards of him. He'd already headed for the showers before I stumbled to a halt outside the exercise chambers.

Master Schorzat wasn't all that far behind me. He gave me a smile. "How are you finding the Civic Patrol?"

"It's interesting, and I'm learning."

"You might think over if there are other ways to do what the Patrol does, and what implications they would have."

I laughed. "Are you trying to get me to think like a field imager?"

"No. That sort of thinking can help you figure out whether procedures can be changed—or why they shouldn't be when someone has a brilliant new idea." He snorted. "Someone always does, and half the time it's a very bad brilliant new idea. A senior imager needs to be able to recognize those. That's all."

"Thank you, sir." I had my doubts whether the reason he'd given me was the only reason why he wanted me to analyze Civic Patrol procedures.

After getting a shower and shaving, and dressing, I hurried to the dining hall, where, just after I appeared, Ferlyn arrived with a graying master I'd seen a few times when I'd been a third, but whom I'd never met. "Rhenn, have you met Quaelyn?"

"I haven't had the pleasure."

"Quaelyn, this is Rhennthyl. He's the newest Maitre D'Aspect. He also has the distinction of having survived more assassination attempts than any third in the history of the Collegium. The last time was when he stopped the Ferran spies from exploding a firewagon near the Council security force." Ferlyn laughed softly. "They had to make him a master after that."

"Ferlyn gives me too much credit," I replied, although I had the feeling he might have been right about the assassination attempts.

"I doubt it, not if you report to Master Dichartyn," replied Quaelyn.

"Might I ask your specialty?" I asked as we walked to the masters' table.

"Me? I guess you'd call me the master of patterns. I look at ledgers and books and rosters, and report what I see in the numbers and figures and . . . everything."

We sat down on the left end of the table. I looked out at the table holding the primes and seconds and could see Shault, sitting next to Lieryns. That was good. Surprisingly, Lieryns looked up, then nodded. I nodded back.

"Just before we saw you," Ferlyn said, pouring tea for Quaelyn and then handing me the pot, "we were talking about the assassinations of imagers. Did you know that we lost another one last night?"

"Another junior imager? Or someone more senior?"

"Thenard. He was still a prime, but he was close to making second."

I recalled Thenard. He'd offered a few suggestions and observation when I'd first come to Imagisle, and he'd been friendly and good-natured. "How did it happen?"

"He just crossed the Bridge of Desires. There's a good patisserie not more than two blocks down the Boulevard D'Council, off a side lane. When he came out of the patisserie, someone shot him. No one saw the shooter."

I turned to Quaelyn. "You weren't discussing this as a coincidence, I take it?"

"No. It is an example of patterns. I'm working with Ferlyn on many of these. I'm not so young as I once was."

"This is getting serious," Ferlyn went on. "We find something between thirty and forty new imagers every year. Master Poincaryt thinks we get about half that are born in Solidar, later, of course. We're fortunate to find even half, but that's the way it is. Maybe ten imagers die naturally every year—on average, anyway. Another ten die because they're imagers and either do something stupid or die as field or covert types, and, like it or not, five to ten get killed every year because some people don't like imagers. Those are the numbers. The problem is that for the past year, we've had close to twenty junior imagers shot, and most have looked to be planned assassinations. And as soon as we stop one group, it's like another pops up."

While he was speaking, I served myself and handed the platter of cheesed eggs and sausage chunks to Ferlyn. "Why do you think that's happening now?"

Ferlyn looked to Quaelyn.

The older master smiled. "Master Poincaryt and Dichartyn have their doubts, but I believe that it's the result of intersecting patterns. Societies and cultures all function because they adopt patterns. Some of those patterns are so ingrained that no one even knows they're patterns. Others aren't so natural, and they need reinforcement. Laws are a form of pattern reinforcement . . ."

I just listened for a time.

". . . as societies or whole lands change, the patterns have to change, and people need to be made aware of the need for change. If they don't see that need and accept it, there's always trouble. Even when those in power try to create greater awareness, people get upset. Those who were well off under the old ways fight change—"

"Like the High Holders?" I asked.

"That is an unfortunate truth," Quaelyn admitted. "Sometimes, those who hold power merely find a way to keep holding power in a new fashion with new patterns. Usually, some fail to change, and they can be most bitter and dangerous. Those who gain power, such as the factors and the manufacturers, often adapt the mannerisms of the old elite, and the same control of power. That is the pattern in Ferrum. When patterns must change and times are unsettled, many turn to what they think of as unchanging."

"Nothing's unchanging, you said," Ferlyn interjected.

Quaelyn smiled patiently. "Follow my words, Ferlyn. I said they turned to what they think is unchanging."

"Faith in the Nameless, or Duodeus, or . . . what's the Tiempran god?" I asked, then dredged up the answer to my own question from somewhere. "Puryon, that's it."

"That is what I surmise," replied Quaelyn. "All theologies seem to embody the idea that because a deity is powerful, if not omnipotent, that deity is eternal and unchanging. That is a pattern of belief that comforts people. That is why it endures. Yet . . . all religions include the point that the deity created the world and the wider cosmos, and we can see how the world changes. Records show where harbors once were that have now silted up. Rivers change their courses. Parts of coasts fall into the sea. The world changes. We age and change. Yet religions all assume that their creator does not change. Such assumed inflexibility is anything but logical." He shook his head. "These days, we live in a time of changes. . . ."

I wished I could have stayed at the table and listened longer, but I had to get to the studio and get set up for Master Rholyn's sitting. So I finally excused myself and made my way through the still-chill air in the quadrangle north to the workshop building that held the studio.

As I went through setting up and deciding which paints to mix, my breath did not quite steam in the chill air of the studio. If Master Poincaryt wanted me to keep painting portraits in the winter months I'd need some heat in the space. Even oils congealed if they got too cold.

Master Rholyn arrived as the bells rang out the glass.

"Rhenn . . . good morning, chill as it is." He paused. "Do you want me standing or sitting?"

"Sitting for the moment." I walked over and studied his face, trying to fix the coloration and shading before I went back to my palette and finished mixing the shade I wanted.

"I noticed you dancing with Madame D'Shendael at the Council's Harvest Ball." Master Rholyn smiled.

"She asked me to dance, sir. It caught me quite off guard." That was true enough.

"Did she say why?" The tone of his words suggested he already knew the answer.

"No, sir. She just said that she required a partner. If you would stand, now, sir, and take that position with your foot on the crate?"

He rose, more awkwardly than I had remembered, but that might have been because the grace and eloquence of his speech colored my memory. "This way?"

"Please turn your head a bit toward me. Good." I eased the tip of the brush into the oils I'd mixed.

"Madame D'Shendael is quite intelligent, Rhennthyl. She never does anything without a reason. Did her words hint at any such purpose?"

"She talked only briefly, about art, and how little it was respected."

Rholyn nodded almost sagely. "She believes in art, but that is not all."

I said nothing, but continued to work on getting the set of his nose and eyes precisely.

"Did she speak of the Council?"

"No, sir, except that she told me that I was an imager, and that it was a silly fiction of the Council that I couldn't even admit it."

"A silly fiction? She would use such a term. You know that she does not approve of the current fashion of selecting councilors?"

"Master Dichartyn mentioned such, sir. He said she would prefer that some councilors be chosen by a form of popular voting."

"As if the populace as a whole would ever choose wisely."

I concentrated on the canvas before me.

"What do you think, Rhenn?"

I didn't want to say what I thought. "It seems to me that the present way of selecting councilors provides a balance among artisans, factors, and High Holders. No one group or individual has control."

"Balance of power . . . yes . . . there is a balance of power, and it is necessary, because those in the Council are far less honorable than those who lead the Collegium. Throughout our history, we've been fortunate that the imagers appointed to senior positions and to the Council by the senior maitre of the Collegium have proven themselves honorable and worthy types." He paused. "I'd best stop talking and let you paint." He smiled warmly.

Master Rholyn was as good as his word and said little after that. As a result, I got a good start on his face, especially around the eyes. Some portraiturists concentrate on the shape of the head and face first, and sometimes I had, but with Master Rholyn, there was a difference in the set of his nose, eyes, and eyebrows that I needed to address first.

I had to clean up the studio in a rush and then make my way to the infirmary to see Master Draffyd. I had to wait in the anteroom for almost a quint before he appeared. The smooth gray stone walls made the space seem even colder than it was, but the anteroom was far better than being in the cold gray individual rooms where I'd already spent too much time recuperating.

Draffyd strolled in with a pleasant smile. "Good morning, Rhenn. This way, please."

I followed him into a small chamber off the anteroom where I removed my waistcoat, scarf-cravat, shirt, and undershirt.

"Does anything hurt?"

"Not any longer," I admitted.

"What was the last thing to stop hurting, and when did it stop?"

"My ribs . . . on the right side. Here." I pointed. "Maybe a week ago."

He poked, prodded, thumped, and pressed and asked more questions before he finally announced, "You look good, and everything feels to have healed.

Clovyl and Master Dichartyn have been asking when you'd be ready to handle more hand-to-hand combat training. You can start on Lundi, but no full-body throws. Make sure that you tell Clovyl that. He can be too enthusiastic. Those will have to wait another few weeks."

"I'll tell him." I didn't want to spend any more time healing. Close to a third of the last year I'd been recovering from wounds and injuries of some sort.

That left me with time for a leisurely stroll back across the quadrangle to the dining hall, where I was the only master there. I ate quickly and went back to my chambers. There I spent some time reading and reviewing court procedures. They were so tedious that I ended up dozing in my chair, and I had to hurry to get ready to leave for Seliora's. I took a hack on the east side of the Bridge of Hopes . . . and no one shot at me.

The hack dropped me off outside Seliora's door at half past four, but that was by design, although I'd originally thought to be there somewhat earlier.

Once more, Odelia opened the door, rather than her younger brother Bhenyt. "You seem to be making a habit of this, Rhenn," she observed warmly.

"Coming here, or arriving early?"

"Both."

"Actually, I had hoped to speak with Grandmama Diestra for a few moments."

"I can ask her."

"With Seliora," I added.

"I'll ask them both."

We walked up the steps to the main second-level foyer, where she left me, heading up to the third level, and I walked around looking to see if there were any new chairs or upholstery designs. There weren't.

Bhenyt was the one who came bounding down the side stairs and skidding out into the foyer. "Grandmama says you're to meet her in the small plaques room upstairs, Master Rhenn."

"I haven't been there. If you'd lead the way."

He grinned and turned. I had to walk quickly to catch up with him, but we reached the top of the narrower side staircase almost together. The small sitting room was almost directly across the smaller upper hallway from the archway from the staircase foyer. The stained oak door was open, and I stepped inside. The curtains were drawn back from the single long and narrow window, and pale white light formed an oblong on the Coharan patterned carpet.

Grandmama Diestra sat in an upholstered straight-backed chair at a small table on which was laid out a complicated form of solitaire. The three other chairs around the table were vacant. She wore a black jacket over a black sweater. Her steel-gray hair—looking almost silver above the black garments—was cut neatly at midneck level. She turned over the plaque she had in her hand and smiled, ruefully, before setting it facedown on the dark blue felt. Her black eyes focused on me.

"Sometimes, you play the plaques, and sometimes they play you."

I wasn't quite certain how to respond to that and had barely inclined my head to Diestra when Seliora stepped through the doorway behind me, closing the door firmly. She smiled, but it wasn't the happiest of smiles. The crimson and black of her wool jacket was becoming, but it also made her look stern when the smile vanished, and her black eyes met mine.

"I'm very sorry," I said, turning to her. "I didn't mean to hurry you, but I've run into one of Grandmama's warnings, and I'm afraid I'm going to need some help. More than some help, I think. It happened late yesterday, so that I really didn't have time to send a note, and what happened I wouldn't have wanted to put on paper."

"Why don't you both sit down?" suggested Diestra, before looking to Seliora. "If you really want him to be part of the family, he has to have the right to ask to talk to me directly."

Her words clearly brought Seliora up short. After a moment, she said, "Yes, Grandmama."

Diestra looked to me. "Your turn will come, when you least expect it. Try to be equally gracious."

I inclined my head. "Thank you for the warning. I will try." Then I turned to Seliora. "I do apologize. I didn't mean to upset you."

Her second smile was warmer, and she nodded and let me pull out the chair to the right of Grandmama Diestra for her. I went to the other side of the plaques table and sat down across from Seliora.

"What is this problem?" asked Diestra.

I offered a sheepish look. "Actually, I have three. First, I have to start working with Lieutenant Mardoyt on Lundi. He handles all the trial preparation for the patrollers. Now that I've seen how offenders are charged, Commander Artois wants me to see how the trials work before I accompany any patrollers." Since I didn't see any great reaction, I went on. "Second, on Meredi, when we were leaving Saliana's at lunch, someone took another shot at me, and the bullet was a heavy sniper type. Third, the riot in the South Middle taudis wasn't something that just happened, and I'd hope that you'd be able to arrange a meeting with that young taudischef I met at Imagisle when he brought his cousin in. His name was Horazt."

"You think all of these are linked together?" asked Seliora.

"The shots at me and the riot might be linked. I can't believe Commander Artois or the subcommander would be involved in the riot, but I feel there's a reason behind my being assigned to observe Mardoyt."

"The obvious reason is that Mardoyt is getting to be a problem, and that the commander wants you to discover something so that the blame falls on you," said Diestra.

"That was my feeling. I thought that Horazt might know something about Mardoyt, and he certainly should be able to tell me about the riot."

"Arranging such a meeting would not be impossible," mused Diestra, "but would it be wise? Why would he agree?"

"He needs to show he has control, even contacts. I can tell him about his young cousin. He might even care."

"Already, you are cynical." Diestra's words were dry.

"I'd also like advice from both of you on dealing with Mardoyt and all the things I need to watch out for."

"The easiest thing," began the gray-haired Pharsi woman, "is to arrange the meeting with Horazt. Between your position and our interest, he would rather have us owing him than the other way around. How is the boy—his young cousin—doing?"

"He seems to be all right. I've been watching from the background, and talking to him once or twice a week. Some of the other primes are watching out for him as well."

"That is good. Betara and I can also make a few inquiries about the riot. That will seem natural, and we can also see if Staelia has overheard anything. The shootings of an imager are not something we should ask about. Such questions from us will do you more harm than good."

"I can see that."

"Mardoyt is another question. Whatever he asks of you, only do what the procedures demand. Nothing else. Be most polite. If he feels slighted, you will become his enemy. You must learn with whom he works. I would suggest that you play the role you can play so well, young Rhenn. That is of the eager young imager who wants to learn and not to offend. Just keep thanking him for every insight and bit of information. But do not ever trust him, even on the slightest of matters. He is doubtless well aware of the weaknesses of imagers." A crooked smile crossed her lips. "It is unlikely that he will do anything wrong or improper while you are around, but that does not mean he will not do such."

That meant I'd have to find evidence of some sort, and Mardoyt didn't sound like someone who left many tracks.

"If that is all, you two can go and leave an old woman in peace." The words were said with a smile.

"Thank you." I stood and bowed to her.

Seliora did not say anything until we were out in the upper hallway, with no one close by. "You didn't tell Grandmama Diestra everything, did you?"

I shook my head. "We—the imagers—have another problem. Someone is shooting junior imagers. Whether it's a group of assassins, or whether someone has offered a bounty for every dead imager, no one knows, but it's happening."

"Most people feel the same way about imagers and Pharsis."

"That may be, but over the past year, they've killed over twenty young imagers—that's about half the number the Collegium finds every year. If someone shot half the Pharsis born in a given year, Solidar would be in shambles."

For a moment, Seliora just stood there in the foyer. "I didn't think of it that way."

"I didn't either, until Ferlyn pointed it out this morning at breakfast. There's another problem—"

"Announcing it will just make matters worse."

I nodded.

"You're going to ask Horazt, aren't you?"

"I'd thought to. I could bring up the fact that I'd like to resolve the problem before Shault is free to leave Imagisle."

"That might work." She paused. "If you don't find anything, Mama and Grandmama could ask if anyone's been promising payoffs for shootings, without mentioning imagers. They might find something. If they don't . . . doesn't that suggest it's someone like the Ferran who was after you?"

"It wouldn't be absolute, but it would seem more likely."

"Good! I'll talk to them." She looked directly at me. "We've both had long weeks. Can we not talk about them and enjoy dinner?"

"Absolutely. That's the best suggestion I've heard." With that, I offered her my arm, and we walked down the staircases.

Bhenyt had hailed a hack, and it was waiting. I slipped him a copper. More, and the family wouldn't have approved. He grinned at me as I offered Seliora a hand getting into the hack.

"Azeyd's," I told the hacker.

"Azeyd's it is, sir."

Once inside the coach, I turned sideways to face Seliora. "I am sorry . . ."

"Are you sorry you did it? Or sorry you upset me?"

"I didn't mean to upset you."

She leaned forward and kissed my cheek. "I accept. You did need to talk to her, but there was time to tell me that was what you needed."

I understood all too well. Offering an apology for a necessary act was hypocrisy, but not apologizing for a rude approach to the necessary was unforgivable. Since I had apologized . . . all was well. I hoped.

Azeyd's was located on a side street without a name off Nordroad, some three blocks to the west of Guild Square. The outside was unprepossessing, just a dark red set of double doors in a yellow brick facade, bound in brass under a short awning and flanked on each side by a set of two narrow windows filled with leaded glass panes that were anything but recent in style or construction.

After helping Seliora from the hack and opening the door, I followed her into the restaurant. The woman standing at the far side of the small foyer tiled in large red and black squares looked to Seliora. "Ah . . . Mistress D'Shelim." Then she looked to me, her eyes clearly measuring me and the imager grays that I wore. "Sir."

"This is Imager Master Rhennthyl. He's a friend of the family." Seliora smiled demurely. "He's an even better friend of mine."

"Then he is certainly welcome here." Her smile to me was warm, yet wary, before she turned and led us to the right into a narrow and long room that held two rows of tables—four on one side and five on the other, each row set against a pale tan plastered wall.

The wall was decorated with a form of art I'd never seen before—thin strips of colored leather braided and worked into designs, ranging in size from a diamond shape less than ten digits on an edge to a leather mosaic mural almost two yards wide and two-thirds of a yard high. The mural showed Pharsi riders charging a line of musket-bearing foot soldiers.

"The battle of Khelgror," Seliora murmured. "The last stand of the Khelan Pharsi against the Bovarians."

"Here you are," offered the hostess, gesturing to an oval table against the inside wall.

"Thank you." Seliora and I spoke almost simultaneously.

A single bronze lamp hung from a bronze chain, positioned about a yard above the center of the table. The linens were red, and a single slate sat on a polished black wooden stand set near the plaster wall and facing outward.

"What do you suggest?" I asked.

"Have you ever had Enazai? It's a traditional ice wine, powerful, but served before a meal." She paused. "Father claims that's because, after drinking it, no one cared what the food tasted like."

"I should try it."

"Two." Seliora nodded to the hostess, who slipped away.

I looked over the menu chalked on the slate. "How is the Bertetia? What is it?"

"Cow stomach marinated for months, sliced and fermented, and then broiled and served with blue potatoes. Grandmama likes it. None of the rest of us have tried it more than once."

"The forest quail sounds better."

"It's one of my favorites, along with venison ragout, but that's very spicy."

The hostess returned with two half-sized goblets of a pale red, almost pinkish, wine. "What will you have?"

"We'll share the priata platter, and I'll have the ragout," Seliora said, "and a red Grisio."

"The quail with a white Cambrisio," I added.

After the hostess left the table, I lifted the small goblet. "To you."

"To us," Seliora replied.

I sipped the Enazai . . . and was glad that I'd only sipped. It didn't burn on the way down, but even that small swallow had a definite impact. Within moments, I could feel the warmth it imparted all over. "I like it, but your father has a point."

"He usually does."

"Like you," I teased.

"And you don't?" she countered.

Since I was supposed to have a point, I had to come up with one. "I heard something at breakfast this morning. One of the older masters was talking about how life and people really operate in patterns and how some of the problems we face are a result of intersecting patterns—old patterns of doing things that clash with new patterns created by the way things change."

"Go on," Seliora prompted.

"Things are changing in Solidar. The number of High Holders is decreasing, and those who are left are more powerful—"

"And more arrogant."

"The larger factors are also getting wealthier and more powerful, and I have the feeling that we're getting more people in the taudis, and they're poorer than before." That was more feeling than anything, but I trusted it.

"There are boys who are smoking elveweed now. Not just men."

"Khethila has seen more men smoking it as well."

"They can't get jobs. We hire from there when we can, for the hauling and rough positions, but we only need a few men. It's hard to find ones who will work and aren't weeded out. Grandmama said it would have been hard for her if she'd arrived in L'Excelsis now."

"Why?"

"Everyone wants to make golds the easy way, and that's trafficking in elve-weed. She wouldn't do anything like that."

At that moment the priata platter arrived. On it were small pastry cres-cents with a dark sauce oozing from the edge where the two sides of the flaky crust joined, large green olives stuffed with some sort of cheese, melon circles wrapped in thin ham, and marinated grape leaves wrapped around some sort of filling.

Seliora lifted one of the crescents, and I followed her example, discover-ing the sweet/sharp sauce imparted a tang to the chopped onion and ripe olive mixture within the crust.

"You said you had a point," Seliora prompted.

Not only did I see the mischievous glint in her eyes, but I could hear a certain interest in her voice. "Besides a good dinner? Oh . . . I was thinking that better steam engines mean we need fewer strong backs and mules and horses, and more people who can do things with powered looms, the way you design fabric patterns, or the way Father can order a fabric more to a clothing factor's requirements."

"Those engines that power the looms and the ironway engines cost more in golds, but they produce more, and so the large High Holders get larger, and the larger factors get wealthier, and there are more smaller businesses like NordEste, and fewer individual crafters—"

"You're not exactly small," I pointed out.

"Compared to the wealth of a High Holder like Ryel? We're nothing."

"But there are hundreds of businesses like yours. Thousands all over Soli-dar, and that will change things. The Council is based on the way things were a century ago."

"Rhenn . . . listen to your own words. The structure of the Council hasn't changed. People still think of Pharsis with distaste, and shopkeepers and trades-people as unworthy of having any real rights. Do you think that the High Hold-ers or the guilds want to give up power? Together, they outvote the factors. Why would they change?"

"Not all the guild members think that way." I was thinking of Caartyl.

"You're right, though. Maybe they won't change, but it's still a pattern of conflict."

By then we had finished off everything on the priata platter, and the hostess appeared and whisked it away, only to reappear with our dinner and wine.

From there on in, we talked about families, the world, food, wine, and each other. Before all that long, or so it seemed to me, I was helping Seliora out of the hack outside of NordEste Design and escorting her to the door—holding my shields so as to protect us both.

"Can I stop by tomorrow?" I asked just before she was about to close the door.

"Why don't you come for lunch—except that it's really a combination of breakfast and lunch? It's at half before noon."

"I'll be there." I couldn't help smiling, and it certainly didn't hurt to see her smile back at me.

The wind had turned much colder by the time I returned to the hack, and as I rode back to the Bridge of Desires, I realized that if I reached my rooms without incident, it would be one of the few times in recent months that nothing had occurred after I had left Seliora.

I didn't relax until I was back in my rooms, but nothing happened. "Not this time," a small voice whispered inside my skull. I had the feeling the voice was right . . . that sooner or later, I'd have an unpleasant surprise, courtesy of High Holder Ryel, but I'd still had a wonderful evening.

Just before eighth glass on Solayi, after waiting for nearly half a glass, I hailed
a hack off the Boulevard D'Imagers and asked the driver to drop me where
South Middle turned off the Midroad, close to four milles northeast of the
Bridge of Hopes.

South Middle angled off Midroad, so that it actually ran almost due east-
west, unlike the Midroad, which angled from the northeast to the southwest.
In practice, the central part of South Middle where I was headed, almost a
mille from the intersection, was the north border of the South Middle taudis,
where the street riot supposedly caused by street preaching had taken place.
I wanted to walk the distance to get a feel for it, and Solayi morning was a
good time. It was bright, if cool with a brisk wind under a sky with only a few
clouds, appropriate for the first day of Feuillyt and the official first day of fall.
Not that many were out on the streets.

The first sign that I was approaching the taudis was a chest-high brick wall
to my right, on the south side of South Middle. The bricks had once been yellow, but now presented a mottled tannish brown appearance. In a few places,
there were patches of faint yellow, where graffiti had been scrubbed off by
one of the penal road crews. The second sign was that I could hear children
playing beyond the wall.

I glanced over the time-smudged brick barrier wall and across the narrow
strip of dirt that had been a parkway decades earlier at the rows of ancient
two-, three-, and four-story dwellings, the wall of one building indistinguishable from the next. Most of the front stoops were empty, but I saw one man
with a tangled beard, puffing on a long pipe of the type used for elveweed. I
glanced farther south along the row of battered brick dwellings. There might
have been another elver on a stoop near the cross street.

I kept walking.

A dark-haired woman with two children, both girls, looked up as I approached.

"Good morning."

"Good morning, sir." She took their hands and did not meet my eyes. Her
shawl and cloak were both spotless, but the wool was frayed in places, and

the pattern an Extelan weave that had not been available since before I had become an apprentice to Caliostrus.

Two boys almost old enough to be working stepped through a gateless gap in the wall. The taller one looked at me defiantly, but only for a moment, until the other murmured something, and both turned and headed back into the taudis.

Just ahead, again on the right and behind the wall, was the first new building I'd seen, a narrow, single-storied, yellow-brick structure with a steeply pitched roof. A cupola of sorts rose on the nearer end above the three sets of double doors that made it look like a meeting house or an anomen of some sort, but I'd never seen an anomen like that, which suggested it was one for another faith, although they wouldn't have called it an anomen.

For the next half mille, I saw no one else at all close to me, and I turned back.

I almost had reached Sudroad before I could hail another hack. This time, I had the driver take me a quarter mille beyond NordEste Design, farther out Nordroad, and drop me off. I didn't know if I'd see or sense anyone with less than savory intentions, but if I did, I had an idea I wanted to try.

The only problem with my idea was that on the entire walk back, I saw almost no one. In fact, I saw fewer people than I had walking past the taudis. I did reach Seliora's a fifth of a glass or so before I was due, but that wouldn't be a problem. I dropped the polished brass knocker twice and waited.

Odelia was the one who greeted me. "Is there anyone you'd like to see before Seliora?" she asked, her tone innocent.

"Not if I expect to leave here with her speaking to me," I replied, knowing that if I were a High Holder, I would have replied in a pleasant tone with words like "Were I not to speak with her first, speaking to anyone else would be an anticlimax."

As she stepped back to let me enter, Odelia laughed at my more direct approach. "I think she's probably in the foyer by now."

Odelia and I walked up the stairs, reaching the foyer just as Seliora stepped out of the archway from the side staircase. She was more casually dressed than on the evening before . . . with a simple black pullover sweater and black slacks. A heavy silver chain and matching silver earrings were the only jewelry she wore. She did smile, openly.

"Everyone else will be down shortly, except Mother and Aegina. They're in the kitchen." She looked at me. "Your face is windburned."

"I went for a walk. I had the hack drop me off farther out Nordroad. I walked back, but I didn't see anyone."

"Good. You shouldn't have. Grandmama got tired of having people shoot at you. She called in a favor, and for a while there will be some old . . . acquaintances watching."

I managed not to shake my head.

"Grandmama won't know until tomorrow at the earliest when you can meet with Horazt. I'll send a note by messenger to the Collegium. That's better, isn't it?"

"Much better. It has to be after fourth glass." I paused. "It doesn't have to be, but it would be a great deal easier if it were."

"We thought as much. Besides, most taudischefs prefer the evening." She paused. "I hope you're hungry."

"I didn't have much breakfast, and I've walked a lot."

"Good." She led me toward the dining chamber.

Seliora had once told me that they never had a formal evening meal on Solayi, except on holidays like Year-Turn. As I looked at all the platters of food spread around the table, I could see why.

I enjoyed the meal and remainder of the afternoon before I had to leave for Imagisle and the evening services at the anomen. In fact, I enjoyed it so much that I felt almost guilty on the hack ride back.

13

Lundi morning, Clovyl was relatively gentle with me in his hand-to-hand instruction, showing me ways to disarm someone with either knife or pistol. I refrained from pointing out that I could just image the weapons out of their hands. My caution was warranted, because he addressed that just before I was to actually try the moves on him.

"One of the reasons you need to learn this sort of thing, Rhennthyl, is because most imagers can't image for a while if they get a stiff blow to their skull. The good assassins and spies know that."

"It would have been nice to learn that earlier."

"You would have, if you'd come to the Collegium a good bit younger than you did," Clovyl replied mildly. "We teach that to the junior primes, but it would have taken years to go over everything with you, and it didn't make sense to hold you back. You really would have done something stupid, then."

"Thank you." My words were not sarcastic. I meant them.

Clovyl looked puzzled.

"No one ever simply explained what you just did. A great deal of my frustration with the Collegium derives from the continual assumptions that I know things I don't. If someone had just said what you did . . ."

"That's probably true, Rhenn, but you have to realize that you're also one of the oldest imagers ever to show up at the Collegium. No one, and I mean no one, has any experience with training a mostly developed imager. Most imagers who develop the skill as late as you did end up dead before the Collegium ever knows about them. That was why you ended up with Master Dichartyn as your preceptor. Usually, he only works with thirds and junior masters."

That made me feel even more stupid, because I really should have noticed more. I'd known I was older than most of the primes, but before I'd had a chance to really think about it, I'd been made a second—and there were many seconds older than I was. There were even graying seconds.

I pushed those thoughts out of my mind and concentrated on learning the moves better. Then I ran the customary four milles and hurried through the rest of the morning routine so that I wouldn't be late to Patrol headquarters.

I wasn't. In fact, I was waiting outside Mardoyt's door when he arrived.

"Have you been here long?"

"No, sir. Just a fraction of a glass."

"Good. Follow me. I'll introduce you to the patroller clerks, and you can go with First Patroller Baluzt and the coach-wagon taking this morning's lot to the courts. He can explain how the procedures work." Mardoyt offered a generous and open smile. "Possibly better than I can."

"You're the one who has to make sure all the supporting documents get to the court?"

"I also have to make certain that witnesses appear for any major offense. Tracking them down isn't always easy, and it often takes a lieutenant and two patrollers to make sure that they do show up. We have another coach-wagon for witnesses." He turned. "This way."

We only walked across the hall into a room twice as large as the commander's anteroom, and far more crowded, with seven writing desks and an entire wall filled with file cases stacked one on top of another. Three of the desks were empty, with files stacked on them. The walls might once have been white, but were now more like a dingy beige.

Only one of the patrollers seated at the desks even looked up, and that was a stocky and balding patroller first. "Sir?"

"This is Imager Master Rhennthyl, Baluzt. He's the new imager liaison to the Patrol, and the subcommander wants him to see how we work. He spent last week on the charging desk."

"Welcome, Master Rhennthyl. We're not the exciting part of the Patrol, but if we don't do our job, offenders get back on the street to cause more trouble."

"I'll leave him in your hands, Baluzt." With another warm smile, Mardoyt inclined his head and then gracefully turned and left.

I stood waiting.

"What we do is simple, sir, and it's the Namer's pain in a sow's rump." Baluzt gestured at the piles of paper in front of him. "I get to make sure that we have all the papers on each prisoner, especially the charging slip, and Fagayn runs down the arresting patroller, the prisoner, and any witnesses that the lieutenant brings. Then I ride the coach-wagon over to the Square of Justice. Most times, we have two of them, one for prisoners, and one for patrollers and witnesses. If we've got a lot of prisoners, we'll run a second load around noon. Then we sit in the chambers and produce prisoners, documents, patrollers, and witnesses when the presiding justice or the magistrate wants them. If we can't, I get to explain to the justice why not. I don't like that, and the lieutenant likes it less. Sereptyl handles the other chamber most days."

"Do you ever deal with cases for districts other than in L'Excelsis?"

"Not unless we have a prisoner who's a witness for them. That's a pain, but it doesn't happen often." Baluzt stood. "You'll ride with me, sir. We got to get this procession moving."

I smiled. "I'll try to stay out of the way." I followed him down the corridor to another set of stairs that led down to the alleyway behind the Patrol building.

The two coach-wagons drawn up and waiting each took four horses. They were long enclosed wagons with but a single door and four rows of bench seats. On top, there was a seat for the driver—padded, if skimpily—and a seat behind the driver. After all the witnesses and prisoners were accounted for, I climbed up the first wagon to sit beside Baluzt behind the driver.

The patroller driver turned the coach-wagon onto East River Road, heading south, until we reached the Sud Bridge, then crossed the river and continued on the Avenue D'Commercia until it intersected the ring avenue around Council Hill. The Square of Justice, with the Hall of Justice and its various courts, was on the south end of the ring avenue. The trip took about three-fifths of a glass.

The patrollers escorted prisoners and witnesses in through a side door guarded by another patroller, and then up a back set of stairs into the justicing chambers. The one where Baluzt led me was not all that large, no more than fifteen yards by eight, with a dais at the north end. Upon the black dais was a wide and featureless black desk. Low-backed benches ran down the center of the chamber, facing the dais. They ended six or seven yards short of the dais. On each side of the open space were three shorter rows of benches.

Baluzt and I sat in the front row of the benches on the east side, with the three witnesses and the patrollers who would testify in the rows behind us. The prisoners, manacled with their hands behind their backs, sat in the benches on the west side facing us.

Shortly after we entered, several advocates appeared, and then the bailiff stepped forward and thumped a heavy oak staff, its uppermost part a bronze sheaf of some sort of grain. Everyone rose, and the presiding justice appeared, wearing a long gray robe, trimmed in black, unlike that of the Collegium justices, whose robes were trimmed in both black and red.

Another thump, and the bailiff intoned, "You may be seated. Bring forth the accused."

Two patrollers marched forward a swarthy but graying older man until he stood before the dais.

"Sactedd D'Rien, you are charged with disturbing the peace and disorderly conduct. Who stands to defend the accused?" asked the justice.

"I do." A man in a gray robe with white trim stepped forward and stood between the west benches and the dais.

"Who presents the case against the accused?"

"I do." The angular prosecuting advocate was a brown-haired, clean-shaven man who didn't look any older than I was.

"State the charges against the accused."

"The accused faces a charge of disturbance and disorderly and using a weapon in refusing to desist in that behavior."

The justice turned to the public defender. "How does the accused plead? Guilty, Not Guilty, No Plea, or For Mercy?"

"Guilty, Your Honor."

The justice looked directly at the manacled old man. "Sactedd, your defender has offered a plea of Guilty. Do you accept that plea?"

"Yes, sir." The weariness behind the words suggested a man for whom a penal workhouse or even a road crew would be a blessing.

"Having pled Guilty, this being your second conviction, you are sentenced to the rest of your natural life at light duty in the penal workhouse at Stuerlt."

The first case was over so quickly that I was still wondering how it had gone so fast when the bailiff thumped his staff. "Bring forth the accused."

The same two patrollers marched forward another man, younger, but clearly not in full possession of all faculties. He swayed as he walked.

"Longtime elver," murmured one of the patrollers behind me.

"Zolierma Aayo, you are charged with public incapacity and use of a banned substance. Who stands to defend the accused?"

"I do." The second of the two public defenders stepped forward.

Zolierma, an outlander of some sort, by his name, also pled Guilty, although I wondered if he had any idea of what he pled, and was sentenced to a penal workhouse as well.

I took more interest in the third case, when the bailiff intoned, "Bring forth the accused," and the two patrollers marched forward two much younger men.

"Hydrat D'Taudis and Chelam D'Whayan, you are charged with disturbance of the peace, disorderly conduct, and assaulting a patroller. Who stands to defend the accused?"

"I do." Instead of the two public defenders, another advocate, older and more dark-skinned, stepped forward.

"How do you plead?"

"They both plead Not Guilty to all charges, Your Honor," offered the advocate.

"Very well." The justice turned. "You may proceed, Prosecuting Advocate."

As I recalled, there had been three men charged with throwing the liquid from slop pots at the patrollers, but I saw only two.

The prosecuting advocate turned toward us. "Patroller Tyenat to the bar."

A tall and muscular patroller stood and stepped forward until he stood below the dais.

"Patroller Tyenat," began the justice, "do you understand that you are required to tell the whole truth, and that your words must not deceive, either by elaboration or omission?"

"Yes, sir."

"Proceed."

The prosecutor addressed the patroller. "Please recount what occurred on the night of Meredi, thirty-second Erntyn, as it relates to the charges against the prisoners."

"Yes, sir. I was just about to start off on foot patrol, when Captain Harraf came into the marshaling room and announced that there was a big disturbance in the South Middle taudis and that everyone was to take the dispatch wagon there. . . ." Tyenat went on to describe how he and nine other patrollers had reached the area just west of the Puryon Temple. ". . . they'd brought in patrollers from all across the city, and there were about fifty of us. That included a half squad of mounted riot patrollers. Three of us were posted at a gap gate in the wall east of their temple . . . the prisoners, those over there, had buckets. They jumped up on the wall. One of them threw the slop in it at us, but it missed. Morgyn told them to go home. They thumbed us, and then threw more shit at us. We charged them. They tried to kick us. Hydrat—he's the short one—pulled a slider knife, but I knocked it out of his hand with my truncheon. . . ."

The prosecutor patiently asked question after question, then stopped and looked to the justice. "That is all for this witness, Your Honor."

"Do you have any questions for the patroller, Advocate?" asked the justice.

"Yes, Your Honor." The defense advocate stepped forward slightly. "Patroller Tyenat, did either of the prisoners show a weapon before you charged them?"

"No, sir. They taunted us, and threw slops at us, and refused to return to their homes."

"How large was this purported slider knife?"

"Your Honor"—Baluzt rose—"the knife was entered as evidence."

"So noted."

The defense advocate asked several more questions, all aimed at trying to establish that the prisoners had done nothing more than be disorderly until they perceived that they were being attacked. Finally, he said, "No more questions, Your Honor."

The justice looked down. "You may return to your place in the court, Patroller Tyenat.

"Are there any more witnesses?"

"We would like to have the accused state their case, Your Honor."

Both Hydrat and Chelam told their stories, which were similar to what Tyenat had said, except that they insisted that they had not assaulted or intended to assault anyone, and that Hydrat had only drawn the knife when he thought that he would be attacked and hurt.

No one else offered anything else, and there was no mention of a third man.

After the defense advocate finished, the justice spent less than a tenth of a glass before straightening and nodding to the bailiff.

The bailiff thumped a heavy staff twice. "The accused will rise and step forward."

The two patrollers escorted the two taudis-men forward until they stood below the dais.

"Hydrat D'Taudis and Chelam D'Whayan, the court finds you Not Guilty on the count of deliberate assault on a patroller, but Guilty of a lesser charge of negligent assault, and Guilty of disturbance and disorderly conduct. The court hereby sentences each of you to one year of service on the road crews of Solidar." The justice looked to the bailiff.

The bailiff rapped his staff twice, and the gaol patrollers escorted the two men away.

Neither taudis-man looked particularly upset.

The rest of the day went on like that, without even a break for lunch, then ended at third glass. In no case were the charges dropped. By the time we gathered everyone together, another quarter glass had passed.

On the ride back, I asked Baluzt, "How soon do prisoners get sent to the penal workhouses or the road crew?"

"Could be as soon as tomorrow. Could be a week. They get sent once a week, usually the same day every week for each place. Tomorrow's the day for Poignard—that's where the dangerous ones go, or those who'll be executed.

Meredi's for the two road crews—they're housed in the south at the Iron Piers gaol or north at Sieuplier."

I didn't have much to say, but I kept thinking about the missing prisoner.

Once the wagons were unloaded, I made my way back up to the justicing preparatory study. Four patrollers were still there.

"Tomorrow's schedule," Baluzt said.

I heard steps and turned to see Mardoyt entering. "Lieutenant."

"How was your day watching the justice proceedings, Master Rhennthyl?"

"Interesting, but long, I must confess."

"It almost always is. It can be much longer if there's an elaborate trial. If that happens, they'll try that case with a senior justice, and cram all the minor cases into the two small court chambers with the junior justices. Means twice as much work for us with three chambers to cover. Fortunately for us, there's nothing like that on the docket this week." He half turned. "Is tomorrow's schedule ready?"

"Yes, sir."

I watched from the side as Mardoyt reviewed the cases scheduled for Mardi and as he and Baluzt discussed the arrangements and patroller assignments.

Before he left, Mardoyt turned to me. "I'll see you in the morning, Master Rhennthyl, but you'll be going with Baluzt again."

After I left Baluzt, I made my way back down to the charging desk.

"Master Rhennthyl."

"Gulyart . . . would you mind if I checked the ledger? I'm trying to recall a case we saw today."

He laughed and pushed the charging ledger over to me.

As I'd thought, there were three names associated with the piss-bucket case—Hydrat D'Taudis, Chelam D'Whayan, and Chardyn D'Steinyn. Once I checked the names in the ledger, I went to the files in the cases behind Gulyart.

There was no sheet on Chardyn. The other two had sheets listing the charges, but not him. As I remembered, he'd been the quiet one of Pharsi-Caenenan heritage. He'd given his name and nothing else.

"Gulyart, when does a record sheet get put in here?"

"Once we charge them, the patrollers working for Mardoyt send down the sheets with the convictions and sentences. Once in a while the charges are dropped. After the trial, they send lists with the names, and when I can, I update the records."

"Do the sheets with the charges arrive here before the trial?"

"They're supposed to, but they don't always."

"Thank you." I had the feeling that the sheet on Chardyn would never show up, but I'd still have to check later. "Good evening. I'll see you later."

Gulyart nodded pleasantly as I left.

I was still pondering the missing records sheet when I got back to my room and found a package wrapped in brown paper had been set inside my door. There was a note on the top.

> *This arrived late this afternoon.*
> *Beleart*

The envelope on top had my name, but was unsealed with nothing inside. I had to cut the heavy cord before I could unfasten the heavy gray paper wrapping. Inside were another envelope, still sealed, and a tattered long brown cloak and a frayed black-and-brown plaid cap whose brown did not match the cloak. I had to smile at that, clearly a touch of Seliora's, but a subtlety I would not have considered.

I opened the envelope to find a plain white card with just a few words.

> *South Middle at Dugalle, sixth and a half, Meredi.*

So now I could meet with Horazt and learn something—if I happened to be fortunate.

What I observed in the justice chamber on Mardi was much the same as what I had seen on Lundi, although there were three separate cases involving the sale of elveweed. Meredi followed the same pattern, except that one prisoner was released because none of the witnesses could be found, and no patroller had observed the reported assault on a taudis-dweller. The purported victim could not identify who attacked him, and three women of what I would have termed dubious occupations insisted that the accused had been with them. The advocate for the accused was not a public advocate, but the same man who had defended the two piss-bucket assailants on Lundi.

I was getting a very definite feel for matters, and I didn't exactly like what I was seeing, but as with other matters I didn't like, there wasn't anything faintly resembling proof.

The caseload at the Square of Justice was heavier on Meredi, and Baluzt and I—and the coach-wagons—did not return to Patrol headquarters until almost fifth glass. I couldn't have walked to the Collegium, eaten, and then taken a hack to meet Horazt, not and be there by half past sixth glass. Instead, I decided that I'd walk to Chaelia's and sample the cooking there. I carried the package holding the cloak and cap. I certainly wasn't about to wear them until after I left Chaelia's.

According to Seliora's directions, the bistro was two blocks east and off Pousaint. Her directions were quite accurate. I'd had the impression that the place was just a common bistro, but it wasn't, not from the outside. The polished light oak double doors were framed by a bright green casement, and the shutters on each side of the sets of leaded glass windows were of the same green. Two large bright brass lamps were set on each side of the door, and the front facade of the bistro was of gray stone, rather than of brick.

I'd barely stepped inside when Staelia hurried forward. She wore black trousers and a gray sweater, with no jewelry. The effect was strangely impressive, perhaps because her skin was just olive-dark enough that her face stood out against the pale gray.

"Master Rhennthyl! I wondered when we might see you."

She spoke loudly enough that several people looked up from the nearby tables to study me. The bistro was mostly full. After a moment I realized that the loudness had been deliberate, and a way of reassuring everyone that I was known and expected. I couldn't help but smile.

"This is the first time I could get away for a meal. I haven't had lunch off all week."

"I'm glad you could come, whenever it happened to be." She led me back through the tables, all of which were covered in pale green linen, and sat me at a small circular table near the rear, but not the one next to the door to the kitchen.

"No one told me what Chaelia's was like," I said as I seated myself in the chair that would let me watch the front of the restaurant.

"Some things are better left undescribed."

Like Seliora, I thought. "You told me what not to order. What would you recommend? I didn't have lunch, but I have to meet someone later."

Staelia nodded. "The fowl with brown mushrooms and grass rice, with the blanched vegetables on the side. It comes with a small plate of greens."

"That sounds good. Cambrisio or Grisio?"

"We have a sparkling Grisio."

"Done." I grinned.

Staelia returned with the wine almost immediately, and I sat and sipped it, studying the others in the dining area. Almost all the diners wore coats or dresses or skirts with jackets. I was the only person dining alone. Couples or sets of couples comprised those at other tables.

In a short time, Staelia returned, placing the "small" plate of greens before me—a full salad with fresh fall apple slivers, toasted almond fragments, and a crumbly bluish cheese.

"Thank you."

"We're glad you came. Would you mind if Taelia and Sartan came over and met you?"

"Not at all." While I couldn't have said anything else, I did want to meet them.

In moments, they were there. Taelia looked to be a year or two older than Khethila, and she took more after her father, shorter, a bit more solid than her mother, with Clyenn's light brown hair.

Sartan was taller than his mother, a shade taller than me, black-haired, and was probably about twenty. His mother's features looked good on him, and there was a twinkle in his eye as he said, "I'm very glad to meet you, Master Rhennthyl. Everyone has been talking about you."

I didn't bother to conceal the wince. "I just hope it's not too bad."

They all laughed. Then Sartan and Taelia slipped away.

"They're good children," Staelia said.

"They look that way."

Someone entered the restaurant, and Staelia nodded and left.

I addressed the "small" salad, and after Staelia had seated the two couples who had just entered and turned them over to Taelia, she eventually returned to my table.

"Did you like the greens?"

"They were excellent. What was the cheese?"

"Blue cave cheese from north of Eshtora. It doesn't take much to give a special flavor to greens. It's a pity it doesn't take heat. You can't use it in most cooked dishes unless you add it at the very end." She paused. "Seliora is my favorite niece."

"She thinks most highly of you." I had an idea what might be coming next.

"You know that Seliora thinks you're very special."

"I think she's more than special."

"That's good. I've never seen her look at anyone like she does you . . . but . . ."

"You have reservations about me?"

"You could be a very dangerous man, Rhenn, and women can be hurt by dangerous men, even unintentionally."

Staelia's words were a bit of a shock. I'd never been called dangerous, and she wasn't flattering me by doing so. Still, she deserved an answer. "I'm involved in a dangerous profession, Staelia, and I've never hidden that from Seliora or her parents."

"I know, but Betara has her reasons."

"I know that, too," I replied softly. "I've thought about it more than a little, and Seliora knows that."

She nodded thoughtfully. "You look the type to have done that." A crooked smile followed, part affectionate and part wry. "That makes you more dangerous and more desirable, and not just to Seliora, you realize."

That was something I hadn't thought about.

"Good! You need to think about that. Now . . . I need to get your entrée." She straightened and headed for the kitchen.

I took another sip of sparkling Grisio, thinking that it was no wonder none of the men in Grandmama Diestra's family strayed. I also wondered if the death of Aegina's husband had been exactly unrelated to the family, despite what Seliora had said about it.

Staelia returned with a platter that she set before me. "I hope you like it."

"I'm sure I will." I was still hungry enough that I started right in. The fowl had been pounded thin and tender, breaded in some sort of savory crumbs I didn't recognize, cooked quickly at high heat while only browning the covering, and then served with some sort of thickened wine sauce with sautéed mushrooms. The side vegetables—beans and carrot strips—were still crisp, yet both warm and tender.

I ate it all, enjoying every bite, and I'd barely finished when Staelia returned.

"How was it?"

"Delicious, better than you said, if anything."

"Good. Clyenn will be pleased."

"I'm going to have to go. I do have this meeting . . . How much?"

"You're almost family . . ."

"I'm also with the Patrol, and not paying . . ." I shrugged. "That could cause me some difficulties. I hope you aren't offended, but I'm a very junior master and need to be very careful."

She smiled, an expression of both understanding and relief. "It would be a silver and one, but we do give all patrollers a tenth off. So just a silver." Her eyes twinkled. "And you don't tip family."

"Yes, Aunt Staelia."

She laughed softly, but she did take the single silver coin.

As I left, I realized that the dinner was one of the best I'd had in a restaurant, and I wondered why Seliora hadn't suggested we eat there. Because it *was* family, or because she hadn't wanted to expose me to Staelia's protectiveness too early? I'd have to tease her about that. In any case, I wouldn't be taking any patrollers to Chaelia's to eat, but not for the reason I'd originally thought, but because most of them couldn't have afforded it, and I couldn't afford to pay for them as well as for myself. In fact, I couldn't afford to eat there often.

It didn't take long to hail a hack. Once inside, I donned the awful wool cloak and the mismatched plaid cap. I had the driver drop me about a mille up South Middle, past the side street that held the Third District Civic Patrol station, but a half mille short of where I was to meet Horazt.

The driver gave me a knowing smile when I paid him. Doubtless he thought I was up to something out of a swash-and-dagger mystery . . . or looking for low pleasures with lower women.

Now that the sun had set, as I walked eastward on the south side of South

Middle, my shields as strong as practicable, I could see more people on the streets, but most of them were men. The worn cloak and the cap seemed to help, because I got far fewer glances than I had when I'd walked the same street earlier in obvious imager grays.

Before I reached Dugalle, Horazt stepped out of a niche in the wall and began to walk beside me. He wore a black cloak, one finer than the plaid I'd donned, but no cap.

"You wanted to talk to me, Master Rhennthyl?"

"I did. First, I wanted to tell you that Shault is doing well at Imagisle. He had a little trouble at first, but now—"

"He wrote Chelya. He said that after you talked to him, no one bothered him. His mother and I thank you for that kindness."

"He still has a long road to walk, and it's not an easy one."

"He'll do better there."

"I think so, but it's not easy."

We kept walking, not slowly, but not all that rapidly, either.

I gestured to the oblong structure ahead and to the right of the chest-high wall. "That's the Temple of Puryon, isn't it?"

"Call it that and the equalifiers get real upset." Horazt's voice carried a sourness. "They want everyone to call it the House of Equality. Don't much like taudischefs or imagers."

"So I've heard. The Patrol said that the riot was caused by street preaching."

Horazt didn't say anything.

"Was it?"

"Nah . . . well . . . sort of. One of their priest-fellows stood on the steps and started one of their rhyme stuff. You know . . .

> "To Puryon all give love and praise,
> To Him all hymns of joy we raise,
> Praise Him, all living here below.
> Praise Him, and all equal things we know . . ."

Horazt broke off. "It's something like that, anyhow."

"You don't much care for the equalifiers, I take it?"

"They're like the stones lining the river, in the shallow water near the edge. You step in, and they're so slippery that you're in up to your neck 'fore you know it." Horazt spat to the side, downwind, thankfully. "They talk about how everyone's got equal stuff inside 'em, but they don't say till later that anyone who's real different belongs to the Namer—well, that's not what they call Him, but He's the evil one that collects the spirits when folks die and freezes 'em so they shiver forever . . ."

"Do the priests in the Temple pay for advocates when the Patrol picks up offenders?"

Horazt just spat again.

"The other day, there was a man who was in the riot. He looked like he was Caenenan or Tiempran. He got the charges dropped, and the other two went to the road crew for a year."

"Chardyn D'Steinyn," Horazt admitted.

"Your doing?"

He shook his head. "He's an enforcer for Youdh. Youdh went to their priest"—he inclined his head toward the Temple building—"and Chardyn came back the next day."

"What does it cost?"

Horazt looked at me hard.

"I'm not a patroller, but I've spent the last few weeks at headquarters, and there are charges dropped and prisoners released without charges. I've got a good idea about who does what, but I want to know how it looks from where you are. I need to know what they pocket."

Horazt shrugged innocently. "I don't do that dung."

"I didn't say you did, but I'd wager that you know what it costs those who do."

"I heard Chefaryl say that the going rate's three golds to kill a minor, ten golds for a major, five golds to drop a major to a minor. Can't pay out of a charge if a patroller's injured. Got to pay quick, right up-front, before they go before a justice."

"Are there special occasions when a taudischef has to pay more?"

Horazt grinned. "Not me. Don't pay. Anyone stupid enough to get caught I don't want. I told my boys that."

"But Youdh?"

"He's like an old-time taudischef. Got favorites. Got lots of golds."

"Who makes the payoffs for Youdh?"

Horazt shrugged.

"Who takes them? It's got to be some lower level patroller, not that they stay there."

"Mardoyt gets them. Everyone knows that. Baluzt is his pocket man. Word is that some goes back to Harraf."

None of that especially surprised me, although I suppose that it would have a year earlier. "And it's all in coin, with no proof of anything. Don't Youdh and the others worry about being double-crossed?"

"It happens. That's why Baluzt is a first patroller and pocket man. Smyrrt got too cocky, held out on Artazt, down in the hellhole. A course right after that, Artazt got mixed up in something with a High Holder. Detazt took over."

"I suppose it works the other way, too."

Horazt frowned.

"Someone gets arrested, and there's no proof, no witnesses. I saw that happen last week. The justice had to dismiss the charges. I don't suppose there's a going rate for that."

"Two golds . . . so I hear. Enough of all that."

I accepted that . . . for the moment. "Did Youdh's people start the riot?"

"They weren't mine or Jadhyl's."

"And Youdh's chefdom is the one closest to the Temple." That was a guess.

"Horses drop dung where they please. Most times in their own stableyard."

"How long before Youdh makes another move for your territory, do you think?"

"He'll pay dear, friggin' sow-sucker."

"Someone's been shooting at patrollers and others with snipers' rifles."

"Don't know about that." Horazt slowed and stared at me. "I'm meeting with you. My turn, now. You walk with me through Youdh's streets, and we'd both better walk out."

"Fair enough." I'd known he'd want something in return, and I hoped I could keep matters from getting too expensive.

"You know when the conscriptors are coming through the taudis?" Horazt's tone was offhand, but his bearing wasn't.

"I haven't heard anything. You think that might cause another riot?"

"Might. Sometimes that'd be the only way to get the young ones away 'fore they get dragged off. There's talk of war, and a couple of black coach-wagons headed out the Sudroad yesterday."

What Horazt said made too much sense, but I still didn't know. "You're probably right, but I haven't heard anything."

He spat once more.

"If you wouldn't mind," I said gently, "tell me more about the South Middle taudis, things everyone here knows, like which part is your territory, which is Jadhyl's, which Youdh's . . ."

"I got the part north of Dugalle . . ."

I listened and watched as we walked a half mille past Dugalle before we got to Feramyo.

Town of Georgina (KESWICK) Public Library

"Here." Horazt turned.

I kept pace with him

"Not so many equalifiers down here," I said.

"Youdh doesn't like 'em."

The buildings were older than those near the Temple—or the House of Equality—and even the handful of better-kept dwellings with recently washed windows seemed to have years of grime caught within the glass itself—at least that was the way they seemed from the lamplight coming from within. The faint but acrid smell of elveweed was more prevalent. With the sun completely set, only a handful of streetlamps lit, and neither moon more than a crescent, seeing more than a handful of yards in any detail was difficult.

Just short of two blocks along Feramyo, two men—barely more than youths—eased from a side alley toward us.

"This isn't your part of town," said the shorter one, revealing a blade.

"Better just turn around," added the taller.

"I'm Horazt. I walk where I please."

"Youdh doesn't care if you're the Namer. We don't either."

"The streets in L'Excelsis are open to all," I said mildly, readying a nonlethal imaging and hoping it would not be necessary.

"We warned you." The shorter one lunged, but his feet slipped from under him on the oil I'd imaged under them, and he hit the pavement hard enough that the knife skittered across the worn stones.

The second one fired his pistol through his cloak. The impact on my shields forced me back a step, but I imaged a bit of caustic into his eyes, and oil under his feet before giving him a shove. He also went down hard. "Shall we continue?" I asked Horazt.

The taudischef glanced at the two figures, one unconscious and the other moaning and rubbing at his eyes. "Another block."

We didn't make it quite a block before three muscular figures in dark brown appeared. They didn't say a word, just began swinging blades—for the moment before I imaged all three blades from their hands and onto the pavement.

One of them backed away. The other two drew old-style heavy pistols. I imaged the cartridges from both before they pulled the triggers.

"You fellows might get hurt if you keep trying to cause trouble," I offered.

One of the two remaining took one step back, then another. The remaining tough, a good half head taller than me, charged. He took two steps before he rammed into the extra-hard shield I'd imaged for just a moment. As he staggered back, his feet went out from under him on imaged oil, and he went down hard. The only problem was that he immediately jumped to his feet . . . and slammed down a second time. When he started to rise a third time, Horazt kicked him in the temple.

He didn't get up after that.

No one bothered us on the way back out to South Middle, but I kept full shields and a wary eye. We walked back along the south side, the way we had come.

As we neared Dugalle, Horazt finally spoke. "You're the first patroller or imager to walk the taudis alone at night in years. Maybe ever."

Possibly the last and stupidest, as well, I thought. "It's not something I plan to make a habit of, but I asked for a favor, and it's best to repay them."

Horazt laughed, a touch nervously, I thought.

"If you do hear of things that don't really belong in the taudis, I would appreciate hearing about it," I said. "That might be best for both of us."

"It might." He paused. "It'll come through Mama Diestra."

"That's fine."

He turned down Dugalle, and I kept walking toward the Midroad.

At that moment, something flashed before my eyes—some sort of fire, I thought, climbing up the side of a brick building. For the moment that I saw the image, I tried to identify what I'd seen.

Had I really seen it?

Or was it just an illusion because my legs were shaky and my vision blurry from too much imaging in a short time? Outside of holding heavy shields, I really hadn't done that much imaging in weeks, even several months, now that I thought about it. I made a mental note to remedy that . . . when I wasn't already exhausted.

As I trudged westward, I hoped I didn't have to do any more imaging anytime soon—and that I could find a hack to hail before too long. But the brief image of the fire climbing the brick wall remained with me, and I tried on the ride back toward Imagisle, without success, to recall anything—or any place—that looked like what I'd briefly seen.

15

I did stagger back to Imagisle on Meredi night, and almost overslept on Jeudi morning. I thought I'd had more dreams about fires, but I didn't remember them at all clearly. The newsheets I picked up hurriedly after breakfast didn't mention any large fires, either, but they might not have, because they were reporting that Ferrum was ready to declare war on Solidar, if our ships insisted on protecting "the enemies of Ferrum." One of those enemies happened to be the Abierto Isles.

There wasn't much I could do about that and, fortunately, all I had to do on Jeudi, again, was watch justicing proceedings, and keep mental track of two more cases where the charges were dropped.

Jeudi night, after Mardoyt was tied up with the final scheduling of prisoners, witnesses, and evidence for Vendrei's hearings, I checked the cases. One charge sheet was missing, and in the other case, the charges were listed as being dropped. That made sense, because the accused already had a record of a year on the road crew, if three years earlier. If his record sheet suddenly disappeared, a few too many questions might be asked.

By Vendrei morning, even after a more spirited hand-to-hand sparring contest with one of Clovyl's assistants, I was feeling back to normal. But I tried to remind myself that there was definitely a limit to what I could image. Vendrei was like every other day that week, with more cases being disposed of quickly by the presiding justice. In only two cases were there Not Guilty pleas, and in one, the justice actually acquitted the accused. That might have been because the case probably never should have gotten that far—the girl had been fast and loose with her favors, but clearly not soliciting, and she'd never used or had a weapon.

When Baluzt and I and the coach-wagons returned to headquarters Vendrei night, through a mist that was threatening to become a full-fledged rain, a patroller greeted me almost as soon as I'd stepped down into the back alley.

"Master Rhennthyl, sir, the subcommander would like to see you immediately."

"Thank you."

Cydarth was standing by the window again, and I had to wonder if that happened to be his favorite position for meeting people. He turned. "Master Rhennthyl, how have you enjoyed your week at the justice hall?"

"It has been informative in many ways," I replied.

"That's good. Both the commander and I felt that seeing the charging process and the trials would give you a better idea of what happens to offenders. Now that you've seen that, the commander feels that you need to see the street side of the Patrol. Starting Lundi morning, at seventh glass, you'll be accompanying various patrollers out of the Third District station off South Middle. Captain Harraf will be expecting you."

"Yes, sir." Seventh glass. That meant a very quick shower and breakfast snatched on the run. Third District was the station with the responsibility for the South Middle taudis . . . and an additional two milles from Imagisle.

"I'm most certain that you will find that duty more interesting, Master Rhennthyl. I won't keep you. If you would tell Lieutenant Mardoyt of your change of duty, I would appreciate it."

"I will, sir." I inclined my head, then departed, making my way down the upper level hallway to Mardoyt's study. I caught him as he was about to leave, probably for the court preparation room.

"If I could have a moment, sir. The subcommander has decided that a week of observing your duties was sufficient. He's assigned me to observe Third District next week."

"What we do"—Mardoyt smiled warmly—"isn't terribly interesting. Necessary, but not intriguing."

"I've learned a great deal." And I had, if not exactly what Mardoyt would have wished.

"You're obviously an imager with a future, Master Rhennthyl," Mardoyt said. "That's clear from the ease with which you've picked up how the Patrol works."

"You and the others have gone out of your way to make sure I understand, and I appreciate that."

"You've been most diligent in checking the charge sheets against the justice proceedings, I also understand."

"I just want to make sure that I understand how things really work, Lieutenant." I smiled pleasantly.

"You're a very bright man, especially for an imager, Master Rhennthyl, and you have quite a future. That Seliora D'Shelim is quite a beauty, I understand. Like a fine blade or a good pistol. You know, a year or so ago, a young man, not much older than you, Master Rhennthyl . . . well . . . he was shot. He was Pharsi, and he wouldn't say anything, but there were only two girls who could have done it. One was Seliora." Mardoyt shrugged. "He got it in the shoulder, but he lived, and no one in the Patrol thought there was any reason to get involved in a Pharsi love spat. Not when no one would say anything."

I wasn't surprised that Mardoyt had made his own inquiries, not after Grandmama Diestra's cautions to me. I couldn't even say I was surprised that Seliora had shot someone who'd attempted to force himself on her. I'd seen her use the pistol to get me to safety.

"Her family has done well, coming up from the taudis," Mardoyt went on, "but I wouldn't be at all surprised if they still didn't have ties to some people there that the Patrol would like to put away for a long time."

"They've never mentioned anything like that."

"I suppose they wouldn't, not to an upstanding young imager like you."

"It wouldn't matter." I laughed softly. "We get all types at Imagisle, from the children of High Holders to those from the taudis. Some have even been brothers to taudischefs. At Imagisle, what you do is what matters, not where you came from."

"I suppose that's true." He shook his head. "It's too bad that the rest of L'Excelsis and Solidar aren't like that. I've seen families suffer, sometimes even to the point of being ruined, when people find out their past." He shrugged. "Sometimes, that past isn't even past. You never know."

I nodded. "That's true." I wanted to add something, but anything I said along those lines, such as that the most respectable-seeming officers were often nothing like that, would have revealed too much. Better to leave the lieutenant guessing. "If you don't have anything else for me, sir, I'll be leaving."

"Best of fortune at Third District."

"Thank you." I walked out of the anteroom and down the corridor to the stairs, then I stopped and stepped back into the alcove beside the steps, erecting an image shield that matched the wall—I hoped.

Before long, Mardoyt appeared, and walked past me and down the steps. At the bottom, he eased open the door, looked, and then closed it, before turning and walking back up and past me. His actions were more than suggestive, but certainly not proof. I waited until he entered the courtroom preparation chamber before slipping down the stairs to the charging area.

Gulyart was still at the charging desk, alone with several stacks of paper.

"Would you like some help filling out some of those?" I asked. "I've got a little time."

Gulyart smiled faintly.

"I mean it." I pulled up a chair. "Just tell me what you want done."

"If you don't mind . . . Ghrisha would be glad that I got home before it gets too dark."

I followed his example, checking the record sheets that had been delivered, and then filing them, after making any necessary changes or entering changes on existing records sheets and then replacing them. Along the way, I sneaked a look at several areas of the files, but the sheets I was looking for weren't there, including the one that should have been on Chardyn D'Steinyn. Only after close to half a glass, when we were nearing the end of the pile, did I speak.

"Someone mentioned a first patroller named Smyrrt who used to work for Lieutenant Mardoyt. I got the impression that something had happened to him."

Gulyart nodded. "He was killed last winter, walking by that new stone building some three blocks up on his way home. Someone knocked over a stack of cut granite . . . fell three stories and hit him. Anyway, he was found under the stone, and his skull was crushed. . . ."

"That sounds like accidental on purpose," I observed.

"Some said it was." Gulyart shrugged. "But Mardoyt looked into it and said it was an accident. Everyone agreed."

"Then it was an accident." I paused. "Have a good weekend."

"I will . . . and thank you for the help."

When I left the Patrol headquarters, I did hail a hack to take me back to the Collegium, and not because of the rain, which wasn't that heavy, but because I wanted to get there in time to talk to Master Dichartyn. I was fortunate enough to find him in and momentarily unoccupied.

"I thought I might be seeing you. Have you been reassigned yet?"

"Third District, starting on Lundi." I eased off my damp gray woolen cloak and sat down in the armless wooden chair across the writing desk from him.

"What of great import do you have to impart?"

I ignored the sarcasm. "Mardoyt's taking payoffs to lose charge sheets or get charges reduced before they're presented to the justices. There's no real proof except for missing charge sheets."

"That's always been a problem, with whoever's held that position. What else?"

"A taudischef named Youdh is fairly close to the Tiempran priests who incited the riots, and they paid for the advocate to represent some of those sentenced, as well as the bribes to get some of the charges unofficially dropped. It's well known that Baluzt is the pocket man for Mardoyt."

"I see that you haven't confined your observations to what has been presented to you, but you'll have to do better if you want to change matters."

"Should I want to change them?"

That brought a frown to Dichartyn's face.

"You pointed out that I was only to be an observer, sir. If the Civic Patrol structure is such that it encourages bribery, that's not exactly something for a liaison to address, is it?"

"No. But proof would help."

I was the one to laugh. "Mardoyt has years of experience in avoiding providing proof. What I know absolutely and what I can prove are two separate matters, and you know that far better than I, sir."

"I'm glad to see you recognize that. Just don't mention what you've told me to anyone except Master Poincaryt until you do have proof." He cleared his throat. "There's one other thing. The Council is having its annual Autumn Ball on Vendrei the thirty-fourth of next month."

"Do they have one every season?"

"Every season except summer. Although Master Schorzat and I both have some reservations about your methods, your ability to discern trouble is extremely good. We have agreed that your presence will be salutary. Since you are no longer officially part of Council security, you will need to wear the black formal jacket of a Solidaran functionary—and the imager's pin, of course. This is not a deception because as both a master imager and a liaison to the Civic Patrol, you are exactly that. The tailor is expecting you for a fitting tomorrow at ninth glass, after you finish your session with Master Rholyn."

"Speaking of that, sir, it's getting rather chill in the studio. If it gets much colder, I won't be able to paint because the oils will harden too much. I'm going to need some way to heat the studio on the coldest days."

"I can see that, but just talk to Grandisyn. I'm sure you two can figure something out."

"I didn't wish to go around you, sir."

"For matters like that," Master Dichartyn said dryly, "please do."

"I have another question."

"Oh?"

"I'd like to paint the portrait of the young woman who saved my life. But since the Collegium paid for everything, from canvases to paints, I don't know how exactly to repay the Collegium. Also, is it possible to have her do the sittings here at the studio . . . if I make sure she only takes the public ways?"

Master Dichartyn laughed. "We're not that secretive, Rhenn, and the Collegium certainly won't have a problem with your painting her portrait or, as you indicated earlier, portraits of other imagers who are friends or acquaintances."

"I didn't want to take any advantage . . ."

"That's very clear . . . and appreciated. Is there anything else? If not . . ." He stood.

"There was one other thing . . . some of the taudischefs are worried about conscriptors scouring the taudis for youngsters."

Master Dichartyn shook his head. "They don't tell me, but it will happen, and sooner than later. The Army and Navy are always short of men, and it's been a good year since the last sweep. I don't feel that sorry for the taudischefs. Most of the boys will fare better outside the taudis, even in war."

He was probably right about that—and I was definitely missing something, something that he wasn't about to tell me . . . as always.

I hurried to the dining hall, only to find that the only convenient space at the masters' table was one to the left of the pattern-finder Quaelyn. On his right was Maitre Dyana.

"Good evening, Rhennthyl," she offered.

"Good evening, maitre, Master Quaelyn," I replied as I seated myself.

"How are you finding the Civic Patrol?" she returned.

"Enlightening in ways that I never considered, but possibly should have." I tried to keep my tone light and wry, accepting the platter of river trout, each wrapped in what passed for parchment.

"A certain practicality, leavened, as it were, by personal necessity?" inquired Quaelyn.

"That's one way of putting it." I poured some of the red table wine. I didn't know what it was, but felt I could use some.

"Practicality and personal necessity. Imagine that," murmured someone.

"What do your patterns say about how the coming war will affect the High Holders?" I looked to the older master.

"Your question, Rhennthyl, contains a number of assumptions, such as there being a war, that such a war will impact Solidar in more than a minimal sense, and that such impacts will indeed affect High Holders as such."

"If you would address Rhenn's assumptions first, then," suggested Maitre Dyana.

"The first assumption is the most reasonable, because whether an actual war is declared or not, there is a definite struggle for economic and military control, but the impacts of such a war are likely to be indirect at best. That is because the Ferrans—or the Tiemprans or anyone else—do not have adequate troop transport capabilities to bring an army onto Solidaran soil.

In the worst case, there will be shortages of certain goods, such as spices, rarer metals, specialty woods, and minerals. Shortages drive up prices of those goods and others as well. Such price increases will impact the poorest in Solidar the most, the crafters almost as much, the factors less, and the vast majority of High Holders minimally." Quaelyn smiled apologetically and somewhat condescendingly.

"I see your reasoning." I smiled. "Thank you." I might be missing something in regards to Master Dichartyn, but I had the feeling that Quaelyn was missing a vital aspect. The taudis already had periodic riots from various causes, and with another conscription effort, followed by higher prices of even a few goods, parts of Solidar—and L'Excelsis—were likely to face more in the way of riots and unrest. He might be right in that such unrest would not extend to the lands and properties of the High Holders . . . but I wouldn't have wagered much on that, although I couldn't have said why.

"With what patterns will the Council respond?" I pressed.

"They will lay the blame primarily upon the Ferrans, and secondarily upon the factoring class, which will respond by pointing out that they did not cause the shortages and that the Council did nothing to anticipate the problems at hand. . . ."

I nodded and kept listening.

16

Samedi morning afforded no rest, not that Samedis ever did. I hurried through everything so that I could get to the studio early enough to set up and—hopefully—to talk to Grandisyn, but he wasn't anywhere around. I'd have to see him on Lundi, then.

Maitre Rholyn appeared in the studio a few moments before eighth glass.

"The standing position?"

"If you would, sir." I paused. "Before we begin, might I ask where it appears the Council stands on the question of war with Ferrum?"

"You can certainly ask, but the Council has declared it opposes war and is unlikely to discuss the matter unless the situation changes."

In short, they'd wait until Ferrum acted.

"Have you thought about my comments of last week?" he asked as he put one foot on the crate.

For a moment I had to search mentally for what he'd said—he'd implied that the Collegium was more authoritarian than even the Council, although his words had been more carefully chosen than that. "Yes, sir. There were several implications behind your words. At least, I thought there were."

"Such as?" He smiled faintly.

"The implication that while some fictions, such as not overtly conceding the obvious in identifying Council security force members as imagers, may be obvious, they are also necessary."

"Oh? How so?"

"Manners are often a fiction, yet without them, all too many gatherings and conversations might well end in violence." I picked up the palette and the fine-tipped brush.

That brought a nod. "Did you . . . ponder any others?"

"I could be mistaken, but I gathered the impression that you implied there was a trade-off between accountability and authority."

Rholyn frowned, as I'd hoped he might. "How did you reach that conclusion?"

"You discussed how the Council must reach a consensus for a decision, but how the Collegium almost always accepts the decision of the chief maitre.

The difference is that all know that the Maitre D'Collegium is fully accountable to the Collegium and can be replaced by a vote of all masters at any time,
whereas councilors serve fixed terms, regardless of their actions. Also, seldom,
if ever, is a single councilor made accountable for a Council action. Thus, it is
clear that while the Maitre D'Collegium is accountable, such sole accountability is far from clear with the Council of Solidar, even when the Executive
Council acts independently."

Maitre Rholyn laughed. I thought the sound was a trace forced.

"In time, you might well represent the Collegium before the Council,
Rhenn."

"I think not, sir. I am not always the best at reserving my views for the
time most appropriate for disclosure."

"That may come with experience." He turned his head. "This way?"

"A bit more toward me."

After that, Rholyn did not mention anything of great import. Once he departed, a few moments before ninth glass, I cleaned up the studio, then looked
once more for Grandisyn, who remained nowhere to be found, and hastened
back to the quadrangle for my fitting.

Based on the way I felt matters would be going over the weekend, after
my fitting with the tailor, I immediately took a hack from the west side of the
Bridge of Desires to see Khethila and Father at the factorage. As soon as the hack
stopped and I stepped out, I could see that something was wrong. There was a
definite odor of smoke and burned wool, and Eilthyr was standing outside by
the front doors, propped wide open, just below the tasteful sign proclaiming
Alusine Wool, set on the yellow bricks of the wall comprising the long front
of the one-story building. The loading docks were in back, more toward the
south end, but still out of sight.

"Master Rhennthyl, we're closed 'cause of the fire, but Mistress Khethila
and Factor Chenkyr are inside."

"A fire? Where?" A coldness flashed down my spine.

"In the back on the north end."

I hurried up the steps to the open double oak doors and inside, where the
heavy acrid odor of smoke assaulted me. I glanced beyond the open area before the racks that held the swathes of various wools. To the right was another
set of racks with the lighter fabrics—muslin, cotton, linen. Behind that was the
raised platform with desks and files from where Father—and now Khethila—
could watch the entry.

Khethila hurried toward me. I didn't see Father.

"Rhenn . . . how did you know?"

"I had a feeling I should come." That was accurate enough. "What happened? How bad is it?"

"Someone pried open the boarded-up window in the small storeroom—the one Father converted—and threw something in—something like a glass jug of lamp oil. Everything there is ruined, but Sherol—the night watch—he stopped the flames. He was burned badly."

"He's dead?"

She shook her head. "Father doesn't think he'll live, but he's still alive. He's at the South Hospital of the Nameless."

"Where's Father?"

"He's in back. The Civic Patrol and the fire brigade left a while ago. The Patrol wasn't that helpful. Oh, they were nice enough, but how can you find someone that no one even saw? It's not like they stole goods that might be traced, or even golds. Even before this, it wasn't that good a week."

"Something happened in Kherseilles?"

She nodded wearily. "One of the properties adjoining the factorage building was sold. The new owner required a survey. He claims the building wall and the courtyard wall were built on his land. He's asking that they be removed—or for five hundred golds to convey the property that the walls were built on. The discrepancy is all of half a yard. Five hundred golds for a strip twenty yards long and half a yard wide."

"Who's the new owner?"

"Rousel doesn't know. The Banque D'Rivages is handling it through the Banque D'Kherseilles."

"How long since Father built the place?" I thought it had been ten years.

"Nine years." She shook her head. "Ten, and it wouldn't matter."

"Can't Father require compensation from the original surveyor?"

"He's dead."

"Oh." I had a very good idea who was behind what had happened, and I wouldn't have been surprised if the surveys and documents presented had even been forged or altered, but, again, with the surveyor dead, and the details almost ten years old, I doubted that there was any way to prove what I instinctively knew.

"Rhenn . . . do you know something?"

"No." I didn't know. "Seliora's family might be able to find out who's behind it. Or I might. Even if I can, though, it will be hard to find any proof."

"That's what Father said."

"He might ask his friend Veblynt, though. He knows people."

"That's a good idea."

"I'm going back to see Father."

"He'll be glad to see you."

I wasn't so sure about that, but I made my way through the racks of woolens, most of which would require a good airing out, if not more. Some of them might not be salvageable.

Father was standing in the doorway of the small storeroom. Two men I didn't know were using large sponges to collect water and squeeze it into buckets that they emptied out through the window that had been boarded shut and pried open by the arsonists.

Father turned. "Khethila thought you might be here." He gestured around the small room. Most of the racks were charred. "A good three to four hundred golds' worth of ruined wool, and a good man who saved us from total ruin who will like as not die."

He turned from the room and shut the door before looking at me. "Do you know who might have done this?"

"It's not someone who knows the business," I said. "They would have forced one of the doors next to the loading docks, and they would have used more oil."

"That means it's someone who just wants to hurt factors—like those Tiempran religious fools or Jariolan sympathizers. Or it's personal."

I nodded. "Has anyone gotten mad at you lately? Or have you had to collect?"

Father shook his head. "Oaletyr's been a season late in paying all year, and there are a couple of tailors I'll never get paid by, but they wouldn't do this. Have you upset anyone?"

"A dead Ferran envoy, and a few dead assassins, but people don't usually attack imagers' families because we can't inherit anything."

"You can't?" His tone of voice told me that he hadn't known that.

"No. And it can't go from you to any children. Now . . . if I married Seliora, her property and golds could go to them, but nothing from my family."

"Then . . . why . . . who?"

"You might ask your friend Veblynt, and I'll see what I can find out." I wasn't about to tell Father what I suspected, because, first, there was no proof, and second, if I happened to be right, no one in my family should know anything at all. I didn't even like telling Seliora, but her family at least had experience in dealing with what I suspected I and mine were facing.

We walked slowly back to rejoin Khethila.

"I've been checking the bolts out here," she said. "Most of them will be all right."

While there wasn't that much that I could do, it was two glasses later before I felt that I could leave, and it took nearly half a glass to get a hack headed back north.

Seliora and I had not made any specific plans for the evening, just that I would arrive around half past four, but the hack dropped me off outside the private entrance closer to a quint past third glass. I held shields and glanced around carefully as I made my way to the steps, despite Seliora's statement a week earlier about Grandmama Diestra calling in some favors. Still . . . no one shot at me.

Bhenyt was the one to open the door and greet me. "You're early."

"Something happened. If you'd tell Seliora, I'll wait in the main foyer, if that's all right."

With a nod, Bhenyt was gone, and another quint passed while I sat on the chair that had been designed for the ruined High Holder Tierchyl, thinking about exactly what I could do and how. I certainly couldn't go running off to wherever Ryel's main holding house was. First, I didn't know where it was. Second, I didn't know where he was. Third, I had no idea exactly how to best do what needed to be done—or what exactly that might be, given the way High Holders clearly held grudges. Fourth, I needed to make sure that whatever I did would not run afoul of the rules of the Collegium, although Maitre Dyana's words suggested I could do almost anything so long as it never became public or linked to me. And, fifth, while I suspected, even knew, that Ryel was behind the arson, if I acted before his acts became known, I'd end up destroying myself, if not my entire family.

When I heard Seliora's steps, I immediately stood and walked toward the archway at the bottom of the staircase. She was wearing deep green trousers, a paler green blouse, and a jacket to match the trousers. Her earrings were silver studs with green stones, and she wore a silver chain with a pendant that looked to be jadeite, matching the earrings.

She gave me a hug and a warm kiss, then wrinkled her nose. "You smell . . . like smoke."

"I'm certain I do. I think I'm going to need even more help. I've just come from the factorage. Last night, someone set a fire there. . . ." I explained as quickly as I could what had happened there—and in Kherseilles.

"It has to be Ryel," she said. "Who else would have the golds—or care that much?"

"I know that, but there's not a shred of proof. Even the card with the silver ribbon couldn't be traced." I stopped. "There's one other thing. On Meredi night after I talked to Horazt . . . Oh, I need to tell you about that as well . . . but, first . . . I was walking back down South Middle, and I felt this flash in my head. That's what it felt like, and I saw flames leaping from a hole in a brick wall—"

"You had a farsight flash?"

"Is that what you call it? I feel so stupid. I didn't even recognize what I was seeing, I mean, where it was. But it's been a good ten years, if not longer since I've really looked at the back of the factorage, on the north end away from the loading docks. There's nothing there, just plain old grimy bricks."

She shook her head. "Rhenn . . . you may be an imager master, but you need help. What do you plan on doing?"

"Nothing . . . not until I learn enough to know what I can do and how. For the moment, I need at least a rough map to High Holder Ryel's estate— the one here, north of L'Excelsis, and a way to get there. According to what Maitre Dyana has said, Ryel won't do anything for a while now. He'll drag it out so that he can be sure that I'll suffer and yet not be able to do anything. That's the way they work. Also, if something happens too soon . . ." I shook my head. "I'm just guessing. If I act too soon, I'll end up in trouble I can't escape, and if I wait too long, I'll run out of time."

She nodded. "He'll be expecting you."

"I'm certain he will be, but he can't very well stop everyone passing by his grounds and gates, and I may find a better approach, but I need to look."

"We can take you there in one of the wagons. We've often delivered things on Solayi."

"Not to Ryel?"

"No, but no one cares what tradespeople do, especially if we look to be working." She looked at me more intently. "You're pale. Have you eaten?"

"No," I admitted. "Not since breakfast."

"We can go over to Terraza. They're open all afternoon on Samedi. It will be quiet. Then we can come back here and discuss what you need and how we can help."

That was fine with me.

17

I arrived at NordEste Design at half before noon on Solayi. I carried a bag inside which were exercise clothes and the field boots that went with them, as well as more than a few sheets of drafting paper, some marker pencils, and a small drawing board.

Seliora was the one to greet me. She wore faded heavy blue trousers and a jacket of similar material. Her hair was up and covered by a dark blue scarf. She looked at the bag. "Working clothes?"

"Such as I have. Exercise clothes and field boots. I need somewhere to change."

"Methyr can show you one of the guest chambers. It's likely to be one of the few times you'll see one." Her smile was sad.

I understood her feelings, because she'd learned early on that imagers could sleep only in lead-lined rooms—or in places well away from anyone else—not for their own health, but for the safety of others.

"Oh . . . I have some good news," I announced, thinking it might cheer her up. "I've worked it out so that I can paint your portrait. We can even do it in my studio at Imagisle."

"You're not placating me, are you?"

"No. I just managed to get approval on Vendrei, and with everything that happened yesterday . . . I forgot to tell you. We could start next Samedi afternoon, and then go out to dinner . . ." Was she upset at coming to Imagisle? "Odelia can come, if . . ." I flushed slightly.

Seliora laughed. "I wouldn't need her in the studio." A more pensive expression followed. "It might be best if we traveled together, at least on those occasions when you aren't with me."

"You think Ryel . . . ?"

"Not yet, but . . ."

I understood that, as well. I was also getting even angrier. Ryel's eldest son Johanyr had been a total bastard, and exactly what right did his mightiness High Holder Ryel have to attack someone who had stopped his son from continuing abusive ways? My lips curled. I knew the answer—the right of power. And the only way to stop such abuse was to remove that power in a way that did not lead back to me . . . and the Collegium.

"That was a rather cruel smile, Rhenn."

"I'm sorry. I was thinking about Ryel." I shook my head. "Thoughts don't count. Actions do."

The sad smile returned to her face. "There's more Pharsi in your background than your mother could ever know."

"And it's the side you don't like," I said gently.

"It's necessary," was all she said.

Necessary? That was a bit cruel. What choice was I being given by either Ryel or the Collegium? If I did nothing, my family would likely be destroyed, and eventually I'd end up dead. I wanted to bring up what Mardoyt had said about Seliora . . . but now wasn't the time. I was too angry to be objective.

"Are you all right?" she asked.

"I'm angry. Not at you. I feel like I'm being pushed into doing things I'd rather not do because the alternatives are worse."

"Sometimes, that's life."

"I know." But I didn't have to like it.

"We'd better get going," she said, turning to beckon Methyr from where he was sitting reading on a settee near the back of the hall.

I followed Methyr up the side staircase to the third level and to a chamber next to the passageway leading to the east terrace, where Seliora and I had often sat and talked over the late summer and harvest. I changed quickly and hurried back downstairs, carrying the drafting paper, markers, and drawing board.

Seliora was waiting. "You look less like an imager."

"My wardrobe is rather limited, since all my work clothes got burned in the fire at Caliostrus's place."

"No one will look that closely. Shomyr's in the courtyard getting the wagon ready. I'll be with you in a bit."

I had to look embarrassed. "How do I get there?"

Seliora laughed. "I forgot. You've never gone that way. Methyr!"

Once again, Methyr led me to my destination, although it wasn't that difficult—to the south end of the foyer and down a set of steps hidden behind a false panel, then along a narrow corridor with doors every so often.

"Those lead to the different workrooms," Methyr said casually.

"Which one do you work in?"

"I like the woodworking best, but I'm supposed to learn something about them all."

At the end of the narrow corridor was another door, which he unlocked and opened.

I stepped out onto a narrow stoop at the top of a set of five steps leading down to the narrow northern end of the courtyard opposite the stables, outside of which Shomyr was checking harnesses on the two mules hitched to the wagon, a simple oblong box, with a frame above, covered with oilcloth that had once been a dark brown, but now appeared mottled with various shades of brown.

After I crossed the paved courtyard and neared the wagon, Shomyr turned from the mules and their traces and surveyed me. "You look more like a factor's son playing at being a workman."

"It doesn't matter, does it? So long as I don't look like an imager?"

He smiled, then walked to the back of the wagon, reached inside, and tossed me a worn, stained, and patched leather jacket. "That should help. Boots are boots, and yours are well worn, and no one looks at trousers."

I set the drawing board on the wagon seat, on top of the paper, and pulled on the jacket, a trace snug, but I didn't need to fasten it.

"You're broader than you look," Shomyr said.

I had Clovyl and Master Dichartyn to thank for that. I glanced into the interior of the wagon, empty except for a single chair, wrapped heavily in cloth.

"One of the sample chairs," explained Seliora, coming up behind me. "In case anyone asks. That's unlikely."

A temporary bench seat had been wedged in place inside the wagon, but just behind the driver's seat. That was for me.

"We might as well get rolling."

Shomyr vaulted up onto the driver's place, and I clambered up and inside, settling onto the bench, in the middle, where I'd be able to look out between Seliora and Shomyr. I set the drawing materials beside me as Seliora vaulted up into her seat with grace.

Shomyr drove the wagon down Nordroad and then turned northeast on the Boulevard D'Este.

"How long will it take?" I asked.

"With the wagon this light, a little more than a glass," offered Shomyr.

"Have you ever been at Ryel's?"

"No. We've driven past the grounds. High Holder Tierchyl's chateau is on the west side of the road a bit farther out." Seliora paused. "Will his family keep it now that he's dead?"

"It depends on what's left after Ryel extracts his pounds of flesh. Tierchyl's family is probably still there for now."

"Not for long, from what we've heard of Ryel," suggested Shomyr.

"What do you recall of Ryel's estate here?" I asked.

"It's near the top of one of the hills to the north, the ones between the higher ground and the valley, but not at the top. At least, the chateau isn't . . ."

I listened until Seliora and Shomyr could say no more, and then we talked more about family. I did tell Seliora that her aunt Staelia was very much her partisan.

While we conversed, Shomyr drove on, through the Plaza D'Nord and along the boulevard for another mille before turning due north on an unmarked but well-paved road.

"To find those with golds, just follow the best roads," Shomyr said cheerfully.

"Or the worst roads with the deepest ruts," countered Seliora.

Before all that long, as the wagon began to head down a gentle slope, Shomyr nodded. "There it is, on the hill ahead, the right side, in the middle of the walls."

I immediately put a sheet of paper on the drawing board and began to study the grounds framed by the wall. The chateau was set on the east side of the road, and dominated the gentler slope just below the hilltop, the building itself a good three hundred yards from end to end. It made the Council Chateau look tiny by comparison, and I would have guessed that it well might be smaller than Ryel's chateau on his main holding north of Rivages. A gray stone wall a little more than two yards high extended around the grounds.

I began to sketch, not wanting to waste a moment, since I was imposing on both Seliora and Shomyr.

From what I could tell as we approached, the structure was laid out in a "Y" shape, with the base of the Y running parallel to the road. The southern extension ended at what looked to be a cliff—one created artificially by digging away the hillside and running a solid stone foundation straight up. A squarish tower was set on the southern-most section of the terrace overlooking the gardens and valley. It appeared no more than five yards on a side, but rose another three levels above the roofed and pillared but otherwise open terrace.

"You could see all the way to Imagisle from the top of the tower," I observed.

"I'm certain that's the point," replied Shomyr. "The terrace offers almost as good a view, and the extensions of the roof allow one to sit there in the late afternoon without getting that warm. They'll doubtless have shades or screens for the time around sunset."

I kept sketching as quickly as I could, trying to put in the various buildings in a quick diagram of where everything was located in respect to the
walls and the gates, and the curving drive from the gates leading to the covered front portico looked as though it fronted a gallery or a grand salon
stretching across the west side of the chateau.

Shomyr let the mules take their time plodding up the relatively gentle, if
long, slope. Neither he nor Seliora spoke as I drew.

Once we passed the gates, I scrambled to the back of the wagon and continued my work. The gates were simple but heavy iron grilles, without even a
crest or coat of arms on them. Two heavy iron bars on the inside secured the
gates. The stone pillars anchoring them rose almost a yard above the top of the
adjoining wall. There was no exterior gatehouse, but I could see the shape of
one against the wall and just inside the gates. The paved drive was wide enough
for two carriages abreast and curved northward to the portico, then circled
back eastward to rejoin itself. In the middle of that circle was a miniature garden, with a fountain statue in the center, although I could not make out the figure in any detail. The ground to the north continued to slope upward. Against
the northern wall, some four hundred yards uphill, was a curved stone structure that puzzled me for a moment, until I realized that it had to be some sort
of cistern or water reservoir, feeding both the chateau and the fountain, and the
water source was probably a spring or a stream even farther uphill.

"There's a turnout at the top of the hill. I can stop there for a bit. That
would seem natural," Shomyr said.

"I'd like that."

I couldn't see all of the chateau from the turnout, but since the wagon
was barely visible from below, I took my time—almost a glass—before I told
Shomyr that I had what I needed.

He turned the wagon back around and headed slowly downhill—as would
any teamster.

I kept drawing and filling in all the details that I could. In fact, I drew all
the way back. When we pulled up in the courtyard of NordEste Design, it was
just past fourth glass. Dark clouds were massing to the northwest, and the
wind had turned chill.

Once the wagon stopped and Shomyr set the brake, Seliora turned in the
seat. "Could I see?"

"Of course." I showed her the first sketch, which was almost a diagram of
where all the buildings were, then the others in turn.

Shomyr looked at the sketches as well, then shook his head. "I didn't see
half of that."

"It takes practice. Master Caliostrus would put an arrangement of fruit or something on a table, and tell me to look at it carefully. Then he'd remove it all, and make me draw it from memory. He got most upset if I left something out. You practice like that for seven years, and you get very good at noticing details." Unless it was something that I hadn't looked at that way, or hadn't known how to study when I'd last seen it—like the back of the factorage.

"Can I help with the wagon?" I asked.

Shomyr shook his head. "You need to change and get back, don't you?"

"I have some time."

"That's all right." Shomyr nodded to his sister.

Seliora took my arm, not saying anything until we were farther away. "He's happy to be able to help. He's also pleased that you offered to do what you could with the wagon, but he likes to handle things in his own way."

I could understand that.

"You go change," she added, "and then we can talk, can't we?"

"For a little," I admitted.

She used a heavy key to unlock the door at the top of the steps, then locked it behind us. Once we were in the main foyer, she turned to me. "Go change. I'll wait here." She took off the scarf and shook out her hair.

For a moment, I just admired her, then headed for the stairs, carrying the drawing board and all the sketches. When I finished changing and made my way back down to her, carrying my bag filled with exercise clothes and the sketches, she had two mugs of hot tea and a plate of biscuits waiting on a side table flanked by two chairs.

"How did you manage that so quickly?" I asked, settling into the chair across from her.

"I didn't. Mother did. She was watching for our return."

"You and your family . . . you're all remarkable." I paused. "Thank you for today. I can't tell you how much I appreciate it." I took a sip of the tea, a small sip. It was hot, very hot. "If I could ride, it would have been easier."

"You can't?" She grinned. "We should teach you."

"You can ride as well?"

"Why wouldn't I be able to? I used to ride messages for Papa when I was little."

"I should learn . . ."

"Good. Next week, we'll put you on the mare."

"Just like that?"

"You can't ride without getting on a horse, Rhenn."

She had a point there.

Her eyes met mine, and she smiled, if briefly, before asking quietly, "After today, what will you do?"

"Keep trying to find out enough to know how to deal with an arrogant High Holder in a way that threatens no one else." Or overtly involved the Collegium.

"If anything happens to Ryel, won't his son . . . ?"

"And his nephew. The possibility that they might is part of the problem."

"That's like Pharsi revenge. Sometimes it never ends." She looked at me. "Unless there's no one left to carry on."

"I hope it doesn't have to go that far." I didn't want to think about that for the moment, or about Pharsi revenge . . . or even bring up the pistol incident. "The biscuits are good." I paused. "Do you want to start on the portrait next Samedi? Can you?"

She nodded, her mouth full, then smiled.

I took another sip of hot tea.

Lundi morning was such a rush that even by taking a duty coach, doubtless stretching the rules, I barely reached the District Three station by seventh glass. The station was anything but impressive, a one-story building whose once-yellow bricks had turned a grayish tan under the impact of time and grime, an impression not helped by the narrow barred windows, or by the overcast and low clouds. I walked quickly through open double doors of the single entrance. They were battered and ironbound oak with equally ancient heavy iron inside hinges.

A young patroller with circles under his eyes looked up from the high and narrow desk set against the wall on the right, then stiffened. "Sir . . . you're Master Rhennthyl? Captain Harraf is expecting you. The first door there." He gestured.

"Thank you."

Two other patrollers on the far side of the open space inside the doors that could have been called an anteroom made a show of checking their equipment, but I could feel their eyes on my back as I walked past the duty patroller, then pushed through the already half-open door and stepped into the small study, little more than three yards by four. Captain Harraf was a small man, not much more than to my shoulder, with bright black eyes that protruded slightly, and short jet-black hair. His pale blue uniform was spotless, as was the top of the desk he stood beside—with the exception of an oblong of folded heavy bluish gray cloth. "Master Rhennthyl."

I inclined my head. "Captain Harraf."

"I'm glad to see that you're the kind who takes punctuality seriously."

"I'm glad to be here."

"We'll see how you feel in a few weeks."

A few weeks—with the implication of a longer time than that? That gave me a definitely uneasy feeling, because Third District was the most dangerous district in L'Excelsis.

"Before I offer you an assignment, I want to be clear on several points. You can't arrest or detain anyone. Only the patroller with you can. You understand that?"

"Master Dichartyn and the commander and subcommander have made that clear."

"Good. A few points about station rules. I'm obviously in command. When I'm not here, Lieutenant Warydt is in charge. Should neither of us be here, the senior patroller first takes command. You won't see too much of the lieutenant in the next few weeks, because he'll usually be here from the third glass of the afternoon until ninth glass, although it's sometimes tenth glass. We switch off on the late shift." He cleared his throat. "For your safety, but also for the safety of the patrollers you accompany, I'm also going to insist that you wear a standard patroller's cloak over your grays. You'll also learn more that way." He picked up the folded gray-blue cloth that turned out to be a cloak, and a new one at that, and handed it to me. "Your cap is close enough that most people won't notice it anyway."

He was doubtless right. From a distance any imager's visored cap didn't look all that different from those worn by the patrollers, just a touch grayer, while theirs were more gray-blue. Both cap devices were pewter, but the patroller's cap held a starburst, while mine held the circled four-pointed star.

"Your first patrol will be one of those less adventuresome. You'll accompany Zellyn along the triangle—down South Middle to the Midroad, then back on Quierca and up Fuosta to the station. There's usually not much happening, but there would be more if some patroller didn't cover it."

"I imagine that's true everywhere in L'Excelsis, but more so in Third District." I slipped on the patroller's cloak.

"Very much more so." Harraf turned toward the door. "Zellyn!"

A patroller hurried in and stopped. "Sir." He was red-faced with a silvering brush mustache and bushy eyebrows above sad and pale brown eyes.

"This is Master Rhennthyl, and he'll be accompanying you on your rounds for the week."

"Yes, sir." Zellyn turned to me. "Master Rhennthyl."

I nodded. "Zellyn, I'm pleased to meet you."

Captain Harraf cleared his throat. "You two had best be off."

As I left the study with Zellyn, one thing was very clear. Captain Harraf didn't want to spend much time with me.

"You ready for a long day on your feet, sir?"

"I think so, but the day will tell."

Zellyn laughed. "That it will. That it will."

We walked out of the station and headed right, up Fuosta toward South Middle, two and a half long blocks away.

"How long have you been with the Patrol?"

"Nearly fifteen years, sir, most of it right here in Third District."

"Would you tell me about your round?"

"We rotate through two or three rounds a year, switch every three months, usually. Means we're familiar with the areas, but that we don't get too friendly, if you know what I mean. This round's the best of the bunch I walk. Biggest problem is the taudis-kids near the shops on Quierca. They'll lift anything that's not chained down. The Pharsis and the Caenenans are the worse. Tiemprans aren't much better."

"How do you tell the difference between the Tiemprans and the Caenenans?"

"Doesn't matter. The darker the tan, the more likely they're trouble. Not all of 'em. Lot of good kids, but the bad ones are more likely to be dark."

Was that because they were poorer? Or because they and their families had less respect for those who didn't follow their beliefs? Or because the patrollers just watched them more closely? Or something else? Whatever the reason, I could tell there wasn't any point in asking.

Small shops clustered on each side of the station, and then eating places— most so small and mean that I wouldn't even have called them bistros, but perhaps taudiscafés. Only the small cafés were open. For a moment, I wondered why they were so close to the station, until I realized that there was a far smaller chance of robbery and theft.

When we turned onto South Middle, walking toward the Midroad, there were few people on the sidewalks, but more than a handful of coaches and wagons passing by, although the wagons were more prevalent, but then, South Middle was a thoroughfare.

"You ever have trouble with the wagons?"

"Only when they're loading or unloading. Those times, it's still not that often because most places have at least two fellows working the wagon. Not much that's small and light, and that's what quick-thieves are looking for." Zellyn waved to a graying and trim man wearing a leather apron outside a shoemaker's shop that could not have been more than five yards wide.

The cobbler smiled and returned the wave.

After we'd walked just a single block west, the buildings on both sides changed from low brick structures, with modest shops, to stone and brick or stone-faced edifices two and three stories high, with larger shops and lace-curtained windows gracing the living quarters above.

Zellyn pointed to one of the iron grates set at the base of the curb and the side of the road pavement. It covered the opening to the storm sewers below. "We're supposed to report any time a grate's been broken or blocked with crap. Sometimes, the penal crews even get them fixed the same week." He snorted. "Usually not."

Another hundred yards on stood an iron pole topped with a blue globe. A heavy iron bar circled the pole at eye height. "That's a pickup point for the Patrol."

I had to think for a moment before I realized what it was—a place where an offender could be cuffed to the railing, if necessary, if a patroller could not march him or her back to the station. "How often do the pickup wagons run by?"

"Supposed to be once a glass." Zellyn laughed.

Walking the first part of the round, back to the station, took about a glass. The second part, patrolling up and down the side streets between Quierca and South Middle, from Fuosta west to the Midroad, took about twice as long, mostly because Zellyn passed pleasantries to various people he recognized. Then we did the first round in reverse, and went back the other way. After that came a bite to eat at Kleonya's, a bistro on Quierca, but a half block off the Midroad. After eating, we continued variations on the round.

Along the way, we helped an older woman who had tripped on a curbing and gotten her scarf caught in a wagon tailgate, listened to a grocer complain about a young thief who had stolen a melon the afternoon before when there weren't any patrollers around, and warned a pair of youths who lounged in an alleyway, clearly eyeing some older and frailer women who made their way to the produce stand on Quierca halfway between the Midroad and Fuosta.

That was my day with Zellyn, and I paid for a hack to drive me back to Imagisle. My feet were definitely sore, and then some. Even after running down Grandisyn and arranging for him to install a small coal heater with a flue, I was at the dining hall a bit early. It had been a few days since I'd talked to Shault, and I hoped to catch him before dinner, but he was already seated with the other primes and seconds. So I walked over. He looked up.

"After dinner by the doors."

"Yes, sir."

I nodded and headed back toward the masters' table, if deliberately.

"What did you do now?" asked someone in a murmur.

". . . probably something from Master Ghaend . . . all the masters stick together . . ."

The masters' table had more than a few there, but rather than sit next to Master Rholyn, I took the place beside Chassendri. Maitre Dyana sat to her right, this time with a thinner pink scarf, but still shimmering and brilliant.

"What are you doing now with the Patrol?" asked Chassendri, passing the wine carafe.

"Accompanying patrollers on their rounds. Last week, I watched justice proceedings, the week before I helped with the charging desk." I poured the wine—a red, but not a Cambrisio—then handed the carafe back.

"Has it changed your view of the Patrol?"

I thought for a moment. "I don't think so. I never saw patrollers much. So I didn't have a good opinion or a bad one."

"That's probably fortunate for the commander," added Maitre Dyana.

"Can you tell what they think of imagers?" Chassendri handed me the platter of fried river trout, not exactly my most favorite of meals.

"They're careful to be respectful, but for most of them that respect comes from fear, I'd guess, and the respect isn't all that deep."

"That makes sense," Chassendri replied.

The faintest smile crossed Maitre Dyana's lips, but she said nothing.

"Maitre Dyana," I asked, "do you recall if Master Dichartyn had any comments on his time as a Patrol liaison?"

"If he hasn't mentioned it, then he has his reasons." After a moment, she added, "Commander Artois was a district captain at that time, as I recall, but he became subcommander shortly after Dichartyn became head of security."

"The previous subcommander was stipended off?"

"As I recall, he developed a lingering illness and died shortly after accepting his stipend."

Lingering illness? Lead imaged into his system? Or something else? Maitre Dyana wouldn't have said anything, let alone have phrased it that way, had matters been natural. I nodded.

Chassendri shook her head. "You covert types are chilling behind those pleasant facades."

"I'm just a junior master trying to learn enough to keep out of trouble," I protested.

"Maitre Dichartyn wouldn't have sent you to the Civic Patrol without a very good reason, and it isn't just for experience," countered Chassendri.

That was doubtless true, but what was also true was that part of the testing and training involved was that I had to figure out the problems to solve and the ways to do so without telling anyone or revealing that I had. That much, I had begun to figure out. If a problem vanished before anyone recognized it was a problem in a way that seemed coincidental or accidental, then far fewer questions were likely to arise. The difficulty, of course, was making sure that it was indeed a problem. And some problems were obvious—like

Mardoyt and possibly Harraf—and it was far harder to find an unobvious solution to an obvious problem because everyone was watching all the time.

"Would you really want to know everything that Maitre Dichartyn does . . . or even what Rhenn here does?" Maitre Dyana's voice remained level and almost sweet as she addressed Chassendri.

Chassendri frowned.

"Would you want the world, or the Council, to know?" pressed Maitre Dyana. "Too many people prattle on about openness and the need for the Collegium and the Council to reveal everything." Her eyes didn't quite roll. "All that means is that they want to know for their own advantage. All ruling and government requires compromise, yet most people only want the other person to do the compromising, and when everything is known, no one will compromise, and ruling then becomes a question of force. Force leads to more force, and eventually to strife, sometimes to rebellion."

"But too much secrecy leads to a land where no one trusts anyone. That leads to rebellion," replied Chassendri.

"That suggests," I interjected, "that an appearance of openness is required, and that some matters be disclosed, but not all."

"You're suggesting effective government is hypocritical." Chassendri's voice was cool.

"Isn't it?" asked Maitre Dyana. "Aren't many effective aspects of society just accepted hypocrisy, such as good manners toward those one detests, being courteous to someone whose treatment of others leaves much to be desired?"

A sour smile appeared on Chassendri's lips. "I may be better suited to research and chemical development. Reagents and reactions don't rely on deception."

"That is true, Chassendri," replied Maitre Dyana, "but people do."

No one said anything immediately following that, but we finally did talk about whether there might be an "official" war between Ferrum and Solidar, but in the end we all agreed that the only way that would occur would be if the Ferrans declared it.

After I finished the lime tart—the best part of the dinner—I excused myself and headed to the corridor outside the dining hall to wait for Shault. I didn't wait long before he appeared.

"Sir? What is it?"

"I met with Horazt the other day. He's glad to know that you're doing well here, and he wants you to work as hard as you can."

"I know, sir. My mere wrote me. Well, he wrote for her. She doesn't know her letters. She said that, too."

"How is your reading coming?"

"It's better, Master Ghaend says. Lieryns and Mayra have helped."

"And your imaging?"

Shault smiled. "I can image good coppers now—but only one a week, Master Ghaend says. I'm really not supposed to image them." The smile vanished.

"Do you want to send coins or a letter to your mother?"

"Can I?"

"I think we can manage something. You have her address, don't you?"

"Yes, sir." Shault paused. "She can't read, and messengers won't go there. I have to post to Horazt, and . . ."

"When he's short of coin . . . you're afraid what you send won't get there?"

The boy nodded.

"For now, until she can come visit you, if you want anything taken to her, I'll make sure it gets there. I'm working not that far away. If you give me her address, the one where she lives, and tell me what she looks like," I added with a smile.

"If you would, sir. Can I give it to you tomorrow? She's not much taller than me, sir. Her hair, it's black. She always wears a chain with the crescent."

"I can remember that." I paused. "No imaged coins, Shault, and don't image coppers and trade them for a half silver, either."

"Yes, sir."

I noted the slightly resigned tone behind the pleasant acquiescence. "Shault . . . don't go against the rules. Every taudis-kid who tried that is dead—not because of the Collegium, either. They either broke laws and got caught or killed themselves because they didn't understand the rules were to protect them as well as other imagers."

I could tell that either my words or tone had reached him, because his eyes widened, but his body didn't stiffen into resistance. So I added, "I want you to succeed. I wouldn't watch you and tell you all this if I didn't. I'm not your preceptor, remember?"

"Yes, sir. I'll find you tomorrow night."

"Good." I smiled and watched as he hurried away. I could only do what I could and hope he didn't end up like Diazt.

19

Mardi was much the same as Lundi, but when I arrived at the station on Meredi morning, Captain Harraf was waiting in the doorway to his study. "A moment, if you would, Master Rhennthyl."

He gestured, and I followed him into his study, not closing the door. He didn't ask me to, either. So I stood and waited for what he had to say.

"So much of what the Civic Patrol does happens at night, but I've been told that you are not available for night duties on a regular basis because of other imager commitments. Yet I am supposed to have you accompany some night patrols as your schedule permits. I had thought that this Jeudi evening might be a possibility . . . just the first two glasses." He raised his eyebrows.

I didn't know why Master Dichartyn—or the commander or subcommander—had indicated that I wouldn't be available on all nights, but I was grateful for that, given Captain Harraf, because I had the feeling that I might have been pulling more than a few night patrols.

"I would be happy to accompany whoever you think would be best Jeudi evening."

"Huerl and Koshal have a round on the north side of South Middle. It should give you a feel for night patrolling without being unduly . . . eventful." He paused. "That's all I had. You'll finish your regular round at fourth glass, and they'll meet you at the station at sixth glass, after they've completed one round. That will give you a little rest and time to get something to eat."

"Yes, sir." It also meant that I'd be doing the patrol after sunset, which was doubtless what the captain had in mind.

"That's all, Master Rhennthyl." Harraf's smile was professionally polite.

Zellyn was waiting out in the open area when I stepped from the captain's study, and we walked out of the station. He didn't ask what the captain had said.

"I'll be doing part of a night patrol with Huerl and Koshal later this week," I offered. "I haven't met them. What are they like?"

"They're usually on the first night shift. From what I've heard they don't seem to have many problems. Except for stupid drunks and elvers."

"The smart drunks and elvers just avoid patrollers?"

"The smart drunks just drink and don't bother anyone. There aren't any smart elvers."

"Do you think there are more elvers than there used to be?"

Zellyn snorted. "When I was your age, Master Rhennthyl, I might go three weeks without seeing an elver, and I was patrolling the center of the south taudis. Today, you can't walk ten yards in any of the taudis without tripping over one."

"Why do you think that's so?"

"Golds. The taudischefs found out they could mint more coins with elveweed than with cheap plonk or their bawds. Then the Pharsis got into it, and all the darkies from Otelyrn, especially the Tiemprans . . ." He shook his head. "The stuff's everywhere."

"It's illegal to import it, but not to use it," I offered.

"How'd you stop people from using it? Make smoking it against the law and throw 'em in gaol and put 'em on the road crews where they'd be useless? The only time we pick up elvers is when they do something else, and we get too many of them as it is."

Zellyn had a point, but then what about all of those who dragged friends and family down to support their habit?

The day, unlike some, was cool enough that wearing the patroller's cloak over my grays didn't leave me too hot. I was thankful I hadn't been doing rounds in the heat of summer, but then I might have just had to wear a patroller's summer tunic with the imager's pin in some unobtrusive place.

As we neared the Midroad, a man in gray, with a darker gray stained leather apron, rushed from a shop on the far side of South Middle. "Patrollers!"

"Burglary last night, I'd wager," Zellyn said quietly, even as he glanced both ways before hurrying across the avenue, after letting a collier's wagon lumber past.

I followed, and when we neared the shop, I caught sight of the small sign—KANTROS & SON, SILVERSMITHS.

"What's the matter, Kantros?" asked Zellyn calmly.

"You ask what the matter is? Come and see!" The silversmith turned and strode back toward the shop, his bald pate and the gray hair that bordered it glistening in the morning sun for a moment before he stepped into the shadows cast by the shops on the east side of South Middle. After he reached the front door, he held it open. "Go see for yourselves."

Zellyn led the way, his truncheon out, through the door set between the still-shuttered glass display windows into the front of the shop, a narrow space with display shelves—empty—on the side walls and a counter less than two yards from the door which extended across from the right wall almost to the left wall, at which point where there was a gap a yard wide to permit access to the rear. Nothing had been touched in front of the counter, but behind it the doors had been ripped off both wall cabinets and hurled against the brick base of the small forge. Four large drawers had been yanked out of a chest and thrown on the floor, with various items that looked to be tools scattered across the ancient stone floor, unlike the polished ceramic tile in front of the counter. A tool case had been up-ended, and the pages from some sort of plan or drawing folder had been ripped and thrown in all directions. Even the glass of the two narrow high windows—too small for entry—had been smashed.

"How did he get in?" asked Zellyn in a matter-of-fact tone.

Kantros led us to the rear door, hanging at an angle by two chains above and below the door bolt. The heavy iron hinges had literally been pried out of the masonry, and there were gouges in the brick above the lower hinge and both above and below the upper one.

Zellyn looked at the dust near the door in the alleyway. "Boots about average size. No other marks. No blood anywhere. Means he didn't cut himself breaking in." Then he nodded and walked back to the counter, avoiding the debris. He looked at Kantros. "Early last night, was it?"

Kantros shrugged. "I don't know. It was like this when I came down this morning."

"What did the thief take?" asked Zellyn.

"Almost nothing. The silver goes upstairs behind all the locks every night. A half ingot of copper, a handful of coppers . . . There might be some small tools missing. Who could tell?" Kantros gestured around the back of the shop. "But look at this! The damage!"

"The thief was angry there were no coins and nothing he could take and sell. That's what it looks like." Zellyn glanced to me. "Has to be a young tough or an elver. Any good thief would know there'd be nothing for him down here." He looked to Kantros. "You're lucky he didn't know that."

"I got double ironbound and barred doors upstairs."

"If you can tell us what's missing, I can put out the word." Zellyn offered a professional and sad smile.

"Much good that will do." Kantros shook his head. "Besides . . . how can I tell?"

Zellyn nodded. "I understand. When you find out, let us know, and we'll do what we can." He pulled out his blue-covered patrolling book and used a marker to jot down notes, then slipped it back inside his tunic.

"Not much good . . ." Kantros was still muttering as we left.

"We'll have to report it, but he'll never tell us what was taken." Zellyn glanced across South Middle, waiting until two coaches rolled past, both heading toward the Midroad. "He probably doesn't know himself."

The remainder of the morning was less eventful, but mornings usually were, it seemed. Even so, when the ten bells of noon began to toll we were both hungry and thirsty, but we were nowhere near any place to eat, and it wasn't until close to half past that we sat down in the rear of a small bistro on Quierca in an alleyway a block off the Midroad. The name on the signboard with peeling paint read Alysna's, but inside was clean—and bare.

I followed Zellyn's lead and had a Domchana—a batter-dipped and fried sandwich that held fowl and ham strips wrapped around mild peppers and a pungent cheese I'd never tasted before. It wasn't bad—but not all that good—if filling. The lager helped.

I'd been thinking about the burglary and finally asked, "You said it was early last night. Why?"

"Kantros likes his brandy at night. Has ever since his son was killed. Young Lantryn ran with a bad crowd and was caught with some silvers that weren't his. He was also probably lifting coins from his father. Justice allowed him to join the Navy, rather than do the road gangs. He was unlucky and got killed in a boiler explosion on the Chedryn. The daughter ran off to Solis, married a coppersmith. After that, Kantros's wife died. He drank a lot before that, but lately . . ." Zellyn shook his head. "Oh . . . that much in spirits means you sleep like the dead for a glass, maybe two or three, then you're restless after that."

"Someone had to know him, then."

"Wager it was one of those fellows who got Lantryn in trouble, but trying to find them . . . don't spend two nights in the same place, and most of them went south to the hellhole. That's not in our district. All we can do is send the patrollers in Fourth District a notice. Sometimes, it leads to something."

His tone suggested that most times it didn't.

"If Kantros didn't keep silver in the shop at night, why were there all the chains and heavy hinges on the rear door?"

Zellyn smiled. "What would keep someone from coming up behind him when he's working?"

Put that way, the chains made sense. I just hadn't thought of it like that, perhaps because for anyone to steal anything of great value from Alusine

Wool would have taken a wagon and a team. Wool was heavier than people realized.

Before that long we were back walking the rounds, looking and being seen. Nothing happened until after third glass, on what would probably be the last round of the day. We were headed up Faistasa when we heard screams.

"Help! Help!"

Both of us hurried up the street for another three houses until we reached one of the narrow wooden dwellings with a half mansard roof of cracked tiles. The house was one of those that dated back close to a century, and that had been turned into dwellings for several families. The wooden clapboards were a faded gray that might have been some other color once, and the yellow bricks in the walk were uneven and cracked.

A man in a ragged brown jacket was beating on the street-level side door, trying to force it open, while the woman screaming was trying to force it closed against him.

He didn't even turn as we approached.

"You patrollers! Get him!" the woman yelled.

At that moment, the assailant turned and lunged toward Zellyn. Behind the attacker, the door slammed.

The patroller's truncheon slammed into the man's temple, and he staggered, but started to lunge again. I delivered a turn-kick to his weight-bearing leg, rather than his knee, and he went down, face-first, into the brick walkway.

Zellyn dropped onto his back and cuffed him so quickly I couldn't believe it, but the man immediately began to kick and squirm.

"If you'd pin his legs, sir!"

I did, and Zellyn wrapped a leather restrainer around both legs, then rolled the man over. His face was scratched and bleeding, but he tried to spit at Zellyn, who promptly clouted him alongside the jaw. "Next time, I won't be so gentle."

"Frigging trolies!"

As I looked at the man more closely, I could see that the irises of his eyes had expanded, or his pupils contracted, so much that the pupils looked to be little more than black dots, and the whites of those eyes were so bloodshot that they looked bright pink.

"Longtime elver," Zellyn said contemptuously, leaving the bound figure on the walk and moving back to the door. "Madame . . . we've got him tied up."

There was no answer.

Zellyn rapped, then pounded. Finally, he shook his head. "No point in breaking down the door. She won't talk anyway. The women around here

never do. We'll just charge him with attacking the woman and attacking patrollers. That'll more than take care of him."

The nearest pickup pole was only a block and a half away, but even with
both of us carrying the squirming elver, covering that distance seemed to take
forever. When we reached the pole, Zellyn didn't attempt to uncuff the man,
just used another strap to tie the cuffs to the railing.

"You . . . trolie bastards . . . sewer-rat sows . . ." From there, his curses
grew fouler and far less inventive.

That made it somewhat easier to ignore him, but it was still close to another two quints before the patroller pickup wagon rolled toward us. After
we lifted the still-cursing and squirming elver onto the wagon, Zellyn looked
to me. "Might as well climb on and ride back. Marshyn won't mind." He
grinned at the burly patroller driving the wagon.

"Nope. I'll even head straight back."

"Only because it's your last stop."

"Next to last."

Since there was no one at the last pickup point, we reached the Third District station about two quints before fourth glass, but it took most of that
time to write up our report and give it to the desk patroller.

Since Shault had given me an envelope for his mother on Mardi evening,
I really felt that I should deliver it, and it would be easier before dark. So as
soon as Zellyn and I finished the report, I hurried off up Fuosta and then east
on South Middle. More than a few taudis-dwellers either looked away or disappeared into alleyways or doors when they caught sight of the patroller's cloak.
Because most of the street signs were either missing or defaced, what should
have taken a quarter glass took me longer. Slightly before half past fourth glass,
I rapped on a door that I thought had to be the right one.

The door itself was age-darkened and cracked oak, without a peephole
that I could see. No one answered, and I rapped harder. I also drew open the
cloak so that my imager's grays and the silver imager's pin would be visible.

A thin-faced woman finally edged the door ajar, but I could see the heavy
chain holding the back of the door to the casement. Her eyes were barely
above the loop of the brass links. As Shault had said, her hair was black, and
she was tiny. I couldn't make out the shape of the pendant at the end of the
silver chain around her neck, but her face was so like Shault's that it was hard
to believe she could have been other than his mother.

"Madame Chelya?"

Her eyes widened more. "Who are you?"

"Master Rhennthyl from Imagisle."

"No! Don't tell me . . . No!"

Did she think I was there to tell her bad news? That her son was dead?

"Shault is fine," I said quickly. "He's doing very well."

The wide-eyed alarm in her face turned to suspicion. "Why are you here?"

"You have a good and devoted son." I eased the envelope through the narrow space between the door and the jamb. "He wanted to make sure you got this."

She took the envelope and opened it. Three silvers dropped into her hand, and her mouth opened.

I was impressed . . . and saddened. Shault had given her everything he had earned since he'd been at the Collegium. Everything.

She looked at the note, almost blankly.

"Would you like me to read it? He gave it to me sealed." I didn't know that she would, but I thought that I should offer.

"Please." She handed me the note back, but not the envelope. She did not loosen the chain.

I took it and cleared my throat, then began.

"Dear Maman,

I am well. I know times are hard. Here are three silvers for you. Master Rhennthyl promised you would get them. He has always kept his word. I can see you on Solayi afternoon—29 Feuillyt, second glass. Ask Master Rhennthyl. I miss you."

Chelya looked at me. "Did he write it? All of it?"

"It's in his hand." I handed her the letter back through the chain and the narrow opening between the door and jamb.

"He is a good boy." She smiled, if sadly, I thought. "He said I could see him?"

"Yes. Solayi the twenty-ninth at second glass. Do you know the Boulevard D'Imagers?"

She nodded.

"Just walk down it to the gray stone bridge over the river. After you cross the bridge, there is a walk and some benches on the left. That is where young imagers meet visitors."

She looked doubtful.

"When I first came to Imagisle, that was where I met my mother," I added. "Imagisle is very safe."

Some of the doubtfulness vanished, but not all.

"I need to go, but I'll tell Shault that you got his letter and his coins." I offered a smile and stepped back.

Slowly, she closed the door.

I kept my eyes moving on the way back to South Middle. For better or worse, I didn't see anyone who looked to be a danger, but I could smell elveweed, and caught a glimpse of two elvers up on a low rooftop. They'd had enough that they certainly weren't looking anywhere near me. Then I glimpsed another one, sitting on a stoop. He looked right at me, or through me, as if he didn't even see me. When I turned onto South Middle, I felt a trace less concerned, but I kept walking until I was almost to the Midroad, where I hailed a hack to take me to Imagisle.

After I got out at the Bridge of Hopes, I crossed it quickly and headed for Master Dichartyn's study. He was in, if standing by his desk and preparing to depart.

"What is it, Rhenn?"

"Captain Harraf has 'offered' me an evening patrol accompanying two patrollers tomorrow night."

"I'm certain he wants you to experience what the patrollers do."

"Captain Harraf doesn't like having me around."

"Most patrollers don't."

I shook my head. "It's more than that."

"That may be, but you'll have to deal with it, at least until you discover why. If you can."

"He also said that he'd been told he couldn't schedule me at night on a regular basis."

"I did mention that to Commander Artois. Once you're more settled in at the Patrol, you will have some additional night duties for the Collegium. That's in addition to your attendance at the Council's Autumn Ball."

"And the Winter Ball?" I didn't ask more than slightly sardonically.

"Assuming you don't encounter another envoy you dislike," he replied pleasantly.

"And what about Ryel?"

"What about him? Has he done anything but send you a card with a silver knot? You can't even prove he sent the card, you know."

At that moment, I realized that the more I said to Master Dichartyn about Ryel, the more difficult it would be for me to deal with the High Holder because saying anything more—about my family or Rousel, especially—would only provide a trail back to me if anything suspicious befell Ryel. And I was more than certain that whatever Ryel did in attacking me and my family would leave no traces leading back anywhere close to him—not in a way that would provide any proof.

"You're right, sir. I should have thought of that."

"Yes, you should." He paused. "Is there anything else?"

"No, sir. Have a pleasant evening." I smiled and left. If nothing else, I did need to tell Shault that I'd delivered his coins and that his mother was fine.

20

Jeudi's rounds with Zellyn were relatively uneventful. As the older patroller had predicted, Kantros never offered a list of what had been taken, or even approached us. We didn't run into any out-of-control elvers, although in late afternoon I could smell the smoke in several places along Faistasa Street. I mentioned that to Zellyn.

"Didn't use to smell it outside the taudis at all. This whole area'll be taudis in another four-five years, if you ask me." He shook his head.

Zellyn had the round calculated to the last fraction of a quint, and we ended up at the station just as the last of the four bells from the nearest anomen tower died away.

I wasn't about to take a hack to Chaelya's to get a really good meal. So I opted for eating at Sneytana's, one of the cafés near the station, not that there was a name posted anywhere, but Zellyn had mentioned it as not being too bad. I had fowl and rice fries, and the meal was edible, but I decided I didn't ever want to eat anywhere that wasn't at least "not-too-bad" according to Zellyn. I took my time, but I still ended up waiting nearly a glass, dawdling over a lager, before heading back to the station. I did leave Sneytana's daughter a larger tip for the time, not that the place was crowded.

A few moments after I entered the station, a tall patroller, about my height, with blond hair streaked with white, stepped out of the doorway beyond the closed door of Captain Harraf's study and walked toward me. He offered a pleasant smile. "You must be Master Rhennthyl. I'm Lieutenant Warydt."

"I'm pleased to meet you, sir."

"I'm glad to have you here, sir," he replied. "If there's anything I can do to help you learn more about the Civic Patrol, don't hesitate to ask."

"I certainly won't." I smiled. "Don't expect any questions until I have a better feel for how the station operates."

"I won't." He paused. "I see Huerl and Koshal coming in."

"Then I'd best meet them. Thank you, sir."

"My pleasure, Master Rhennthyl."

I turned and walked toward the two patrollers. They looked close to what I'd envisioned. Koshal was a few digits taller than I, broader in the shoulders and looked like he'd have little trouble heaving a wrecked wagon or carriage out of the way. Heurl was thin and wiry, and half a head shorter.

"Master Rhennthyl," offered Huerl.

"I'm pleased to meet you both," I returned.

Both nodded, almost as one.

"Shouldn't be too bad tonight," offered Koshal. "It's cold for early fall, but it's not an end-night, and not a pay-night, either."

"Didn't smell any weed on the first round, either," added Huerl.

I fell in with them, and we walked out of the station and back up Fuosta in the vestige of twilight remaining, although the sun had set more than a half glass earlier.

By the time we reached South Middle, only a thin band of lighter purple remained on the western horizon, and the avenue was lit but intermittently by the tall iron streetlamps, a good third of which were not working. Few shops and dwellings had outside lamps, and that meant a patrol through uneven light.

Koshal crossed the avenue and headed eastward.

"Does the round go all the way out to the plaza?" I asked.

"Just halfway there, maybe a block past the heathen Temple, except it's on the south side. There's just one round through the taudis at night, and it takes a three-man team. Ciemyl runs it." Huerl shook his head. "Wouldn't want that round."

Were three men enough?

As if to answer my question, Huerl went on. "The taudischefs could take any team, but if they hit one member, we'd hit back. If they took out all three, then we could go in and level anything we wanted. They know that. No one except the elvers and the stupids gives Ciemyl trouble, and that's fine with Horazt and Jadhyl. Youdh doesn't like it, but doesn't make trouble. Not often, anyway."

South Middle was not deserted so early in the evening, but most of the traffic on the avenue consisted of occasional hacks and private coaches, and a very infrequent rider, usually one of the private couriers. There were even fewer on the sidewalks, except around the bistros, but there were no bistros once we neared the taudis, just two lonely cafés across Dugalle from each other on the north side of South Middle.

"You need to eat on the round," offered Huerl, "take Aylsim's. That's on this side. That Tiempran slop Rivara serves over there . . ." He shook his head. "It'd be a real long night."

The two patrollers moved at a moderate pace, not ambling, but not striding, their eyes constantly moving, checking the closed shutters of the shops on the avenue, as well as the alleyways we passed. At times, they stopped and listened.

Before long, we turned up Elsyor, which ran north and actually, if we were to walk far enough, would have taken us to the Anomen D'Este, where my family attended services. We didn't walk that far, only to Marzynn, before turning back east. Marzynn was better lit than South Middle and flanked by stylish row houses that gave way to a range of equally stylish trade shops, including the milliner Mother frequented, once we neared the Midroad.

Abruptly a scream rang out, and then just ahead of us, a woman ran down a narrow lane to our right, passing directly under one of the streetlamps. Part of her blouse looked to have been torn away. She vanished down the lane, followed moments later by a larger figure, who did not pass so directly beneath the light.

Another scream echoed from the lane.

"Frig!" Koshal looked to Huerl.

"We've got to look."

"Don't rush," muttered Koshal. "Take it a step at a time."

I followed the two down the narrow lane between two taller three-story buildings. The first streetlight was out, as was the second, but the glow from the third one allowed some relief from the shadows and gloom. The building to the right looked abandoned. I took a closer look and realized that it was being rebuilt, with the third level being added.

Ahead to the left was a pile of discarded roofing shingles and broken timbers, forcing us more to the right. Thankfully, there weren't any crannies or niches, just a relatively even brick wall on the ground level, although there were windows—without casements or glass—on the second level.

I dropped back slightly as the two patrollers skirted the pile of construction debris.

"See anything?"

"Nothing."

At that moment, something slammed into me from overhead, and stars flashed before my eyes. I took two steps and whirled as I heard steps on the stone behind me.

I didn't have any shields. That I could sense, and two figures were running toward me from a doorway half concealed by the rubbish pile. The man on the left slowed, while the one on the right, who carried a club or pipe with a padded grip-end, charged right at me. He raised the pipe, and I ducked under it and inside, and in that moment, the moves that Clovyl had drilled into me for months took over. That was the way it felt. My left forearm came up under his arm and blocked the downswing of the pipe. My knee came up, and my elbow came across. The pipe dropped with a dull clunk onto the stone, and the attacker doubled up, silently gagging . . . or trying to.

I kept moving, delivering a side-kick to the weight-bearing knee of the second assailant. I didn't hear the crack, but could feel it through my boots. I had to dodge the wild swing of the long knife, but grabbed the back of his arm and used his remaining momentum to help him into the wall, temple first. He just lay against the brick wall.

Only then did I glance around.

Huerl and Koshal stood there. Both had their truncheons out. Koshal's mouth was open, and his eyes were focused behind me. I turned quickly.

The alleyway was empty—except for a pile of cut stone almost knee-high that was fragmented in places and scattered across the alleyway in others. I glanced up. The stone had to have fallen from a broken platform beside a chimney at least two stories up. I swallowed, then gestured to the two bodies. "You happen to know either one?"

Huerl moved forward, looking at the ruffian with the crushed throat, who had stopped moving. In fact, he'd stopped breathing. Huerl bent down, then straightened and shook his head.

Koshal checked the other dead man. "Chykol. Used to be a bouncer at the Red Ruby. Haven't seen him for a good year. Fleuryla said he got too heavy into the plonk."

I was still seeing flashes like miniature stars, and despite another effort, I could not raise my shields. I couldn't image anything. "Now what?"

Huerl shrugged. "Well, sir, if it'd just been me and Koshal, we'd report that they got in a fight over the girl and killed each other, and she ran off."

I nodded. "It seems to me that Chykol fought off the other man, protecting her, and then got hit with the stone. Maybe their fighting loosened that platform up there."

"That'd do," replied Koshal. "Make Moalyna happier, too."

"Moalyna?"

"Chykol's girl . . . maybe his wife, now."

"What do we do with the bodies?" I asked.

"Not much we can do but get a pickup," said Huerl. "I'll stay here, and you two go back to the pole off Florrisa."

"What if I stayed with you?" I asked. "This lane isn't all that well lit." That was an understatement; it was barely lit at all, with only the single light farther to the south.

"Might be better," replied Huerl.

"Good idea," seconded Koshal. He turned and hurried off back out onto South Middle.

"We ought to look farther down the lane. Just in case," offered Huerl. "She's probably long gone, and one of the ones you stopped was one of those after her."

I suspected that as well, if not for precisely the same reasons as Huerl voiced.

I moved up beside the veteran patroller as we began to check out the lane ahead.

No shields. Yet how could I complain about continuing the round with Huerl and Koshal? They'd never had shields, and they made patrols every night. Still, I wasn't about to hint anything was wrong, not after the occurrences of the evening.

I focused my attention on the lane, checking the more deeply shadowed spots.

When we reached the end, at Dysel, Huerl turned to me. "She could have gone anywhere."

"She probably did."

"Might as well go back and see if they left any traces."

We headed back down the lane, and I was listening for any sound, as well as checking windows above, but I heard nothing but the faint echo of our boots on stone.

The doorway of the building where the two had hidden—or from which they'd emerged—was locked and barred from the inside, and no one answered our pounding. No lamps were lit within, and there were no signs to indicate the building's purpose or use.

As we waited for Koshal and the wagon, I could only hope that the rest of the round was less eventful—far less eventful.

21

When I woke well before fifth glass on Vendrei morning I tried to create shields—and ended up with a blinding headache that forced me to drop them immediately. How long would it be before I recovered from all that stone dropping on my shields? Effectively, I'd gotten a concussion from the shields, but that was better than being dead. Still, the fact that I could raise shields for a moment suggested I would recover, but not as soon as I'd prefer.

The other question, one that I'd pondered the night before, was whether the attack on me had been set up by Harraf or Mardoyt—or both. Either Harraf or Warydt had to be involved, because they were effectively the only ones who'd known where I'd be patrolling. I doubted that either Huerl or Koshal knew anything. They'd both been as surprised as I'd been. I somehow didn't think Warydt was involved, but I had nothing but feeling to support that conclusion, and I certainly could be wrong. But whether it was Harraf or Warydt, by making sure the two patrollers didn't know, whoever planned it was avoiding any direct links. Also, there was the case of Smyrrt, who had died suspiciously under exactly the same kind of circumstances, according to Gulyart. Since Smyrrt had worked for Mardoyt, that suggested a certain collusion between the officers. But why would they have used the same method?

It could only be because they had planned on an imager being assigned to the Civic Patrol, and that method, someone knew, might work against imager shields. Also, dropping stone on me was one of the only sure ways to disable my shields without my seeing what was happening before it occurred. That also suggested that Mardoyt knew what I'd discovered, and Harraf was afraid of what I might find out.

I wanted to shake my head. There was no way I could prove what I'd learned and figured out, and I didn't see that I'd ever come up with enough proof to bring before a justice, not unless I spent months or longer working out of the Third District station. After my last conversation with Master Dichartyn, I also didn't see much point in running to tell him what had happened. All I had were surmises, and he definitely wasn't interested in those. All he wanted was hard proof.

Pondering the unlikely wouldn't help, and I had a long day ahead of me.

In the fall gloom, I struggled from my bed, dressed, and headed out for Clovyl's exercises, sparring, and running. After the night before, I had to admit I was grateful for his tutoring, but I still didn't have to enjoy the process.

All in all, after exercises, sparring, running, showering, dressing, and eating, I managed to get to the station slightly before seventh glass, and before Zellyn. As I waited for the older patroller and looked around, I saw Captain Harraf.

He stepped toward me and asked, "How was your patrol last night?"

"Except for the two footpads and the screaming woman, it was uneventful." I kept my tone ironic.

"Oh . . . that. The night reports from Lieutenant Warydt mentioned that Huerl and Koshal had come upon the end of a fight between two ruffians, but that they killed each other. Wasn't that what happened?"

"In summary. One was chasing the woman and apparently ran into the other. One of them killed the other, but in the process they knocked a scaffold or something loose, and he got his skull crushed by the stones piled on it."

Harraf nodded. "Those things happen when people aren't aware of their surroundings."

"That's very true, sir. Anyone can be surprised, and sometimes things don't go the way they're planned." I smiled pleasantly.

He smiled in return. "You're learning about the Patrol. Next week and the week after, I'd thought I'd pair you with Alsoran. His partner has leave, and that will allow us not to leave some areas less patrolled."

"What area does his round cover?"

"The east end of the taudis and the area farther east to the Avenue D'Artisans."

I nodded. Again, I couldn't say I was surprised.

"I've told Alsoran, but you'll need to keep your eyes open more than usual. We haven't heard anything official, but there are rumors that there will be a conscription sweep through our area sometime this fall. Before long, some of the taudischefs will know, after that . . ." He shrugged. "Who knows?"

"I appreciate the word, sir."

"I thought you would." He turned and headed to his study.

Zellyn was waiting for me to finish with the captain.

We headed out. Once we were clear of the station, he looked to me.

"The captain wants me to pair with Alsoran next week."

"He's a good man. Lousy round, but a good man." He paused. "What about Lyonyt?"

"He said Lyonyt would be on leave."

Zellyn just nodded to that, and we continued on our way, going down Fu-osta to Quierca, reversing the direction of the initial round.

Although in midafternoon Zellyn and I stopped at the silversmith's, Kantros insisted that nothing of import was missing, and in the end, unlike my rounds with Zellyn on Meredi or those with Huerl and Koshal the night before, Vendrei was thankfully most uneventful.

For more than a few reasons, including the fact that trying to image still brought on a headache, if not quite so severe as had been the instance that morning, I took a hack back to Imagisle. For the past weeks, I'd not been saving much of my pay, just because of the number of hack rides I'd taken, and that bothered me. It was getting so that everything was bothering me, and that bothered me as well.

As I hurried across the Bridge of Hopes, I thought about reporting to Mas-ter Dichartyn, but decided against it, because I was more than a little tired of being told, in effect, not to bother him unless I had some sort of proof.

When I finally did get to the dining hall, I found Maitre Dyana waiting outside. That was no coincidence.

"Dichartyn suggested we might have a conversation over dinner." Her smile was pleasant, and there was a sparkle in her eyes that intimated I was about to learn something else less than to my liking.

"If both of you agree, I'd best listen carefully." I smiled in return as I walked beside her into the dining hall and to the masters' table. Ferlyn was already there, seated with Chassendri on one side and Quaelyn on the other. At the center of the table sat Maitre Poincaryt with a dark-haired older imager I had not seen before. "Is Master Poincaryt with a chief maitre of one of the other collegia?"

"Not a bad surmise, and accurate this time. That's Maitre Dhelyn. He's from Westisle." Dyana guided us toward the end of the table, away from the others, but to where two carafes of wine had been placed.

After we had seated ourselves, I asked, "Red or white?"

"The red, please."

I poured red for both of us, then took a sip—after she did.

"For a young imager, even a young master, Rhennthyl, you're compara-tively bright, and you tend not to make the same mistake twice. Also, there are gaps in your education, and the combination leads older heads to assume that you know more than you do. You also don't always see the import of what you have been told. Together, these create certain problems." She looked to me inquiringly.

"I have a tendency to act, and not always wisely, because I don't know things obvious to those imagers my own age who have been imagers far longer."

She nodded, then waited as one of the servers offered her a platter on which rested slices of skirt steak stuffed with mushrooms, onions, parsley, and herbs, and covered with a cream sauce. She took a single slice.

I took two slices. It had been a long day.

Once we had served ourselves, with both the meat and the leeks and squash and fried brown rice that followed, she looked to me again. "What do you think the silver knot means?"

"A High Holder has declared me as an enemy. Beyond that, very little, except from what you've said, and what I've heard, when a High Holder sets out to ruin an enemy, obtaining the death of that enemy is almost secondary to assuring that the enemy and his family will not remain as High Holders. At least, that seems to be the goal."

Dyana did not respond until after she took another sip of the wine, a rather tart Grisio. "In the 'ideal' sense, the successful pursuit of ruination first destroys the assets of the opponent, then all friendships and alliances that would allow rebuilding, and then the suicide of the enemy because everything is lost. Often matters do not go that far, but often they do. There is, however, another aspect that is seldom mentioned."

"Which is?" I asked because I didn't know and because the question was clearly expected.

"Should the one who issues the notice die, every male heir, in turn, is obligated to continue the effort."

For a moment I said nothing. Finally, I spoke, trying to hold in anger. "I asked you about this earlier, and you told me we would talk if Ryel proceeded beyond the card."

"Has he?"

What could I say? The last thing I wanted to do was admit to Maitre Dyana that while I knew Ryel had been behind the arson, I could prove nothing. "There's no proof of anything yet. Not that I know of."

"Then you have time, don't you?"

There might have been a hint of irony there, but I couldn't tell. So I swallowed my anger and ignored the thrust of her words and went back to what she'd said earlier. "So the one being attacked must either ruin the attacker or kill every male heir? Or both?"

"Exactly." Her smile was cool.

I hadn't exactly planned on that in dealing with Ryel, and how could I possibly ruin him commercially? I had no idea even what all his holdings were. I definitely didn't have any economic power.

"The Council and the Collegium support this?" I found that hard to believe.

"It provides a certain, shall we say, balance of power. While you may not notice this, you can take it as a granted that seldom do High Holders declare factors or tradespeople as enemies. There are several reasons for this. First, they consider those exclusively in commerce beneath them. Second, the factoring associations will unite to refuse to trade or buy from any High Holder who attacks a member. That is one reason why few factors refuse to join the associations or pay their annual fees. Third, the gain obtained from attacking any single factor is seldom worth the cost, and there is little satisfaction from the result. Fourth, it provides a way for pruning out truly incompetent High Holders."

I could understand all that, but what I really wanted to know was why the Collegium didn't stand up to the High Holders the way the factors did. Maitre Dyana was assuming I knew, and I didn't. For a moment I took refuge in my food. The skirt steak was tender and flavorful, but the onions and leeks were overcooked. I finally asked, "Why doesn't the Collegium react the way the factors do?"

"I have a question for you, Rhennthyl. How many imagers do you think have an ability with shields similar to yours?"

I'd actually thought about that when I'd considered the numbers of young imagers that had been killed by the assassins hired by the late Ferran envoy, Vhillar. I also had been wondering if the newest Ferran envoy had been trying to continue those policies, although it had been something like two weeks since someone had fired at me. "I have the impression, maitre, that very few have that ability outside of those reporting to Master Dichartyn, either directly or indirectly. There may be some others, such as you." That was safe enough.

"How many do you think that might be?"

I knew there were only about five hundred imagers in all of Solidar, and there were only ten to fifteen in the counterspy area, and perhaps as many field operatives reporting to Master Schorzat. "I'd say there might be forty with strong shields, and another forty who could muster some sort of shield."

"That is close enough. How many High Holdings are there?"

"Over a thousand."

She smiled politely. "You should find those numbers interesting, I would think. You know, the Collegium as an institution has never had to confront a High Holder . . . or all the High Holders. I have no doubt you understand why that is so."

A cold chill went down my back. I understood exactly what message I'd been given—that the Collegium would not risk itself for a single individual unfortunate enough to cross a High Holder—but I did reply. "I assume that it is for the same reason that only a single imager represents the Collegium in the Council."

"In a manner of speaking." She smiled. "How are you finding being a liaison to the Civic Patrol?"

"I'm still being rotated through various duties in order to gain a better understanding of how the Patrol works." And how it didn't, but I was more than certain she knew that as well.

"Understanding is a two-edged blade."

"I'm discovering that." I managed a laugh, even as I wondered how long it would be before I regained my imaging abilities, and even as I managed to damp the anger that her words about the Collegium and High Holders had raised. Mama Diestra definitely had been right about the Collegium not being my friend, especially in dealing with Ryel.

22

When I awoke on Samedi, I again tried to raise shields, and found that I could, but with an immediate, if dull, headache. That was both a frustration and a relief, because I was improving, just not as quickly as I would have liked. I'd been thrown into a wall by an explosion outside the Chateau, and that hadn't affected my ability at all, but a load of granite crashing down on me from above had destroyed my ability to create shields for days? The only thing I could figure was something Maitre Dyana had said months earlier—about the angling of shields. There had been no way to slide the impact of the stones because they had dropped directly down on me, whereas I'd been at an angle to the explosion. But . . . again, that suggested someone knew far too much about imager limits.

Putting those thoughts aside for the moment, I pulled myself from bed, donned exercise clothes and boots, and headed out to deal with Clovyl's regimen. Under a sky graying with approaching dawn, the air was chill, almost cold enough for frost, and I thought that was unusual for so early in the year—until I realized it was fall. So much of the year had slipped by without my really knowing it.

Clovyl worked us so hard that the cool was more than welcome for the four-mille run that always ended the early-morning sessions. The cold shower that followed wasn't nearly so welcome, and even after I donned the gray imager's garb that had seemed so hot during summer and harvest I took a while to warm up as I crossed the quadrangle.

Dartazn and Martyl were standing outside the dining hall when I got there. I had missed their company at meals, and I walked over to them. "How are things going with the Council—besides your being overworked?"

Martyl grinned. "Overworked? How could you say that, sir?"

"No 'sirs' between us. I wouldn't have the position if they hadn't had to get me away from the Council." I wouldn't have been surprised if Dartazn and Baratyn both were Maitres D'Aspect, anyway, their rank concealed as was the case with many working for Master Dichartyn. "Is the Council doing anything?" That wasn't an idle question. Outside of reading *Veritum* and *Tableta*, I hadn't done much to keep up with events between Solidar and Ferrum. War hadn't been declared, but there had been minor naval incidents off the coast of Jariola.

"Nothing that anyone can see." Dartazn's tone was dry. "There are lots of Navy couriers, and Councilor Rholyn has made at least two quick trips from the Chateau to the Collegium in the middle of the day."

"Something's about to happen, then."

"That'd be our guess." Martyl shrugged. "What about you? How do you like the Civic Patrol?"

"It's more eventful. You know . . . burglaries, weeded-out elvers, toughs killing each other. And lots and lots of walking. Oh, I forgot, boredom in watching justice cases, and lots of excuses when people are charged."

"Almost makes you want to come back to the Chateau, does it?" asked Dartazn.

"The company at the Chateau is much better. So is the food, and far cheaper."

"You have to pay for your own lunches?"

"So far, anyway." I paused. "Has Master Dichartyn found anyone to help you?"

"Not yet," replied Martyl. "I don't think he's hurrying, either."

"Any new kinds of attempts to attack councilors?"

The two exchanged the quickest of glances.

"Cannons?" I pressed. "Gunpowder devices?"

"Someone tried to drive another wagon through the gates," Martyl admitted. "Like the one you exploded. It was filled with black powder and grapeshot. Dartazn, here, got it to explode outside the gates. Two guards were injured, and they had to put down a half-dozen dray horses. Good thing it was on a day when only the High Council was there."

Did that mean that it had been a Jariolan plot? Or a Tiempran one? Would anyone ever know?

We talked a bit more and then went to our separate tables. I sat with Ferlyn, but he didn't know as much as Dartazn and Martyl had. After breakfast, I hurried back to my studio, not because I had that much to do in preparation for the sitting with Master Rholyn but because I wanted to start on some design sketches for Seliora's portrait. Her portrait wouldn't be one where she was seated, although most were, but Seliora had too much energy for that. I wasn't certain how to capture her standing, either.

By the time Master Rholyn arrived just after ninth glass, I'd gone through something like four different design sketches and found each of them lacking.

I was ready to set them aside for the task of working on finishing Rholyn's face, or as much of it as I could.

"Good morning, sir," I offered.

He only nodded as he took off his heavy cloak and walked over to the low crate. "The same position?"

"If you would, for a moment."

I decided not to ask any questions while I worked on the part of the portrait dealing with his neck and chin. After perhaps two quints, when I'd done what I could and he was getting stiff and tired, I said, "If you'd like to sit down, sir."

After several moments, while still painting, I said, "I heard that someone tried to send a wagon filled with explosives into the Chateau."

"It was rather hard to miss . . . the explosion, that is."

"Do you think it was the Jariolans or the Ferrans?"

"The Jariolans are most secretive, and it's rather hard to find out things when the Solidaran embassy in Ferrial is closed, even temporarily," replied Rholyn. "The Ferran parliament, if you can term it such, was not exactly pleased at the demise of their previous envoy, accidental as it may have appeared."

"That sounds to me like the death of envoys, however accidental, is unacceptable, but the death of tens of imagers is . . . from the Ferran point of view, at least."

"The deaths of imagers are always acceptable, anywhere in Terahnar." Rholyn raised his eyebrows. "Haven't you learned that yet?"

"I've learned it, sir, but I'd hoped such deaths wouldn't be that acceptable within the Collegium." I was baiting Rholyn a bit. That was probably unwise, but I'd gotten more than a little tired of a leadership attitude in the Collegium which seemed to regard junior imagers as expendable targets and lures.

"That is an assumption that you lack the facts to support, Rhennthyl."

"That's quite possible, sir. Would you be willing to affirm that my personal experience or the killing of more than ten junior imagers by assassins so far this year are completely at odds with the Collegium's actual practices?"

Rholyn actually sighed. "Master Dichartyn did mention that your inquiries could prove difficult." After a lengthy interval, he finally spoke. "Let me reply in this fashion. It is not widely known, nor do we wish it known, that some two hundred years ago, the chief maitre of the Collegium protested, both in word and action, the practice of local patrollers and others who engaged in killing young imagers. More than two-thirds of the imagers in Solidar were seriously injured or killed. Close to two hundred High Holders died as well, and more than a thousand factors and artisans. The fleet was less than united or effective, and the Ferran autocracy was overthrown and replaced by the commercial barons who now rule Ferrum. You will find little mention of anything like this in the histories, only the mention of the Navy's inability to affect events in Ferrum. At that time, there were close to four hundred imagers in the Collegium—before the pogroms. Less than two hundred survived. You can check the figures by going through the old rosters of the Collegium. I'm sure that Master Poincaryt would open them to you. With the widespread use of firearms now, we are possibly even more vulnerable. You would doubtless survive, but what of those who cannot raise the shields that you can?"

I didn't have a quick answer to that. In fact, I didn't have any good answer.

"Difficult as the present situation is, Rhennthyl, any action the Collegium takes independently and as an institution that suggests it would or could arrogate itself over the Council, the guilds, the factors associations, or any government anywhere on Terahnar would result in extreme danger to every imager, especially those you would protect. The Collegium as a whole must always be seen to support the Council and never to oppose any of the three groups it comprises."

"As a whole . . ." I mused half aloud.

Rholyn smiled. It was a cold expression. "Personal difficulties must be handled personally and in a fashion that can never involve the Collegium as an institution, nor be seen to involve it. That is how it has been for the past two centuries and how it must be, for the sake of all imagers, not just those who have the imaging strength to stand against armed force."

"I see, sir. Thank you." Both Maitre Dichartyn and Maitre Dyana had been more than clear on that policy, but not the full reasons behind it. I almost asked why, but after a moment I understood. The issue arose only for the handful of imagers with abilities such as mine, and we could be handled as discrete individuals, while raising the point that Rholyn and Maitre Dyana had for all imagers would only emphasize the Collegium's vulnerability. I also realized another reason why the Collegium guarded the Council members—to remind them that there was power in the Collegium and that such power served them.

Needless to say, I asked no more questions, but just worked on the portrait, then partly cleaned up after Master Rholyn left. I didn't have to put everything away because Seliora would be sitting for me in the afternoon.

At lunch, I listened to Ferlyn and Quaelyn as they discussed the patterns of where imagers had been born. I hadn't even realized that the Collegium kept such records.

After I ate, I hurried off to wait for Seliora. On the previous Solayi, she had agreed to meet me at the end of the Bridge of Hopes at the first glass of the afternoon—but only if I agreed to spend a glass on horseback in the courtyard at NordEste Design before we could have dinner. I pondered just how well I might do as I stood on the middle of the bridge a good quint before the bells rang out from the Imagisle Anomen.

A coach for hire pulled up at the east side of the bridge, and three people emerged—Odelia, Kolasyn, and Seliora. I immediately hurried toward them. The bells began to peal the glass, their sound both more mellow and yet sharper in the cool fall afternoon. As we neared each other, I could see that Seliora wore black split skirts, a simple red blouse, and a black jacket also trimmed in red.

We hugged each other briefly, then separated, and I turned toward Odelia and Kolasyn. "Thank you for accompanying Seliora."

"It was our pleasure," replied Kolasyn. His voice suggested that he definitely meant that.

"But we do want to be among the first to see the portrait," Odelia added.

"You will be," I promised.

"Until later, then," Odelia replied.

Seliora and I watched from the middle of the bridge as the two walked back toward the Boulevard D'Imagers.

"They look good together," I offered.

"He's good for her," Seliora said.

I understood all too well what she didn't say—that nice as he was, Kolasyn didn't have the strength to replace Shelim. Nor did Shomyr. I turned to her again. "You look good."

"Simple, you mean." The mischievous smile appeared. "I don't want a portrait that shows me in something I'd never wear."

"I could still paint it that way," I said teasingly.

She raised her eyebrows.

"But I'd better not." I laughed. "I thought we'd take the scenic walk to my studio, around Imagisle, so that you could see more of it."

"I'd like that."

I took her arm, and we turned northward and began to follow the stone-paved path on the east side of the isle that paralleled the river, if some five yards back from the granite river wall.

"That's the administration building, and those are the quarters for primes and seconds. I had a room on the second level there." I pointed.

"It looks rather severe," Seliora replied, "although it's pleasant enough with the oaks beginning to turn. I imagine it's more austere in full winter." She paused. "There aren't that many trees this old left in L'Excelsis."

"Some date back to the founding of the Collegium."

We walked farther north, past the small docks that held two modest training steamboats, on one of which I'd done my first public imaging, although I couldn't distinguish which of the two it might have been.

To our left was an expanse of grass, surrounded by the ancient oaks, and farther west were the armory and the building holding the various workshops. Before long, we reached the houses for the married imagers. The larger dwellings fronted the river on both the east and west sides of the isle, but all were of two stories, and of solid granite with tile roofs, and with garden courtyards behind them and stone lanes flanked with grass and hedges between. While the exteriors were similar, from the window hangings, flower boxes, and various small touches, the sizes varied somewhat, and it was clear that those who lived there had very differing tastes. I wondered which might belong to Master Dichartyn.

"That's where the imagers with families live. The larger dwellings are mostly for the senior masters, but they're not nearly so grand as NordEste Design," I said with a smile.

"They have a great deal more privacy, Rhenn."

"I can see that, and there are a few that are spacious."

Seliora stopped. So did I. She looked at me. "They're built so that imagers can live safely with their families, aren't they?"

"Yes."

"Could an imager . . ." She didn't finish the thought.

"It's rare, but I once lit a lamp in my sleep. I was dreaming, but thought I was awake."

She nodded thoughtfully.

North of the houses was the park with the open grassy spaces for play and walking and, of course, the hedge maze. I would have liked to have played in one of those as a boy. Most of the time I'd walked there, I hadn't seen many people, but perhaps because it was a Samedi afternoon, there were at least half a dozen families there. Four or five children were running through the head-high boxwood maze, occasionally shrieking and having a wonderful time.

We reached the northern tip of the isle, where there were several shaded benches with a view of the gray waters of the River Aluse. Seated on one of those in the middle were Shannyr and his new bride. I couldn't remember her name. Although I hadn't seen her before, he'd told me about her. He'd also been more than friendly at the time of my difficulties with Johanyr, one of the few seconds who had been truly supportive.

"Shannyr?"

He turned, then rose. "Master Rhennthyl."

His wife stood almost immediately as well. She was slender, but with a round face and pale green eyes washed out somewhat by the dark blue woolen coat. She grasped his hand.

"I haven't ever had the honor of meeting your wife." I smiled, looking at her. "I have heard him speak most flatteringly about you."

She flushed ever so slightly as Shannyr said quickly, "Ciermya, this is Master Rhennthyl."

"I'm pleased to meet you, sir." She smiled, a trace apprehensively, I thought.

"And I you. This is Seliora," I said.

Seliora offered a warm smile, then said, "I'm glad to meet you. All I've seen here are men."

"This is the first time she's really seen Imagisle," I added. "How are you finding it, Ciermya?"

"I like it very much, sir. Our quarters are lovely, and it's a short walk to work . . . so long as I keep working, leastwise."

"You do . . . drafting, is it?"

"Yes, sir."

"She's outstanding at it," added Shannyr proudly.

"I'm sure she is." I could tell Ciermya was not exactly at ease, so I smiled again. "We won't keep you, but I did want to meet you after all Shannyr said. He won't tell you, but I appreciate all that he did to help me."

"I just did—"

"You did more than anyone else then, and I won't forget it." I could tell he was embarrassed, but I wasn't about to let him minimize his actions.

As we began to walk along the west side of the isle, I looked to Seliora.

Her eyes met mine, and she nodded.

"What was that supposed to mean?"

"He's older than you, a good five years or more, but he respects you. She fears you."

"Am I so fearsome? I didn't do all that well at the Council, and now I'm pounding the stone pavement of L'Excelsis with patrollers."

"You did very well at the Chateau. It could be that you did too well."

I almost missed a step as the combination of her words and what Master

Rholyn had said earlier struck me. Did Master Dichartyn—or Maitre Poincaryt—worry that my inability to conceal my imaging might unsettle the Council? Or had I been removed as a purported disciplinary action to show the Council that the Collegium did not approve of "accidents" occurring to foreign envoys, regardless of provocation?

"Frig . . ." I barely murmured the words. It made far too much sense.

Seliora stopped, still looking at me.

"I just realized something. I'm going to have to be far more circumspect than I've been before. Master Rholyn hinted at that earlier today, but what you said made me think about it in a different way."

"How so?"

"What I did at the Chateau was too much a reminder to the Council of how powerful an imager can be, and the Collegium does not want that."

"Wasn't it acceptable, in protecting them?"

"I'm sure it was. Once, or very occasionally."

She nodded again.

I pointed across the river to the west where the gleaming white walls of the Council Chateau, sitting on its hill, almost sparkled in the fall afternoon light. "We do have a good view of the Chateau."

South of the park was the armory, set almost next to the gray stone river walls on the west side of the isle. The massive gray-walled building with the workrooms was next.

"What's that?"

"That's where we're headed. My studio is a small converted workroom, on the northeast corner—right there." I pointed.

"Do they all have outside doors?"

"Most of them, and they're all lead-lined, with leaded glass windows, and leaden sheets in the center of the doors."

"That's not true of the houses, is it?" She frowned.

"Just one sleeping chamber, I'm told." I led the way to the studio, where I opened the door and gestured for her to enter.

Once Seliora was inside, as I closed the door, she glanced around the studio, her eyes alighting on the sheets of paper that held the various design sketches that I'd worked on earlier. "Can I see?"

"Be my guest. I wasn't happy with any of them, and I decided that I needed to have you here to do a decent design."

Then she looked to the uncompleted portrait of Master Rholyn. "I saw your study at the Guild Hall, but this is the first portrait I've seen."

"It needs more work."

"It will be good, better than he deserves."

"How do you know that?"

"There's a cruelty there. I can see it, even now. You paint what you see and feel, Rhenn. Isn't that so?"

Cruelty? I studied what I'd portrayed so far. Perhaps there was a hint of that. Certainly, there was a hardness to the set of his eyes that combined with the strong jaw and the too-full lips to create an image of . . . what, I still wasn't sure. When I finished the hair and forehead, and the one side of the neck, I'd know more.

"This afternoon is for your portrait, not his. I'd like to work on some more sketches. If you'd take off the scarf and drape it loosely over your left shoulder . . ."

"Like this?"

"That's good."

From there on, I began to sketch.

The third design had something, but it was too head-on; so I did a fourth . . . and the angle was perfect.

"Good. Just hold that."

She didn't say a word.

I called a halt when I realized that the bells had rung half past second glass. "I'm sorry. I didn't realize . . ."

"That's fine." She shook her head, then shrugged her shoulders, trying to loosen them. "Posing is hard work. How much did you get done?"

"The design, and I got that all on the canvas, just a light outline, as well as the lines of your face, the eyes, the cheeks. It's a very good start, but it could take several months because I'll need you to sit, and we can only do that on end-days." I began to clean up, not that I had that much to do, because I hadn't used any oils, just the fine-lined drawing pencil.

"How about tomorrow?"

"I can't. I'm the duty master, and I really shouldn't be this far from the administrative building."

"Oh . . ."

"I'm sorry. I should have told you."

"That's all right."

It wasn't, but her tone was forgiving.

"I owe you a dinner for all your hard work."

"First, you owe me some time on horseback," she reminded me.

"Can we go to dinner afterward? Somewhere like Chaelya's," I suggested. "That would be family-approved, would it not?" I followed my words with a grin.

"Aunt Staelia would be pleased, and the food is good."

"You have some reservations? Or were we supposed to meet Odelia and Kolasyn somewhere?"

"No . . . they're having dinner with Shomyr and someone he's interested in. Haelya is her name."

"You're more interested in torturing me on horseback, is that it? Or do you have a feeling it wouldn't be good to have dinner there?" That was a guess, but with Seliora's Pharsi farsight, that was always a possibility.

"Not farsight . . . but a feeling."

"Azeyd's, then? We went to Terraza last week."

"That might be better. Next week we could go to Chaelya's with either Odelia and Kolasyn or Shomyr and Haelya."

"Besides, I'm growing very fond of Pharsi fare, all kinds of Pharsi fare." I didn't quite leer.

"Rhenn . . ." She laughed and shook her head.

For a number of reasons, including my inability to hold shields for long, we walked over the Bridge of Desires and hailed a hack on the west bank of the Aluse. The wind had turned chill during the course of the afternoon, and Seliora's jacket wasn't that heavy. She was shivering by the time we got into the coach. As the coach crossed the Nord Bridge, I looked out at the river, its dark gray water topped with whitecaps, thinking that we might be in for an early snowfall.

Back at NordEste Design, I got a lesson in saddling and putting a bridle on a very gentle mare, who snorted only once or twice at my incompetence. Then I managed to mount and ride around the courtyard until my thighs ached and my ears were numb, and my nose began to run.

Finally, my task-mistress relented and let me dismount, but I still had to stall and unsaddle and curry the mare. Then I had to wash up as well. We were both cold by that time.

It was well past sixth glass when we finally ended up at a cozy corner table at Azeyd, close enough to the hearth that Seliora stopped shivering, but not near enough to roast me.

"Do you want some hot mulled wine?" I asked.

"No, I'm already warm enough. A red Cambrisio, please," she told the server, a black-haired Pharsi girl several years younger than Khethila, "and I'll have the harvest greens, and the lamb pastry roll."

"The red Cambrisio also," I added, "and the harvest greens, but I'd like the cumin-cream lamb with the rice."

"Yes, sir." The server smiled and slipped away.

"She's cheerful," I offered.

"Her parents wouldn't have it any other way."

"She's the daughter of the owners?"

"Martica and Chelaom are much stricter than Mama and Papa."

I offered a wince.

Seliora laughed softly.

Once our wine and greens arrived, I began to explain, keeping my voice very low, what I'd learned over the week from Master Dichartyn, Maitre Dyana, and Master Rholyn, ending with, ". . . in short, I've been told that my problems with Ryel are mine and mine alone, and that I need to resolve them by myself and without any tracks leading back to the Collegium—or to you and your family."

"My family? Oh, because too many people know we're close, and that would lead back to you?"

"I don't think we need both the Collegium and the High Holders after you and your family." I tried to keep my tone dry. "Although I did hear from Lieutenant Mardoyt that you were more than capable of protecting yourself."

"Grandmama said that would come up." Her words were not quite defiant. "When did he tell you this?"

"This last week." That was a bit of a stretch, but not that much.

"He's an evil man and not to be trusted." She offered a wry smile. "But it is true. Ricardio attempted to take some liberties with me. He ripped my blouse right off me. I shot him in the shoulder. Then I told him that if he said a word about it, he'd never say another. He said I was a bitch." She sighed. "I didn't want to shoot him. That's why I had to."

"What?" I didn't understand that.

"I kept trying to discourage him gently. He wouldn't discourage. I even warned him. He laughed and lunged for me. Some people only understand force. It's best to avoid those altogether . . . if you can."

"Because, in the end, you have to use force to stop them?" I asked.

She nodded.

By that token, if I'd had any sense, I should have avoided Johanyr totally—except he hadn't given me that choice.

"Do you think I'm terrible for that?" Seliora asked quietly. "I suppose I should have told you, but . . ."

"You hoped I'd understand, and feared I wouldn't?"

She nodded again.

"Dear one . . ." I smiled. "If anyone understands being pushed into doing something necessary and unpleasant, I'm certainly getting to that point. Sometimes, there aren't any alternatives."

"There are always alternatives," she replied, "but if we accept them, we become less."

I'd thought about that, if not in her case.

"What can I do to help you?" she asked after a moment, a question that also asked if we could leave the shooting behind.

"Could you find out what you can about Ryel's commercial enterprises, especially in L'Excelsis? I'm fairly certain he has interests in or control of the Banque D'Rivages." I paused. "But I'd rather have no information than have anything leading to you and your family."

"I can see that. I can ask, and we'll talk it over." Seliora nodded slowly. "Can I ask what you have in mind?"

"In a general sense. I'm trying to figure out what might be called misdirection. I can't wait too long, because the greatest pressure Ryel can put on me is through my family. If he presses your family right now, he offers an opportunity he doesn't want to give."

That was clear enough to me, because Seliora and I weren't even betrothed, let alone married. If Ryel acted against them, now, they certainly could use their taudis contacts against him and his family, and it was unlikely that the High Holder—his heirs, especially—would get much support for attacking a crafting family not involved in his feud. That also meant that I had to deal with Ryel before I could even consider marrying Seliora.

"I see that. Still . . . I should tell Mama and Grandmama to be prepared if he does act against us." Her smile was cold.

There wasn't much more to say about that, not really, because I had only a vague idea of how I would actually attempt to carry out what I had in mind. So I looked at Seliora and smiled. "How are your greens?"

"Good. And yours?" The mischievous smile reappeared.

"Excellent, if not quite so good as those prepared by those in a certain kitchen off Hagahl Lane."

We would enjoy the rest of the evening. About that, I was determined. I was also relieved to have heard Seliora's words about the shooting. It did confirm what I already knew. She wasn't about to be demeaned or abused, regardless of the cost. Her reaction also strengthened my own feelings about dealing with Ryel.

Because I was the duty master on Solayi, I could do more thinking and read-ing, and planning, but not much else. The day was uneventful, except for having to get up early. No would-be imagers appeared. No one reported any imagers killed or missing, and the dining hall was so deserted at midday that I was the only master there.

Even though I'd already told Shault that I'd delivered his coins and mes-sage on Meredi evening, I did motion him aside after lunch.

"How are your studies with Master Ghaend going?"

He didn't quite meet my eyes.

"You're having trouble with the reading?"

"Yes, sir."

I didn't know how to respond to that because, to me, reading had come almost naturally. "Is it the letters or the way they sound?"

"No, sir. It's the words. I can sound them out, but there are so many that I don't know what they mean."

"Haven't you heard of a dictionary?"

He looked absolutely blank.

"Come with me."

As we walked, I began to explain. "A dictionary is a book that has all the words one could ever use, and it explains each word in smaller words, usu-ally, anyway. . . ."

While the library was dark, as it always was on Solayi, I found a diction-ary and signed it out to Shault, cautioning him that he'd have to pay for re-placing it if he lost or damaged the book. Then I sent him on his way, but he seemed almost relieved.

A dictionary—something so simple that it was obvious . . . except to a very bright boy from the taudis and one who was still fearful enough that he didn't want to ask anyone, and who would seemingly tell only me, and only if questioned.

Thankfully, that was the most eventful happening of Solayi.

I did have to get up earlier on Lundi to fit in both Clovyl's exercises and sparring, as well as report on the duty to Master Schorzat. But I managed to arrive at Third District station before seventh glass in time to meet Alsoran before the morning patrols began.

Alsoran had definitely been picked for his patrol round on the basis of physical appearance and capability. He stood a good ten digits taller than me, and his shoulders were far broader. There wasn't the faintest trace of extra flesh or fat around his midsection. His black hair was cut short and still faintly curly below his visored cap, and his eyebrows were thick and bushy, almost meeting above his nose.

"Good morning, Master Rhennthyl."

"Good morning, Alsoran."

"You ready?"

"As ready as I can be." That meant that I was only holding very light shields, with triggers, because anything more caused a pounding headache. That wasn't exactly ideal, but letting anyone know I was less than fully able would have been worse. I thought that it was unlikely that Mardoyt or Harraf would try anything too soon after the last incident, and I hoped I was right.

Without another word, we walked out of the station and headed south-west on Fuosta. We'd almost reached Quierca before Alsoran spoke again.

"I heard about what happened when you went with Huerl and Koshal." Alsoran's slightly high-pitched voice was mild. "I recall something like that happened to a first patroller out of headquarters, except he got killed instead of the brigands."

"I'd heard that. I was assured it was an accident." I laughed. "I'm not fond of accidents."

"Being as you're an imager, I'd wager you aren't, sir. It does seem strange that they've got you walking rounds, not that I'm complaining, mind you." The bushy eyebrows rose.

"The commander wants me to understand everything that you patrollers do. I got the feeling that he worries that if I don't have that understanding, I might recommend something that might cause more problems than doing nothing."

Alsoran shook his head. "Doesn't hold on this round. In the taudis, some-one's always doing something wrong. You do something, and you got prob-lems. You do nothing, and you got more problems."

"You're speaking from experience. How long have you had this round?"

"On and off, for six-seven years. They rotate us, but I always get rotated back here." He laughed. "Suits me. The elvers and the taudischefs in my round know the rules, and they don't give us problems. It's always the young toughs, and most of them don't last." He shook his head good-naturedly. "Some of them get it, and they work out, but the others . . ."

I let a moment of silence pass before I asked, "How do you set up your round?"

"Always do a circle on the edges first. That way, you get a feel for the day and what's happening before you get really inside the taudis. We go out South Middle or Quierca, doesn't much matter, and then along the Avenue D'Artisans. The stretch along the avenue and the two streets behind it are the only part of the round that aren't in the South Middle taudis. From the plaza or from Quierca, depending on which way we go, we head back to Mando— that's the west end of the round. Lyonyt always says that Mando's the border between nasty tough and really evil."

"And your round takes in all the really evil side?"

"Nah . . . our side is just tough. But you can't stop looking. The moment you do . . . that's when trouble starts."

We'd walked two blocks along Quierca. On the south side of the street were row houses, most with heavy shutters or bars on the lower windows, but the dwellings—mostly of faded and soot-stained yellow brick—were neat. Through the occasional gaps between the duplexes and triplexes, I could see hints of gardens and trees in the rear courtyards. On the north side, where we walked, there was the chest-high wall at the back edge of the sidewalk. The ground between the wall and the dwellings was mostly bare, except for strag- gly weeds. Still, after the first four blocks, most of the windows on the lower level had heavy shutters, and almost none had windows boarded shut, al- though I could see traces of smoke coming from chimneys of the few houses with boarded-up windows.

"Quiet this morning. Usually is on Lundi," observed Alsoran.

Even the Avenue D'Artisans seemed to have fewer wagons and coaches, but that might well have been because I'd never been there so early in the morning before. The shops were still all shuttered. The walk back down South Middle was equally quiet, but the row dwellings on the south side, in the taudis, looked even more dilapidated than those off Quierca.

When we reached Mando, Alsoran looked to me. "From here on, don't stop looking."

"I won't." Especially since I was in no shape to hold full shields.

Mando was more like a lane than a street, and an odor of wastes, human and otherwise, drifted up around us.

"Don't work on the sewers here much," said Alsoran. "Can't say I blame 'em."

Town of Georgina (KESWICK) Public Library

The lane ran three long blocks, then turned almost at a right angle and ran another three long blocks back to Quierca. We didn't see anyone on the lane itself all the way, but a block or so short of the end I caught the smell of elveweed—a strong odor.

"Elveweed," I noted.

"From the brown place there on the left," replied Alsoran. "Always smell it there in the morning. Haven't had any trouble, though. Not yet, anyway."

"How long has it been that way?"

"Two-three years."

"Have you noticed more elvers?"

"The captain just rotated us back here a month ago. Spent four months on a round east of the Guild Hall. Must be twice as many elvers since we were here last. Younger, too. The young ones steal more. Older ones work as loaders, smoke when they're off. Youngers can't be bothered to work."

We turned back out Quierca to the next street. I couldn't tell the name because the paint on the wall had been scratched away.

We made it to the last lane at the east end of the taudis area before we ran into trouble. Two blocks in on Saelio, a burly youth a half head taller than me leaned against a brick post that might once have held a lamp. He had a straggly beard that did little for his appearance, and the nearly new yellow and red plaid cloak did even less.

"Alsoran! You got a newbie." The tough spat in my direction, but not at me.

I smiled. "You do that again, and you won't have teeth to spit through."

A long knife appeared. "Says who?"

"Don't you think that's an assault on a patroller?" I asked Alsoran, keeping my eye on the youth.

"Old man . . . stay out of it," the tough warned. "What you going to do, newbie?" He spat again.

I cheated, admittedly, because I lifted full shields, if against my body, before I disarmed him, swept his legs out from under him, and dumped him on the stone pavement. The knife clattered to the stones. I kicked it away.

Inadvertent tears welled from his eyes as he massaged what was probably a sprained wrist. "Trolie bastard . . . get you . . ."

"No, you won't. All you had to do was not spit and not draw a knife. I could have smashed your kneecap so you'd never walk right again," I said in a conversational tone. "Consider it a kindness. Also consider that if you try it again, you just might not wake up after your face smashes into the pavement, rather than your backside."

His eyes dropped to the gray imager trousers, then widened, and he scrambled to his feet, backing away and holding the injured wrist. "Yes, sir."

I watched as he scuttled toward the narrow alleyway between two houses with crude heavy shutters over the lower windows.

"Gave you special training, did they?" asked Alsoran.

"Not that special. There are probably fifty others as good as I am. I'm just the newest."

"You didn't image anything."

"Generally, I'd rather not." That was true, if misleading.

"Better that way. He'll remember that you took him without it."

I hoped so. Even from the momentary use of shields, my head ached.

Fortunately, while we began to see people on the streets and lanes of the taudis during the second round, most were older.

One graying woman called from her front stoop. "Alsoran . . . Fedark got promoted. He's a boatswain third."

"I'm glad to hear it. Give him my best!"

As we continued on, Alsoran said, "Her boy was too smart and too good to stay here. I talked him into enlisting. They give a better deal to the enlistees than the ones they conscript."

"That's true of the imagers, too." Very true, because imagers who didn't come to the Collegium often ended up dead.

After the second full round, we stopped to eat at Elysto's—a small bistro in the one good section of the round, just off the Boulevard D'Artisans—and I enjoyed the batter-fried lamb and onion croissant and the rice fries with the balsamic vinegar.

Then we were back on our feet once more, reversing the direction of the round.

For a good half glass, nothing occurred, although there were more people on the streets. We headed down Mando once more, where I caught sight of three taudis-toughs leaning against the low brick wall of a front porch.

One of them called out, "Such brave trolies. We do like our brave trolies."

Another sang,

> "See our trolies prance and go
> Till the scripties start their show . . ."

"Such brave trolies."

Alsoran flushed, but said nothing, not until we had almost reached South Middle.

"Hate the conscription teams. Most of the ones they pick up here just end up in the Westisle penal crews, and it takes weeks for things to settle out after they leave."

"Do you think it could be worse this time, with the Tiempran priests stirring up things?"

"Sure as the Namer won't be better."

We walked through another round and more. It was close to third glass when we started up Kyena from Quierca toward South Middle.

Just as we neared a lane that was more like a narrow alleyway, I heard a faint click. A taudis-tough stepped out with a pistol aimed in our direction. I threw up shields, even as I snapped, "On the right."

Except that it wasn't on the right. As the one tough fired, three others charged from the left.

Crack! Crack! Crack!

The shots slammed into my shields, driving me back. The impact felt like knives driving into my brain, and for a moment I couldn't even see. Any imaging was definitely not a possibility.

As my eyes cleared, I saw that all five of the toughs had iron bars, and the bars had pointed ends.

I charged the one on the left, so that I could get under the bar before it swung down. My block was good enough that he dropped the bar to the pavement. It landed with a dull clang, but I'd already put an elbow through his throat, and he staggered away.

I used a side-kick on the next tough, right on his knee, and he pitched forward.

Alsoran had used his truncheon on one, who'd gone down, and had slammed it down on the wrist of a second with a sickening crunch. Another iron bar clanked on the uneven stones of the sidewalk.

The last tough vanished up the side lane.

Two figures lay on the pavement. The one hit with the truncheon on the head was unmoving and not breathing. The other had a leg twisted from the knee down and a bruise across his forehead. He was breathing.

Alsoran scooped up the pistol dropped by the one tough and slipped it somewhere under his cloak. Then he picked up the wounded taudis-tough and slung him over his shoulder like a sack of meal. "We'll have to leave the other. One of us needs to have both hands free."

It might have been better with me lugging the wounded tough, but I didn't feel like saying so. My head was throbbing, and intermittent stabs of pain ran down my spine.

The remaining block of Kyena was eerily empty. So were the two short blocks from Kyena down South Middle to the nearest pickup point, where Alsoran laid the tough out on the ground next to the pole.

"He's not going to wake up soon, maybe not at all." Alsoran straightened, shaking himself to relieve sore muscles. "Those weren't local, not from this part of the taudis."

That didn't surprise me. They had to be from the territory to the west of where we had been attacked, that part controlled by Youdh. That meant I had more to do after I finished my round with Alsoran. I realized that I had more than a few bruises, but I hadn't felt being hit. Mostly I was angry. Every which way I turned, someone was after me for something. There wasn't even much I could say as we waited by the pole for the pickup wagon.

"You didn't image," Alsoran finally said.

"I did. I blocked the shots from the pistol. After that, there wasn't time. You have to be able to concentrate." Again, that wasn't totally true, but close enough.

He frowned.

"We do much better one on one," I said, "or when there's some distance between us and an attacker. Why do you think they train us to use our hands and feet?"

"For a middling-sized fellow, Master Rhennthyl, you do wallop folks." He glanced down at the tough.

Even though I was taller than most, I guessed that I was just middling-sized to the massive Alsoran.

By the time we got back to Third District station with the still-unconscious tough, our round was supposed to be over, but it was close to two quints past four before we finished the round report and the initial charging sheet.

After that, I left the station and walked back up South Middle to Dugalle. My head still ached, if not quite so sharply. I saw one of the typical taudis-toughs, young with ragged-cut hair. He just looked at me as I walked closer.

"You know Horazt?"

"Yeah."

I flipped a silver into the air. "That's yours if you'll find him and tell him Master Rhennthyl wants to see him. Now."

The tough stiffened, then looked at me more closely, seeing the gray trousers and black boots for the first time. His eyes went back to the blue patroller's cloak that I wore.

"I'm assigned to the Patrol for now. He knows that."

"How do I know—"

"I can get word to Horazt in other ways, but it takes longer. If I have to do that, you won't want to stay anywhere in L'Excelsis."

"See what I can do." He moved away, not quite ambling, but not hurrying too much, not in my sight, anyway.

I waited a good half glass for Horazt, and the sun had already dropped behind the taudis-dwellings south and west of South Middle before he appeared, accompanied by the younger man. As they sauntered toward me, Horazt's almost-squat form was partly concealed by the black woolen cloak he wore.

"Here's the silver I promised." I tossed it over to the younger tough, who caught it.

"Bougyt . . . you can go."

This time, the younger man hurried away.

"Master Rhennthyl. Must be important for you to come here so late, and to spend a silver just to find me."

"I thought you'd like to know that your nephew Shault is doing well. He's very bright, but he's having to work hard."

"That'd be good. Not why you came, I'd wager."

"It's not. Something happened that could matter for both of us. Five taudis-toughs attacked another patroller and me earlier this afternoon. We were patrolling the west end of the taudis. One's dead, one's been charged with assault on patrollers—if he lives."

"You're with that Alsoran . . ."

"He said that they weren't from there, that they didn't belong to the taudischefs in his round. I'd guess they didn't belong to you, either."

"If you know that, why come to me?"

"Because you might be able to tell me if they were Youdh's men and why he sent them against Alsoran and me."

"Don't know."

I waited, my eyes on the young taudischef, my thoughts suggesting that he'd be far better off telling me.

"Word is that Youdh's got a deal with Harraf. Do favors for each other."

"So Youdh's got deals with the Tiempran priests and the captain?"

"That's the word." Horazt shrugged.

"And?"

"Word is that the taudis might get off easy when the scripties come if an imager isn't around."

I laughed. "Harraf can't do anything about the conscription teams. Neither can the Collegium. They're usually Navy, with naval marines doing the hard work, and they don't even tell the Civic Patrol or the imagers when they're coming. Even if Harraf knew, he couldn't do anything about it."

"What I figured," Horazt said, "but I'm just a young taudischef, don't know sowshit." His words were delivered with a cheerful banter, but I suspected there was a bitterness behind them that would have curdled fresh cream.

"What will Youdh do?"

Horazt smiled. "Kill the ones who failed. If anyone asks him, he'll claim that he had nothing to do with it."

I'd almost expected that. "What would happen if something happened to Youdh?"

"Saelyhd would take over. He's worse. Stupid and vicious."

I didn't need that, either. "That's too bad. Might be better if he vanished before anything happens to Youdh."

Horazt looked at me.

I ignored the look. "Will they try again soon?"

"Wouldn't think so. Youdh wouldn't want to lose too many with Jadhyl and Deyalt both wanting more territory."

"They're the taudischefs to the east of Youdh?"

Horazt nodded. "Best I be going. Good evening, Master Rhennthyl."

I headed back down South Middle to where I could find a hack to take me back to the Collegium. I didn't stop looking and studying every shadow in the twilight, not until I was in the coach and well clear of the area around Third District station.

So now what was I supposed to do?

24

Most, but not all, of my headache had departed by the time I dragged myself out of bed in the near-darkness of Mardi morning. I still had no real idea how to deal with Mardoyt and Harraf. I had no proof at all that they were involved, but who else could be? And how did the attacks on Alsoran and me by Youdh's toughs fit in? Beyond that, I had only the vaguest idea of what to do about High Holder Ryel. In fact, if I wanted to be honest with myself, I was having trouble just staying alive and in one piece . . . and I hadn't had to deal with anything involving Ryel yet.

I managed not to think too hard about that through the morning exercises or breakfast, but when I got to the Third District station just before seventh glass, Captain Harraf gestured for me to join him in his study. I didn't close the door, and he didn't ask me to.

For a moment, he said nothing, just looked at me.

I waited for what he had to say.

"The man you brought yesterday died before he could say anything. It's a pity you couldn't have been more gentle. Alsoran does his best, but you as an imager . . ."

"I protected him against gunshots and after that we did our best against five taudis-toughs, Captain. As the report stated, they didn't say a word to us. They started shooting and then attacked."

"Surely they must have had a reason."

"I'm most certain they did, but since neither Alsoran nor I had ever seen any of them before, whatever that reason happened to be was not based on personal contact with us. It might be the result of decisions you or the commander made or just because they were feeling like they wanted to make an example of two patrollers, or because they're worried a conscription team may be sweeping the taudis before long. I couldn't say." I could sense Harraf stiffen, but I just smiled politely. "You certainly have a better idea of such matters than do I."

"I'm so glad you grant me that, Master Rhennthyl."

"You have far more experience than I do, sir. I'm here to learn."

For some reason, he paused at my words, if only momentarily. "That you are. I trust you will convey what you learn to other imagers. Still, it was unfortunate that there was no one to question."

"Yes, sir." It was indeed unfortunate—but not for Harraf, I thought.

"That's all I had, Master Rhennthyl."

"Thank you, sir." I smiled and slipped out of his study, wondering why he'd even brought the matter up at all. Was he that stupid to think I didn't see? Or was I that stupid in not overtly recognizing how much power he wielded in the Third District?

Alsoran was waiting as I walked into the front area of the station.

"How are you feeling this morning?" I asked as we left.

"I'm fine. Still can't figure out why those toughs attacked us yesterday."

"It could be that someone told them I was an imager, and they don't like that."

"If they'd been from that part of the taudis . . . maybe . . . but they were intruding."

"Could it be that they wanted to cause trouble for the taudischefs on your round?"

Alsoran considered that for several moments before saying, "It's possible."

"But you don't think that's it."

"Nope. Couldn't say why, though."

I could, but I wasn't about to say that it was Youdh's doing at Harraf's prompting. Or that if I'd failed to protect Alsoran, matters would have been worse for me and the Collegium.

While there were more people on the streets as we walked the round, especially on South Middle and the Avenue D'Artisans, no one even gave us more than a passing glance, except for the handful of older women who smiled at Alsoran or passed pleasantries.

We were near the end of the first pass through the east end of the taudis, on Saelio, when I caught sight of three men, all wearing dark green cloaks, walking slowly toward us. They stopped a good ten yards away.

"Jadhyl," murmured Alsoran.

"You were right," I murmured back.

"Good morning, Jadhyl," offered Alsoran. "Have you met Rhennthyl? He's filling in for Lyonyt for a while."

"I cannot say that I have."

"I'm pleased to meet you, Jadhyl." I inclined my head politely. While Jadhyl's speech was precise, far better than any of the taudis-toughs I'd heard, there was a hint of an accent, and his skin had a trace of a golden tinge that I'd never seen before. His hair was also an unusual golden brown.

"I wanted to inform you that no one associated with me was involved in the unfortunate incident yesterday afternoon. That would not be in my interests, nor Deyalt's."

Alsoran nodded. "Master Rhennthyl and I sort of thought that, but it's good to hear it from you."

"I appreciate your not reaching an untoward conclusion. Thank you." He nodded, then turned, flanked by the two others. They disappeared down the next side lane.

Once they were out of sight, we continued onward.

"I wouldn't be surprised if he ends up the head of all the taudischefs here," I said quietly.

"That's what the captain's afraid of," replied Alsoran. "You notice the streets here?"

"They're neater. Not perfect, but better than those to the west."

"Look at the windows. Close."

I did as we walked along the block, and then it struck me. I'd half noticed it before. There weren't any boarded-up windows. Some had very crude shutters, stained rather than painted, but shutters. "Is that Jadhyl's doing?"

"Couldn't say, but that tough you handled yesterday . . . you see him today?"

"No."

"He's been leaning on that post for two weeks, every morning. Wager you won't see him again, one way or the other. Wager I won't, either."

I wasn't about to take that wager.

Later, when we had reached the end of our second round, I asked, "Who patrols the part of the taudis between the station and your round? During the day?"

"That'd be Melyor and Slausyl. You thinking about those toughs again?"

"I was."

"I asked them if they thought they might be Youdh's. They didn't know. Slausyl's heard word that Youdh wants to be a sort of head taudischef over the whole South Middle taudis. He might want to see if we'd do something against Jadhyl or Deyalt."

"That's possible." Or had the point really been to see if they could get me . . . and failing that, get Alsoran and discredit me?

While we kept a careful eye on the narrower lanes and alleys for the rest of the day, we weren't looking so much for the locals, but for crazy elvers or those who didn't belong. We didn't see either, not that there weren't elvers and more than the occasional odor of the weed by late afternoon, but no one smoking it ever came close to us.

I kept thinking over what I'd seen. Why was Harraf worried about Jadhyl? Because he might end up controlling the entire taudis? Or because he wouldn't funnel payoffs to Harraf? How did the priests of Puryon fit in?

Just before we headed back to the station, I finally asked, "Do you know how Jadhyl gets along with the priests of Puryon?"

"Can't say as I know for certain, Master Rhennthyl. Heard it said that anyone from his area who uses their advocates goes over to Youdh. They do, and they have to move out of here, though."

"Jadhyl looks different."

"His folks came from Stakanar."

The more I saw and heard, the less I liked what seemed to be going on in Third District. Yet . . . it was all vague. The one thing that was clear, once Alsoran had pointed it out, was that the area controlled by taudischef Jadhyl was far more orderly and better kept. But that didn't prove anything about Captain Harraf.

Because we hadn't had any more troubles, I was able to leave the station just after fourth glass. I hadn't seen anyone in the family for over a week, and since I was already closer to the house than I would have been at Imagisle, I took a carriage for hire out to the house.

Khethila was the one to open the door.

"Rhenn . . . I didn't expect you, not in the middle of the week." She stepped back.

I followed her inside, closing the door behind me. "I would have come on Solayi, but I was the duty master and couldn't leave Imagisle."

"Mother's over at the neighbors', and Father won't be home for a bit. He wanted to check some of the inventory after they closed."

"Are you still enjoying doing the accounts?"

Her smile was brief. "That part is good. I even figured out a way to ship woolens to Solis and Asseroiles faster and cheaper."

"Oh?"

"Most people don't ship on Samedi, but if we have the shipment ready on Vendrei night, we can send it down to the ironway freight depot first thing on Samedi morning and have the wagon back by midday. I negotiated a ten percent discount that way." She shrugged. "It won't work on urgent shipments, but it does help."

I didn't like the sound of that.

"Is there anything new from Kherseilles?" I was almost afraid to ask.

Khethila was silent for a long moment. "Unless things get better, Father will probably have to close the factorage there." She kept her voice low. "He doesn't want to admit it, but we're losing more golds every month there."

"It's that bad?"

"The Abiertans reneged on their contracts because the Council won't send a fleet to protect the port, and our ships won't steam there, and theirs can't afford to approach Solidar. Rousel has been relying on the Abiertans for trade with Tiempre and Caenen, and all the cargo space on Solidaran merchanters heading to Otelyrn has been bought up. The Caenenans and Tiemprans aren't sending that many vessels north." Khethila pursed her lips, then continued. "Rousel can't seem to find anyone to tear down the warehouse wall and rebuild it where it should be, and the new owner of the adjoining land is threatening to have it done—and it's in the middle of the fall rains there. Rousel missed one major shipment because the dray wagon broke the trace pole and he couldn't get a replacement in time, and he couldn't hire any other teamsters to carry the bales. Whether he'll get paid for the delayed shipment . . ." She shrugged.

All that sounded like Rousel, never quite following through, never quite making sure of the details. Yet after what was happening to me, I almost questioned whether it made a difference. I'd tried to be careful, and I was still in trouble.

"Can you do anything?"

"I'm afraid . . ." She stopped. "Father wants to extend more credit. I've told him we can't afford it. We could. This time." Her eyes met mine. "Am I wrong?"

How could I answer that? Finally, I said, "Do you remember how I got strapped for not trimming the hedge properly?"

"I just remember you punched Rousel, and Father strapped you again."

"He was supposed to use the small shears and follow up. He never did. He went off to play, and Father punished me for not catching him. If I'd caught him, he would have complained that I hurt him. That sort of thing happened more than once."

"You're saying that if I . . ."

I nodded. "You'll only make it harder for Father."

"Rousel will plead that the problem with the wall wasn't his fault and that he just needs a little more credit and time."

"I'm sure he will. He hasn't paid out anything for the wall or rebuilding, has he?"

"No. Not yet." She sighed. "I see what you mean. I knew it, but it's so hard."

I knew that, too, and I knew Ryel would find a way to make it harder. I just didn't know how.

25

Compared to previous days, Meredi was uneventful, and I didn't even see Captain Harraf. Nor were there any taudis-toughs waiting on corners or by posts. We did have to deal with a window smash-and-grab at a small silversmith's off the Avenue D'Artisans in the afternoon, but the thief made the mistake of smashing the glass when the owner's son—who overtopped me—was returning to the shop. All we had to do was cart the thief away. He was an elver, desperate for coins.

When I woke on Jeudi morning, I could actually lift shields without a headache. One blow to my shields from above, and I'd been limited for a week.

After completing my now all-too-regular prebreakfast routine, I walked quickly to the dining hall. I was about to enter when the large headline type from the topmost newsheet in the full boxes caught my eye: "War Looms!" I immediately hurried over and picked up a copy of *Veritum*, then scanned the lead story quickly.

A Ferran fleet had attacked a Solidaran flotilla off the harbor at Teusig, wherever that was, using fog as a cover and apparently taking our ships by surprise. The losses had been heavy on both sides, with only two Solidaran ships out of eight surviving. Reportedly, some fifteen Ferran ships had been sunk. The Council was expected to declare war imminently.

The Abiertan Isles had declared their neutrality, insisting all merchant vessels were welcome, but no warships. That cut off one of the major refueling ports for the Solidaran Navy and meant more colliers would have to accompany the fleet. The newsheet said that several advisors to the Council had raised the question as to whether Solidar should take over the port at Abierta— or the coaling station operated there by our Navy.

After folding the sheet and thrusting it inside my waistcoat, I entered the dining hall. Ferlyn was the only other one at the masters' table, and I sat down beside him. No sooner had I poured my tea than Chassendri joined us.

"What do you think about war with Ferrum?" I asked.

"It had to happen sooner or later," Ferlyn replied calmly. "The Ferrans don't like us, and they don't like the way we run our country, and we're the ones who might keep them from annexing the chunk of Jariola that they want. They've been trying to provoke a war for months."

I offered the teapot to Chassendri because her mug was on the side away from me. "And you?"

"It won't solve anything, really. They think they won a battle, but they destroyed six older frigates and lost fifteen of their own. The Council will declare war. The war will destroy the Ferran fleets and much of Ferran commerce, and weaken ours. All the more repressive regimes will benefit, and that will assure that political change across Terahnar will take longer and require more rebellions and bloodshed. In the end, we both lose."

"Aren't you the cheerful one," replied Ferlyn dryly. "You've obviously been listening to Maitre Dyana."

"She's right more often than not."

"And she has a way of letting us know it without saying a word," Ferlyn replied with a laugh.

"I wish I were that effective," I said.

"You do rather well yourself." At least Chassendri smiled when she spoke.

We didn't decide much at breakfast . . . or agree, and I ate hurriedly.

Then I used a duty coach to get to Third District station because I'd decided that I shouldn't be paying for transportation required by the Collegium. I'd still have to use a hack or my feet to return, but halving the cost was better than bearing it all myself.

The station didn't look any different that morning, even with the possibility of war hanging over everyone. I didn't even see Captain Harraf, and that was fine with me.

I didn't have to wait long for Alsoran, and we walked out into a chill breeze that had seemingly risen in the short time since I'd entered the station. I was glad that I was wearing the heavier winter waistcoat under the patroller's cloak.

We walked almost to Quierca before I asked Alsoran, "What do you think about the Council declaring war?"

"They'll do what they will. It's not as though we can do anything about it. I'm just glad my son's only nine. Be trouble for Third Station, because the conscription teams will be here sooner and more often."

"Next week?"

"More like two, I'd wager. Or three."

Throughout the day, even when we patrolled the Avenue D'Artisans, I didn't hear anyone talking about war or Ferrum. I overheard a few comments at Elysto's, most definitely Alsoran's favorite place to eat lunch.

". . . Ferrans won't learn . . ."

". . . good at counting golds, but not at counting shells . . ."

". . . think our Navy's that good?"

Even when we returned to the station just after fourth glass, when the shifts were changing, I didn't hear a word about the coming war. Did it matter that little? Or did all the patrollers feel the way Alsoran did? Or was it just that they fought their own skirmishes, day after day, with little or no recognition?

When I returned to my quarters, I found that my black formal jacket and trousers had been delivered and laid out across my easy chair and that an envelope had been slipped under my door. Inside was a note with a single line: "Meet me at fifth glass. D."

I reached his study just before fifth glass. The door was open. I stepped inside. "Sir?"

Master Dichartyn turned from the window. "If you'd close the door, Rhenn."

I did. Although my feet were sore, I did not sit because he remained standing.

"Did you hear that the Council declared war on Ferrum?"

"No, sir. I saw the newsheets this morning, but I hadn't heard anything more. I had the feeling they would."

"They don't have much choice. Ferran forces have invaded Jariola, and the Ferran fleet attacked our other flotilla, with far less success than in the earlier battle. The Jariolans will likely be pushed back or retreat, even after our main battle fleet arrives."

"How will that help? We aren't going to invade Ferrum or send troops, are we?"

"We won't have to. Once the Ferrans lose their fleet, and we confiscate the majority of their merchanters for damages, it's likely that their Assembly might see matters rather differently." He shrugged. "If not, a blockade on the ports will eventually bring them to their senses. If that doesn't, the Jariolans will, once full winter hits."

"Won't that just create an opportunity for smugglers?"

"It doubtless will, but smugglers can't bring in large quantities of anything. They'll bring luxury goods and small high-value items that will damage the Ferran economy even more."

"Won't the fighting in Jariola continue, though?"

"For months, if not far longer, but the Jariolans have more troops, and they'll be fighting in winter in the mountains of their own land. All that heavy equipment of the Ferrans won't be that useful in snow and rugged terrain."

"Isn't this going to be . . . costly? For us, I mean."

"Very much, Rhennthyl. Very much. But if one goes to war, one does it right, so that future adversaries understand the dangers. It's been almost a century since the Reduction of Stakanar, and that's about as long as people choose to remember. Now . . . there are likely to be agents of various sorts appearing in L'Excelsis, and the Tiemprans may want to cause trouble, if they see an opportunity. If you see someone who might be such, unless he attacks or threatens you, do nothing except observe and report to me. If you cannot find me, tell Master Schorzat."

"Yes, sir."

"Now . . . what do you have to report about your Patrol activities?" Master Dichartyn's voice dropped into a tone somewhere between tired and bored, as if nothing I said would matter all that much.

"Five taudis-toughs attacked me and Alsoran on Lundi. They weren't from within that round and didn't belong to the local taudischef. We injured two, killed two, and the one uninjured and two injured ones escaped. They were most likely Youdh's men, acting on behalf of Captain Harraf."

"That's a serious charge. Do you have any proof?" His tone was skeptical.

"Not much. The local taudischef came out and told us that the men weren't his. They weren't Horazt's, either. Beyond that, it's unlikely that I'll ever have any proof. That doesn't make it any less true."

"As far as the Collegium goes, Rhennthyl, only that which can be proved is true."

"Would you rather I not report what I can't prove?"

"No. If you feel you have to tell me, just say that it's a possibility without proof. Never put anything in writing without proof behind it."

"Yes, sir. I'd like to report, verbally, that five taudis-toughs fired pistol shots at us, then assaulted us with pointed iron bars and that it is a possibility that they acted under orders from taudischef Youdh. The word among the other taudischefs, which is only rumor, is that Youdh and Captain Harraf have an arrangement of some sort, and that Captain Harraf and Youdh also have a similar arrangement with the Equalifier priests of Puryon."

"You know, Rhennthyl, it might be better if you were somewhat more circumspect in your speech."

"That might be, sir, but it's rather difficult to be circumspect when so many people are trying to kill one, and when one has been informed that such problems are strictly one's own."

"The Collegium, as you well know, cannot take a position that will endanger all imagers, now and in the future, for the sake of one."

"I understand that. Perfectly. I would ask, sir, that you not expect me to show great pleasure about that policy. While I understand its need, it does present certain rather significant difficulties for me." Not to mention for my family, but there wasn't any point in declaring that.

"All imagers face difficulties. That is the nature of the world in which we find ourselves. You might remember that you are far from the first to be placed in such a situation."

I barely managed to refrain from asking that if there had been so many in that position, why the Collegium had not done something about it.

"Rhennthyl . . . although you should have asked, it is proper to take a duty coach in the morning. You are undertaking duty."

"Thank you for the clarification, sir."

"Do you have anything else to report?"

"Elveweed use is continuing to rise, but mainly in the taudis area controlled by Youdh."

"That's not surprising. He has connections to more smugglers. Anything else?"

"No, sir."

"I may not be around for a time. If I'm gone for more than a week, get in touch with Master Schorzat." With that, he nodded a dismissal at me.

I left, and I didn't close the door behind me.

Then I made my way back to my quarters, where I tried on the formal wear that I'd have to wear to the Council's Autumn Ball. It fit. I hung the coat and trousers up in the wardrobe in my sleeping chamber, which held little enough, and settled into the chair behind my writing desk. While I had some ideas for dealing with Ryel, I knew I could not implement them until something else happened that could be linked to Ryel, and I had no ideas—except the most unpalatable—for handling Harraf and Mardoyt.

I frowned. I couldn't be certain just how guilty Harraf was, not for sure. I paused, knowing that there was something . . . something I wasn't quite seeing.

Finally, I shook my head. I knew Mardoyt was definitely fixing charges and pocketing golds. I could start there . . . and Horazt might be able to help.

On Vendrei, Alsoran and I finished the last round at half a quint before fourth glass, and I was on my way out of the station even before the glass struck, heading up toward South Middle to see if I could find Horazt or one of his toughs who could locate him. Of course, because I was finally working out something, where time might be a factor, I didn't see anyone except elvers on stoops and bent women with baskets and laundry, and a handful of boys who scurried away when they caught sight of the blue patroller's cloak.

So I opted for the fallback plan, and that was to go to Chelya's place. After two wrong turns, I came to what I thought was her door. I rapped several times. Finally, it eased open, just a crack.

I opened my cloak to let the imager's gray show. "Shault's doing well. That's not why I came."

Someone widened the crack, if just slightly, and enough light fell on her face for me to confirm that Chelya stood there.

"I need to talk to Horazt, but I don't know how to reach him. If you see him, I'd like to meet him on South Middle on Solayi at the first glass of the afternoon."

She just looked at me.

"I'm asking a favor, one I'll pay for. I need some information from Horazt, and nothing that would hurt him or you. Would a silver help?"

I thought she nodded, and I extended a silver. She took it, almost reluctantly, as if she disliked being beholden to me, even for a service.

"I will see what I can do, Master Rhennthyl."

"You will come to see Shault a week from Solayi, won't you?"

"If it does not rain or snow I will come."

"He may not say so, but he would be glad to see you."

There might have been a hint of a smile behind the sadness in her face, but then, I might have imagined it.

"Thank you." I inclined my head to her.

She inclined her head in return and slowly closed the door.

As I headed back toward South Middle, I hoped that Horazt would be there on Solayi. One way or another, I'd find him, but Solayi would be better, far better, than later.

On the way out of the taudis, I still saw no one who looked like one of Horazt's men. Once I was back on South Middle, headed west, as I passed Dugalle, I could see a pair of patrollers ahead. As they neared, I recognized Huerl and Koshal, heading eastward.

"Good evening," I offered.

The two stopped, although Koshal glanced past me, as if to indicate that they had rounds to make. I ignored the glance and smiled politely.

"Evening, Master Rhennthyl," offered Huerl.

"I was wondering if anything ever came of those two who killed themselves that night I patrolled with you."

"No, sir. Never heard anything." Koshal looked past me again.

"Have you noticed any spread of elvers into your patrol round? Or any more break-ins?"

"No, sir."

"Thank you. I wondered because some of the taudis-toughs have been attacking folks outside their usual territories."

"Alsoran said something about that," replied Huerl.

"He thought that Youdh might be trying to expand his territory, and the word seems to be that he's not happy about something."

The two exchanged glances.

"Hadn't heard that, sir," said Koshal. "Wouldn't be good, that wouldn't."

"I won't keep you. I'd just wondered if you'd seen anything like that."

"No, sir."

I kept a pleasant smile on my face and nodded, then continued back up South Middle.

It took longer than usual to hail a hack, possibly because the wind had picked up, and a light rain had begun to fall. That meant that I was more than a little late for dinner, close to half a glass, but when I entered the dining hall, Maitre Dyana beckoned for me to join her.

"Thank you," I said as I took the seat to her left.

"I'm glad to see that you're actually working late. You were working, I trust?"

"Searching out information, at least." I decided on hot tea because the wind and rain had picked up and I had gotten chilled on the walk across the Bridge of Hopes and the quadrangle.

"That's always a start, but only a start." She smiled, passing the platter of curried ribs. "Most people don't respond to information by itself. They tend to dismiss it if it doesn't fit their opinions, or ignore it in favor of those facts presented by someone who is more powerful."

"You're suggesting information is useful only in determining what action to take, then?"

"I don't recall saying exactly that."

More word games from Dyana? "Or are you saying that one can only use information after conveying a sense of power?"

"That can be effective, but as you've already discovered, being perceived as powerful can also make one a target."

I managed a smile, then took several bites of the ribs, slightly overcooked, followed by seasoned yellow rice that was moist and savory. I took another sip of hot tea before I spoke. "You have great experience, Maitre Dyana, and I'm afraid that you have the better of me, because, upon considering your words, I seem to be able to come to no other conclusion than the fact that information is effectively useless without power, and yet having power makes one a target, and being a target will eventually destroy one's power, because targets usually do get destroyed in time."

"Your logic is good, Rhennthyl, but you are missing one point. I'm not going to tell you what that is, not tonight anyway, because you need to think it through." She smiled again. "How are you finding the Civic Patrol?"

"As it is, I trust. So far, from what I have seen, some patrollers are dedicated. Others do their job, and a handful shouldn't be patrollers at all."

"That is true in all fields."

"That is my impression, maitre, and I suppose that it applies to High Holders as well."

"Very much so, although High Holders tend to be less tolerant of those who squander their heritage or whose actions threaten other High Holders for no worthwhile reason."

"That makes sense." For all that it did, I didn't think that she had said it as a pleasant observation.

"It does indeed. Oh . . . I must congratulate you on the portrait that you did of Maitre Poincaryt. I saw it in the receiving hall earlier this week. It's not only an excellent likeness and lifelike, but it also conveys a sense of power."

"Thank you."

After that, the most interesting topics were the weather and the decline of portraiture in Solidar. When I left the dining hall, I picked up a copy of *Tableta* and read the lead stories, but in the first paragraphs there was little real news about the war, except that the last elements of the "northern fleet" had steamed out of Westisle on Jeudi. Not until I reached the end of the story did I come across an interesting section.

> . . . to increase the Army and to assure greater safety in the cities of Solidar, the Council approved a measure, effective immediately, to allow increased conscription levels of young men without permanent trades, positions, or advanced education.

I didn't like that implication at all, especially since it appeared I'd be working out of Third District station for a time yet.

In fact, I didn't like the implications of most matters affecting me. High Holder Ryel was clearly trying to squeeze my family, and while I had my own qualms about Rousel's overall competence, his shortcomings and Ryel's machinations, unless stopped, would ruin my father and my family. And, like it or not, either Mardoyt or Harraf, if not both, seemed to want to have most unfortunate difficulties befall me.

My efforts to date, based on my observing during the official "working day" of the Patrol, weren't resolving that problem, and I had yet to put anything in action to deal effectively with High Holder Ryel.

I was going to have to spend a lot more time on the problems facing me . . . before they overwhelmed me and everyone for whom I cared.

27

Samedi morning was foggy, and it had rained during the night, leaving the grass and the walkways damp when I headed out for the obligatory exercise and sparring session. None of the older masters was there except for Schorzat. That left less than half of the normal complement—Baratyn, Dartazn, Martyl, and me. I ended up sparring with Baratyn and getting bruises that would turn sore indeed by the end of the day.

"Not bad, Rhenn," he told me.

If I hadn't done badly, I certainly didn't want to do worse. But then, Baratyn had a good ten years' experience on me.

With so few older imagers undergoing Clovyl's exercise session, I wasn't exactly surprised to find myself alone at breakfast with Heisbyl, a Maitre D'Aspect far older and grayer than I, who almost never ate in the dining hall unless he was the duty imager, but I had to wonder because Samedi wasn't usually a duty day.

"Good morning," I offered politely as I poured my tea.

"Good morning, Rhennthyl. A mite cool outside, wouldn't you say?"

"It's not too bad, not if you keep moving."

"That's fine for you young fellows." He frowned. "You were a portraitist for a time, weren't you? For Caliostrus?"

"I was, and that was when he did the portrait of your daughter."

"A good work, if dear. I saw your portrait of Maitre Poincaryt for the first time this morning. Rather fine, I fancy, and I daresay it cost the Collegium far less than what I paid Caliostrus for Verinya's portrait." He laughed.

"Far less, at least in coin," I replied lightly.

"Oh, all of you young masters think you've cost the Collegium dearly, and so you have, but so has anyone who's made master. One cannot make master without self-confidence, and self-confidence combines with youth and ability to make mistakes, and those are costly both in coin and blood."

I couldn't argue that . . . and didn't. I just offered an exaggerated shrug and set to eating the fried cakes dowsed in syrup along with the slab of bacon.

After I excused myself and rose to leave, Heisbyl smiled faintly and said, "It remains to be seen whether you'll be a greater master imager than you could have been as a master portraiturist. Ability, self-confidence, and dedication suffice for a master portraiturist. They aren't enough for an imager."

"I'll keep that in mind," I replied politely.

"I hope you do." The smile faded. "I did not."

"Thank you," I added.

As I walked northward along the west side of the quadrangle in the cool and still air, Heisbyl's last words still echoed in my thoughts, as did the sadness behind them. Especially after those words, I didn't mind getting to the studio early. I'd already wanted to look over what I'd done on both Master Rholyn's portrait and the one of Seliora that I'd barely begun.

When I walked into the studio, I saw a small iron coal stove that sat almost against the outside wall. An iron chimney had also been installed, with new brickwork around where it went through the wall. A full coal scuttle stood on the stone floor. After opening the stove door to load it, I realized that the ashes were warm and that the studio, while not warm, was certainly not as cold as it had been. That meant Grandisyn, or someone, had been fueling and watching the stove while I was working with the Patrol. After loading the stove, I did manage to image some of the coal into flame.

After that, not only did I get everything set up, but I worked for more than a glass on the background of Master Rholyn's portrait before he arrived in the studio. By then, the air was far warmer than when I'd first entered the studio, so much so that Master Rholyn had his heavy winter cloak off even before he closed the door behind him.

"Rhennthyl . . . this morning I can only sit for half a glass. I've a meeting with Master Poincaryt."

"If that would press you, sir . . ." I offered.

"No . . . a half glass will allow me more than enough time."

"I imagine that the events between Ferrum and Jariola—and the Council—have created more than a few problems," I offered, gesturing toward the crate. "If you don't mind taking the standing position . . ."

"That's fine. I'll be sitting for a good long time after I leave you, I expect."

I touched the oils on the tray with the brush tip and began to work on an unfinished section where his neck met the collar of his gray shirt. "What will happen now that the Council has declared war on Ferrum, sir? Besides the northern fleet attacking Ferran warships and merchanters, I mean."

"No one on the Council wishes to land troops anywhere in Cloisera, either in Jariola or in Ferrum itself. High Councilor Suyrien is deeply concerned that Solidar not be perceived as showing favoritism to the Jariolans. He and

Caartyl have already drafted a communiqué insisting that the Oligarch and his council immediately begin reimbursing Solidar for its efforts in assisting Jariola." Rholyn raised his eyebrows. "What does that indicate to you, Rhenn?"

"The Council wants to make clear that the war is about the actions taken by Ferrum, and not about a preference for the Jariolan system of government."

"That is certainly one purpose."

I decided against asking what the real purpose was, not directly. "Will the Jariolans actually reimburse us, or is that just a posture?"

"I doubt that they can."

"But if I might ask why, sir . . ."

"When they demur, we will most likely request a ninety-nine-year lease on Harvik—that's a small isle off the port of Jaaslk—along with a guarantee of coal sales and shipment, at the prevailing price. The isle does have a harbor, but virtually no inhabitants, and a single pier. But it will make a good sheltered anchorage for the new northern fleet, and we could build our own port there and garrison it. It's less than a day's steaming to Ferrial from there."

"The Council must anticipate problems there for some time to come." I kept my voice even, trying to concentrate on painting.

"For several centuries, Maitre Poincaryt believes."

"Problems lasting that long will not please the Council."

"Lengthy expenditures on anything seldom do." A quick wry smile crossed his face, and I tried to hold it in my mind, because that expression captured a certain essence of Maitre Rholyn. I stopped working on his neck and switched to his mouth and cheeks. Neither of us spoke for a time.

Then . . . I had the expression, and with the brush itself, and not imaging. Just those touches, and it brought his face to life, not that I didn't have a great deal more work to do. I even got his neck and collar just right before the bell announced the half glass.

At lunch, I joined Ferlyn and Heisbyl, and we talked about the war, and what might occur once the northern fleet reached the waters off Cloisera. After eating, I took my time walking across the quadrangle and to the Bridge of Hopes, where I stood in the damp chill and waited.

Shortly before first glass, Shomyr escorted Seliora to the east end of the Bridge of Hopes. She was wearing a black cloak over the same outfit she'd worn the week before and carrying a flat parcel of some sort. I walked toward her, and Shomyr waited until we were together. Then he turned and waved, returning to the coach that had brought them.

"That was good of Shomyr."

"Aunt Aegina, Mama, and Odelia went to a luncheon for Yaena, and he didn't want them to have to worry about me."

Yaena? Then the name came to me—Seliora's cousin who'd gotten married the day after I'd nearly gotten myself killed at the Council's Harvest Ball. I hoped that the Autumn Ball in two weeks would be far less eventful.

"Oh." Seliora handed me a large envelope. "This is what Ailphens could discover."

"Ailphens?" The weight of paper suggested more than a few documents.

"The advocate for NordEste Design. We thought going through him would obscure matters sufficiently."

After she'd explained, I recalled the advocate's name as one she'd told me months before. I wished I'd recalled it before she'd had to tell me again. "Have you read what's in here?"

"Yes. It's typical for a High Holder. He's got the main holding, and ownership of various other sections of land across Solidar, but most of his known interests outside his main holdings are in various banques."

"Such as the Banque D'Rivages and the Banque D'Kherseilles."

"If you knew that, why did you ask . . ."

"I didn't know. I suspected, but it was only a guess."

"You knew. You just couldn't prove it." Seliora looked at me. "Did you see it, or just know it?"

"I knew it. The only thing I've seen is the fire at the factorage." So far.

"You'll see more. You will."

"Is that a promise?" I laughed softly.

She flushed. "You are . . ." Then she shook her head.

I held the package in my right arm and offered the left to Seliora. We walked off the bridge and along the lane and then across the north end of the quadrangle before turning north toward the workrooms and my studio.

"What about dinner? We'll meet Shomyr and Haelya at Chaelya's?" I asked.

"At half past sixth glass. That will give you more time to paint . . . and to learn a bit more about riding."

"You've seen me riding—Pharsi farsight—haven't you?"

"Just that. Nothing frightening, but it can't hurt for you to know a little about riding."

"I doubt that I'll ever know more than a little. I know enough to ask for a gentle horse."

On the stone walkway coming toward us were two young imagers. I recognized them both—Gherard and Petryn.

The two looked at Seliora, exchanged knowing glances, then stopped.

"Good afternoon." I paused. "And yes, she is beautiful, and might I present Mistress Seliora D'Shelim. I'm painting her portrait."

"Good afternoon, sir, mistress." Their words were not quite synchronized, and they looked away from Seliora.

"Good afternoon, imagers," Seliora said, her voice warm, her eyes on Gherard.

The older imager inclined his head. Then, so did Petryn, before the two stood back to let us pass.

"There will be rumors all over Imagisle by tonight." She smiled at me.

"Among the seconds and thirds, anyway."

"Not among the masters?"

"Even at meals, we don't see much of each other. Well . . . I might at midday, but I'm not here then. Sometimes there are only one or two of us at the masters' table. Most are married, and they eat with their families at breakfast or dinner, unless they have work on Samedi or duty on Solayi."

"It doesn't sound like there are that many masters."

"There might be fifteen or twenty here."

"And you led me to believe that you've done nothing special?" She raised her eyebrows. "In less than a year, you've gone from being a prime to a master, and there are only twenty masters out of four hundred imagers?"

"I was fortunate to have a great deal of imaging talent."

Seliora shook her head. "Do you really believe it's just that?"

I was glad I didn't have to answer, because we'd reached the studio door, and I opened it. Before I started painting, I opened the stove door and shoveled more coal inside.

The position I'd finally decided on was one where Seliora looked like she'd been walking, then stopped and half turned to look at something. When I got to painting the split-skirts, I knew that I'd depict them as still flared, as if she'd just turned and they hadn't settled back down.

This sitting, though, I was concentrating on her face.

One of the hardest parts, as I'd known it would be, was to get the right skin tone. Seliora was fair-skinned, but her face was not that pale bluish white that many women of Bovarian heritage—such as Ryel's daughter Iryela—flaunted. Nor did Seliora have either an olive complexion or the dark-honeyed look of many Pharsi women, yet her skin held the faintest trace of a bronze-gold. I'd have called it goddess-gold, almost, but I kept that thought to myself.

After working on her face for the entire time, I called a halt to the painting at half past three. That gave me half a glass to clean up the oils, the studio, and myself—and a quick stop by my quarters to drop the information package inside. All that actually took a quint longer, but we were still at the NordEste Design stables by half past four.

This time, Seliora rode a gelding beside me, and we chanced some of the side lanes to the northeast of Hagahl Lane. I managed to stay in the saddle, but I still felt awkward. I was certain I looked even worse than I felt.

After we returned, Seliora didn't make me groom the mare, but let the ostler do it, noting that she'd prefer not to have to bathe again before we dined, although we both did wash up.

"Now . . . you could actually ride the mare somewhere and arrive," she said.

"I'm not up for much more than that."

"No, but that's all you'll probably need."

I hoped I didn't need even that, but that was hoping against hope, I feared.

In the end we made it to Chaelya's just slightly after half past six.

We had barely stepped inside the door when Staelia hurried forward to meet us. "It's so good to see you!"

"We'd hoped to come last Samedi," I offered, "but things didn't work out. Shomyr and . . . Haelya . . . they were supposed to meet us here."

"Four of you, then? We can take care of that." Staelia immediately escorted us to a circular table in an alcove near the rear of Chaelya's. "You two sit down, and I'll have Taelia bring you each a glass of something special."

"You don't have to . . ." I began.

"We want to." With a smile, she turned.

"Is that why we can't eat here often?" I asked.

"She'd do anything for family, no matter what it cost her." Seliora paused. "Would you like to come to brunch tomorrow?"

"I'd like that very much. I do have to meet Horazt at the first glass of afternoon, and I should stop by to see my parents. I saw Khethila earlier this week. Matters aren't going well in Kherseilles."

"Ryel, you think?"

"Ryel and Rousel's lack of attention to details. The combination is anything but good, but I can't say anything about either."

"You learn failure with details is expensive in crafting."

"It's expensive in factoring as well. He just isn't ever the one to pay the full price."

"Rhenn . . . I feel sorry for him."

Sorry for Rousel? I just raised my eyebrows. I didn't want to say what I really thought.

"People like your brother go through life not understanding the true costs of anything. He didn't have to pay with pain or patience or much of anything for the love of a woman. He didn't have to learn factoring from the bottom up with a whipping or loss of coins for failure."

"That's true."

"When you don't pay, you don't know what something's worth. You only think you do, and you make mistakes. That's why I feel sorry for your brother. He may never learn the worth of what he has."

I hadn't quite thought of it that way, but I couldn't say more because I saw Shomyr and a woman following Staelia toward our table. I rose just before they arrived.

"I'm sorry we're late," offered Shomyr with an embarrassed smile. "We were delayed."

"My parents wished to talk," added the woman, who was close to a head shorter than Seliora with orange-flame hair, freckles, and a figure with curves excessive for her height. She also had an open smile and exuded warmth.

"This is Haelya. Haelya . . . Master Rhennthyl. You've met Seliora."

"I'm pleased to meet you, Haelya." I gestured for her to take the seat to my left. "We just arrived ourselves."

As soon as everyone was seated, Taelia appeared with a tray holding four goblets of an amber wine. The first goblet went to me, the second to Seliora.

"The special tonight," said Taelia, "is capon marinated in walnut oil and naranje, with special spices, then grilled and served in Father's special naranje cream sauce. We also have the flank steak especial and a poached sole . . ."

In the end, both Seliora and I ordered the special capon, with greens topped with crumbled cheese and walnuts. Shomyr ordered the flank steak and Haelya the sole.

Once Taelia retreated to the kitchen, I lifted my goblet. "I don't have a specific toast, except to family."

"To family." The others raised their goblets as well.

I sipped the wine, which held a hint of cinnamon and butter, as well as just enough sweetness so that it was not bitter. It was good, but I think I would have preferred a white Grisio.

"How is the portrait coming?" asked Shomyr, looking to his sister.

"I don't know. I haven't looked," Seliora replied.

"Portraits take time," I said, "and I can't work on it that much."

Haelya looked confused, but said nothing.

"Haelya," I asked, "how did you and Shomyr meet?"

Seliora laughed.

I glanced at her.

"It's always better to ask the woman," she replied.

"At the apothecary shop," Haelya said in a low voice. "He was always so kind and cheerful."

"And she was always so helpful, especially with the liniments for Grand-mama," added Shomyr. "Her family has four apothecary shops here in L'Ex-celsis, and they have a separate formulation building. That way, the products are the same in all the shops."

"Father will be opening a fifth before long," added Haelya, "a street be-yond the Plaza D'Nord."

At that moment, Taelia reappeared with four plates of greens, three of the mixed with walnuts and one of fall fruits over greens. That was for Haelya.

"How did you two meet, if I might ask?" Haelya looked from Seliora to me and then back to Seliora.

"It's not that mysterious," I offered. "I was a portraiturist before I became an imager, and Seliora and I attended the Samedi get-togethers at the Guild Hall. . . ."

"But I had to ask him to dance the first time." The mischievous grin ap-peared. "And the second."

"I was a slow learner."

Haelya looked puzzled, once more. "But you're a master imager."

"A very junior master imager from a very conservative wool-factoring family. Seliora has taught me a great deal."

Shomyr grinned.

Seliora raised her eyebrows.

Conversation for the rest of the evening revolved around such topics as Haelya's family and siblings, the range of crafting handled by NordEste De-sign, the relative taste of the various dinner entrees, and the early coolness of autumn.

After a lengthy and good, but not exquisite, meal, I made a coachman for hire relatively happy by paying him to deliver Haelya to her home, on one of the lanes on the lower slopes of Martradon, Shomyr and Seliora to their place, and me to the foot of the Bridge of Desires.

Once I reached my chambers and undressed, I was tired enough to fall into bed and find sleep quickly.

28

"Ryel will ruin my family, if not worse." I looked across the study to where Master Dichartyn sat behind his desk. "And the Collegium will do nothing? When I was the one attacked by Johanyr?"

"Rhennthyl, you must understand. The Collegium simply cannot allow you to destroy a thousand years of hard-fought effort that has created the only protection for imagers anywhere in the world." Master Dichartyn looked calmly at me.

"I'm supposed to sit by and watch this arrogant High Holder destroy my family one person at a time, while the Collegium does nothing?"

"We're supposed to hazard the lives of hundreds who cannot protect themselves for the sake of a few people?" countered Dichartyn. "Do what you will, but do not involve the Collegium."

"That's fine for you to say." I could feel my anger rising.

"You seem to think that you're special, Rhenn, and that the world and the Collegium should accommodate to your view. You seem to think that good deeds are always rewarded, and that evildoers are always punished, and that there's no price to be paid. . . ."

The sardonic belittling in his words touched something . . . somewhere . . . and from I knew not where flame exploded across the study. The entire study was enveloped in it.

Heat flared across my face.

I was lying in my bed . . . and the front of the armoire was aflame.

After a confused moment, I ran to the corridor and grabbed the bucket of damp sand—there were usually five on every corridor—and dashed back into my bedchamber. I immediately imaged a thin layer of sand across the armoire. Most of the flames died away.

I imaged the rest of the sand across the remaining patches of flame, until there were only a few embers. Then I used a towel wetted in the water pitcher to make sure all traces of embers and flame were gone.

Only then did I sit down for a moment, shivering and coughing.

My room stank of smoke, but I slowly rose and managed to open the louvered windows wide enough so that when I imaged cold fresh air into the bedchamber several times, the odor was bearable.

Then I imaged all the ashes and sand into the waste bin and carried it out into the corridor and down to the main level and out to the enclosed rubbish area, where I dumped it all into one of the large waste-wagon beds.

All in all, it was a good two glasses before I got back to sleep. I didn't sleep well, and I didn't sleep all that late, and I woke up wondering if I was worrying so much that I'd have more nightmares that called up imaging. That brought a shudder.

I sat up and decided to read through the information gathered by Ailphens before breakfast, although I had to light my desk lamp because the heavy clouds hovering over L'Excelsis made it seem more like the glass before dawn, and I could still smell smoke. I concentrated on the papers Seliora had given me. I had to. The nightmare just added to my concerns.

Ryel's main holding could only be described as massive—an expanse that stretched roughly some sixty milles east to west and forty north to south and included prime growing and grazing lands, more than a score of small towns, and two coal mines and one iron mine, not to mention the ironworks itself. He or his forebears had never sold any lands within the holding, and the leasehold rentals alone amounted to close to a quarter million golds annually. Based on the finance taxes paid on his earnings from the holdings in ten banques, his banking income was triple that. There was no way to calculate the revenues from the annual sales of grain and livestock, or the proceeds from the mines and ironworks, but the indications were that those exceeded the revenues from leasehold fees several times over. Ryel was also extremely conservative, with no known borrowings or debts.

Considering that an annual net income of a thousand golds a year was more than all but a few thousand people in L'Excelsis—out of more than two million—made, one obvious conclusion stood out: No one was going to be able to ruin High Holder Ryel commercially, not without destroying Solidar itself.

That didn't leave me too many options, but I'd known that all along. I just hadn't really wanted to deal with it. I kept thinking about the implications and the possibilities as I shaved, showered in water that was all too chill, and then dressed. I kept thinking all the way to the dining hall.

There, Maitre Dyana was the duty master, and since it was Solayi, she and I were the only masters at breakfast. So I sat beside her, and poured a healthy mug of steaming tea.

"I had a nightmare last night, and I awoke with the armoire on fire."

"That happens . . . occasionally." Her voice betrayed concern. "You obviously found a way to deal with it."

"I did, but . . . I have a rather charred armoire."

She laughed softly. "You're not the first. You won't be the last. Just tell Grandisyn, and they'll replace it. That's a contingency that the Collegium has anticipated."

"Do we . . . lose imagers?"

"Seldom. Those who are strong enough to do such damage are usually strong enough to contain it once their imaging wakes them." She paused. "It is a reminder of why we always sleep alone and behind leaden walls—or with the help of drugs."

I'd almost forgotten why all the quarters had lead sheets behind the walls. Almost.

I took a sip of tea, but only a sip because steam was still rising from the mug.

"How are you finding Third District, Rhenn?"

"About as I expected, maitre, with an exception or two."

"Oh?" She adjusted the silver and crimson silk scarf, almost not looking at me.

"I met one of the taudischefs—Jadhyl. He was extremely well spoken and had the air of education."

"You expected stupidity in a taudischef?"

"Hardly." I laughed. "I expected a combination of strength, cunning, and intelligence . . . and the ability to inspire others, but not refinement."

She actually paused, waiting for me to say more.

So I did. "The part of the taudis he controls looks better than the others, and some of the people actually talk to the patrollers." I thought about the enforcers in green, but didn't mention them.

"A mailed fist in a velvet glove?"

"More like a reluctant mailed fist, I think."

"He won't last long, then."

"Why not?"

"If your description is accurate, he has judgment and cares. That approach will gain him support and followers. Support and followers will make him a threat, for differing reasons, to both the Patrol and the other taudischefs."

"Are you suggesting an unspoken agenda to keep the taudis disorganized and poor?"

"I don't believe I suggested anything at all. Were I into suggestions, however, why on earth would I suggest something like that to the Collegium's liaison to the Civic Patrol?"

Keeping a polite face, rather than laughing outright, was difficult. The alternative would have been anger. Neither would have been productive, I was learning. I took refuge in another sip of tea before replying. "I beg your pardon. It was foolish of me to think that the guilds, the factors, and the High Holders would even consider measures, particularly covert measures, that effectively keep the cost of day labor lower for those without contacts or guilds. I cannot imagine that I might have thought that someone without an association with the guilds or factors might marshal political and organizing skills in a way to unsettle a political system that has worked so well for so long."

"Ill-timed imagination can be more deadly than gunpowder, or imaging," she replied dryly. "Your fancies about this taudischef might well amuse us, and in a calmer time, they might indeed entertain Master Rholyn and most members of the Council."

"Not to mention High Councilor Suyrien."

"Indeed." She served herself an omelet from the platter held by a server. "I understand these mushroom and cheese omelets are quite excellent. They're not something my cook does well."

"Nor mine," I quipped, since I had no cook and was unlikely to have one anytime soon.

"The bacon is also good."

I got the message and concentrated on eating.

Once I finished breakfast and took my leave of Maitre Dyana, I made my way back to my chambers, where I considered the difficulties facing me and which steps I should take to deal with each. Part of my problem was that I had too many separate difficulties. Could I address that multiplicity? I was beginning to do so, but I needed to speed up my efforts.

By the time I stepped out of the hack on Hagahl Lane at two quints before ninth glass, I had a better idea of what I needed to do.

As soon as I stepped to the door and dropped the polished knocker, young Bhenyt opened the door. A blast of chill wind almost pulled the heavy oak door out of his hand before he grabbed the brass lever with both hands. "Come in, Master Rhennthyl."

I hurried inside, and he closed the door quickly and shot the bolt. We walked up the stairs, but I only had to wait a few moments in the main second-level foyer before Seliora appeared. She wore a red sweater-vest over a black long-sleeved silk blouse whose shade and hue matched her black trousers and boots.

"You're not dressed for riding in this weather." Those were her first words.

I almost missed the glint in her eyes, but managed to reply, "Neither are you, not in silk, and I fear I still need instruction."

She laughed, then stepped forward and hugged me. I held on longer than I should have, but she felt so good against me, especially after the way the day—or the very early morning glasses—had gone.

When she stepped back, she said, "I was serious, if not about today."

"You foresaw me riding in the rain?"

"In bad weather," she admitted.

"It could come to that. If you and your family will agree, I may have to borrow a horse."

"I'm glad you mentioned me." The smile I loved appeared. "The mare is mine."

"I do love propertied women." I grinned.

"Just for that, you can sit next to Methyr . . . or the twins."

"If you sit across from me . . ."

She didn't carry out on the threat, thankfully, but I did end up between Aegina and Betara, both of whom were most interested in the portrait of Seliora. I really didn't like discussing unfinished work, but I didn't want to be rude.

"When will it be done?" asked Betara.

"Several months," I replied.

"What do you think about it, Seliora?" asked Aegina.

"I haven't looked at it yet," Seliora replied. "I don't like people looking at my designs until they're done, and Rhenn deserves the same courtesy."

My only serious question to Seliora's mother was about the taudis. "Do you know anything about two taudischefs—Youdh and Jadhyl?"

"No one knows much about Youdh. They say that few have ever crossed him and lived. He's been taudischef for close to ten years now. Jadhyl . . ." She frowned. "He's an outlander, but Mama Diestra says he's the most trustworthy of the taudischefs. He won't tell us much, though, but he's planning to be taudischef for a long time."

"Why do you say that?"

"He goes out of his way not to make enemies, and those he can't charm, and who continue to cause trouble for him . . . they vanish." Betara smiled ironically.

"A very polite local despot."

"Less of a despot than most, and he doesn't let his men take liberties with the locals."

"What about Youdh?"

"He's more like the older taudischefs. He doesn't take slights easily, and he doesn't think much of women or those less fortunate."

In the end, I did enjoy the meal, as much for Seliora's presence as anything, but I left while most everyone was still at the table, although I didn't see Grandmama Diestra anywhere.

The clouds outside were darkening when I hailed a hack, but because I'd caught the coach earlier than I'd calculated, I had the driver drop me almost directly outside Third District station. Then I hurried inside through a rain so fine, but so wind-driven, that the small droplets stung my face and neck like needles.

The antechamber was empty except for Sansolt, the patroller on the duty desk. I'd only passed a few words with him over the past weeks. Taciturn as he'd been, he'd seemed solid.

"Master Rhennthyl . . . you aren't supposed to be accompanying someone today, are you? No one told me—"

I shook my head. "I have to meet someone near here, but I was thinking, What do you know about the taudischefs?"

Sansolt glanced toward the door, although no one had entered the station, then cocked his head to one side. "You hear a lot. Some of it might be true. Some might not. There's four right now in the taudis—you're talking about our taudis, right?"

I nodded.

"Horazt is the new one on the west end. Grausyn and Lykyt patrol that round. They haven't had any trouble, but the equalifiers and the Temple types don't like him, and that could be trouble before long. The chief before him disappeared just before the riots. The east end, there are two, Jadhyl and Deyalt, but Deyalt might as well be the subchief because he goes along with whatever Jadhyl wants. But you're patrolling with Alsoran, aren't you?"

"I am. Jadhyl talked to us last week. He said the toughs who attacked us weren't his."

Sansolt frowned. "Alsoran said that. Guess I believe it, but . . ."

"You think Youdh was trying to set up Jadhyl or Deyalt?"

"I wouldn't put it past him. Don't know as there's anyone with a good word to say about him."

"So why is he still taudischef?"

Sansolt laughed. "Anyone who crosses him ends up dead real quick."

"Have you ever seen him?"

"No one's ever seen him. I mean, no patroller ever has. Not that I ever heard."

"Has the captain ever met any of the taudischefs? To get the plaques on the table, face up, so to speak?"

"When he was a lieutenant, he met with Worazt, the taudischef before Youdh. That's what Melyor said, anyway. Didn't do much good. The next week some toughs tried to take out a patrol on rounds. The captain hasn't said anything about meeting any of them since."

"Thank you. Everything I can learn helps."

"Sir . . . some say you know Horazt."

"I do, but not from working with the Civic Patrol. He brought his nephew to Imagisle on a day when I was on duty. The boy is an imager. He's very young, but he has promise."

I didn't like the idea that someone was circulating word that I knew Horazt, because I'd told no one. The most obvious answer was that Youdh had gotten word to Harraf—or someone—at the station because of the time I'd openly walked through the taudis with Horazt.

"An imager . . . from the taudis?"

"Imagers can be born into any family. My father's a wool factor, but I've known several imagers whose parents were High Holders."

I could tell that surprised Sansolt, but he only nodded and said, "Hadn't thought of that, but you say so, it must be."

"Thank you again." I smiled and turned, heading out of the station.

The wind and rain were stronger as I walked up Fuosta toward South Middle and then east to Dugalle. The Puryon Temple ahead seemed empty, but I wouldn't have been surprised if people were watching.

A bell struck, the sound coming from an anomen I couldn't see, announcing the first glass of the afternoon. Of course, Horazt was nowhere to be seen.

I kept moving, walking a ways east on South Middle, and then back, back and forth, for what seemed like glasses, but was probably closer to two quints, before a figure emerged out of the mistlike hard rain.

"Afternoon, Master Rhennthyl."

"Good afternoon, Horazt."

"You paid coin to get a message to me. Must be urgent." He turned and began to walk westward, back toward the Midroad.

I took two quick steps to catch him, then matched his pace. "It might be. Youdh's put out the word that you don't like the equalifiers and the Temple priests."

"So?"

"It doesn't sound like Youdh's any sort of friend of yours."

"Taudischefs aren't friends with other taudischefs."

"You know what I mean."

"Not much I can do about what he feels."

I waited to say more until we passed an old man trudging eastward. He didn't even look in our direction, just kept his head down against the fine rain.

"Do your men have something that identifies them as your taudis-men? A kind of belt buckle, a certain cloak, like the green cloaks that Jadhyl's men wear?"

"You think I should tell you?"

"I'm not asking what it is. I'm thinking that each taudischef's men carry or wear something like that. I'd like to know if you know what Youdh's men use, or if Youdh sends messages with a special seal or sign."

Horazt laughed harshly. "The only message he sends is a slashed throat, with a wide-bladed dagger through the voice box. That's how he deals with squeals."

"No tattoos for his men? No jackets of a special color?"

"His enforcers wear purple jackets. That's only the top ones."

"Can you get me—"

"You don't think—"

"Not a jacket. Just a small piece of the material." I held my fingers barely a digit apart. "Just a shred like that. I'll pay a gold for it." Once I had it, I could always image something just a bit larger.

A sly grin crossed his face. "Might be worth the risk at that. If I can get it, I'll send it with Chelya when she goes to see Shault. You and me, we been seen too much together."

"I'll be there. No one will think that's strange for her first visit." I'd have to be there, because I didn't want Shault to see what I had in mind. "Do you want me to give her the gold?"

"You can owe me, Master Rhennthyl. You're good for it." He slowed and looked at me. "You really think Shault can make a life as an imager?"

"He has the talent, and he has more chances than anyone I know of from the taudis, but he has to want it. It's not easy for a taudis-kid because the best imagers are those no one sees."

"You're good, or you wouldn't be a master, and people know who you are."

"I've also been shot at and attacked more times than any other master, and I could have died twice. I wouldn't want Shault to go through that."

"He'll want to follow you."

I didn't bother hiding the sigh. "We're all afraid of that, but we'll help him all we can."

"His grandfather was quiet. So was his uncle. They both died young."

"I understand. Quiet doesn't always work in the taudis. I can only tell you that I'll do what I can."

"That's all anyone can ask." Horazt raised his hand. "Later. Don't get too wet." He turned and crossed South Middle, walking into a narrow lane on the other side and disappearing into the misty rain.

I kept walking until I was on the Midroad. Eventually, I managed to hail a coach for hire.

By the time I reached my parents' house and walked up under the portico roof, my cloak was more than a little damp. I lifted the knocker and let it drop twice before the door opened.

Mother stood there. "Rhenn! I thought it might be you. Come in before you get any wetter." Her eyes went over me. "From the look of your cloak, I don't know that you could."

Once inside, I immediately shed the cloak.

"Dear, let me hang that up in the kitchen. The stove is still hot."

"Thank you. Are you here alone?"

"Oh, no. Your father's in the parlor. Khethila's over at Brennai's this afternoon, but you did see her last week when we weren't here." Mother bustled toward the family parlor and the kitchen beyond.

As I followed, I ignored her attempt to inject guilt into the conversation. "I can't always come every Samedi. I was painting until late yesterday."

"Whose portrait?" asked Father from his chair, setting down the book he had been reading.

"I've been working on several, but the important one is Master Rholyn's. He's the Collegium councilor."

"Khethila said that you were working hard." Mother stopped at the door to the kitchen. "Can I get you some hot mulled wine or some tea?"

"Tea would be good. I can only stay a glass or so."

"The kettle's still warm. It shouldn't take long." Mother scurried into the kitchen.

I settled into the chair across from Father, grateful for the warmth from the hearth stove. "I haven't seen you for a bit. Is there anything new happening?" I doubted that Father would say anything about the problems in Kherseilles.

"There is one thing." Father beamed. "That dinner we had with Veblynt and Ferdinand last month actually led to a contract from the Navy. One of the supply commanders said that Veblynt had recommended me, and he asked me to bid on a large contract. That was several weeks ago. On Meredi, I received notice that the bid had been accepted." Father smiled. "That was most welcome."

"Will it be profitable?"

"A solid profit's to be had, but the margin on military contracts is lower. Always has been, but it's not to be sneezed at."

"No contract backed by the Council is to be ignored," Mother added, returning with a mug of tea.

I took the mug and held it under my chin, letting the steam warm my face for a moment before taking a sip. "Thank you."

"You're welcome, dear."

I turned back to Father. "I suppose Veblynt showed up on Jeudi to congratulate you?" I kept my tone idle.

Father frowned. "On Vendrei, actually." After a pause, he went on. "He congratulated me on getting the bid, but he also said that you were to be equally congratulated for your efforts in dealing with his wife's most distant relations."

Mother looked up sharply. "You didn't mention that, dear."

"I'm certain I did, Maelyna."

"Perhaps you did." Mother's tone indicated that he had not, but that she was not going to make an issue of it—not at the moment. Instead, she looked to me. "What did Veblynt mean, do you think?"

"I don't know. I suspect that he was referring to my avoiding problems with the daughter of High Holder Ryel."

"Why would there be problems?"

"Iryela is most determined, extremely good-looking, and to be as safe as possible, she needs a husband who cannot inherit from her. Imagers fit those criteria. By not angering her, and by choosing Seliora, I hoped to avoid involvements of that sort." All that I said was true, if somewhat misleading.

For whatever reason, Veblynt had steered the wool contract to Father. While I did not know the reason, I had the feeling that it was strictly to give me time to deal with Ryel . . . or at the least to make Ryel work harder to ruin me and my family. Then, it might have been to force Ryel into making a mistake. I had strong doubts that it was merely to help Father, but how could I tell? I wasn't about to ask Veblynt . . . not now, at least.

"Seliora is beautiful and well endowed . . . especially coming from a crafting family," Mother offered.

What she really meant was that she was still surprised to find a Pharsi girl who was as beautiful and well off as Seliora. She was also suggesting that I might have done better to look more closely at Iryela.

"Indeed she is, and her brothers are far more welcoming than Iryela's brothers would have been. High Holders would prefer not to have imagers privy, even indirectly, to their family and their affairs."

"That's a pity," Mother said. "Is this . . . heiress . . . attractive?"

"She's quite attractive, if in a cold and calculating fashion," I replied. "You know I don't do well with that." I took another sip of the tea.

"Maelyna, even I know that Rhennthyl needs someone warm and kind, especially since he's become an imager. All the gold in Solidar doesn't warm a home or a bed."

That comment from my father surprised me, although it shouldn't have, because, for all his bluster at times, he'd always been appreciative of my mother, and seldom said anything unkind. He also didn't tolerate anyone else saying anything negative about her.

"You and Seliora haven't had dinner with us recently," Mother said.

I had to think about that, but she was right. It had been over a month.

"You could come next Samedi. Culthyn has never met Seliora, you know?"

"Could we make it for sixth glass?"

"Of course, dear."

"I'll have to send her a note." Seliora had agreed that we'd go out, and I hoped she wouldn't mind. "Plan on it, and I'll let you know if there's a problem."

"It would be nice to get to know her better."

That might well be, but it would be nerve-racking for me. I just smiled.

"Will you keep painting?" Mother asked. "Khethila mentioned something . . ."

"I've finished one portrait. That's of the head maitre of the Collegium. They hung it in the receiving hall. . . ." I went on to talk about Maitre Rholyn's portrait, but not Seliora's. It wasn't far enough along that I felt comfortable discussing it yet, although I'd certainly have to by the next Samedi.

29

Lundi morning, Clovyl canceled the running, but not the exercises and spar-ring, because so much water had pooled all over the isle and because tree limbs had fallen everywhere in the high winds that hadn't even awakened me during the night. I hurried through cleaning up and breakfast so that I could post the note to Seliora about our change in dinner plans, run down Gran-disyn to request a replacement for my armoire, and so I could get to Third District station earlier than usual. Grandisyn didn't even seem surprised, but he did say it would be a few days.

I made it to the station early only because I had the use of a duty coach. I also carried a small bag that held the frayed and worn brown cloak and brown-and-black plaid cap. I didn't see many hacks on the road. Captain Har-raf must have switched to supervising the late shift, because Lieutenant Warydt looked up from talking to a patroller on desk duty and nodded to me as I en-tered the station and put the bag in the square cubby that had been assigned to me.

I didn't see Alsoran, but that was secondary for the moment. I was look-ing for the pair who had the round covering that part of the taudis controlled by Youdh. It didn't take long to run down Melyor and Slausyl, although I only knew them by sight and in passing.

Slausyl was about my height, with blue eyes, blond hair, and a round boyish face on which the deep lines on his forehead seemed out of place. Melyor was shorter, squatter, with washed-out and limp brown hair and sad hazel eyes.

"A moment, if you would," I offered as I stepped toward them.

"What did you want to know, sir?" asked Melyor.

"Whatever you can tell me about Youdh. Alsoran may have told you what happened . . ."

"Yeah," replied Slausyl. "It doesn't make much sense."

"About Youdh?" I prompted.

"We've never really seen him—except at a distance—if he was even the one. He looks to be big, but not so tall as Alsoran, maybe not quite so broad, either."

"Does he always have guards with him?"

"You aren't thinking . . ." Melyor glanced to Slausyl.

I shook my head. "It seems to me that an imager or a Civic Patroller's taking out a taudischef would just create a bigger problem. I'm just trying to learn enough so that things make more sense to me."

"Sometimes the toughs with him wear purple jackets," said Slausyl. "There's always one in purple."

"Probably his enforcers," I speculated. "How does he handle enemies?"

"Has 'em killed. How else?" asked Melyor.

"But is there anything to show that's why?"

Both patrollers exchanged glances.

"Why else would they be dead?" Slausyl finally asked.

"Lots of reasons." I paused. "I've heard that the Tiempran priests—the ones who believe in equality—they'll cut their heretics into two equal halves. The High Holders leave silver knots to make sure people know why something happened. Does Youdh do anything like that?"

"Oh . . . that," replied Melyor. "Don't know as it always happens, but we've found a couple of bodies in the middle of where two lanes cross with their throat cut and a dull knife through their voice box. That's for squealers."

"I'd heard that Youdh makes deals with the Puryon Temple priests."

"That'd be hard to say, sir," said Melyor. "Sometimes one of the advocates that the priests use will show up in court for someone that might belong to Youdh. But who could tell whether they were working for the priests or Youdh?"

"Or both," I added.

Melyor looked at me, as it to ask if I had any more questions.

"What do you think will happen if a conscription team enters your round?"

Both patrollers laughed harshly.

"Nothing Namer good, sir," Slausyl finally replied.

"Do you know when they will?" asked Melyor.

"They don't tell anyone, especially not imagers . . . or patrollers. Since I'm considered both right now . . ." I let the words hang.

"Too bad."

"Exactly." I nodded. "Thank you both."

"Our pleasure, sir," replied Melyor.

No sooner had I stepped away from the two patrollers and turned to look for Alsoran than Lieutenant Warydt stepped away from the duty desk and began to walk toward me.

I was getting leery of Patrol officers. Whenever one approached me, the results were seldom good, but I smiled and said, "Lieutenant."

"Master Rhennthyl . . . how would you feel about accompanying Lyonyt next week on the round you've been doing? That would be a real help. We just found out that Alsoran's been made a patroller first, and he's being transferred to Fifth District. We won't get a replacement by then, and it might be longer."

"I'd be happy to help." What else could I have said?

"The captain and I appreciate that very much. Thank you." With a smile, he turned and headed toward his study.

By then, Alsoran had arrived, and I walked to join him. I didn't say anything about his pending promotion until we were outside and walking down to Quierca. "I understand congratulations are in order."

Alsoran offered an embarrassed smile. "I guess I was fortunate."

"I'm sure you deserve it. What have you heard about Fifth District?"

"It won't break my heart to spend some time there. That's the area that includes Plaza D'Este, and there's no taudis or taudis-types around. I won't have as many stories to tell, but that's just fine." Alsoran grinned.

"I'm glad for you."

"Not as glad as my wife."

We'd walked more than five blocks southeast on Quierca, just about two blocks short of where the round started, when I noticed a taudis-tough leaning against the wall. He made no attempt to conceal the fact that he was watching us.

"Do you know him?" I asked Alsoran.

"I don't recall seeing him before, but that's Youdh's territory."

The man said nothing, but I could feel the tough's eyes on my back after we passed. A little more than a block farther along was another tough, leaning against a stone gatepost. Like the first, he watched, but said nothing.

"They're looking at you, sir," observed Alsoran.

They were the only taudis-toughs we saw all day, and the only difficulty we had was with a smash-and-grab by a muddled elver in late afternoon. I had to chase him a block, but I couldn't claim much credit because he looked back at me and ran into a lamppost and went down. The old woman got her bag and wallet back, and the elver went off to gaol, and we rode the pickup wagon back to the station.

After I finished the round report with Alsoran, I reclaimed my bag and then walked up Fuosta and out to the Midroad, where I waited nearly half a glass to catch a hack. The driver didn't say much, but I could sense he didn't like taking me to the intersection of Fedre and East River Road, because he'd end up on the wrong side to pick up fares. While I was in the hack I donned the brown cloak and plaid cap and slipped my visored uniform cap into the bag.

Once I'd paid the driver, and I did give him a few extra coppers, I dodged through the welter of coaches and wagons, and the occasional rider, back across East River Road. As soon as I turned up Fedre, I began to build concealment shields, just enough so that anyone who looked in my direction would see a workman in mismatched cloak and cap, without really picking up much more than that.

The sky was hazy and overcast, and the sun was only a faint glow in the west, already dropping behind the buildings on the west side of Fedre. When I neared Patrol headquarters, I eased closer to the buildings and began to increase the concealment of my shields. When I reached the main entrance I eased back against the stone wall and waited.

Nearly a glass passed, and while I saw both the commander and the subcommander leave, I didn't see Lieutenant Mardoyt. Had he taken the day off? Or was he on leave? I couldn't afford to ask about such. So I decided to keep waiting and watching.

Close to two quints passed before I saw him hurry down the steps and turn toward the river. I followed, maintaining concealment shields and trying to stay close, but not too close. The fading light helped, or at least I thought it did, because no one even seemed to see me.

When Mardoyt reached East River Road, he stopped and began to signal for a hack.

Once Mardoyt was inside, I swung up on the luggage rack in the rear, hoping that the trip wouldn't be long or rough . . . and that the driver wouldn't take undue notice of the extra weight.

The coach followed East River to the Avenue D'Artisans, then headed east, but only for a mille or so, when it came to a halt. When I heard the coach door open, I slipped off the luggage rack, but waited at the rear of the coach where, even had I not been using shields, it would have been impossible for the driver to see me.

Mardoyt glanced around, then began to walk up the side street, whose name I couldn't make out in the dimness. He turned right at the second cross street, which had to be Saelio, although this portion of the street was a good two milles, if not more, from the part that bordered the taudis near Third Station, and somewhere southwest of Sudroad.

Both sides of the street were filled with modest row houses, either duplexes or triplexes. They were established enough that the trees lining the narrow strip next to the walk were older and would offer considerable shade during the day. Almost all were oaks.

Mardoyt walked up the walk of the fifth house, the left side of a duplex, which had a covered porch on the east side. A girl opened the door, and Mardoyt stepped inside.

I moved under a tall and not quite ancient sycamore, one of the few softwoods, and leaned against the trunk.

From what I'd seen of Mardoyt's schedule during the time I'd been at headquarters, if he were meeting with those outside the Patrol, it most likely had to occur after he left headquarters or before he arrived. I knew very few people, except imagers working for Master Dichartyn, who were that active in the early morning, and I was wagering that if I followed Mardoyt long enough, I'd learn something.

Although I watched the house for close to two glasses, no one entered or left, and I finally walked back to the avenue and waited another half glass to pick up a hack. It cost me double because it was so late.

When I got out of the duty coach outside Third District station on Mardi morning, the pale blue sky was clear and crisp, and the wind had died away. I nodded to Melyor and Slausyl as they headed out of the station, and to Zellyn, who was just inside the station door. He gave me a smile.

Alsoran arrived right after I stowed my bag in my cubby, and we immediately walked out of the station and up Fuosta to South Middle. Well before Dugalle, we passed the first of three toughs, all on the edge of Youdh's "territory," and all of whom watched me as we passed. I thought I caught a hint of purple under the nondescript dark brown cloak of the second tough.

Once we were past the third tough—who was barely visible and indistinct from where he watched from within an alleyway—and started on the round proper, Alsoran cleared his throat. He didn't quite look at me as he spoke. "Looks as you did something that Youdh didn't like. Any idea what that might have been?"

"The only thing I've done recently is ask some of the other patrollers what they know about Youdh. I asked Melyor and Slausyl because that's their round."

"Good men, and they do their best." He paused again. "No one else?" His tone was casual.

"I did ask Sansolt about Youdh on Solayi. He was on the desk."

"Sansolt knows a great deal. He talks to everyone."

The flatness of Alsoran's tone suggested even more than his words.

"I'll have to keep that in mind. Is there anyone else you think I should talk to who might know why Youdh's men are watching me?"

Alsoran didn't speak for several steps, then fingered his chin. "You know, Master Rhennthyl, I can't think of anyone who'd be helpful besides the ones you've already talked to. No patroller worth his stipend wants to get too close to the taudischefs. Folks believe the worst. The taudischefs think you're out to get them somehow, and everyone else thinks you're getting something from them. No way to come out ahead."

I laughed. "It's too bad, but it makes sense. It seems to me that a taudischef like Jadhyl wants the same thing as the Patrol. He wants things to be orderly and go smoothly."

"He also wants to line his wallet."

"That's true, but who doesn't? The question is how people do it. Youdh likes to kill people if they don't pay him. Does Jadhyl? You've patrolled here. What do you think?"

"Jadhyl will . . . I think, only if he has to. Someone's disappearing every week around Youdh. That's what Melyor says. Is it true? Who knows? We don't find bodies, and that's fine with the captain."

I had doubts about that policy, but I wasn't the captain.

Meredi was again comparatively uneventful, although we did have to investigate a break-in at one of the bistros. A side of beef was missing, along with flour and oil and an empty cashbox that had held only a handful of coppers, but it had happened in the middle of the night, and the thief hadn't left many traces except where he'd pried the bars away from a window opening onto the alley.

Since we didn't bring in any malefactors near the end of our round, I was able to leave the station close to fourth glass. Again, I hailed a hack to take me to Patrol headquarters. This time, I didn't put on the cloak and cap in the coach, but left them in the bag. I didn't slink around, either, but had the driver deliver me right to the building. I actually walked right into headquarters to the charging desk. Gulyart was still there.

"Working the late glasses again?"

Gulyart looked up from the charging sheet. "Master Rhennthyl." He shook his head. "It takes longer by myself. I heard you were still at Third District."

"I am, but I thought I'd stop by and see how things were going here."

Gulyart shrugged. "Same as always." He looked at me. "Maybe not quite. We're not getting as many prisoners from Third District."

"I wouldn't know. I've been walking rounds with patrollers, mostly in the taudis areas. The patrollers haven't said much about numbers."

"There aren't as many." He gave a crooked smile. "Could be that some of them don't want to try anything with an imager."

I shook my head. "From what I've seen, offenders don't think about patrollers or imagers."

"They don't, but the taudischefs might."

I just shrugged. What else could I have done? My next words were far lower. "Has anything changed here?"

He was the one to shake his head. Then he glanced toward the closed door that led to the upper level and Mardoyt's study. After a moment, he asked, "Have you heard about when they might send in the conscription teams?"

"No. They wouldn't tell me or anyone I know. I'd have to believe that it won't be long, but who knows?"

"Be nice if they'd let us know."

We both knew that the Army and Navy would do what they'd do.

At that moment, the door from the upper level opened, and Baluzt stepped out, hurrying toward the charging desk. "Gulyart, do you have the charging sheets—"

He actually stopped in midstride, and his mouth opened, if for just a moment before he smiled. "Master Rhennthyl, I didn't expect to see you here."

"I missed headquarters," I replied cheerfully.

"It'll be another quint," Gulyart said to Baluzt.

"I'll be back then." Baluzt nodded to me. "It's good to see you, Master Rhennthyl." Then he turned and headed back through the doorway to the staircase, closing it behind him.

I had no doubts at all that Baluzt was reporting my presence to Lieutenant Mardoyt, and that suited my purposes.

"I won't keep you, Gulyart, but I did want to stop by and see how you were doing." I smiled, not out of calculation, because I liked Gulyart and thought he was doing the best he could.

"I'm glad you did, sir."

Once I left headquarters, I raised concealment shields and waited.

While I still waited close to two quints, Mardoyt left headquarters close to a glass earlier than he had on Lundi. I used the same technique, holding on to the luggage rack at the back of the hack. I managed to get the brown cloak out of the bag and on, and to switch caps before we reached Mardoyt's destination. This time, the lieutenant took the hack two blocks farther from the river on the Avenue D'Artisans before leaving the coach. There he stopped by a flower stall and purchased a large bunch of yellow chrysanthemums and then walked, whistling cheerfully, back down the avenue and then to his house.

Several times he paused, looking back. Once he shook his head.

Yet . . . I didn't have the feeling he was looking for me, or at least not in my direction. I looked around as well, but I didn't see anything. Who would have seen me through shields?

A girl, perhaps the one who had opened the door the night before, stood waiting for him in the twilight on the porch. Holding the flowers in one hand, he gave her a hug with his free arm. They entered the house together.

Because it was earlier in the evening than when I had seen the dwelling the night before, I had a better chance to study it. Although it was a row duplex, it was a good fifteen yards in width, and deeper than that, rising three stories. The third level was probably cramped and smaller, but the dormers suggested that there was at least one usable room there.

Whether the lieutenant leased the dwelling or actually owned it, given what I recalled about Patrol pay scales, he would have had difficulty paying for such lodging, unless he'd inherited money or had other income. I was wagering on the latter, based on what I'd observed when I'd been assisting on the charging desk and observing the justice hearings, but I did need to get a copy of the pay scales and see if Seliora could have her advocate find out who owned the house in which Mardoyt lived.

Once more, I watched the dwelling for more than two glasses, until the lamps were extinguished on the lower levels and only a faint trace of light escaped from one room on the second floor.

On Meredi morning, right after breakfast, I stopped by the receiving hall and asked Beleart when he expected Master Dichartyn to return.

"Not for several days, sir. He didn't say when exactly. He said it would be late this week."

"Thank you."

I headed for Master Schorzat's study, hoping to find him in—and I did.

"Rhennthyl . . . what can I do for you?" He did not rise from behind his writing desk.

"Sir, I was wondering if you happened to know where I could lay my hands on the pay schedules for civic patrollers."

"Pay schedules?"

"I'm looking into something, and Master Dichartyn said I needed proof. Part of the proof happens to be what a civic patroller makes."

"If you're looking for proof of bribes, pay alone won't do it. They'll claim legacies, inheritances from widowed uncles without children, even gaming wins."

"That may be, sir, but I have to start somewhere."

Schorzat nodded. "I'll have a copy made and left in your letter box." He paused. "By the way, I do like the portrait you did of Thelya. I hadn't realized you'd been the one to paint it."

For a moment, I wasn't sure what he was talking about, but then realized that it was the portrait of his niece, Thelya D'Scheorzyl. "She was a very sweet girl."

"She still is."

"Do you have any idea when the conscription teams will begin their canvass of L'Excelsis, sir?"

"They started in the western quarter, out beyond Council Hill, on Lundi, but they don't say where they'll go next. It usually takes a good week for each area."

"Thank you, sir."

"You're welcome." As soon as he finished speaking, his eyes dropped to the stack of papers before him.

I slipped out of the study and eased the door closed behind me. Then I hurried toward the duty coach station, still carrying the bag with the brown cloak and plaid cap. Because two wagons had collided and created a welter of carriages around the intersection of the Avenue D'Artisans and Sudroad, it was slightly after seventh glass when I arrived at Third District station.

Alsoran was waiting outside the station. In the shade, his breath almost steamed. "I was wondering . . ."

"Two wagons collided on the avenue," I explained. "We couldn't get to the side roads for a bit."

"Both teamsters blaming the other, I imagine."

"I wouldn't be surprised, but I didn't try to find out." I matched my steps to Alsoran's, and we headed toward Quierca.

Unlike Mardi, there were no taudis-toughs watching as we walked down Quierca past the section of the taudis that Youdh claimed as his. Why would they be watching one day and not the next?

I didn't have all that much time to think about it, because the day was busy. The same thief as the one who had burgled the silversmith—or one using the same methods—had broken into a tavern just off the Avenue D'Artisans, and as soon as we finished talking to the owner, we had to subdue an older elver who'd mixed beer and weed and who'd decided that he wanted to pull shutters off a tinsmith's shop.

After that, a teamster on a wagon carrying lamp oil broke an axle, and one of the barrels rolled off and smashed. With oil in the gutters, we had to make sure no one was smoking or had anything that would cause a fire until the fire brigade arrived with a sand wagon and a clean-up crew. We ate quickly at Florena's, and with the gut-aches I had for the next three glasses from her special ragout, I decided I never wanted to eat there again.

On the second round of the afternoon, we happened on two youngsters having at each other with knives, but I flattened one with a shield and Alsoran disarmed the other before they had more than a minor cut or two. One of Deyalt's enforcers showed up, and we let him escort them off. Neither one of us wanted to charge them. Someone might have to later, but it was worth the risk, given what I'd seen about Jadhyl and Deyalt. If they didn't learn, they'd end up dead, or on a penal crew for life.

All in all, it was a long, long day, and I wasn't looking forward to tailing Mardoyt yet another night, but Baluzt's reaction on Mardi had convinced me that I was on the right track. So, after more than a half glass of writing out reports, I took a hack back down to East River Road and Fedre and donned my disguise on the way.

For better or worse, Mardoyt left headquarters later that evening and only took a hack as far as he had on Lundi. Once more, I rode on the rear luggage rack, but there was a trunk with a rounded lid fastened there, and I was more than glad when the hack finally stopped.

I eased up next to a post in order to allow my shields to blend me into the background because Mardoyt didn't immediately cross the avenue, but stood there for several moments, glancing around. Once he crossed, he didn't look back, not once, but he didn't rush, either, just walked deliberately down two blocks or so and then up on Saelio toward his dwelling. I let him have more space, now that I knew where he was headed.

That turned out to be wise, because slouching against a gatepost, across Saelio, was a figure in a black cloak, and that figure looked to be a taudis-tough, although I couldn't tell if he happened to be one of those who had been watching me on Mardi.

"Over there," hissed someone.

I turned in the direction of the sound, to see another tough, one who looked to be wearing a purple jacket under yet another nondescript black cloak. The second tough was looking in my direction, but not at me. I took another step, and at the scuff of my boots on the sandy stone, his head turned more toward me.

Then something twisted at my shields, and I staggered for a moment. Another imager? After me? I strengthened my shields and tried to determine from where the attack had come, just as something exploded against my shields, rocking me back again.

Whoever the other imager was, he was powerful, but I could sense the lack of technique. I dropped behind a scraggly hedge, trying to see through the dimness. Could it have been the second tough?

Dust flared into a column, just on the other side of the hedge.

"Now!"

With that single command came a flurry of shots, all aimed at the dust column. Most missed, but several hit my shields, and one twisted me around, and I sprawled on the ground behind the hedge.

I decided not to move, and held my shields as I watched and waited. After a time, perhaps half a quint, I heard footsteps. Then I could see the first tough moving through the late twilight across the street and toward me. He held a pistol.

Given his intent, I didn't wait any longer, but imaged air into his brain and heart vessels. He convulsed and pitched forward onto the walk. The pistol dropped onto the dirt beside the walk. I grabbed the weapon, aimed it at his head, and fired.

After that single shot, I heard boots on stone, running, followed by voices, and someone yelling.

I got to my feet, dropped the pistol by the dead tough, and eased around the hedge to the street. The second tough had vanished. So had Mardoyt, and his house was unlit.

Holding concealment shields, I walked back toward the avenue, thinking about what had just happened. Mardoyt had known he was being followed, and he'd gotten word to Youdh. That didn't surprise me, but what did was that one of the toughs, seemingly one of those working for Youdh, was an imager of sorts, and had the ability to detect another imager.

That was anything but good, especially since Mardoyt had to know that I was looking into his activities.

I kept walking until I reached the avenue, where I turned westward, still watching around me and thinking. I'd been shot at, attacked by an unknown imager, and I still had no proof of anything at all—even though I knew Mardoyt was connected to Youdh and the unknown imager. I thought about reporting the imager to Master Dichartyn . . . and decided against it. First, I didn't have the kind of proof he wanted. Second, I didn't even know where to start as far as identifying the imager, and third, Master Dichartyn wasn't even around, and I wasn't about to report so little to anyone else. Besides, then I'd have to explain too much about what I was doing . . . because I didn't have any real proof to back that up, either.

Even though I'd walked all the way back to Imagisle on Meredi night, trying to puzzle out what I should do next, and arrived footsore and tired, I didn't sleep all that well. My dreams were filled with imagers I could not see, and whenever I tried to move toward them, Master Dichartyn appeared between me and what I could not see. I tried to image a light, and he imaged darkness around it. When I woke on Jeudi, I definitely had the feeling that I was not only fighting against Mardoyt and Harraf and the unknown taudis imager, but the Collegium itself—and that didn't even take into account my problems with High Holder Ryel and his efforts to ruin me and my family. At that thought, I had to wonder what Ryel might be planning next . . . but I had to deal with the Civic Patrol problems first.

After breakfast, I did remember to check my letter box, where I found two items. One was the copy of the Civic Patrol pay schedules and the second was an envelope note addressed to me in Seliora's handwriting. On seeing the pay schedule, I had the definite feeling that I should not have asked for it, although I couldn't have said why, and not just because of what Master Schorzat had said. I slipped it into the inside pocket of my waistcoat and opened Seliora's note, not without some qualms.

> Dear Rhenn,
> I am so pleased that your mother wants us for dinner. I hope that you have already accepted. I look forward to seeing you on Samedi.

The closing read, "With love."

I took a deep breath. I hadn't really expected anything else, but . . . I also knew I wasn't necessarily that good at predicting how women might react. Then I hurried back to my quarters and dashed off a quick note to Mother to confirm that we would be there, rushed to the reception hall, because Beleart could post the note from there for me, and hurried to the duty coach.

All in all, I made it to the station just before seventh glass, but not before Alsoran.

"Good morning, Master Rhennthyl."

"Good morning." I glanced back toward the study doors of the captain and the lieutenant, but didn't see either. "Has anything happened?"

"According to the duty desk, it was real quiet in the taudis last night."

That didn't surprise me. At least some of the toughs had been elsewhere. "Let's hope it continues that way until you get to Fifth District."

Alsoran smiled and turned toward the door. "I wouldn't be arguing against that."

"I didn't think you would."

The first and outer round was as quiet as the night before had been reported. Then, halfway through the second round, we heard screams and found an elver trying to batter his way into a dwelling that wasn't his. It took both of us to subdue him and keep him restrained until the pickup wagon carted him off.

After that, there were more people on the streets and lanes, and two times when older women reported grab-and-runs. We couldn't find either youth.

Lunch came, and we ate, and then went back to walking the round.

In midafternoon, I happened to ask Alsoran how he'd worked out the way he'd developed of patrolling the round.

He grinned. "Just did."

"You must have put some thought into the order."

"All things have an order. That's true. My papa told me that time after time when I was little. You do things in the wrong order, and you run into trouble. If you try and it doesn't work, maybe you forgot to do something first. He was a great one for doing it step-by-step." Alsoran laughed. "Sometimes that works, and sometimes it doesn't. It's always worth trying."

I nodded slowly. That didn't seem to be my problem.

"The thing I learned here on the Patrol is that sometimes you do the opposite."

"The opposite?" I had an idea what he meant, but I wanted to see if I did.

"You put in too many steps." He shook his head. "Take elvers who've gone crazed. The procedures say that we're supposed to tell them to halt and that we're patrollers. There's no elver who's overweeded that'll hear anything. You try to talk to them, and before you can say three words, they're either running from you or at you. You have to know what steps to skip."

As we finished the last round of the day, Alsoran's words kept echoing in my thoughts. That could have been because Master Dichartyn—all the maitres, really—had pressed so hard on me the need to proceed logically, to go through all the steps, one by one. There were more than a few problems with that. First, any logical progression would lead back to me. Second, no matter how hard I searched, I would never have the kind of absolute proof that Maitres Jhulian and Dichartyn had kept stressing. But . . . that worked two ways. And it meant that I never should have asked for the pay schedule.

It also meant that there was little point in following Mardoyt until I made another set of preparations. So I just took a hack back to Imagisle.

As I sat in my quarters before dinner, I continued to think about Mardoyt. I knew that he was changing charges, even eliminating the records of any charges in some cases, or sending back notes that the charges had been dropped. He was also connected to taudis-toughs and a taudischef, most likely Youdh, and those toughs had tried to kill me. Twice—through imaging and shooting at me. Equally important, I hadn't done anything to threaten anyone. I'd only followed Mardoyt.

I also had to wonder if imaging had been used to topple the pile of granite that had left me without shields for almost a week. If that were so, it suggested most strongly that both Harraf and Mardoyt were linked to Youdh, but in the case of Harraf, I had less information. I certainly couldn't call it proof.

At dinner, I ended up sitting between Chorister Isola and Quaelyn.

"How is your pattern analysis going?" I asked Quaelyn, after we had served ourselves from the platters brought out by the servers. I hoped he might reveal something of interest.

"There are always patterns." He smiled. "Sometimes we can read them, and sometimes we can't."

"Do you analyze patterns that affect the Ferrans?"

"I have, but there's little point in that now."

"When we're at war?"

He shrugged. "Their response will be to build as many weapons, ships, and landcruisers as they can and train as many soldiers and sailors as possible. Ours will be to deny them effective use of all that matériel. Because we control the sea after last week's battles, they will turn their fury against the Jariolans on land. The Jariolans will let them attack until they are overextended, and until winter is at its height, when the steam engines of the landcruisers have a tendency to freeze up, and they will counterattack. That is what the patterns indicate."

"People aren't patterns," Isola pointed out.

"No, honored chorister. People *are* patterns. We could not function without routines, schedules, and habits, and the confluence of these create patterns in every society. Success in war is being able to maintain your vital patterns and to deploy others the enemy cannot replicate or counter while anticipating and disrupting all his patterns." Quaelyn shrugged. "Those words make it sound far simpler than the strategies and tactics necessary to do so, but in the simplest terms, that is what war is all about." He smiled at Isola. "One of the patterns that few recognize is that of titles and naming, but I would judge that you as a chorister would see that."

I recognized that titles formed a pattern in any society, but what did that have to do with war? I didn't ask, but I might as well have, because Isola read the inquiry in my expression.

"You have to remember, Rhenn, that names and titles are like chains. Some few people wear them like fine light jewelry links that can be snapped in an instant, but for most the links are heavy enough to bind them within the confines and expectations that their name and title impose on them. The more traditional or formal a society is, the stronger those links, and both the Ferrans and the Jariolans are like that."

I frowned. "And we aren't?"

"The Council is, and much of Solidar is. The Collegium, or those who lead and direct it, is not . . . and yet is. Think about your training."

While I was thinking, she went on.

"This is also true in families. Names come with expectations. Parents don't say that the eldest child should be especially responsible, but the way in which they act effectively adds that expectation to the child's name, perhaps every time that the child hears his name."

I hadn't thought of it in quite that fashion. Then, I was more interested in the implications of what she and Quaelyn had been discussing . . . and how it related to me.

There was a silence. A thought had occurred to me. "You know so much about this . . . but you're here in L'Excelsis . . ." I looked to Quaelyn.

He laughed. "I'm an analyst of patterns, not a military commander." After a pause, he cleared his throat and added, in an almost embarrassed tone, "Every year, I teach a course at the staff college in pattern recognition and analysis. That's for senior officers."

"Oh . . . I didn't know."

"There's no reason you should have," he said gently.

It was just another example of something else that the Collegium did that appeared nowhere in writing.

After dinner, I did not return to my quarters, but instead walked to the south end of Imagisle, past the anomen, to the west side, where a stand of ancient oaks formed almost a second barrier between the grounds and the River Aluse. I had an idea, but as I was discovering, not all ideas translated into practice in the way I had envisioned.

I walked up and down the line of oaks, under the all too faint light of Artiema, only half full. Erion was full, but already low in the western sky, his grayish red light far less helpful, although it gave a sinister look to the abandoned and partly burned-out old mill across the river. I looked away from the mill, concentrating on the trees. The second oak from the north end had several large branches near the top that appeared to be dead.

After studying them more closely, I set to work, beginning near the branch tip, and imaging out a section of wood. The branch wavered, but did not break.

I imaged out a bit more of the dead wood. Nothing happened.

Another attempt brought a cracking, and then the branch broke, but only hung.

After wiping my forehead, I took a deep breath. Like everything else, making my idea into a practical device was going to take more work and skill than I'd thought. But I kept at it for more than a glass before I finally learned how to make the heavy wood fall in the general, and then the specific area where I tried to direct it.

33

Vendrei was misty, with intermittent rain, and a damp chill that suggested a bitter late autumn, although winter proper was a bit more than a month away. I slipped several times on the four-mille run, but Dartazn slipped more, and I managed to finish closer to him than usual. Master Dichartyn wasn't there for either the exercises or the run, and I wondered when he would be returning to Imagisle . . . and where he had been.

After a cold shower and a shave that left my face blue, it took two full mugs of steaming tea at breakfast to lift the chill from my body, but I got to the duty coach early enough that I arrived on time for my last day of rounds with Alsoran. I even had to wait for him.

He was smiling when he walked into the station.

I couldn't help smiling back. "Good morning. Ready to head out?"

"Why wouldn't I be?"

I shrugged, and we left the station and started off up Fuosta.

"Will you miss any part of Third District, do you think?" I asked.

"I'll miss some of the patrollers. Lyonyt was always good to do rounds with, and Zellyn's a good fellow. Some of the others, too. But they say that Captain Telleryn runs a good station." He smiled. "Jotenyr told me I'd eat a lot better out in Fifth District, and that he sees a lot more pretty women."

"That sounds promising."

"Have to admit I could stand better food than the bistros on this round."

With that I could definitely agree.

As was usually the case in the earlier part of the morning, we didn't see any taudis-toughs on the first two rounds, and only sniffed a hint of elve-weed when we were two blocks or so past the Temple of Puryon on the first leg of the first round.

Youdh's territory, I thought.

"Have you heard anything about the scripties, Master Rhennthyl?"

"All I know is that they've started somewhere in L'Excelsis, but I don't know much more than that, except it's west of the river."

"They usually start in one of the taudis. That'd be Caniffe, most likely."

"Then where?"

Alsoran shook his head. "Might do the nicer districts in the west or go straight for the hellhole. Can't ever tell, and that's the way they like it. They just move in and cordon off something like a ten-block square and move from house to house. We have to charge and send to gaol anyone who tries to attack them—if they don't shoot 'em first."

I hadn't heard that aspect of the conscription teams. I'd only seen them twice, when they'd visited our house when I was something like eleven and then again when I'd been an apprentice for Master Caliostrus, just before I made journeyman. "I didn't see a cordon when they've been through before."

"They don't use full force in some parts of the city, just in the trade and taudis quarters."

We kept walking and watching, but the second round ended without incident. By the second round, we'd both removed our cloaks because the sun beat down more like summer, and the air was getting hotter and steamier by the moment.

"You never know what to expect this time of year." Alsoran blotted his forehead. "You wear a summer uniform, and you freeze. You put on the heavier wool, and you roast."

By the third round, the usual toughs were beginning to appear, but all of them either ignored us or provided Alsoran with a quick nod. Clearly Jadhyl and Deyalt didn't want trouble with the Patrol, or with Alsoran. Somewhere near the end of that round, I realized that I'd never seen the tough who'd drawn a knife on me nearly two weeks earlier.

I insisted on buying Alsoran his lunch at Parmiens, one of the better bistros on the avenue section of the round, as a sort of promotion and transfer present. He tried to object.

"Promotions don't come every day, or even every year," I pointed out. "And, this way, if no one else says anything, you can tell your wife that someone noticed. Besides, it's Vendrei, and we deserve a good meal."

In the end, he capitulated.

Not only was Alsoran pleased, but I didn't have gut-aches for the rest of the afternoon, something that had occurred more than I would have preferred when we had eaten in some of his "favorite" places.

When we walked up the walk to the station at the end of the last round of the day, I stopped just outside and clasped Alsoran's hand. "I do wish you well in Fifth District."

"I'd be wishing you well, too, Master Rhennthyl. If you don't mind my saying so, with some more experience, you'd be a good Patrol captain. You settle things down, somehow. Zellyn said the same thing."

Settle things down? It seemed to me that I was always being forced to stir things up.

Once we entered the station, Captain Harraf, whom I hadn't seen in days, beckoned to Alsoran, then smiled at me before escorting Alsoran into his study and closing the door.

After I left Third District station, just after fourth glass, I took a hack to the Avenue D'Artisans and had the driver drop me off midway between the two points where Mardoyt had left the hack when I'd trailed him. Then I made my way westward to Saelio, moving in from the north under conceal- ment shields. With the sun getting lower in the west, and the shadows from the old dwellings and oak trees, no one seemed to look in my direction as I took my time getting into position two houses away from Mardoyt's duplex. His daughter was playing with dolls on the porch, then disappeared inside when someone called her as the shadows merged with twilight.

As I continued to wait, not exactly comfortably, I studied the old oaks, pick- ing out several as possibilities, and testing them gently. The twilight deep- ened into night, past the time when other men, and some women, returned to their houses. Twice, I had to ease out of people's way, but they either didn't see me through my shields, or if they caught a hint of something, they really didn't want to look in my direction.

In time, the lights on the lower level of the house were snuffed out, except for a single lamp that remained lit in the front hall, barely visible through the large window behind the porch. I kept waiting, until close to midnight, or perhaps past it.

It was a long, long walk back to Imagisle, since there were no hacks about, and my feet ached by the time I opened the door to my quarters. I almost stepped on the note that had been slipped under my door, but bent over and picked it up. Then I closed the door and imaged the desk lamp into flame be- fore opening the envelope and reading the single line.

I'd like to see you.

Under the five words was the initial D.

I couldn't say that I was surprised.

34

I was so tired on Vendrei night that it took me a moment to realize that my old charred armoire had been replaced, but my clothes had been merely laid out on my bed. That meant I had to put them away before I went to sleep. Before breakfast on Samedi morning, I immediately stopped by Master Dichartyn's study. He wasn't there, and I left word with the duty prime—Olseort—that I'd been by to see him. After breakfast I stopped by once more, but unsurprisingly he wasn't there.

So I headed out to my studio, where I fired up the stove to take the chill off, prepared for Master Rholyn's sitting, and then began to work on the background—which didn't require his presence. Several times, I glanced outside, where the morning sun was warming the damp ground and grass and fog was rising into a clear pale blue sky.

Right around half past seven, while I was finishing up the foreground at the bottom of Master Rholyn's portrait, Master Dichartyn walked into the studio.

"Rhennthyl . . . I thought I might find you here. You're so very predictable. Dutiful, too, for the most part."

I smiled my polite smile, the one Maitre Dyana had called almost supercilious or some such. "Yes, sir. I do try."

"You're also trying." He sighed. Loudly. "You asked for a pay schedule for the civic patrollers. Fortunately, you asked Master Schorzat. What would have happened if you had asked the Patrol commander or subcommander?"

"I realized I shouldn't have—"

"Of course, you shouldn't have. And it's all well and good to be contrite after Master Schorzat pointed out the problems." He didn't raise his voice. "Sometimes, you offer such promise, and then . . ."

"Sir . . . I understand. You pointed out to me when I first arrived at the Collegium, and that was slightly more than half a year ago, that I would be required to learn not only the written and formal rules of the Collegium, but the equally important and unspoken ones as well. That is all well and good, but I can learn what is unspoken only if I can observe, or if I can deduce from what I do not see, what I should or should not do. From Master Schorzat's reaction and other observations I have made, I realized that requesting any such documentation from anyone in the Patrol would be a mistake, and I have requested nothing from anyone in the Patrol." I didn't see much point in stating that I had observed enough documents to learn what I needed.

His face softened, just slightly. "You don't really expect anyone in the Patrol to adhere to the standards of public conduct expected of imagers, do you?"

"No, sir."

He paused. "What else have you noted?"

"About the conduct of the Civic Patrol and its officers, I've seen nothing new in the way of what might be termed proof. The patroller with whom I've been doing rounds for the past two weeks has been promoted and transferred. I agreed to do rounds with his partner, who has been on leave, for the next week. After that, I have no idea what either Captain Harraf or the commander or subcommander have in mind for me."

"Has anything occurred with regard to the High Holder?"

"Nothing has changed there, either, sir." That was true enough. I had learned more, but it hadn't changed the situation at all.

"What have you been doing, then?"

"Learning as much as I can, sir, but as you have pointed out, if what I have learned does not qualify as proof, that knowledge, by itself, does not change the situation."

Abruptly he laughed, shaking his head. "You sound like Maitre Jhulian." The laugh faded all too quickly. "Patrol Commander Artois is concerned that you are concerned with issues beyond learning about the Patrol."

This time I laughed. "I have not spoken to the commander since the first day I was at headquarters. Nor have I spoken to the subcommander in almost a month. The only three officers I've exchanged words with are Lieutenant Mardoyt, Captain Harraf, and Lieutenant Warydt. I find that most interesting, sir."

"Oh . . . it's interesting enough, and I know what your suspicions are. But suspicions aren't proof, and in the meantime, even assuming, just assuming, that they're correct, you've been unable to come up with proof. When the working of an institution is at stake, or its integrity is, one must have proof of wrongdoing, or come up with results to correct the problem if one cannot properly charge a malefactor, and those results must seem accidental and unrelated to you or the Collegium."

"Yes, sir."

"Now . . . there is one other item . . ."

I didn't care much for it when he was almost done and then said, "Now . . ." It usually meant a reprimand or a very pointed question. "Yes, sir?"

"You know the Ferran envoy—Stauffen Gregg?"

"No, sir. I never met or saw him. I would have thought he would have left L'Excelsis after the Council declared war on Ferrum."

"He and his staff left L'Excelsis for Westisle on the twentieth, but they did not actually leave Solidar proper until earlier this week, Mardi, in fact, because of the difficulty in obtaining passage on a neutral vessel that would take them somewhere from which they could hopefully take a Ferran ship to Ferrial. That will be risky indeed. But . . ." Dichartyn paused meaningfully. "Certain investigations revealed that some of the Ferran staff serving the envoy had vanished. Our first thought was that they had gone underground. But when we captured and interrogated some of the Ferran agents we have been following, none had ever heard or seen the missing staff members. They truly vanished. Interestingly enough, about the time they did, the shootings of imagers ceased. Did you happen to have anything to do with this?"

"No, sir. I can say in all honesty I did not even know that any Ferrans had vanished, let alone that they belonged to the envoy." That was absolutely true, even though, in retrospect, I had a very good idea what had happened to them. "Do you know what they were doing?"

"We suspect that they were the ones who killed Thenard and one other junior imager. There were a number of shootings . . . and then they stopped. As I recall, you were shot at twice."

"Yes, sir, and it's just as you said. In fact, I'd been wondering about that. I mean, I've taken shots since then, but those have been Patrol- and taudis-related. The first ones were when I was in public places."

"You didn't have anything to do with what happened to them?"

"No, sir." And I hadn't.

Dichartyn nodded. "We'd best leave it at that."

He suspected what I knew, but neither of us had any proof.

"That's all for now. On Vendrei, you can take one of the duty coaches with me to go to the Council's Autumn Ball. Don't forget to wear the imager's pin, either." At that point, he walked past me to where he could see the easel. "It does look like him, even unfinished."

I forbore saying that creating a lifelike resemblance was precisely the point of a portrait, but just nodded and watched as he left. I'd gotten his message, all right, as if I hadn't already begun to understand. I understood. I definitely did.

After a time, I shook myself and went back to painting.

Master Rholyn appeared just as the bells were striking eighth glass. "Good morning, Rhennthyl. There's a definite chill in the air this morning, isn't there?"

"That there is, sir."

Rholyn took the position on the crate, and I began to paint.

After a time, he spoke. "You'll be at the Autumn Ball?"

He had to know that, but I merely said, "Master Dichartyn has insisted that I be there."

"It might be best if you did not attach yourself closely to any envoys, Rhennthyl."

"I had not thought to seek any out, sir." Before he could suggest more, I added, "Did you meet the second Ferran envoy?"

"Only briefly, when he presented his credentials to the Council. It is highly unlikely that he was an imager, or that anyone on his staff was." Rholyn smiled politely. "But that matters little, since he departed as soon as we declared war. He did have to take an Abiertan ship. I might point out that it is most likely that envoys from almost all the other lands involved in the current unpleasantness will be at the Autumn Ball."

"Including a Caenenan envoy?"

"Hardly. They conduct all diplomatic affairs through the Gyarlese envoy, and he's an equalifier of Puryon, because no true believer in Duodeus will live anywhere in Solidar."

I frowned, if inadvertently. "I thought they sent an envoy to work out trade terms some months back."

"He was officially a negotiator, and he stayed at the Gyarlese envoy's compound." Master Rholyn's tone carried an edge.

I decided not to press. "Thank you, sir. I did not realize that the Caenenan dislike of Solidar even permeated the question of envoys."

"It does, and it has, and the Council may yet have to consider Councilor Caartyl's proposal to remove our envoy from Caena."

Caartyl again. His name had cropped up more than a few times with regard to issues not exactly favorable to the High Holders' interests, and now Master Rholyn was suggesting that Caartyl was not exactly one of his favorite councilors.

I concentrated more intently on finishing the right side of Master Rholyn's face.

He said little more, beyond pleasantries when he departed, except to confirm that he would be available for another sitting the following Samedi.

I worked almost to lunchtime, as much to see what I could do to complete

Rholyn's portrait as well—and as quickly—as possible. While I didn't particularly like Master Dichartyn or his outlook, I did respect him. I was coming to realize that I neither liked nor respected Rholyn, even if, again, I had little of what Master Dichartyn would have called proof to support my feeling. I also understood something else, something that Master Dichartyn would never say directly. Proof was what was necessary to act officially. It wasn't necessary for other actions—so long as they seemed accidental or someone else's fault, but if such actions failed, the imager would always be held totally at fault if they ever came to the official attention of the Collegium, the Civic Patrol, or the Council.

That realization only gave me more to worry about.

The damp and chill morning had given way to a sunny, if crisp, day, and the walk down the west side of the quadrangle cheered me. When I entered the dining hall, I saw a familiar face at the thirds' table. Kahlasa was standing, talking to Meynard and Reynol. I immediately walked over and joined them.

"I'm glad to see you back," I offered, noticing that her curly blond hair was longer than when she'd left, and that there was a darkness behind the brown eyes. Had it always been there, and I'd failed to notice it, or was it the result of her last mission? Or did all field imagers hold that darkness in their eyes? That wasn't something I was about to ask.

She turned. Her smile contained pleasure and sadness, almost in equal measure. "Rhenn! I heard that you're now a master. Congratulations."

I nodded. "I'm fortunate to be in a position where my talents are openly recognized." I paused just slightly. "You must have had a difficult set of tasks with all that's going on in the world."

"Not so difficult as Claustyn."

"His death . . . I was . . . he'd been so helpful to me," I finally said.

She smiled more warmly, then inclined her head to Reynol. "I heard."

"I also have my doubts that your tasks were any less difficult."

"You're kind."

I shook my head. "I think not. How long will you be here, or do you know?"

"We never know, but Master Schorzat has promised me at least two months and until after Year-Turn. It could be longer. There are . . . matters to be considered."

After we talked pleasantly for a time, I finally inclined my head to her and slipped away to the masters' table. Just from her bearing and choice of words, it was clear to me that she was at least a Maitre D'Aspect, but held it as a hidden rank, as Claustyn had. That bothered me, but was that because she was a woman, who had probably had to work far harder? I wasn't certain I wanted to know what she had been doing . . . even if someone had been willing to tell me.

Chassendri and Isola sat on one side of the masters' table, and I joined them. Chassendri stopped whatever she was saying and looked to me. "I hadn't seen the portrait of Maitre Poincaryt until today, Rhenn. It's good."

"Thank you. But I have to say that he made it easy for me to depict him."

"That's one of his talents," she replied.

"It's a skill that's helpful for whoever is in charge of something like the Collegium," added Isola.

I almost responded, but instead I thought over her words. If making things easy was necessary and important, why did so many people, like Mardoyt, Subcommander Cydarth, and Harraf go out of their way to make matters difficult? For that matter, why did Master Dichartyn?

With Master Dichartyn, I thought I knew, but how he reacted to what I had in mind would settle that one way or another.

"You look rather thoughtful," observed Isola.

"I've discovered a few things about which to be thoughtful," I said with a laugh. "That's what comes of discovering you're an imager comparatively later in life."

"Having been an artist first must be an advantage," suggested Chassendri.

"It's a mixed blessing. That training made it easier to visualize objects, but as an artist, in a way, you feel things, but you also stand outside them. You're not supposed to act in other people's lives, just observe them, but all too often what an imager does affects the lives of others." I shrugged. I didn't want to say more.

"Especially if you report to Master Dichartyn," said Chassendri dryly.

I laughed again.

The remainder of lunch was less introspective, and we actually talked about art. I enjoyed it enough that I lingered somewhat and had to hurry to get to the Bridge of Hopes.

My hurrying didn't matter, because Seliora didn't arrive until a quint past one, and she emerged from the hack by herself. Her determined and quick stride suggested all was not well.

I hurried to meet her. "Is everything all right?"

"I had to explain to the wife of the younger son of High Holder Devoult why she could have the pattern she wanted or the price she wanted, but not both. She didn't want to understand that at the price she wanted, if word got around and everyone else demanded the same, we'd lose so much that we wouldn't be in business. So her threats to have her father-in-law drive us out of business were meaningless. Her husband is slow, but not stupid, and he finally managed to explain the problem." Seliora shook her head. "Some of those men . . . why do they marry such idiots?"

"Because they probably have no real choice. They can't marry out of their class, and their parents and older brothers don't really want them to marry anyone with brains, not unless the younger son has none." I leaned forward and kissed her cheek. That was as much as I thought wise, given her mood.

"And then, Shomyr ran off to see Haelya, and left all his worksheets scattered all over the design spaces."

"You've definitely had a long morning."

"Today was calm, compared to yesterday . . ."

I took her arm and guided her toward the more direct walkway that led to my studio, the stone path that angled across the north end of the buildings on the quadrangle. I listened as she continued.

". . . the Ealityr mill in Kephria sent five bolts of fabric with the wrong shade of blue . . . they'll have to replace it . . . but that means another three weeks, and the penalty clauses won't repay all of our costs . . ."

We had almost reached the studio before she turned and looked at me. "I'm sorry. I didn't mean to rail on and on at you. You didn't do any of this."

"I can certainly listen. You've listened to my frustrations enough." I sincerely hoped that the problems with the mill weren't a result of more interference by Ryel, but I had no way of knowing whether NordEste Design was suffering from mere incompetence at the mill or worse.

She smiled wryly. "There are reasons for your problems. Mine come from people's stupidity."

"That is a reason as well," I pointed out.

Seliora did laugh.

"After the sitting, and before we go to my parents . . . do you suppose we could take a wagon out to Ryel's estate?"

"No." Her voice lilted, though, and I caught sight of a glint in her eye.

"Why not?"

"Because it's a pleasant afternoon, and it would be better to ride out there. It would also be faster, and we wouldn't have to wash the wagon and clean up nearly so much. That will also give you practice. You need it."

"I'm certain I do. I'd best bring a spare outfit, then."

"That might be a good idea."

No one intruded while I was working on the portrait, not that I expected it, and I finished most of the right side of her face, and her neck. Painting a woman's neck is difficult. It was for me, anyway, because of the changing curves and the muscles and because unless the neck is correct, the face always seems wrong. In that sense, the neck is part of the face.

That left me at a good stopping point, and I had Seliora sit down while I cleaned up.

Then we went back to my quarters—or I did. She waited in the entry below while I quickly folded another outfit into the carrying bag.

We actually reached NordEste Design before half past two.

There, I learned more about saddling the mare, a patient creature, as Seliora instructed and watched as I struggled with blankets, and girths, and the saddle. Eventually, I did manage all those details, and we rode out of the courtyard, me on the mare, and Seliora on a much friskier chestnut.

We took the direct route, and in roughly half a glass, the Plaza D'Nord was behind us, as well as most of the carriages and wagons that had thronged the Boulevard D'Este. I wouldn't have claimed that I rode well, but I was finally developing some sense of what I was doing.

"Is the ride helping put the past days behind you?" I asked as we turned northward on the paved road leading to the estate.

Seliora's first response was a faint smile. "I'd already done that."

"You're worried, still."

"Knowing you, how can I not be worried?"

"Farsight?"

"Not really. Not mostly. You've made an enemy of one of the more powerful High Holders. You're a powerful imager. He's too arrogant to back off, and that leaves you with no choices."

I'd known that for a long time. So had Seliora, I suspected.

"Rhenn?"

"Yes?"

"High Holders don't believe in mercy or fairness. Their honor is based on power. Nothing else. I understand that. Please remember that I understand."

"You're one of the few outside the High Holders and the Collegium who does. Or who's willing to say it."

"My whole family knows." Her tone declared that they knew personally, and that she'd tell me when the time came. And that such a time might never come.

I nodded.

We reached the low rise to the south of the one on which stood Ryel's chateau, and I studied the lands once more. Even at a glance, I could see that there was but one gate in the long wall around the estate—that part I could see—and that was the massive entry gate. Again, I was struck by the tower that rose off the terrace at the end of the chateau's south wing, overlooking the formal gardens that stretched a good half mille down to the stream flowing in a swale whose far southern side was less than a hundred yards from the southern wall.

To the east of the gardens was what looked to be an orchard, and then a small woodland farther east. From what I could determine, the grounds were modest—for a High Holder—roughly three-quarters of a mille north to south and possibly twice that from west to east.

Once we followed the road down and into its lowest point between the two rises, I eased the mare to the right side of the road, letting her walk slowly as I studied the wall that surrounded the estate. The wall stood close to two and a half yards high, but the top was set with a mortared surface from which protruded all sorts of sharp objects—broken glass and crockery, nails, the edges of shattered blades. The gray stone had a slightly irregular finish, but not rough enough to afford handholds. The only break in the wall occurred where the stream—a small river—flowed between two stone pillars. There the walls turned at a right angle and ran back another five yards or so along the stream, but they had been set so that they constricted and deepened the stream and so that it rushed through the gap and down a short rapids before entering a culvert that continued under the road.

Beyond the stream, the road rose more steeply, so that if I looked forward, I couldn't see the chateau from the side of the road. I glanced around. While there were a few low bushes, there were no trees. Some of the bushes looked fairly sturdy.

Beyond the wall, I could hear dogs—a combination of deep barks and baying. Doubtless, the beasts ran free at night, although since all the sounds came from one general area, I felt they were presently kenneled.

When we rode past the gates, I scarcely looked at them. Although there were no guards stationed outside, I had the feeling that someone watched us through the iron grillwork.

Neither Seliora nor I said anything until we were a good hundred yards past the gate.

"That's just his small estate in the capital." Her words were light.

"Set among another hundred or so of lesser holders, I'd judge."

"His is among the more impressive I've seen, but he's one of the wealthiest High Holders."

There was little to add to that. I just said, "We can stop and rest the horses at the turnaround."

"There's a trough there. We can water them some, but not too much."

"I leave that judgment to you, dear lady."

My words, or my tone, did bring a brief smile to her lips.

While we watered our mounts and tarried a bit, I studied the grounds even more, if not obviously, I hoped. From the north side, I could see the tower in perspective. Its uppermost level was almost level with the hilltop turnaround . . . or so it seemed.

When we headed back, I realized, as with all too many things I'd planned in recent weeks, that I'd underestimated the time required. It was close to sixth glass when we reined up in the NordEste courtyard.

"We're going to be late," I confessed as I dismounted.

"What time are we supposed to be there?"

"In about a quint."

Seliora just looked at me.

"It's my fault."

Then she grinned. "So long as you tell them that."

"I promise."

How we managed it, between stabling and grooming and washing up and changing, I wasn't quite certain, but it wasn't that much past half past six when the hack rolled up before my parents' dwelling.

Seliora looked beautiful—and far more composed than I felt when I lifted and dropped the knocker.

Mother immediately opened the door. "I was getting worried."

"I know. I'm sorry we're a bit late. That was my fault."

From where she stood behind Mother, Khethila laughed and looked at Seliora. "You're definitely good for Rhenn. He'd never have admitted that a year ago."

"He wouldn't have admitted it three months ago," Seliora replied cheerfully as she stepped into the house.

I closed the door and followed them into the family parlor. That was a good sign.

Even before we could sit down, Khethila asked me, "Dare I ask what you were doing?"

"She's teaching me to ride, and I thought we could go farther than we should have. I didn't listen to someone." I shrugged. "Horses get tired, too, and it takes longer to return . . . and to groom them."

"Greetings, Seliora," Father said as he rose from his armchair. "We're glad you're here."

"I'm glad to be here."

Father half turned to me, gesturing for everyone to sit down. "It seems to me that you're being trained, or training yourself, more like an Army commando than an imager."

"Imaging is far more work than most people could believe," I answered. "I've never ridden before, and when I mentioned it to Seliora, she decided that it was a good idea. I'll probably be sore enough tomorrow that I won't be so sure that it was a good idea."

"What's a good idea?" asked Culthyn, slipping in from the kitchen with a smudge of something on his cheek.

"Have you been in the tarts?" demanded Khethila.

"Rhenn was late. I was hungry."

"And you couldn't have had a piece of bread or a biscuit or an apple, I suppose?" asked Father.

Mother looked hard at Culthyn. "Then you have had your dessert. Please join us." She patted the settee and the open space between her and Khethila. "I don't believe you've met Seliora. I understand she has a younger brother close to your age."

Culthyn as much as slunk onto the settee as seated himself. He kept his eyes averted from Mother and me.

"Methyr is two years younger, from what Rhenn has told me," Seliora said. "You both share a fondness for sweets. Last night, he shaved a slice off Odelia's pie when she wasn't looking."

"Is he still walking?" I asked.

"He was moving a little stiffly this morning, I thought."

Culthyn's eyes widened a touch, and Khethila concealed a smile.

"Rhenn was a bit more indirect, as I recall," Mother said. "He'd take the dough, before it was baked, and roll it around something sweet—jelly or jam or honey—when no one was looking. It took a while for the cook to figure out why the pastry was often short when he was around."

"I never heard that," said Khethila.

"See? I wasn't the only one." Culthyn's tone carried the same self-justification that I'd heard too much from Rousel.

Seliora smiled at me.

Dinner would be fine. That I knew.

35

Because we were both tired, Seliora and I hadn't stayed all that late after dinner, and we'd been fortunate, although I'd hoped for it, that Mother had paid Charlsyn to work late and take Seliora back to NordEste Design and me to the Collegium. I had held Seliora quite closely on the first part of that trip.

I'd also slept past breakfast on Solayi, and I took my time getting cleaned up and dressed, thinking over what I wanted to do and what I needed to do. Seliora had a number of "family things," as well as some work she'd put aside to spend the day with me on Samedi. So I had Solayi to myself, except that I needed to meet Chelya when she came to visit Shault, something that I'd almost forgotten, perhaps because my plans had changed somewhat, and the cloth scrap wasn't as vital as I'd originally thought it would be, although I still might be able to use it.

Once I'd planned out my schedule, I left my quarters, enjoying another sunny, if crisp, day. The benches on the quadrangle were empty, except for a few primes and young seconds. Then, I saw Ferlyn walking toward the dining hall for lunch and hurried to catch up with him.

"Duty, once more?" I asked, rhetorically and dryly.

"What else?" He shook his head. "I don't mind it that much. I'm not married, and I'm not struggling through all the extra duties that Master Dichartyn lays on you security types, so it's not as though it's a great imposition."

"Aren't you learning things from Quaelyn?"

"True enough, but there's time for most of that during the week, when I'm not supervising and checking the armory imagers and their work."

"You have the skill to use imaging to compare things to exact tolerances, or something like that?" That was a guess, but I couldn't figure out what other skill would have made him a master so young, since he was probably only five or six years older than I was.

He shook his head, if ruefully. "Master Schorzat warned me about you, Rhenn. He said that you had this talent of discovering things with no facts at all to support you."

I didn't point out that I'd had two facts. "What can I say?"

"You can't." He laughed. "But let's say you're close enough."

"Can you tell me what you know about the war—based on what the armory is doing?"

"Not really. The Navy doesn't say much, but I don't think matters are going as well as they'd hoped." He frowned. "That's not quite right. They're pleased with the . . . with what we're doing, but I get the impression that while the Ferrans are losing ships and taking heavy losses, there's no slacking in the fighting."

I held the outer door to the dining hall and followed him into the corridor inside. "From what I've heard, there won't be until winter, and then everything will come unraveled for them."

"That will mean more casualties for both the Ferrans and Jariolans."

"And less golds for our factors—because the shipping's been largely cut off."

"That hasn't seemed to bother the Council," Ferlyn said.

It probably hadn't, because the longer the war dragged on, the less likely either land would be able to create future problems for Solidar. If the Oligarchy merely survived, the High Holders on the Council would be relieved that another land had not become governed by mercantilists, and the factors and guilds would be happy to see Ferran competitiveness reduced.

Just after we'd seated ourselves, alone at the masters' table, Shault entered the hall with two other primes. The three talked animatedly, and I caught a few fragments of what they said.

". . . wouldn't do any good. No master's that strong . . ."

"Then why are the Caenenans and Tiemprans so afraid of imagers?"

". . . against what they believe . . ."

". . . belief doesn't make it so," Shault replied.

I had to smile at that.

"That Shault's a handful," observed Ferlyn.

"He was petrified when he came here."

"That was just you, Rhenn. All the juniors think you're a later version of Cyran."

Cyran—one of the handful of Maitres D'Image—the one who had removed Rex Defou? "Me? I'm always polite and thoughtful."

"The word's gotten around that you defied Master Dichartyn and took out those Ferran agents outside the Council Chateau by yourself. No one has ever defied him. Then you survived an explosion that killed everyone in an entire block and went to a wedding the next day."

"But I didn't defy him," I protested. It was true that I'd taken out the Ferran envoy without Dichartyn's permission because Vhillar was an imager who'd arranged for the killing of more than ten junior imagers. But I hadn't actually defied Master Dichartyn.

Ferlyn laughed. "Sometimes, the facts aren't the truth."

I almost winced at his perception, but I managed to laugh.

Lunch, as often happened on Solayi, was a form of tarted-up leftovers, in this case, a pastry-covered pot pie. But it was hot, filling, and tasty, and I could still recall the dry and unsatisfying meals prepared by poor Madame Caliostrus.

When Shault left the dining hall, I excused myself and slipped out. While he might not be heading to the waiting area west of the Bridge of Hopes, I didn't want him to encounter his mother before I was there.

Although Shault headed back in the direction of the primes' quarters, I immediately walked past the administration building and then toward the Bridge of Hopes . . . and then out to the middle of the bridge, where I looked down at the gray water, its surface not quite sparkling in the midday sunlight. The breeze was cool, but light, and out of the north. Occasionally I glanced back toward the Collegium, but I didn't actually walk back to the waiting area until Shault appeared.

As I neared him, I could see that he had grown some and filled out. His demeanor was reserved, but not fearful . . . a good change, and one I was happy to see.

"Good afternoon, Shault."

"Good afternoon, Master Rhennthyl."

"How are your studies going with Master Ghaend?"

"They're better. I'm reading better, and that helps. Thank you for the dictionary."

"Did it help?"

"Yes, sir . . . but not the way . . . Well . . . it was just easier to start reading it."

I almost shook my head. "How did Master Ghaend take that?"

"I didn't tell him. But he lets me image little things." Shault grinned. "I could do a good copper now, but I promised Master Ghaend I wouldn't."

"Please keep that promise."

Shault looked toward the empty Bridge of Hopes, then back toward me with a quizzical glance, as if to ask why I was there.

"I told your mother I'd be here the first time she came. She seemed to want some assurance that it would be all right for her to visit." That wasn't literally true, but I had seen her concerns on her face.

"Oh . . . she worries some. She doesn't think I see that, but I do."

"Are you happier here now?"

"Yes, sir." He paused. "I still miss Ma." He glanced toward the bridge.

"You should miss her. She's your mother, and she loves you." I just hoped that Chelya would come, whether or not she had anything for me from Horazt. Shault deserved that.

"Things have been hard for her."

"Things are usually hard in the taudis," I said. "What part of your studies do you like the best?"

"The science stuff. The words are hard, but I like learning how things work."

"And the hardest subject?"

"Politics . . ." He looked at me.

"Why is that hard?"

"It's false, sir. It's all pretend. It's like they're all taudischefs with fancy names and lots of lands or people working for them . . ."

I could see how a taudis-kid would be skeptical of the necessary hypocrisy and falseness of government, but I just nodded and listened, prompting him with a question or two, the way Master Dichartyn had prodded me.

At a good quint past first glass, a woman in a brown cloak crossed East River Road and started across the bridge. Her steps were both deliberate and reluctant.

"You can meet her halfway," I told Shault.

I waited until the two of them walked back, then addressed Chelya. "I'm glad you came. You should be proud of your son."

"He is growing." She did not look at me as she went on. "Horazt asked me to give this to you." She thrust a grayish object at me.

"Thank you." I took the worn woolen bag, crudely cut and sewn from what had probably been a discarded garment. "I appreciate your bringing it."

Shault's eyes widened.

I nodded to him. "Imager business."

He nodded back solemnly.

I turned to Chelya. "I hope you will come again to see Shault, until he's free to leave Imagisle." I hoped that wouldn't be too soon, because I really didn't want the boy walking through the taudis as a junior imager.

"We'll have to meet in the public gardens," Shault said. "But I can go to the ones near the Guild Square, and we'll have a real dinner at a bistro."

Chelya's eyes were bright.

It was time for me to leave. "Have a good afternoon."

I started out, taking my time. With my shields in place, I strolled across the bridge, down East River Road two blocks where I paused to open the woolen bag. Inside was a rough-cut small square of purple wool. From what I recalled, it matched the jackets of the two toughs that had attacked me near Mardoyt's house. I replaced the fabric in the bag and slipped both into the inside pocket of my waistcoat.

I followed the walk on the river side of the road until I reached Fedre, then walked up it past Patrol headquarters. I saw no patrollers. Then I took Aslym across to Saelio. There I turned northeast, in the direction of Mardoyt's house. A block or so short of his dwelling, I raised partial concealment shields. Even if Mardoyt weren't there, I didn't want the neighbors seeing me clearly.

It didn't surprise me that no one appeared to be home. On Solayi, more than a few people visited friends or relatives, at least until time for services in the evening.

After watching the house for a time, I walked out to the Avenue D'Artisans, where I hailed a hack and rode to the Plaza Sudeste, where South Middle intersected the avenue.

I walked the length of South Middle from the plaza all the way to the Midroad. I didn't see a single taudis-tough, although in places, especially near Dugalle, the odor of elveweed was close to overpowering. I also didn't stop by the station.

Then I took a hack back to the Collegium, arriving a good glass before dinner. That gave me time to rest tired feet and to think some more. Dinner was quiet, and I walked alone to the anomen for services, standing forward and to the side where I could easily hear Isola.

Her homily addressed something I'd never heard a chorister mention before.

"... the other day I was asked by a young imager why we cremate those who have died, and why what we do makes any difference in the eyes of the Nameless ... Were you to go to an anomen in Caenen, except they call them churches, you would find a large grassy expanse behind the building. Covering that space would be stone monuments, each topped with the forked columns of duality. On the face of each monument, carved into the stone, would be a name and an inscription. And what would you find in the ground beneath each monument? A body ... or the remnants of one." Isola paused.

I could hear indrawn breaths of repugnance from some of the younger imagers. I didn't like the image her words evoked, either. Buried and rotting in the cold, damp ground? I supposed it wouldn't matter, though, not if I were dead. Still ...

"I can sense the distaste that image creates," she went on, "but what is the reason behind this practice? We all know bodies, once dead, do not come to life again, and that, for all the old folktales, there are no necrimagers. Certainly, the Caenenans do not even believe in imaging. So why are there monuments and bodies beneath them?" After another pause, she continued. "This practice is yet another variation on the sin of naming. We all seek meaning in our lives. We want our thoughts and deeds to live on after us, and if we have expressed worthy thoughts and done worthy deeds, we believe they should live on after us. But carving a name in cold stone, over a lifeless and decaying body, is mere vanity. A name is not the deeds of whoever bore the name. A name is not the worthy thoughts of whoever bore the name. A name, once whoever bore it has passed on, is nothing more than an assemblage of letters, an empty vanity. . . ."

Was that really so? Wouldn't I want others to remember me? To remember Rhenn? And didn't the Collegium list the names of imagers who died in service on plaques? Like Claustyn, who'd been so supportive of me when I'd first made third. Or were those names carved in stone more to illustrate that they had died *doing* deeds?

"The Nameless cares for us, for what we have done, for how we have loved . . . for those are what comprise us, not a name, nor a label. We are the sum of our acts and thoughts and feelings, not mere names to be set on dead stone. . . ."

I had to wonder if, in a way, that was why I preferred portraiture to sculpting, because the goal of the portraiturist was to create an image, an impression, of the sum of the personage as he or she was in life, an image that also touched and changed the lives and views of the beholder in the way I had never found that cold stone could do.

I would remember Claustyn for his warmth and friendliness, not for his name.

Wouldn't I?

36

On Lundi morning, I'd barely taken three steps into District Three station, carrying the bag that held the brown cloak, the plaid cap, and the smaller bag with the purple scrap of wool, when Captain Harraf appeared at his study door and summoned me with a peremptory gesture. He said nothing until he had closed the door behind me.

"You haven't heard anything about the Navy conscription teams, have you?"

"I asked about them, but all I was told was that they're likely to begin conscripting in L'Excelsis shortly. The Collegium hasn't been informed when they might start in specific areas of the city."

"Shortly? Is that weeks or days?"

"I got the impression that they would begin in L'Excelsis sooner rather than later, but no one could tell me an exact date."

"Rather convenient. I suppose that even the liaison to the Civic Patrol isn't exalted enough to be privy to such."

"So far as I can tell, Captain, even the Collegium councilor doesn't know."

He looked hard at me.

I had no doubts that Rholyn didn't know. Master Dichartyn might, but not Rholyn.

Finally, he said, "You expect me to believe that, Master Rhennthyl?"

"Captain, you can believe whatever you like, but the councilor told me that he didn't know, and if he doesn't, I don't know when the conscription teams will be doing anything, or where—except that I do know they will be operating in L'Excelsis before long."

"It appears that the Navy trusts the Collegium as little as I do." He smiled coolly. "That was all I had for you, Master Rhennthyl. I imagine Lyonyt is waiting outside for you."

"Do you know when you'll have a replacement for Alsoran?"

"He's not the kind of patroller to replace. A new man is scheduled to be here a week from today. It may be that you will be rotated to another station before long, as well, but no one has informed me."

That was also understandable, from what I'd seen. Neither the subcommander nor the commander really knew what to do with me, and I'd gotten the impression that Artois didn't want to talk to me and Cydarth didn't want me in headquarters. "I'll help as I can here, sir, until the commander decides."

Harraf nodded. "You'd best find Lyonyt."

I didn't bother replying, but smiled, turned, opened the door, and departed, leaving the door open behind me. I stowed the bag in the cubby and went to look for Lyonyt.

"Master Rhennthyl?"

I turned.

"Lyonyt, sir." He stood almost a head shorter than did I, with a wiry build, and brown eyes that never seemed to remain fixed on anything, even while he was looking at me.

"We're to be patrolling together this week, I understand."

"Yes, sir."

"I'm sorry I'm late, but the captain had a question." I looked toward the station door. "I suppose we'd better get moving."

"Yes, sir." Lyonyt seemed to bounce as he moved.

I didn't say more until we were striding up Fuosta toward South Middle. "You've been on leave."

"Yes, sir. I have to thank you. The captain said I only got it because you were available to help Alsoran."

"I'm not sure he needed much help."

"Could be, sir, but it meant a lot to me. Anacherie was so ill after little Marie was born, and then with my father dying right after that . . ."

And Harraf wouldn't allow Lyonyt leave without a replacement? Was Third District that short of patrollers? "I'm glad it worked out." I paused. "How long have you been with the Civic Patrol?"

"Be nine years next Ianus. Best thing I ever did, quit being a butcher's apprentice and apply to the Patrol. Wasn't the cutting. That was fine. Always have liked knives." He drew a long shimmering blade from the sheath on his heavy belt, a sheath partly concealed by his short patroller's cloak. "Times a knife'll do you better than a truncheon." The knife vanished. "Always got fidgety halfway through the day. Caymeyrl was always telling me to settle down. Said a good butcher had to be solid. . . ."

We kept walking, turning east on South Middle. I listened, but kept my eyes moving. For all his chatter, Lyonyt didn't stop looking, either.

Just after we passed the Puryon Temple, I caught sight of another tough, this one some twenty yards up Weigand—the first through street to the south past the Temple. He watched us until we were out of sight. I didn't look at him but once, but could feel his eyes on my back.

I didn't see a purple jacket under the nondescript brown cloak, but I would have wagered he was wearing one.

". . . Sansolt always listens, but he never says anything . . . gets to a fellow after a while. Now, Jaovyl, he's a good man . . . got the round east of the Guild Hall this rotation. . . ."

Before long, we reached the Avenue D'Artisans, and after less than two quints with Lyonyt, I could see why he'd been paired with the quiet and solid Alsoran.

"That place there. It's called Yualtyn's. Don't eat there. Wasn't bad when it was Gosmyn's. Hetyr fixed a good honest ragout. Yualtyn bought him out two-three years back. Now all they serve is that Tiempran shit that burns your mouth before you open it. Over there, Chapytoc—good bootmaker. Does good resoling, too. . . ."

Lyonyt did suggest a different place to eat at midday, a patisserie called Jehan's, which served a folded fried flatbread filled with lamb and mint with a cucumber sauce. I didn't know that I'd have wanted it every day, but it was tasty and filling and a definite change.

After we ate, we reversed the direction of the rounds, but outside of the increasing odor of elveweed, something that happened late every afternoon, the remaining rounds were without any major incidents.

Once I left Lyonyt at the station, I walked down Fuosta and north on Quierca until I could hail a hack. I had the driver drop me in front of Alouette—a patisserie on the Avenue D'Artisans not all that far southwest of Sudroad. If I were to wait for Mardoyt as long as I might have to, I needed something to eat. I settled for a heavy almond-filled croissant and a mug of tea. The tea was merely hot and adequate. The croissant was good enough that I'd come back, perhaps even pick up some to take to my parents and Khethila . . . and, of course, I'd have to make sure there were two for Culthyn.

I took my time walking down the avenue and then across it and wending my way to Saelio, raising concealment shields more than three blocks away from Mardoyt's duplex. When I reached the vantage point from where I could observe the oak in front of the house, I settled into the lengthening shadows and prepared for a long wait. Most of the oaks' leaves had turned, as had the leaves of the other seasonal trees along the street, and possibly a third had fallen onto the grass and the walks, but they were not dry enough yet to rustle that much when someone walked through them.

I took out the scrap of purple cloth and imaged a larger duplicate, concentrating on replicating the warp and weft of the weave, as well as the weight of the threads. Then I studied what I'd imaged. Even as someone who'd been raised to appraise wool, I could detect no noticeable difference between the smaller sample and the larger imaged section of cloth.

Then, I imaged out some sections of the selected oak limb, one that was already dead and hung over the walkway leading to the duplex, not enough that it would break, except in a storm, but enough to make the next step easier.

I kept waiting. I felt I had to, because I needed to resolve the problems Mardoyt was causing before the problems Ryel was causing got even worse. Sooner or later, Mardoyt had to come home, if not tonight, then on Mardi or Meredi, or even Jeudi. I was getting more than a little irritated that I was having to spend so much time dealing with a Patrol officer who was so corrupt, and about whom no one seemed to want to do anything. More than a few patrollers knew what he was doing, and I didn't see how that helped the Civic Patrol maintain any sort of standards in the slightest.

I waited, but Mardoyt still did not appear.

The sun dropped low enough in the west that the entire street was in shadows. Then, roughly a quint after the bells of the nearby anomen rang out sixth glass, a figure in a blue cloak turned the corner and walked up Saelio. It was Mardoyt, his head down, clearly thinking, as if he was worried. He was so preoccupied that I doubted he would have seen me even if I had not been holding concealment shields.

I imaged away the remaining key sections of the oak limb before Mardoyt was even close to the walkway to his house. It took even more effort to use an extension of imaging shields to hold it in place while he neared.

Then, as he turned, I released those supports, and projected shields to hold him in place. The limb toppled, seemingly slowly, but it took all the imaging effort I could muster with extended shields to direct the limb so that the heavier end twisted and slammed into Mardoyt. Just before the limb hit, I released the shield around him, but he couldn't move fast enough to avoid the limb's impact as it smashed across his left shoulder and then crushed and pinned his left leg.

Still behind concealment shields, I slipped up to the unconscious officer and left the imaged scrap of purple in his hand. I also accomplished a last touch of imaging.

I stepped back, realizing that I was soaked in sweat. I could feel my control of my shields slipping away. So I retreated into the shadows and tried to move quietly down the street.

I'd made it less than five yards from the mass of limbs and foliage when I heard a scream from the front porch—that of Mardoyt's daughter. The sound went through me like a knife—or more like the assassin's bullet I'd taken. I kept moving, trying to keep in mind that the patroller whose death Mardoyt had arranged had certainly had those who loved him, and I hadn't done anything to Mardoyt when Youdh's toughs had started attempts on my life. That didn't count the attempt with the granite stones.

Besides, I kept reminding myself on the long and chill walk back to the Collegium, I hadn't killed Mardoyt. If . . . if things went as I'd planned, he'd live, and he'd receive a stipend. He just wouldn't keep his position and be able to take bribes and arrange murders.

If . . .

When I woke on Mardi, I had my ability to raise shields back, and a dull headache that faded after breakfast. Mardi's rounds with Lyonyt were much the same as those on Lundi—until we finished the last round and were heading back west on South Middle, through an autumn mist that wasn't quite a light rain. We crossed Weigand, with the Puryon Temple ahead.

"Over there, Master Rhennthyl!" Lyonyt's voice was low, but insistent. "Left, up maybe thirty yards."

Two men, wearing purple jackets, and not cloaks or waterproofs, despite the mist, stood on a stoop of a house with boarded-up windows. They looked directly at me. Both were old for taudis-toughs, close to my age. One might have been the imager-tough, but I couldn't be certain.

Neither man said anything or moved as we walked past. They just watched us.

"That's not good, Master Rhennthyl. Means they got it in for us."

For me, most likely, but I didn't voice the thought. "These days, they may have it in for everyone, what with a conscription team coming sometime this fall or winter."

"That's what I been hearing. You don't know when, do you?"

"No. The captain asked me yesterday. I didn't know then, and I haven't heard anything since."

"That'll bring more trouble. Always does."

We certainly didn't need more trouble. I knew I didn't.

Once we'd reached the station, we completed the round report, and I signed off on it. Then, I left the station, after a nod to Lieutenant Warydt, who returned the nod with his usual smile, and walked down South Middle until I could catch a hack back to the Bridge of Hopes. On the ride back to Imagisle, I couldn't help worrying about the two toughs. I worried a bit about Mardoyt, but mostly hoped that his injuries were as I'd planned . . . except I could still hear the scream of Mardoyt's daughter.

A thin prime was waiting for me on the Collegium side of the bridge.

"Master Rhennthyl, sir?"

His presence could only mean that Master Dichartyn was looking for me, but I just replied, "Yes?"

"Master Dichartyn would like to see you, sir, right now, sir. If you wouldn't mind, sir . . ."

Three "sirs" strung together like that meant more trouble.

"He's in his study?"

"Yes, sir."

"Then I'll head right there."

The frightened prime followed me, if at a distance, until I knocked on Dichartyn's door.

"Master Dichartyn. It's Rhennthyl. . . ."

"Do come in and close the door, Rhennthyl."

I did.

He was standing by the window. He just looked at me for a long time before speaking. "This afternoon, I had to spend some time with Commander Artois. He was not exactly happy with the reports he had received from Subcommander Cydarth."

"Did something I do displease them?"

"Did you?"

"I did a normal patrol round yesterday, sir. I don't see how that could disturb anyone. Captain Harraf did ask me if I knew when the conscription teams would reach the Third District, and I told him that I didn't know, except that it was likely they would begin in L'Excelsis in the next few weeks. He wasn't happy that I didn't know more."

"How did you know that?"

"Last week, Master Schorzat said that they'd already begun in the west of L'Excelsis." I paused, then added, "Captain Harraf has kept asking about the Navy conscription teams."

For just a moment, there was a flicker of something in Master Dichartyn's eyes. "Most of the teams direct the conscripts to the Navy." He cleared his throat. "Last week, you asked for a patroller pay scale. Why?"

"Might I ask why Commander Artois was displeased, sir?"

"Patience, Rhennthyl. We'll get there in good time." His tone suggested that I wouldn't be happy to get where he was going. "The pay scale?"

"I was still concerned about Lieutenant Mardoyt. He—or someone working for him—has been altering the charging records of the Patrol. Statements come back to the charging desk that charges have been dropped. Some of those charges were dropped while I was observing the justicing administration, and while I was present in the hearings, and they were never brought up before the justice. There aren't any records to support the entries, either, in many cases. After seeing Lieutenant Mardoyt's house—"

"How did you manage that? Following him?"

"Yes, sir."

"Go on."

"He has a house on Saelio below Sudroad. It's a duplex, but a large one in a good neighborhood. It struck me that it would have been difficult to rent or buy such a house on the pay of a lieutenant, but I didn't know because I don't know what a lieutenant makes. So I went to find you, and Beleart said Master Schorzat—"

"We've talked about that. Go on."

"Yes, sir. He said that the pay scale wouldn't prove anything. I realized that but thought I might as well know the pay rates, in any case."

"So why did you attempt to kill Mardoyt?"

"I did no such thing. When did this happen? Is that what Commander Artois was suggesting? Or the subcommander?"

"I will note for the record that you denied attempting to kill one Lieutenant Mardoyt. What did you do with regard to Mardoyt?"

"I told you. I've been following him, trying to see whom he met, trying to figure out how he was doing what he did. You have been very clear with me, sir. You said that you did not want to hear anything from me that I could not prove. I admit fully that I have been following Lieutenant Mardoyt. He is the only member of the Patrol associated with a death caused by an almost identical method as was attempted on me—granite falling from a height. The first patroller under him was killed that way. Likewise, he has changed or removed charges from records. In addition, he knows all about the young lady I have been seeing, in more than fair detail, and he was clear in letting me know that. . . ."

That did catch him by surprise.

Before he could say anything, I went on. "Yet, only Captain Harraf knew where I would be when the granite blocks 'fell' off a scaffold and nearly killed me. Now . . . as you have pointed out, all this does not constitute proof. So I've followed the lieutenant after work a number of nights to see if I could come up with something that might be acceptable as proof. Last week—on Mardi—while using concealment shields slightly down the street from Mardoyt's house, I was attacked by two taudis-toughs. Both were wearing the purple jackets of Youdh's toughs under their cloaks. One was an imager—not terribly well trained, but strong. He used a dust spray to show my position to the gunman and battered at my shields. The gunman fired and hit my shields. I fell and waited. When he came close enough, I dropped him and shot him with his own weapon. I left the body and the weapon there, but the tough who was the imager was already gone."

"Rhennthyl." He used my name as an epithet.

"Master Dichartyn, sir . . . you cannot have it both ways. You cannot tell me that you do not want to hear what I cannot prove and then object that I have not told you what I cannot prove. I was trying to discover the connection between Mardoyt and Harraf and found that there was one between Mardoyt and Youdh. Oh . . . I forgot one other thing . . . two other things. The day I was attacked, three of Youdh's toughs watched me on the patrol round. It was so obvious that Alsoran asked me what I'd done to offend Youdh, but I've never met Youdh. I wouldn't know what he looked like if he appeared here in the study with us. Again, this afternoon, two more toughs were watching Lyonyt and me when we returned to the station. One of them might have been the imager-tough, but I couldn't be sure. I never saw his face, and he didn't have shields."

"You're certain that there was an imager?"

"Yes, sir."

"That's all we need—a renegade imager in the taudis, and one we cannot identify or find. And you said nothing?"

"You weren't here, and what exactly could anyone do until he acted again? No one knows who he is or where he is."

"Rhennthyl . . ."

I just waited.

He shook his head.

"What happened to Lieutenant Mardoyt, sir? You never told me."

"Why do you care? You don't seem to have a good opinion of the man."

"I don't, but I also don't want him dead. So long as he's alive, we might be able to find out more of what he's been doing."

"How did you manage to mangle him with a tree branch?"

"Sir, I'd like to point out again that I had no intention of killing the lieutenant. Since I had no intention of doing so, why would I attack him with something like a tree branch, which might not injure him at all or might easily kill him? How is he?"

Master Dichartyn sighed, mostly for effect, I thought. "The physicians think he'll live. If he does, he won't ever use his left arm for much, and he'll need a cane and a leg brace to walk." He looked at me. "Didn't you know that?"

"No, sir." I knew what I'd done, but not whether it had worked out as I planned.

"Mardoyt said that he heard a crack and that he couldn't move, and then an oak limb fell on him. His wife found a scrap of purple cloth in his hand." Master Dichartyn's eyes narrowed. "You know, Rhennthyl, taking bribes isn't that unique an offense, and it's not one of particular concern to the Collegium. Besides, and more important, his place will be taken sooner or later by someone else who will take bribes."

"Given the structure, that's a possibility, sir. But it's not the bribes that concern me the most. What bothers me, and should bother you, is that both Captain Harraf and the lieutenant have a link to a renegade imager in the taudis, and it's highly likely, proof or no proof, that they have been paying off that imager to kill Patroller Smyrrt and to attempt to kill me. Or that they're trading favors or worse. I also find it interesting that all of the displeasure with me gets filtered through Subcommander Cydarth—who was the one who assigned me to Third District where there is an imager-tough who seems to have connections with two other officers. On top of that, there are more than a few indications that more is going on, possibly including the Equalifier priests. Otherwise, why would there be so many attempts to kill me? Also . . . I'm rather curious about one other thing, sir. You say that a tree branch fell on the lieutenant. Isn't it a bit strange that the commander immediately expresses his displeasure at me? Especially through the subcommander. Why would he even consider that I might be involved?"

"You should have asked that question first."

"It's still a good question, sir. I don't have near the experience that you do, but I know that you and Maitre Poincaryt keep telling me that part of my duties are to be a lure. That may be, but I'm being accused of causing an accident that happened to a Patrol officer who is taking bribes and tied to a taudischef, and probably to attempts to kill me, and I've done nothing but look into a real problem."

"Rhennthyl . . ." He shook his head. "Are you suggesting that I tell the commander we have a renegade imager who's being paid off by his officers, possibly even his subcommander, with no proof whatsoever?"

"No, sir. I'm certain that you could tell him something far more palatable. But you might point out that there have been three attempts on my life since I was named as Patrol liaison, and that doesn't reflect very well on what's happening in the Patrol."

He smiled, if coolly. "That's exactly what I did tell him. He was even less pleased. Next time, if there is a next time, and I do hope that there isn't, you should start your explanations where you ended." He looked at me. "It would also help if you could find a way to resolve these . . . difficulties before too long. It would also be good to have more than your word about a renegade imager."

"I'm doing the best I can, sir." And that didn't even take into account my problems with High Holder Ryel.

"You need to do better." He paused. "That's all, Rhennthyl."

"Yes, sir."

"Close the door on your way out."

I did.

Once again, I'd gotten another lesson, if not the one that Master Dichartyn had intended. Still, he knew I'd injured Mardoyt. The fact that he'd gone through the motions meant that he didn't think much of Mardoyt, either. He just hadn't cared for my way of handling it. What else was I supposed to do? Keep looking for nonexistent proof until I got killed?

I stopped by my quarters, leaving my patroller's cloak behind, and then headed to the dining hall. Because I was a bit early, I stopped by my letter box, not that I really expected anything. But there was a letter there, and it held the red stripe. Who would be sending me an urgent message by private courier? I looked at the writing . . . and swallowed. It was Khethila's—and that was anything but good. I didn't quite rip the envelope open.

Dear Rhenn,

I am writing this because Father and Mother did not have time to. We have just received word that Rousel has been badly injured in a wagon accident in Kherseilles. We don't know how it happened, but his legs have been crushed, and he has other injuries.

It seems so unfair. He had just written that he had managed to get a stonemason to rebuild the wall on our property. He had worked all night and day with the mason to meet the deadline stipulated by the legal agreement in order to avoid a 500 gold penalty, and there are other problems as well.

You cannot do anything, I know, but you should know. Father and Mother have already left on the ironway for Kherseilles with Culthyn . . .

I lowered the letter. I had no doubts that Rousel's injury was anything but an accident, and that Ryel had been behind it. Then I slipped the letter inside my waistcoat and left the dining hall, heading across the Bridge of Desires, because that was the closest place to find a hack. The mist had turned into a light rain and I was damp, but not soaked, by the time I was inside a coach and headed to see Khethila.

Why Rousel? Even as I asked myself that question, I knew the answer. Because he was Father's heir to Alusine Wool and because Ryel was a typical sadistic High Holder who wanted to prove that he could destroy my family, slowly and deliberately, without a shred of proof to link anything illegal to him. Everything he'd caused to happen would show as either perfectly legal or connected in no way to him.

The rain was heavier when I left the hack, and I gave the driver a few extra coppers for his trouble, then hurried up under the portico roof, where I gave the knocker several sharp thraps. After several moments, the door opened slightly, and I could see the chains.

"Khethila . . . it's me. I just got your message, and I came immediately."

She opened the door. "Oh . . . Rhenn . . . you didn't have to." The tone of her voice contradicted her words.

I stepped inside, closed the door, and put my arms around her.

She sobbed silently for a time, then stepped back and blotted her eyes. They were blotchy. "Thank you."

"It's all I can do right now." That was more than true, unfortunately.

She looked at me. "You didn't eat, did you?"

"No. Why?"

"You're pale. We can go into the kitchen. You can eat, and we can talk. There's some cold fowl and cheese and some fresh bread. I didn't have cook fix a supper . . ."

"Anything would be fine." I followed her through the family parlor and into the kitchen.

Before long, I was sitting on one side of the table in the breakfast room, lit by a single wall lamp, and she was on the other. I had slices of bread, cheese, and fowl on a plate, and we each had a glass of Grisio. She needed it more than I.

"What happened?" I asked, after taking a bite of the sharp white cheese. I was hungry.

"I don't know much more than I wrote. Rousel was hit by a horse that spooked and knocked him under a brewer's wagon that was moving. Remaya sent a dispatch by ironway. Father talked to someone he knew to get a compartment on the afternoon train." Khethila took a healthy swallow of the Grisio. "It's almost like the Nameless or the Namer is after Father."

"Or some commercial rival," I suggested.

"Could anyone . . ." She let the words die away for a moment. "Of course they could. Some people will do anything. But who?"

"It could be someone with an old grudge, who just waited until the time was right to hurt the family the hardest." That was as close as I was going to get because, with what I planned, no one in my family, especially Khethila, could afford to know why it was happening.

"It could be Rousel, too," she said softly. "He hasn't always been as careful as he should be."

"You need to think about it. So will I. You'll keep me informed?"

"I promise."

After that we talked, first about Rousel and the factorage in Kherseilles and then about less consequential things, but I did mention I'd been required to attend the Autumn Ball, and that led to a few questions about Madame D'Shendael, none of which I could really answer.

Then, as it got close to eighth glass, I rose to go.

"You can't stay tonight . . . can you?"

I shook my head. "I can't stay anywhere at night besides the Collegium."

"That's a stupid rule."

"No. Unhappily, it's not. Imagers can image in their dreams, and dreams aren't always under control. Especially at a time like this." I'd never been told I couldn't say that, and she needed a real reason, tonight more than any other.

"Oh . . ."

"I'm sorry. Please don't tell anyone else that. It's not something the Collegium likes known, but tonight I didn't want to just say that it was a rule."

That brought a shaky smile to her lips. "I won't . . . but thank you." After a moment, she said, "Charlsyn can take you back. I'll let him know."

I didn't argue, even if it meant that Khethila would end up paying him more for the week.

Town of Georgina (KESWICK) Public Library

38

I didn't sleep well on Mardi night, not with nightmares about more fires in the factorage, and runaway wagons, and lightning striking the house while Khethila was in it, but at least I didn't image any more fires in my sleep. It was a relief to get up and deal with the simple physical tasks of exercising, sparring, and running. For that time, at least, the effort kept me from dwelling on my worries about Rousel and Father. I was quiet enough at breakfast, but no one noticed because Ferlyn was talking about how the Northern Fleet had destroyed another Ferran flotilla.

When I finally got to Third District station, I didn't see either the captain or the lieutenant, and that was fine with me.

Lyonyt was waiting, bouncing from one booted foot to the other. "Master Rhennthyl."

"Good morning, Lyonyt."

"A good morning it is, sir. Not a cloud in the sky, and but enough breeze to keep a patroller comfortable on his rounds."

I hadn't brought anything with me, nothing to stow in the cubby that was temporarily mine. So I gestured to the doors, and we headed out. As had seemed to be the case in all the rounds in the area of the taudis, we saw very few people on the first round—and none of Youdh's toughs. Their absence bothered me, because it suggested the time for observation was over, and I resolved to be as alert as I could be throughout the day. I did have to make an effort not to get distracted by worrying about Rousel.

We were finishing the second round, heading down Mando, the unofficial boundary, Alsoran had told me, between Jadhyl's territory and that of Youdh, or the bad part of the taudis and the really evil section. West of Mando, the ground rose, not a great deal but a good two or three yards over the next block, so that when I looked westward up the alleys opening on to Mando I couldn't see the end of the alley. This section of the taudis had to be ancient because the alleyways were barely wide enough to fit a single large wagon.

The row houses were all old and weathered, and the faintest odor of elveweed drifted unevenly in the air, an odor that would strengthen with each round in the day. But none of the houses on the east side of the street had empty windows or those that were boarded over. Admittedly, many of them had crude shutters, often only of oiled wood, but they did have shutters. I thought that reflected well on Jadhyl, or at least better upon him than the shabbier conditions of the area to the west did upon Youdh. Youdh was truly an old-style taudischef of the sansespoirs.

We walked down the east side of Mando, and I glanced up the next alley, only to see a large wagon, its wheels blocked in place at the top of the rise, and so broad that there was less than a hand's width between the wagon bed and frame and the high brick walls of the courtyards adjoining the alley.

"Help! Help!" A frantic high-pitched scream echoed down the alleyway.

We both turned.

A dark-haired woman, scarcely more than a young girl, was pressed against the rough bricks of a second-level terrace by a man in shabby clothing. She struggled to get away, then ducked under his arm, but he grabbed her blouse and ripped it open, leaving her mostly naked from the waist up. I couldn't help but notice she was well formed and most attractive, before she tried to wrench away from the far larger man once again.

"Help!"

It was too far to image anything accurately, and they were moving about so quickly I might hurt the wrong one if I tried. Even as I hurried across Mando and up the alley, followed by Lyonyt, I kept looking in all directions, although I thought it was probably early for most taudis-toughs. I saw no one anywhere, except for the screaming half-naked woman and the man trying to assault her. Even so, I checked and strengthened my shields.

Lyonyt's knife was out, shimmering in the midmorning sunlight.

When we reached the courtyard wall below the terrace, a good twenty-five yards from the street, I discovered that the high side wall to the courtyard below the terrace had no gate.

"Help me!"

Up on the ancient roof terrace, the attacker was ripping away the girl's skirt.

"Help!" Her voice rose into a shriek.

But there was something wrong . . .

At a low rumbling sound, almost like thunder, I glanced up the alley, only to see that the enormous wagon was rolling—more like hurtling—down the stone-paved alleyway at us, less than ten yards away and already moving far too fast for us to outrun it. I could also see that it was loaded with stone and rocks, and that the axles and the wagon bed were too low to dive under the middle and let it pass over.

"Down, flat, against the wall!" I snapped and dropped to the alley pavement, carrying Lyonyt down as well, so that we lay stomach down beside the brick wall. I strengthened my shields and tried to tie them not to me, but to the cracked stone pavement beneath us and the brick wall against which my shoulder and side were pressed.

The rumbling thunder crashed over us, pressing us down, and then passed.

"Stay down," I hissed, not moving.

The next sound was that of the wagon impacting something, most likely the stoop or the front of a house on the other side of Mando, and wrenching and splintering wood and the diminishing lesser rumbles of stones coming to rest.

"Keep still . . ." I was wagering that whoever had set up the attack would want to check out the carnage, and I wanted them close—very close—before I moved. I was getting very tired of being attacked, especially when I hadn't even been chasing or investigating Youdh, but Mardoyt.

I didn't move, but kept my eyes open.

After a time, it could have been as long as half a quint, two figures began to walk down the alley. Both wore the purple jackets.

I wasn't in any mood for fairness. I just waited until the pair were less than five yards away when I imaged oil and grease under their boots, and a blast of air to unbalance them. They both went down, but not as hard as I would have liked. I scrambled to my feet, glancing around in all directions, but seeing only the two toughs nearby . . . but several near the part of the alley that was the top of the rise.

The taller one immediately did something I didn't expect, not exactly. Rather than even get up, he just looked at me, and then five rusty knives impacted my shields before dropping to the pavement. The shorter one scrambled to his feet and fell again, then regained his footing and raced away from Lyonyt, yelling something to the two taudis-toughs farther up the alley.

Before I could even think what to do next, another set of weapons slammed into my shields—this time, what looked like iron crossbow bolts. They were followed by flaming oily fireballs.

"Spawn of the Namer!" blurted Lyonyt.

Then came three large spiked objects, so heavy that when they struck my shields, I was slammed back against the brick wall. One of them dropped from my shields and splintered the heavy stone of a paving stone. Another stuck with a point wedged between two paving blocks.

At that point, I'd had enough. Even so, I didn't want to overdo it, because

I wanted the imager alive. I imaged salt and caustic into his eyes, not in the massive amounts that had killed Diazt, but enough, I thought, to blur the imager's vision or blind him for a quint or so. As I did so, I charged him, putting a knee into his chin and snapping his head back. He just tumbled back onto the ancient cracked and uneven paving stones, mumbling.

". . . can't see . . . Ravyt! Ravyt!"

The man who lay there trying to rise and rubbing at his eyes was the tough who had escaped me at Mardoyt's house, and the same one who had observed me when I walked past the Puryon Temple early in the week.

"Get him tied up, Lyonyt. Quickly."

At that moment, the imager-tough rolled on his side and then started to rise and lunge away. I dropped on his back with both knees, slamming him into the pavement again.

He was still, or mostly still, while Lyonyt and I manacled his hands behind him. I kept my weight on him while Lyonyt bound his feet at the ankles. Then, I concentrated, as well as I could, enough to image a length of black cloth—not very good wool, but sufficient for my purposes—and I immediately began wrapping it around his upper face and across his eyes.

Only after he was secured did I glance up at the terrace—silent and empty. The two, or at least the man, had been creating a distraction—enough of one that we had not been able to escape the stone-weighted wagon.

"Sir? The cloth?"

"He's a renegade imager, but he has to see to image."

"Sir . . . that's Youdh."

"How do you know?"

"The one who ran off . . . he was yelling to the others that you'd gotten Youdh."

Youdh? The imager was Youdh himself?

I couldn't say I was surprised.

"Sir . . . what do we do now?"

"We tie him up really tightly and cart him to the pickup point and have the pickup wagon take him to Imagisle. Imagers who commit crimes are subject to the laws of the Collegium. Besides, no gaol can hold an imager without special procedures."

"Ah . . . yes, sir."

"Do you have another suggestion?"

"No, sir."

Youdh was neither light nor cooperative, and he squirmed a great deal. We carried him for a time, then rested, and carried him farther, until we reached the pickup point. But I wasn't about to give him any vision and any leeway whatsoever, not after he'd tried to kill me so many times.

While we were waiting, I decided to see if he'd talk, but I didn't want to ask him anything that dealt with possible Patrol corruption, not with Lyonyt standing beside me.

"Youdh . . . why did you keep trying to kill me?"

"Friggin' imager-patroller, spawn of Namer-sow and cursed canine . . . friggin' everything up . . . couldn't find a teat on a copper cow . . ."

"What do you get from the equalifiers . . . or do you have to pay them?"

"Give more 'n the Patrol types."

That was suggestive, but I wasn't going to pursue it. "So they do pay well. A few golds a month?"

"Frig you . . ." The mutter was low, but clear.

After that, he said even less.

Almost a glass passed before the wagon arrived. When I told the driver where we were headed, he looked at me, then at Lyonyt, almost helpless.

"Take us where Master Rhennthyl wants," Lyonyt finally said. "You really want to be the one to bring a taudischef imager to the station?"

With the clarity of those words, the driver swallowed and said, "Yes, sir."

Although Youdh didn't seem to have much to say, except mutter, I watched him closely on the slow wagon trip down the Midroad and then the Boulevard D'Imagers, thinking. If Youdh was an imager, why couldn't he have used his abilities in little ways to help the people in his area of the taudis? Or couldn't he afford to reveal that to anyone except his toughs because the equalifier priests, whom he needed, opposed imagers? Or was he like Diazt, who would rather have been the meanest and least powerful taudischef than a respected imager?

Once the wagon finally came to a halt outside the receiving hall on the east side of Imagisle, I hopped off.

"Lyonyt . . . if he does anything, hit him hard on the head with the truncheon. Do you understand?"

"Yes, sir." Lyonyt's voice was resolute, but he was far from happy. I couldn't say I blamed him, but I had no idea where the Collegium's equivalent of a gaol was. That hadn't been on the map I'd memorized, or if it had been, I didn't remember.

I walked into the reception hall. I barely knew the prime on duty and had to struggle with his name. "Jakhob, is either Master Dichartyn or Master Schorzat here?"

"Master Dichartyn, sir, but . . ." He gulped.

"But what . . . ?"

"He's meeting with someone, sir."

"In his study?"

"Yes, sir . . . but . . ."

"I'll take care of it." I turned and walked down to the study, where I rapped smartly on the door.

There was no answer. So I rapped harder.

"I'm not to be disturbed." The words were snappish.

"It's Rhennthyl, and I have the renegade imager trussed up and blindfolded out in a Civic Patrol wagon outside the receiving hall. Exactly what would you like me to do with him?"

As he opened the door, Master Dichartyn glared at me, possibly the first time his expression had ever held such hostility. "Rhennthyl. Is this some jest?"

"No, sir. I have with him a certain amount of physical proof, including five identical rusty knives that he imaged at me, six identical iron crossbow bolts, and three large items that resemble morning stars. I also have the patroller who was with me when he attacked us with a large wagon filled with stones and who saw all the imaging attacks." I paused. "And, by the way, this renegade imager also happens to be taudischef Youdh himself, which might explain a few things."

"Why didn't you—"

"Because you gave me the impression that, first, you were rather dubious about my insistence that I was facing a renegade imager, and second, that some form of proof was necessary. Given that situation, I thought it best that I deliver the renegade to the Collegium, along with all the proof I could provide. I also thought his trial might prove useful. You might find out what else he knows. I'm doubtful about that myself. He's been awake for most of the trip down here, but he's only muttered various expletives having to do with my heritage. Oh . . . his vision is probably somewhat impaired. I did image some caustic there, but not nearly so much as in past cases."

Abruptly a series of laughs issued from the study behind Master Dichartyn.

"Ask and you shall receive, Dichartyn. You might as well open the door."

I recognized the voice of Maitre Poincaryt.

Master Dichartyn's glare faded from burnished steel to blank obsidian. Then he shook his head, ruefully, as he opened the door. "You might as well come in."

I did, inclining my head politely to Maitre Poincaryt. "Sir."

"Rhennthyl." The head maitre of the Collegium studied me. "Tell me. What was it that Dichartyn did that so angered you?"

"Sir . . . I know that there's much I don't know—"

Master Dichartyn's expression indicated disbelief or disagreement with my words.

"But when I tell a senior master I've encountered an imager, I do know enough to recognize one. I've even uncovered one that he'd met and hadn't recognized. My techniques are rough, and my knowledge of the finer points of many aspects of imaging is doubtless lacking, but when I report two or possibly three senior officers of the Civic Patrol are corrupt and two are deeply involved with the taudis and bribes and killings . . . don't tell me I don't know what I'm talking about. You can certainly tell me to ignore it, or that there are other considerations, or that someone else will handle it, but don't expect me to believe what is not true."

Maitre Poincaryt raised his eyebrows and looked to Dichartyn.

"He's asked me to take a great deal on faith, sir," Master Dichartyn said.

"Has he been wrong?"

"Yes, sir," I admitted. "I have been, but it's been because I didn't know other information. I needn't have killed Diazt, but I thought I was facing him and Johanyr alone. I thought that the corruption in the Civic Patrol was limited to Mardoyt and Harraf, and I still can't prove that Cydarth and Harraf are involved."

"Enough." Master Poincaryt's voice was firm, but I sensed tiredness behind it. He looked to Master Dichartyn. "Try this renegade, and make it public and quick. Find out what you can about his ties to the Patrol, but don't make those public. For the moment, only we three need to know that." He looked at me. "I'd appreciate it if you'd be a little easier on Dichartyn. You're still young and worried and upset about your situation. Imagine what it would be if you were handling three times that amount, if not more. You worry about one renegade imager and one High Holder being after you. I doubt that Master Dichartyn has ever had that few enemies in the last ten years. In addition, unlike you, he has a wife and two daughters as well." He paused. "I'd also appreciate it if both of you trusted each other more."

Then he nodded and stepped past me and down the corridor.

I turned to Master Dichartyn. "I'm sorry to have upset matters, sir." And I was, but what else could I have done?

He shook his head once more. "Rhennthyl . . . you could be such an asset to the Collegium, if we all survive your learning process." Then he actually smiled, genuinely, if ruefully. "Let's take care of your captive imager."

I did appreciate his momentary kindness, even if the rest of the day turned out to be very long. First, I had to send a Collegium messenger to Third District station with a note informing Captain Harraf or Lieutenant Warydt what had happened and why neither Lyonyt nor I would be back for the rest of the shift. I ended up directing a group of primes and seconds who functioned as scriveners to take the statements of Lyonyt and the driver. Then, while Master Dichartyn and Master Jhulian were questioning Youdh, since I could not, having been part of the events, I had to write out my own statement, as well as a description of the evidence.

After that, Master Jhulian questioned me in great depth—but, interestingly, only about the events of the morning. I had a good idea how the hearing was likely to go, but I'd have to see.

The worst part, I realized, was how little I'd accomplished.

Baluzt was probably continuing what Mardoyt had been doing. There was no real evidence to lead to either Captain Harraf or to the subcommander.

And, worst of all, I'd been able to do nothing to address the problems with High Holder Ryel. I could only hope that I could discover something at the Ball—assuming that he or Iryela or his son or nephew even attended.

39

Again, on Meredi night, I didn't sleep all that well. The nightmares were more vivid, a mélange of scenes with Patrol officers, severe-faced maitres, High Holders, and Khethila. Although I couldn't recall details when I woke, the impression they left with me was that whatever I did was too late or not enough, or both. I had to work to get past the feelings raised by the nightmares as I tried to think out the day on the coach ride to Third District station, but there were so many unresolved matters.

The first thing I did after I arrived at the station was read over Lyonyt's official Patrol report of the incident with Youdh, with Lyonyt hovering at my elbow.

"I think I got it all down, sir. Some of it happened real quick."

"The important things are all here." I smiled, then signed below his scrawl. "I need to talk to the captain for a moment. I won't be able to be here tomorrow, and he needs to know."

"Sir?"

"The justice hearing for Youdh. It's tomorrow."

"Oh . . . yes, sir."

I turned and walked straight into the captain's study. "Good morning."

He didn't rise from behind his desk. "Good morning, Master Rhennthyl. You and Lyonyt had a busy day yesterday. I would like to say that we won't have as many problems with the middle section of the taudis." His smile was forced. "I fear that we will have more and different problems. Much as they are problems, strong taudischefs maintain order in ways that the Patrol cannot."

"That they can, sir. I'm not certain that Youdh was a strong taudischef. He was personally powerful, but that doesn't always translate into strong and effective leadership. As you have said, we will see." I smiled politely. "I fear that I am going to create a small problem for you. I will not be able to accompany Lyonyt tomorrow. My presence is required at the justice hearing for Youdh."

"So soon?" Harraf frowned. "Usually, there's at least a week between charging and the hearing."

"You haven't had a chance to read yesterday's report. One of the reasons Youdh's caused so much trouble is that he's actually an imager who was never discovered. Imagers fall under Collegium justice."

"Oh . . . and what might that be?"

I kept smiling. "The penalty for using imaging in committing any significant crime is death. There are no exceptions and mitigating circumstances.
The only question is whether Youdh committed a crime, but since he used
imaging in attempting to kill a patroller and an imager . . ." I shrugged.

"I don't imagine he's said much or confessed to anything. Most taudis-
types don't."

"He had quite a few comments upon my breeding and background and
why I deserved to be dead, but little more than that. But I'm not trained in
obtaining information the way some imagers are. They may find out more,
but even if they do, I doubt if I'll know for some time."

Harraf nodded, then spoke. "Subcommander Cydarth sent a message in-
dicating that you would be available to assist Third District for another two
weeks, and possibly longer, depending on other circumstances. I had thought
that next week, with the possible unrest in the taudis, you could accompany
Lyonyt and Fuast—he's Alsoran's replacement, fresh from training."

"I'll plan on doing that, sir."

"You haven't heard anything more on the progress of the conscription
teams, have you?"

"There's a rumor that they've started in the west of L'Excelsis, but I've
heard nothing to confirm that, sir."

"The west? Much help that is." He glanced past me.

"If you'll excuse me . . ."

He nodded again, and I departed.

Harraf had not been surprised in the least that Youdh had been an imager.
He hadn't even tried to counterfeit surprise. That strongly suggested that he'd
known and, more important, that he knew that I knew he knew. He also
knew I had no proof that he'd done anything wrong.

"Sir?" asked Lyonyt as soon as I rejoined him. "Did he say anything about
tomorrow?"

"He didn't. I will be patrolling with you and Fuast next week, on some of
the days, at least." That wasn't what Harraf had said, but the way matters were
going I had an idea I might need to be elsewhere.

When we walked past the Temple I saw no sign of any taudis-toughs,
in purple jackets or otherwise. On the first patrol round, the one that
made a circuit, we saw only the usual morning people—women sweeping
stoops, small children on porches, a few older women walking toward the
avenue.

We'd gone a block farther along on the second round, leaving Saelio, when I caught sight of two men in green jackets, standing beside a gatepost next to an alley.

"Jadhyl . . ." murmured Lyonyt.

I'd half expected the well-spoken taudischef, if somewhat later in the day, but all I said was, "Let's see what he has to say."

Once we were within a few yards, I halted and said, "Good morning, Jadhyl."

"Good morning to you, Master Imager." Jadhyl looked at me, appraisingly, before continuing. "It is said that a wagon filled with stones rolled over you, and that you got up and walked through a hail of knives, and arrows, and brushed aside spiked cannonballs. Then you brought Youdh to his knees and then trussed him up like a piglet for slaughter."

"Something like that," I admitted. "It wasn't that exciting. Youdh had tried to kill me several times before that. It was time to put a stop to it."

He inclined his head. "Were you a Patrol lieutenant, Master Rhennthyl, or a captain, the taudis would be far safer."

"If you were a taudischef of more blocks, Jadhyl, people would live better."

"Deyalt and I do what we can." He nodded to the muscular man beside him.

"So do I, and so do most patrollers." I smiled politely. "I appreciate your being willing to talk and your efforts to make things better in the taudis."

There was a moment of silence.

"Has it been decided," I asked, "who might succeed Youdh? Or take over his territory?"

"Of that I would not know," replied Jadhyl. "We have made it clear that we will do our own patrols on both sides of Mando. I have heard that Horazt may watch over another block east toward Dugalle. Those between us will decide what they will do."

"And the priests of Puryon?"

"They will decide what they will decide." Jadhyl's voice was cold. Then he smiled, politely, but not coolly. "We did wish to express our pleasure that you are well and continue to patrol."

"Thank you for your kind words. We will continue to do what we can."

He nodded, and I nodded, and we resumed our patrol round.

Lyonyt looked sideways at me, but did not speak for a time as we kept walking. Finally, he said, "Begging your pardon, Master Rhennthyl, but could I ask . . . ah . . . you're a real master imager, and you're doing patrols, like the lowest patroller."

I managed a smile. "How would I know what you do if I don't do it? Words . . . names . . . they don't convey what it feels like when you have to watch every corner and every alley . . . or wonder if you're going to walk down a street and find an old lady being strangled by an out-of-control elver, or find taudis-toughs attacking you."

"Folks can't hurt you."

I laughed. "I've been shot in the chest and almost didn't live through it. I've had my ribs broken in an explosion, and at one time or another just about every part of my body has been bruised. My skills just make it harder for people to hurt me, but it doesn't mean they can't and haven't. Youdh was an imager, but we managed to subdue him."

"A good thing, too." He looked at me again, but I just smiled, and he didn't ask any more questions about how I might get hurt.

When we walked down Mando, I noted that the wreckage of the large wagon had vanished totally, although there was sawdust in places in the gutters, as well as wood chips. The broken building stones and bricks had been placed in a single pile. There were no intact bricks or building stones left.

All in all the rounds of the day were most quiet, and when we finished the last round and returned to the district station, I didn't see either the captain or the lieutenant.

I was more tired on Jeudi night when I got to the dining hall than I had been the night before. Thankfully, there were no red-striped letters in my box, but I had the sinking feeling that sooner or later there would be. Ryel was nothing if not thorough, and yet I was still flailing, and trying to work out how I could respond without overt traces back to me . . . and I feared that others would pay the price. Yet, without knowing more, I couldn't take any action that would not be hasty and futile.

Belatedly, as I headed toward the masters' table, I realized that it had been quite a while since I'd eaten two dinners in a row at the Collegium. Maitre Dyana beckoned to me in a quiet way that could not be denied, and I settled into the seat to her left. Ferlyn and Quaelyn were to her right, with Chassendri and Isola beyond them.

"Good evening, maitre."

"Good evening, Rhenn. I understand that you have been rather dogged in ferreting out what many would prefer not to be ferreted out."

"I imagine that's a matter of opinion."

"So it is. You're going to the Autumn Ball tomorrow, are you not?" Maitre Dyana's words were polite and mildly curious as she straightened the comparatively subdued black scarf, trimmed in gold.

"Unless Master Dichartyn changes his mind," I replied with a smile. "Would you like the red or the white Grisio?"

"The white goes better with the veal. The cream sauce is usually a touch heavier than it should be. But then, cream applied heavily enough can sweeten anything."

"That's something I've observed with Maitre Poincaryt." I chuckled wryly, after half filling her goblet. "He can deliver a reprimand with such gentleness that you almost don't feel the welts—except they don't go away. I suppose that's just another reason why he's the Collegium Maitre." I could have been less direct, but I wasn't as good at it as she was, and she had something in mind.

"A series of cuts delivered with a sharp knife has the same delayed effect, but there's more bleeding. Poison in a dessert wine is also a favorite of some High Holders. It's best to remember that the meal isn't over until it's thoroughly digested."

I supposed that was the same as saying that the last laugh was the best, but since High Holders seldom laughed, not in honest enjoyment, anyway, they wouldn't have said anything like that.

"Tell me, Rhennthyl. How long do you think that taudis imager had been imaging?"

"I have no way of knowing, but I'd judge at least ten years, if not longer."

"Yet he revealed himself to you, if indirectly."

"Not exactly," I replied. "I discovered his abilities when he didn't know who I was, and then, after he'd revealed those abilities, the attacks on me began."

"I thought it might have been something like that. Even in games of plaques, when one must only keep track of cards, it's a pity that often revealing one's abilities leads to greater difficulties . . . unless, of course, one reveals limited abilities and holds greater capabilities in reserve."

"The problem there, maitre, as I see it, is that one can do that only once, perhaps twice, even in plaques."

"Precisely." She smiled. "The seasoning on the pilaf is almost piquant."

I'd definitely gotten a message. Whether I could translate the implications of her conversation was another question entirely, since I'd already revealed my abilities to a greater degree than was wise. I avoided frowning, though, as I realized that it was highly unlikely that High Holder Ryel knew the extent of what I could do—and Maitre Dyana's comments had been prefaced with remarks about the Autumn Ball.

40

Between Youdh's hearing and my required attendance at the Council's Autumn Ball, I knew Vendrei would be a long day—a very long day—beginning with the strenuous exercises and sparring under Clovyl's watchful eyes.

I was at the Collegium Justice Building at half before eighth glass, as Master Dichartyn had told me to be, and found myself sitting alone in the witness chamber adjoining the hearing area. Except for Youdh, who had not appeared, there were no other witnesses, because Master Dichartyn had taken their statements for the hearing record.

As I waited, I stood in the open door to the witness chamber and glanced through the archway up at the wooden high-backed gallery benches set on tiers that rose behind a low wall that separated the hearing area from the gallery. A central set of steps split the benches, rising from the wall to the upper entry on the second level. My eyes dropped to the justicing area. At the east end was a dais a yard high, with a black desk in the middle. The floor was entirely of gray seamless stone, except for a walkway of black stone that ran from the archway where I stood to the foot of the dais.

"Rhennthyl . . ." offered Master Dichartyn, gesturing toward the witness chamber.

"Yes, sir." I edged back into the small room and sat down on the bench on the east side.

I'd been seated for only a moment, when two muscular obdurate guards in their black uniforms marched Youdh in and sat him on the other bench, blindfolded and manacled. The guards remained standing on each side of Youdh, who said nothing.

Outside, the bells began to ring the glass.

A few moments later, I could hear the voice of the bailiff, Master Ghaend, faintly through the now-closed door. "All rise."

There was silence for what seemed to be a long time. Although I could not see what was happening, I knew that the justice, most likely Master Jhulian, walked to the dais and seated himself behind the desk.

"You may be seated," announced Master Ghaend. The door to the witness chamber opened. "Youdh D'Estaudis, step forward to the bar."

Youdh did not move. The two guards said nothing, but hoisted the taudis-chef to his feet. After that he did walk, in a fashion, out of the witness chamber. Master Ghaend closed the door, and I could hear nothing.

I knew he'd be charged with one count of attempted murder of a patroller, two counts of attempted murder of an imager, two counts of assault, and one count of failing to report to Imagisle as an imager. Since all of the charges, except failure to report, involved the use of imaging, each one of which he was convicted could carry a death sentence.

I felt that almost a full glass passed before the door to the witness chamber opened and Master Ghaend announced, "Master Rhennthyl to the bar."

As I stepped out of the witness chamber and through the archway, I could sense that the gallery was filled, which meant close to two hundred fifty im-agers, from primes to graying masters. I walked deliberately forward to the bar before the dais.

The justice seated behind the desk on the dais was Master Jhulian. He wore a long gray robe, like the Council justices, except his was trimmed in both black and red, instead of just black. The prosecutor for the Collegium, standing before the small table to the left, was Master Dichartyn. To the right was Master Rholyn. Seated behind the small table on the right was Youdh. I noticed that he was now gagged and bound to the chair.

I halted short of the bar and inclined my head politely.

"Master Rhennthyl," said Master Jhulian, looking directly and intently at me, "do you understand that you are required to tell the whole truth, and that your words must not deceive, either by elaboration or omission?"

"Yes, sir."

"Proceed." Jhulian looked to Master Dichartyn.

"Master Rhennthyl, please describe what occurred on the morning of Meredi, the thirty-second of Feuillyt, as you were patrolling with one Patroller Lyonyt." Master Dichartyn could have been reading a textbook, for all the lack of emotion in his voice.

"We had made one patrol round, heading out Quierca and then up the Avenue D'Artisans, and then down South Middle, before we walked back to Saelio and began patrolling the inner streets of the round. The last street on the second round was Mando . . ." I went on to describe exactly what had happened, from the first scream of the woman until we had delivered Youdh to the gaol at Imagisle.

Master Dichartyn did not interrupt me once. After I finished, he said, "I have several questions, for clarification for the Collegium. Why did you remain lying on the pavement after the wagon passed?"

"There was no one nearby, and I wanted to see if whoever had aimed the wagon at us would investigate. I thought that if we got up immediately, we would drive them away."

Master Dichartyn lifted a rusty knife and carried it over to me. "Is this one of the knives that was imaged at you?"

I studied it. "Yes, sir. There were five, and they were all identical, even to the pattern of rust and the gouge on the grip."

"Thank you." He set the knife on the justice's desk and picked up an iron crossbow bolt. "Do you recognize this?"

"Yes, sir. It's one of the crossbow bolts that Youdh imaged at me."

He asked the same questions about the morning stars, and I replied. Then he asked, "It would have been within your purview as a master imager to have killed Youdh then and there. Why didn't you?"

"I had reported the possibility that there was an imager-tough in the taudis, and that report was received with some skepticism, sir. I attempted to capture him for two reasons. First, I thought the Collegium should have the opportunity to question him. Second, I wanted it verified that much of the recent difficulty in the area had been caused by an imager."

"Thank you, Master Rhennthyl. No further questions."

Master Jhulian looked to Master Rholyn. "Do you have any questions for the witness, Advocate for the Defense?"

"Just a few, Your Honor." Rholyn stepped forward. "Master Rhennthyl, you said that you had anticipated there was an imager in the taudis. Did you have any idea as to the actual identity of the imager?"

"No, sir. In fact, even after we captured the imager, I didn't know who he was—except that I'd seen him twice before without knowing who he was. Lyonyt told me who he was."

"Given his lack of training, don't you think that you could have captured him without injuring his vision?"

"He kept imaging things at us, and I didn't sense that he was at all tired. I also didn't know whether his toughs would return if I spent too much time trying to subdue him gently. With everything he was throwing in my direction, it would have been difficult and dangerous to approach more closely. I did try not to inflict permanent damage to his vision, but that seemed the safest way to stop his imaging so that we could capture him."

Muffled sounds issued from the gagged Youdh, and his chair bounced.

None of the masters looked in his direction.

Master Rholyn turned to Master Jhulian. "No further questions."

"You may leave the chamber for the anteroom, Master Rhennthyl," declared Master Jhulian.

I inclined my head in respect, then turned, and walked back along the black stone, stepping through the archway and back into the witness chamber.

As bailiff, Master Ghaend closed the door behind me.

As I sat there thinking, I realized something else, another reason why Youdh was most likely behind the granite blocks falling on me. Someone had known that my shields might have been impaired by a blow coming downward . . . but I had told no one that my shields had been hit by the stone. Only whoever had done it—Youdh—or someone familiar with imagers—Harraf perhaps—would have known that and arranged for toughs to use pistols against me in the days following. Again . . . it wasn't proof.

Only about half a glass passed before I heard Master Ghaend's voice coming through the door of the witness chamber. "All rise!" From the timing and the firmness in Ghaend's voice, Master Jhulian was about to announce his findings and sentence, not that there was any question as to either.

Ghaend eased the door to the witness chamber ajar, clearly so that I could listen, and I rose from the bench and eased over to the door, hoping to hear more clearly.

"Youdh, imager of Estaudis, this court finds as follows. First, the facts and testimony confirm that you did in fact commit the offenses with which you have been charged. Second, given your lengthy misuse of imaging, acceptance of a plea of For Mercy is not warranted. Third, the penalty for conviction on each of the major charges is death."

I could hear no sound from either the court area or the gallery.

A faint clank echoed through the space. That had to have been when Youdh fell after Master Jhulian executed the sentence.

I waited by the door to the witness box, knowing that the two obdurates were lifting the body. Before long, I could see through the narrow space between the door and the jamb as they walked past with Youdh's still figure on their shoulders.

Then came the words from Master Jhulian. "The sentence of the Collegium has been enforced. Justice has been done. So be it."

He would leave through the smaller archway at the rear of the dais, I knew, and I waited while Master Rholyn and Master Dichartyn turned and walked toward the archway closest to me.

Master Dichartyn opened the door and stepped into the witness chamber. For a moment, he just looked at me.

I looked back at him.

"You've made matters easier for the Collegium," he said. "They won't be any easier for you. Not after today."

"That depends, sir."

He raised his eyebrows. "Oh?"

"If the Collegium is more willing to accept my observations—not my judgment—just my observations, matters could be much easier."

"You've made it clear that we don't have much choice." His face twisted into a wry and sour smile. "But you're still going to be the Collegium liaison to the Civic Patrol, and every taudischef will be wary of you, as will all of the Patrol officers. The everyday patrollers will expect more out of you as well."

"Your words suggest that most of the officers are corrupt. Otherwise, why would they worry?"

"Many of them are, if in minor ways. Some, as you have discovered, are more so. You'll need to keep that in mind." He paused, then added, "Meet me at the west duty carriage stop at half past seventh glass."

"Yes, sir."

He nodded and left the antechamber.

I took a deep breath, then walked out as well, heading back to my quarters through the blustery winds that suggested colder weather was on its way, although the start of winter was still a month away.

When I got to my rooms, I realized that it was only a quint until noon. So I headed back out and across the quadrangle to the dining hall.

Ferlyn and Chassendri cornered me even before I reached the masters' table, and I ended up sitting between them. We were early enough that the servers had only brought out the carafes of wine and the teapots.

"How did you know he was an imager?" asked Ferlyn.

"I didn't. As I said at the hearing, I only knew that there was an imager. He kept himself concealed as one of the toughs. I mean, he presented himself in public as one of the taudischef's toughs, not as the taudischef, and he always used imaging, from what I could tell, when no one else was around or when no one else could see what he was doing."

"That sounds rather clever," observed Chassendri.

"Why was he gagged?" I asked, trying to avoid questions I didn't want to answer. I wanted a glass of wine, or more, but I didn't dare, not with the rest of the day to come, and I settled for a mug of tea. It wasn't all that warm outside, anyway.

"Why? You were there . . . Oh . . . you weren't, were you?" replied Ferlyn.

"I was in the witness chamber."

"He called Master Dichartyn a ball-less bull and said that the Collegium was a creation of the Namer and worshipped Bius—"

"Bius?" questioned Chassendri.

"The black demon who opposes Puryon," I explained. "That's the god of the Tiemprans and some of the Gyarlese." That also confirmed for me that Youdh had indeed been close to the priests of Puryon. Most taudis-toughs wouldn't have known or cared who or what Bius was. "Then what?"

"Then Master Jhulian cautioned him, and he said that since they were going to kill him, what did it matter? They gagged him after that."

"How did you think of using shields like that to escape the wagon?"

"I don't know, except I knew that the wagon had to go someplace, and that we'd be squeezed too thin if I tried to use shields between the wagon and the side walls."

"How did he learn to be an imager . . . ?"

I tried to answer or deflect the questions, either with careful words or by retreating into eating the gravied pork chops and rice fries, but I was more tired after lunch than I'd been before I'd eaten.

When I left the dining hall, I saw Shault waiting in the corridor outside. After a single quick glance at me, he didn't look at me again, but he didn't move, either.

I walked over to him. "Shault?"

"Yes, sir?" His eyes avoided mine.

"Horazt isn't an imager, and he hasn't done anything to upset the Collegium. The Collegium doesn't have anything against taudischefs if they don't create trouble for us. Horazt hasn't done that, and he certainly hasn't tried to attack any patrollers. He's helped me several times."

The boy looked up, finally.

"I know you worry, but you don't have to worry about that." I paused. "How is your mother?"

"She's fine, sir." He glanced to one side. "I need to meet Master Ghaend soon, sir."

"I won't keep you, then."

"Yes, sir." He swallowed, then murmured, "Thank you." He hurried away without looking back.

I'd always wondered about Horazt and Shault, but now I knew.

41

Given what likely faced me that evening, when I finished eating lunch in the dining hall, I returned to my quarters to think and plan. After thinking and rethinking for almost four glasses, and trying not to think about Rousel and what I feared was inevitable, and then hurrying over to the dining hall and eating dinner quickly, I returned to my rooms and dressed carefully in the black formal attire I'd received earlier. I was careful to slip some poison imaging detection strips inside my jacket and to place the silver imager's pin on the left breast of the formal black jacket. As with the Harvest Ball, the Council's Autumn Ball began officially at eighth glass, which was why I had to meet Master Dichartyn at half past seven.

I did arrive at the duty coach stop before he did, if only by a few moments. Already, the evening was promising to be chill and windy, but clear. There were two coaches waiting, and Master Dichartyn gestured to the first one. "Baratyn and the others can take the second."

After holding the door for him, I climbed up into the coach and closed the door.

Once we had pulled away, he looked at me. "You know that High Holder Ryel will be there tonight?"

"I'd thought he would be."

"Nothing must happen to him this evening."

"I had not planned on anything, sir, except dancing with his daughter, should she be here."

"She is on the guest list, as is Madame D'Shendael. Madame D'Shendael has requested that you invite her to dance with you, for some reason."

"I expressed sympathy at the loss of her father, without ever overtly connecting them." I didn't ask how Master Dichartyn had come to receive that request. He would have told me if he'd wanted me to know, and I was tired of begging for scraps of information and being refused.

"If you would be so discreet with other matters . . ."

"I intend to be the soul of discretion this evening, sir, but I will continue to keep my eyes and abilities ready for any other troublemakers."

He laughed. "Was that intentional?"

"Me, sir?" I smiled innocently. "I'm merely the son of a factor who has much to learn about High Holders and their society and comings and goings." That was totally true, in more ways than the words conveyed.

"Rhennthyl . . . when you talk like that, I must confess to a certain concern."

He should have a concern, I thought, but not tonight, at least not on my account. "I understand my position with regard to High Holder Ryel and the Collegium, sir."

He nodded, but I could sense a certain skepticism.

Once the coach arrived at the curb of the ring road around Council Hill, opposite the side door used by imagers, I followed Master Dichartyn through the side gate and past the guard and up the narrow steps, inside the Council Chateau and past a second guard.

"Good evening, maitres."

"Good evening," replied Master Dichartyn.

I echoed his salutation.

We walked along the lower corridor that led to the foot of the grand staircase. When we reached the ceremonial guards, standing just forward of the two statues of winged angelicas rising from the pedestals that formed the bottom of the rose marble balustrade, I smiled. I couldn't help but recall my comments to my father the first time I'd seen the winged figures with their impossibly small wings and equally impossibly large individual feathers.

Master Dichartyn didn't pause but began to climb the stairs. I walked beside him.

"You don't have any fixed station tonight, not that such has hindered you before," he said dryly. "If you see trouble, try to handle it quietly . . . please."

"Yes, sir."

We stood by the archway into the great receiving hall, waiting.

The first carriage arrived in the drive usually restricted to councilors at a quint before eighth glass, followed within moments by another, for almost none wanted to be the first to arrive. Another quint passed before figures appeared in the main floor grand foyer and began to pass the ceremonial guards and ascend the grand staircase, slowly and deliberately, taking far more time than necessary on the grand staircase.

Master Dichartyn nodded to me, and we retreated into the hall proper.

"Councilor Alucion D'Artisan and Madame D'Alucion!" The deep voice announcing the first arrival boomed from the same small balding man who had announced arrivals at the last Ball and whose name I still did not know. He stood at the left side of the center archway into the great receiving hall.

Behind him, inside the hall, were the three councilors on the Executive Council, who formed a receiving line of sorts.

Baratyn stood against the east wall of the hall, past the councilors, while Dartazn and Martyl were along the west wall.

"Councilor Sabatyon D'Factorius and Madame D'Sabatyon!"

"Commander Artois D'Patrol and Madame D'Artois!"

That surprised me, because Commander Artois hadn't been at the previous Ball, or if he had, I'd missed his name, which was possible since I'd had no idea then that I'd become the Collegium liaison to the Civic Patrol.

"Councilor Ramon D'Artisan and Madame D'Ramon."

Once more, it didn't take long before I began to lose track of all the names, although I did remember and recognize more than at the previous Ball, but I doubted that I had any real idea of all who were present. I kept waiting for a particular set of names. Finally, they came.

"Ryel D'Alte and Madame D'Ryel."

"Alynat D'Ryel-Alte and Mistress Iryela D'Ryel-Alte . . ."

Alynat? That had to be Ryel's nephew. Where was Dulyk?

I watched as the Ryels made their way into the hall and over to the three councilors.

Madame D'Ryel could indeed have been the sister or cousin of Factor Veblynt's wife, although Madame D'Ryel was slightly more angular than Madame D'Veblynt, it seemed to me. Also, compared to her mother, Iryela seemed more petite, and her hair was more white-blond. Iryela wore a gown of shimmering black and silver—the High Holder's colors—which did not suit her as well as the blue and silver I recalled from the last time we had met. Her scarf was of the same glittering silver, however, trimmed in black. It could have been the same scarf, for all I knew.

Alynat was more muscular than either Johanyr or Dulyk, and rounder of face, but his mien carried with it the same sense of smallness and pettiness, although he was close to my height.

As Iryela and Alynat stepped away from Councilor Caartyl, the last of the three on the High Council, her eyes crossed mine—and held them, if but for an instant—before she let them pass as if nothing had occurred. The two moved toward the smaller group of younger people on the east side of the hall, coincidentally just a few yards from the sideboards that held various vintages, with uniformed servers already providing goblets to those who wished them.

"Shendael D'Alte and Madame D'Shendael."

I watched as Juniae D'Shendael smiled graciously at each of the High

Councilors, her short-cut mahogany hair not even moving as she nodded to each.

"The Honorable Dharios Harnen, Envoy of the Abierto Isles, and Mistress Dhenica Harnen."

I paused, remembering that Harnen had brought his daughter to the previous Ball, and I wondered if he happened to be a widower.

From the temporary dais at the south end of the hall, the sounds of the orchestra drifted across the scattered groups of people.

"Go ahead and dance, if you like," said Master Dichartyn. "I intend to."

His voice caught me off guard, because I'd been concentrating on those entering the great hall. "I suppose I should."

He offered a faint smile as he moved away.

I edged along the side of the dance floor, then, surprisingly, I saw a familiar—or semifamiliar figure, not that I would have recognized her except for her height. While Alynkya D'Ramsael-Alte stood beside another couple, she was clearly alone. I also noted the totally black scarf. Her mother had been ill at the time of the last Ball, and the scarf suggested that Alynkya was in mourning, but fulfilling the public social role of her mother for her father, the High Holder and councilor from Kephria.

"Mistress Alynkya, might I have the honor of a dance?"

Her eyes widened slightly, and then she smiled, taking in the silver imager's pin. "You might." Her smile held a certain relief, but curiosity.

As we joined the other dancers, she said, "You know, you never told me your name, Master Rhennthyl." While I felt my dancing had improved, so had hers. She was no longer a charmingly awkward girl, and that saddened me, because I suspected she'd had to grow up a great deal in a season.

"You seem to have discovered it well enough, mistress."

"Alynkya, please. Father discovered it for me. I had thought you were an imager, but he did not mention that you had become a master imager."

"Occasionally, that occurs." I laughed lightly, guiding her around Envoy Harnen and his daughter.

"You are young to be a master, aren't you?"

"I'm one of the younger masters."

"You're one of the better ones, then."

She hadn't made her words a question. So I asked, "Are you staying long in L'Excelsis?"

"Yes, I'm studying at the Universite. Since Father maintains the house here . . ." She let her words drift.

"A house? Or a chateau or an estate?"

"A small mansion. Very small, as they go, not far from the Plaza D'Nord. We're Bovarian by descent."

"He must be one of the few High Holders who can claim that." It also suggested that High Holder Ramsael was one of those with more modest lands. Modest, comparatively, at least.

She smiled shyly. "I'm glad you asked me to dance."

"How could I resist?"

"You're teasing me." Her face held the slightest trace of a pout.

"I'm not."

"Oh?"

I would have shrugged had we not been dancing. Instead, I shook my head. "I asked you to dance at the last Ball because you looked unhappy, but you danced so well. Tonight, you looked so much more self-possessed that I couldn't resist asking you. And you dance even more gracefully."

She inclined her head at the compliment, trying to hide a blush.

I did not speak for a time, just enjoying the dance.

When the music stopped I touched the edge of her scarf. "You had mentioned . . ."

She nodded.

"I'm sorry. It has to have been difficult for you."

"Coming from anyone else, that would be a pleasantry. From you, I accept it in the way it was meant." Her eyes brightened for a moment.

"You're the oldest, I assume?"

"The only daughter, too."

When her father cut in on us, after another dance, he did not smile patronizingly, as he had at the previous Ball, but merely politely. I supposed that meant I had risen in his estimation.

I decided that it was time to begin what was necessary, and I eased around the edge of the dancers to where Iryela had been. She was not there. I studied the dancers, watching until she passed, in the arms of a slender man with short-cut blond hair and the bearing of a High Holder, most likely some holder's son. The young man was clearly attentive, and at times actually seemed to lose his hauteur. After the dance ended, he returned Iryela to a position beside Alynat, who seemed indifferent to her reappearance.

After waiting for a moment, until the music resumed and Iryela had looked away from the others momentarily, I stepped forward and around Alynat, who in attitude could have been the twin of the missing Dulyk, with the same studied arrogance and supercilious smile, contemptuously ignoring the others at the Ball, except for the other young man with whom he was conversing.

"Who . . . ?" murmured Alynat, the single word conveying the sense of a sneer.

"Mistress Iryela, might I have the pleasure of a dance?" I asked, inclining my head in greeting.

Iryela turned and smiled, as if she had been expecting me all along, which I was certain she had. "Master Rhennthyl . . . that would be most pleasant."

"Imagers . . . no breeding . . ." Alynat's murmur was just low enough that he could have denied making it.

As well as I could, I swept Iryela out into the dancers. "You are striking this evening, wearing the family colors, but I must confess that I preferred the blue and silver."

"You are gallant, as always, Rhennthyl. Did you say something equally charming to Mistress Alynkya?"

"I noted she was in mourning and only asked her to dance."

"So kindhearted of you."

"I can be, as can anyone when not threatened or concerned. I noted you enjoying the company of a young man on the previous dance. He seemed rather interested in you."

"Oh, Kandryl. He's very sweet and attentive. As a younger son, he has to be. He does have some redeeming qualities."

"Such as?" I raised my eyebrows. "Being willing to accede to your wishes and desires?"

"I did say he was sweet, but enough of that."

"I note that Dulyk did not choose to escort you."

"It was decided that Alynat should have that experience, especially if there might be the possibility that you would be here."

"Oh?"

"I told them that you were certainly among the suitable choices for a husband. You're handsome and talented, and there is no way that you could ever inherit any of the holding. I intimated that such might be of interest to them, rather than . . . other possibilities."

"You flatter me, but certainly the High Holding of Ryel is expansive enough for more than a single heir."

"Oh, indeed, but not if Ryealte is to remain unchallenged in its scope and grandeur. More than a single heir?" Her glance was withering, yet there was something behind it.

"Or an heiress?" I suggested blandly.

"That is beyond jesting, Master Rhennthyl."

"It has happened," I pointed out. "I do believe that Junaie D'Shendael inherited her sire's holding."

"It is exceedingly rare, as I am sure you know."

"That I do." I laughed. "Yet if you were such an heiress, I'm certain that you would know what to do far better than either Dulyk or Alynat."

"Let us not talk of the impossible."

"By all means. About what possibilities would you like to converse?"

"I leave that to you, Rhennthyl. I'm but a mere woman, who can do little about possibilities, or even impossibilities." Her eyes fixed on me intently, once again, if but for a moment.

"Tell me. What does your younger cousin do? Does he hunt? Or draw? Or play the pianoforte? How does he amuse himself while he's avoiding your father and Dulyk?" I kept my tone light.

"He rides, or he takes his racing trap over hill and dale." Iryela laughed. "He'd like everyone to think that he's reckless, but he's rather good with both trap and mount."

"On the main roads?" I raised my eyebrows.

"Where else could he frighten the unwary?"

"I see."

"And Dulyk just follows your father, learning everything he can?"

"My brother is a dutiful son, Master Rhennthyl."

"How indeed could he be otherwise?"

"How indeed."

The music began to die away.

"Rhennthyl . . ." There was a pause. "Should you wish another dance, please do not make it the last dance. I prefer not to save anything to the end. That is so predictable."

"I would never wish to be predictable. When one is an imager, predictability can be . . . unfortunate."

"Unless it is unthinkable. The unthinkable is often predictable, but because it is unthinkable, it becomes unpredicted."

"Circles within circles." I smiled. "Will you introduce me to your sire?"

"I thought you would never ask."

I escorted her toward her parents, although she was actually leading me.

Ryel was an older and gray-haired version of his eldest son, except that his blue eyes were glass-hard, and the thin lines that radiated from the corners of his eyes were the laugh lines etched in his face by years of cruel jests. His wife nudged him, and he half turned.

"Sir," offered Iryela. "I thought you might wish to meet Master Imager Rhennthyl."

"I appreciate the opportunity to see you in the flesh, sir." I smiled pleasantly, inclining my head to that degree that was just short of insult, according to Maitre Dyana.

"And I, you, Master Rhennthyl. For a comparatively young master imager, you have a certain presence."

I kept smiling. "You honor me, sir, but I fear that my presence pales in your light, and in view of your reputation."

"Do you hear that, Irenya?" Ryel inclined his head to his wife. "Master Rhennthyl would tie me up in my own reputation. What a terrible thing to do." His eyes took me in for a moment, and there was the slightest of nods. "It is indeed a pleasure to meet you, Master Rhennthyl. Oh, and by the way, my condolences on your brother's accident, and my best wishes for his speedy recovery."

I managed not even to look startled. "I appreciate your words, sir, and we all wish him an uneventful and healthful recovery. Thank you." I inclined my head just enough. "I will not intrude further."

He smiled, and I smiled, and I turned as he did, so that he could not obviously dismiss me.

After I left Iryela and her sire, I caught sight of Madame D'Shendael, near one of the sideboards. She had requested a dance, and her husband was talking to another High Holder, though he did stand beside her.

I moved toward her, then inclined my head. "Madame, might I have the honor of a dance?"

Her eyes took in my black formal dress and the silver imager's pin. "You might, Master Rhennthyl."

I took her hand, and we began to dance. Her husband scarcely seemed to notice that she was gone.

"Has your sister yet read *On Art and Society*, Master Rhennthyl?"

"She recently got her own copy, but I've also read most of it. There is a copy in the Collegium Library."

"Yes, there would be, buried in among all the other treatises on the organization of society. And how does a master imager who must work with the Civic Patrol as a common patroller reconcile such an attempt at lofty prose to the mundanity of each day?"

"What we do, I believe, madame, is not all that we are, nor all that we could be. Reading opens one's eyes to the possibilities."

"Ah, yes, to the cruelty of possibilities seldom realized. Did you know that Vhillar had three small children?"

"No, madame, but I do know that the more than ten junior imagers whose deaths he arranged might well have had small children, had they lived long enough to reach that point in life that Vhillar had already attained. I know that Emanus might have enjoyed a few more years of life."

"Would you call his life enjoyable, truly, Master Rhennthyl?"

"I could not speak to that, madame, but he did tell me that he had no regrets about what he had done. It was clear that he referred to giving up his position in the guild."

"Just that?" Her voice was casual.

"I do not know how he managed to arrange matters, but he was happy to do what was necessary to protect his daughter and to make her secure. Of that I am certain." That was as close as I dared to allude to the fact that she was his daughter.

"You are rather young to presume that, are you not?"

"I presume nothing, madame. I only listened."

"He would not have said that."

"I listened to the words he did not say and combined them with what I could see about his artistry and how he had acted."

"You will be disappointed in life, Master Rhennthyl. For one so young, you see well beyond what appears on the surface. Few do."

"I suspect that, madame, and that may be why I am accompanying common patrollers."

"Emanus . . . he said that, even for a portraiturist, once the painting was begun, hesitation was only an invitation to failure. Imaging, I would think, is similar to portraiture, especially in dealing with the Council or High Holders. You are both portraiturist and imager, are you not?"

"Yes, madame."

"How would you view his observation?"

"As accurate in every particular. But when anyone, even a High Holder, thinks a portrait has been begun is not always when the portraiturist has truly begun or taken the steps to capture the image."

"You have an interesting way of interpreting matters, Master Rhennthyl. I do hope that I will see you at the Winter Ball. Your company is far more interesting than, say, that of High Holder Ryel. I saw that you persuaded his daughter to present you."

"It was convenient, and I thought it the proper thing to do."

She smiled, faintly and sadly. "I fear that you will soon be beyond help, Master Rhennthyl, either following those other younger imagers or having become too terrible to imagine." After the slightest of pauses, she added, "I do believe that my husband has at last noticed my absence. If you would not mind . . ."

"I would be delighted." We danced to the edge of the floor, and I escorted her back to Shendael. Then I inclined my head, in far greater respect than I had given Ryel. "My thanks, madame."

She nodded in return. With the nod was another smile, a knowing one that held a hint of sadness.

I eased along the edge of the dance floor for a time, but then saw another young lady, obviously alone, but attired in a shimmering muted violet that matched her eyes.

"Might I have this dance, mistress?"

She nodded politely, but did not speak, not until near the end of that dance when another young man—a Holder heir, I suspected—cut in. Then she smiled and said, "Thank you."

I circled the dancers, studying them as I passed, as well as those at the side of the hall who chose not to dance.

As the last bell of ninth glass echoed, then faded, High Councilor Suyrien stepped toward the table set on the middle of the east side of the dance floor. A drumroll rose from the dais holding the orchestra, followed by a quick trumpet call. Three bottles, corked and sealed, awaited the High Councilor. He pointed to the one on the left, and the server removed the foil and cork from one of the bottles, then set a goblet down and poured the sparkling white wine into it.

I watched the goblet, but there was no trembling, and no sign of any imaging. I could see Master Dichartyn watching as well.

Suyrien D'Alte picked up the goblet, raised it, and declared, "For Solidar, for the Council, and in thanks for a pleasant and productive autumn!"

Then he lowered the goblet and put it to his lips.

Thankfully, unlike the last Ball, this time nothing happened.

"For Solidar, for the Council, and thanks for a pleasant and productive autumn!" echoed from the bystanders, less than enthusiastically.

After smiling politely for several moments, Councilor Suyrien set down the goblet, left the toasting table, and rejoined several other High Holders to the side of the table.

Master Dichartyn eased through the crowd toward me.

I waited, smiling.

"Much less eventful than the last Ball," he observed. "I saw that you asked Madame D'Shendael to dance."

"As was requested, sir."

"And?"

"She hinted that my options were rather limited. It was kind of her. She also expressed indirect appreciation for my concerns about her family."

"That was all?"

"That was all." It was far more notice than I had received from other High Holders, except, of course, Iryela.

"Interesting." He smiled and slipped away.

I didn't feel like dancing, and I went to one of the sideboards, where I took a goblet of Grisio. Since I was not an expert on vintages, I did take the precaution of using a testing strip and imaging a drop of the wine onto it. The strip showed no poison.

A quint passed as I sipped the Grisio, slowly, and watched the dancers, and those moving to and from the sideboards. Then it was time to claim my second dance with Iryela.

She saw me coming and eased away from Alynat—and her parents—meeting me on the edge of the dance floor.

"Might I?" I asked, inclining my head politely.

"You might, especially since you are so kind as to heed my request." She eased into my arms.

As good a dancer as she was, she didn't compare to Seliora, and I wished that I could have been dancing with Seliora, necessary as the dance with Iryela was.

"Alynat seems less than thrilled."

"We are polite to each other, as cousins must be."

"It might be that he was required to attend," I suggested. "Or perhaps he would rather be racing his trap through the night."

"Never the night, Rhennthyl. Who would see him? These days, he prefers showing such speed on the road from the estate to the Plaza D'Nord—generally in midweek around midday."

"Will he attempt such with a sled after the turn of winter, or will he do that at Ryealte?"

"He will have to give that up for the winter. The ice in the north is far too hard on the horses. Even Alynat can occasionally be made to understand that there are some challenges that are less than useful or worthwhile."

"That's a lesson Johanyr never learned," I said dryly.

"There are always those who do not know which challenges to take and which to avoid."

Her casual dismissal of her elder brother, cruel bastard that he was, still bothered me, and suggested . . . something. "And you?"

"I'm a woman, Rhennthyl. Women do not have such choices. We must live by the results of the choices of others."

"If you did, I would suspect you would choose wisely."

"You are too kind." Her words were dry.

"Merely truthful as I see it." I smiled politely. "Will you return to the main holding for the Year-Turn?"

"Only a few days before the end of Finitas. Ryealte is rather boring in a grand fashion. We all—excepting Mother—prefer L'Excelsis." She arched a single eyebrow. "Where else could one dance in perfect safety with a notorious imager?"

"Notorious? I fear that you vastly overesteem me, mistress."

"Iryela, please. How could I possibly do that, Rhennthyl, when I am but viewing you as my sire does?"

"And your brother?"

"He has said nothing."

"I suppose your sire will do much entertaining before the Year-Turn."

She laughed archly. "Well before that. Two weeks from now is the Foliage Festival, and of course there is a full week of dinners at the end of the month before we leave for Ryealte, one after another . . . every night. And once we return to L'Excelsis, the winter season begins. I shall see you at the Winter Ball, I trust."

"We shall see, shall we not?"

"So we shall."

"What is the Foliage Festival?"

"That is what my sire terms it. He has his . . . whims. He and Dulyk and those he invites will climb the tower and see whose tree in the garden has the most leaves remaining. He assigns the trees by lot before the guests arrive. The winner sits to his right at dinner."

"Then he must be inviting lesser High Holders, not that all are not such."

Iryela gave a trace of a nod, so slight I would not have seen it had I not been watching.

"And you, will you have a tree?"

"My dear Rhennthyl." She smothered a laugh behind a bright smile.

I had thought I knew the answer, but I wanted to make sure. "Your gardens must have hardy trees, or is he choosing evergreens?"

"There are always a few leaves, well past Year-Turn. His guests are always pleased to be honored to share ancient vintages with him on the tower. Except for that day, the tower is for family alone."

"You are allowed on the tower?"

"Not when other High Holders are present, but at other times. The view to the west is rather spectacular, especially at sunset, and just before, although one can see nothing in the gardens because the sky is so bright."

"Often the light of the rising and setting sun obscures matters, although the poets claim both clarify."

"What do the artists think?"

"Each artist has his own vision. Which is true? Who knows?" At that point, I could see Alynat sliding between the dancers toward us.

"Your cousin approaches, and I thank you for the dance, Iryela." I inclined my head.

"And I you. I look forward to seeing you at the Winter Ball. I trust I will not see you before then."

"It's rather unlikely." I stepped back and nodded to Alynat. "The lady is yours for the dance."

He actually froze for a second, then took Iryela's hand and swung her back into the flow of dancers.

I smiled as I eased my way back toward the sideboard where I saw Master Dichartyn standing.

"Good evening, sir. You will note that I have followed every formality."

"You have, and you could not have made Ryel more determined to destroy you had you planned it," offered Master Dichartyn.

"No," I replied. "He had already determined that." His comment about Rousel had made that clear, because he could not have known had he not been involved. "Nothing I did tonight would change that. Groveling would only have gained contempt."

"Are you now a High Holder?" The gentleness of his voice only intensified the sarcasm.

"No, sir. I am an imager. I will always be one."

Surprisingly, he only nodded. "The duty coaches will be outside waiting at a quint past midnight. We should observe as the guests leave."

I followed him toward the archway that opened onto the open area at the top of the grand staircase. I could see that as many as a third of the guests had already slipped away.

42

Samedi would have been a good morning to sleep in, what with the chill and the wind gusts that splattered icy rain against my windows, but I didn't. By the time I'd finished breakfast and was on my way to the studio for Master Rholyn's sitting, the clouds had blown over, leaving a chill and pale sky, and the wind had gotten even stronger and colder. I was grateful for being able to sit at the masters' table, because I'd been alone, with no one to ask me about the Ball.

I'd glanced through *Veritum*, after seeing headlines that had proclaimed a Jariolan victory. The Jariolans had taken advantage of a severe early winter storm to launch a counterattack that resulted in the destruction of more than forty Ferran landcruisers and more than four thousand Ferran casualties. Unless I missed my guess, over the winter those losses would become greater because the Ferran machinery wasn't up to the Cloiseran winters. I put aside the new-sheet after I entered the studio and loaded and stoked the stove, then set to work.

Master Rholyn arrived almost a quint before eighth glass, but I was ready for him, since I'd been working on some touches to his waistcoat.

"Good morning, Rhenn. Yesterday's hearing was rather interesting."

"I wouldn't know, sir. I spent most of my time in the witness chamber. They let me hear the verdict, and that was all, except for when I was testifying."

"I'm not sure Dichartyn was all that enthused about having a public hearing with a renegade imager. He does prefer a quieter resolution of such matters." Rholyn moved to the crate and took his position. "I thought that the total intransigence of the taudischef provided an important illustration, especially to those in the Collegium who don't have to deal with people like that. Too many imagers think that the world outside Imagisle is a reasonable place, and that there's always a solution that doesn't hurt too many people. Most people aren't reasonable, and every solution hurts someone."

"Many aren't reasonable, I've discovered." I wasn't certain I thought that of most people, but it seemed to be more true of those with power.

"The fellow had such imaging ability. Such a waste. Yet . . . so few of the ones from the taudis actually are able to become successful imagers. You saw that with the one . . . Diazt, was that his name?"

"Diazt came out of the hellhole, and that's one of the worst, I understand. Still, I'm hopeful for young Shault."

"Ah . . . yes. The dark-haired one. He works hard, Ghaend says. But then, he's younger than those few we usually get from the taudis." Rholyn tilted his head. "How did we come by him so young? You were the receiving master for him, weren't you?"

"I was. I had the duty. His uncle brought him in."

"For the golds, I imagine?"

"He didn't turn them down, but I had the feeling that the man was actually trying to do what was best for the boy. His mother has visited, and I'm fairly sure that Shault is giving much of his earnings to her."

"Dichartyn says that he looks up to you."

"I don't know why, but I've tried to be supportive."

"You settle him down, Ghaend said. After the hearing yesterday morning, he was very upset, but he was calm that afternoon. Ghaend asked him, and young Shault would only say that you explained things to him."

"I tried. I wasn't sure I was successful, but I'm glad to hear that he settled down." I looked at him closely. "If you'd turn your head just a touch away from me . . . there. That's good."

After that, I just painted, and Rholyn didn't say much more, or ask any questions. As he gathered his cloak and prepared to leave, he did ask, "How many more sittings, do you think?"

"Not more than two. If things go well next week, it could be the last."

"Good. No offense, but . . ."

"Yes, sir. I know. It takes time."

He smiled politely, nodded, and departed.

I continued to work on his portrait until close to noon, when I hurried over to the dining hall. Maitres Dyana, Chassendri, and Ferlyn were all there, beckoning to me.

"How was the Ball?" asked Ferlyn, even before I slipped into the seat beside Maitre Dyana. "I saw you leaving the Collegium last night. Rather splendid, you looked."

I smiled and glanced at Maitre Dyana, who was wearing, as usual, a brilliant scarf, this one of purple, edged in pink. "The red or the white?"

"White. It is midday." A faint smile lingered on her lips.

I poured us each a half goblet from the carafe, then let her hand the carafe to Chassendri. "Do you think we'll see an early snow?"

Ferlyn snorted. "Now you sound like Maitre Poincaryt. That's what he does when he doesn't want to answer a question."

"Does he?" I kept my voice innocent.

Ferlyn shook his head, then said to Chassendri in a lower voice, "All of the security types are the same. They just tell you what they want you to know."

He was right, but I'd come to see why. I grinned. "It was a quiet evening as such events go. There were scores of people dressed far more impressively than I was. There were no accidents and no explosions, and only a few young ladies needing dance partners when they'd been inadvertently left standing alone."

"See what I mean."

I laughed. "I can't tell you what didn't happen."

Ferlyn snorted, but poured red wine for himself and white for Chassendri. "We will have an early snow, but not this weekend."

"I'm so glad to hear that," replied Maitre Dyana sweetly.

At that point, the cutlets arrived, with a light brown sauce, followed by roasted potatoes and a steamed cabbage. The cabbage was sweet, as it only was in autumn, and the dessert wasn't bad, a rather plain cake drizzled with congealed heavy blueberry syrup.

For the rest of lunch, conversation centered on the latest events from Cloisera. In one way or another, they all expressed the idea that the Ferran attack on Jariola so late in the year had been unwise. There was such unanimity that I wondered if I might have been mistaken, because unanimous opinions, I'd begun to believe, were usually in error.

After lunch I made my way to the Bridge of Hopes. This Samedi, Shomyr did escort Seliora, but he stayed only long enough to see that I met her before he departed.

I found myself embracing Seliora tightly in the middle of the bridge, my arms almost pinning her inside the heavy black wool cloak.

"Are you all right, Rhenn?"

"I'm glad to see you." I slowly released her, then kissed her gently on the cheek.

"What's happened?"

"I'll tell you, but not in the middle of the bridge."

We walked off the bridge and to one of the stone benches where I'd waited so often the previous spring. I stopped by the bench, gesturing, then stopping. "It's wet."

"I can stand. Tell me what happened." She took my hands in hers, and it was as though warmth flowed from her and released a chill I had not even known had encased me.

I turned to face her. "The patrol rounds on Lundi were all right, but that night I went to deal with Mardoyt—"

"The Patrol lieutenant Grandmama warned you about?"

"The same one . . ." I explained all that had happened before and what I had done. "Then, on Mardi night, Master Dichartyn called me in. He told me that he'd been asked to talk to the Patrol subcommander. He wanted to know why I'd tried to kill Mardoyt. I denied trying to kill him, because that wasn't what I'd had in mind. . . ."

Seliora's mouth opened. "How did any of them know unless . . ."

"Exactly. The subcommander, Mardoyt, and Harraf—and Youdh—all had to know—"

"Youdh? The taudischef?"

"He's an imager. Or he was." I had to explain how that had developed. I ended with what kept coming up. "Except for Youdh being an imager, there's no real proof of anything."

"That's why Grandmama has held on to her contacts. By the time there's proof, too often it's too late. The innocent are destroyed, and the lower-level evil ones are caught, but the people who are responsible walk away untouched."

"Speaking of those who are responsible . . . that was just the beginning. That same night, I walked over to the dining hall after dealing with Master Dichartyn. There was an urgent message from Khethila in my letter box. Rousel was badly injured in a wagon accident in Kherseilles. My parents had already left with Culthyn by the time I got the note. I went to see Khethila immediately, but she hadn't heard more."

"That's not a coincidence."

"No. I'll explain that in a moment. On Meredi . . . I've told you about Youdh's attack and the hearing. Vendrei was the Autumn Ball . . ." I didn't go into full details about what Iryela had said—or what she had implied—but I did mention Ryel's words about Rousel's accident.

"He wants you to know that he'll destroy your entire family." Her eyes did not so much flash as smolder with solidified rage. "He wants to grind it into you."

That was all too possible.

"Do you think she's suggesting that marrying her would end this feud by her father?"

"That doesn't feel quite right," I admitted. "There's something else there. She has her own schemes."

"She could be throwing you up at them so that she can have a say in choosing a husband."

"That could be. Or it could be something else."

"I wouldn't trust a word she says. These High Holders play with people like they were dealing plaques." Seliora looked at me. "What do you need from me? From us?"

"I'll need to borrow the mare, possibly several times over the next two weeks. Also, I'd like for both of us to stop by the factorage after I spend a glass or so painting you. . . ."

"You can still paint with all this . . . ?"

"I *need* to do that." And I did. I wanted to finish her portrait. If things didn't go right, and well they might not, she deserved that, cold comfort as it might be.

She tightened her fingers around mine, and we just stood in the chill, silently, for a time.

Finally, I took her arm, and we began to walk. "I do want to finish your portrait, and it's not getting done out here."

"I don't want just a portrait."

I knew what she meant. "I want more than that, too, but I'm not going to let things slide because of corrupt Patrol officers and vengeful High Holders. Besides, I do have plans."

"I never doubted that. Will you tell me?"

I shook my head. "I can't. I haven't worked out everything yet." I still had trouble with the full implications of Ryel's feud, and the fact that I might well have to deal with not just Ryel, but Dulyk and Alynat as well. Just because I'd partly blinded Johanyr, I was facing either losing my family or ruining another?

"You will tell me?"

"Yes." And I would.

We walked more quickly toward the studio. North of the center of the quadrangle, we passed two seconds headed toward their quarters. One was Vanjhant, the blond and chubby imager who'd been a witness at the ill-fated Floryn's hearing the previous spring.

"Good afternoon, Vanjhant."

"Good afternoon, sir, mistress."

After they passed, I caught a few words, carried on the wind.

". . . does something with the Civic Patrol . . ."

". . . looks like he'd be the type . . ."

Did I really look that way?

"Yes," replied Seliora, although I'd not said a word. "Even your father said something about it, Khethila told me. You never looked like a portraiturist, and now you look much more like a very fit and physical naval officer."

"Not an Army type?"

She shook her head.

Once we got to the studio, I helped Seliora out of her cloak, then held her tightly. The kisses that followed were not short, but not overly long, and she eased away from me.

"There was something about a portrait . . ."

The smile in her eyes warmed me, and I posed her, then went to the easel.

I only worked on Seliora's portrait for a little more than a glass, but by then I had her face completed, except for a few touches, and some of her jacket. It still took close to a quint before I'd cleaned up everything and closed up the studio.

"I'll be glad not to have to wear this every Samedi afternoon," she said as we walked toward the Bridge of Desires—the closest bridge for hailing a hack to go to the factorage.

"You can wear a different blouse next week. That part's done." I grinned at her, except it was close to a leer.

She blushed. "You can be impossible."

"Not impossible. Merely difficult."

We were both chilled by the time we crossed the bridge and managed to hail a coach. The ride south to Alusine Wool was not much warmer, because the wind was strong enough to whistle around and through the rattling windows. There was a single coach outside Alusine Wool when we emerged from the hack, but when I'd paid the driver and turned, the coach had pulled away. I hoped whoever was inside had expended more than a few golds purchasing wool.

Seliora stood and studied the front of the building for a moment, and at the letters of the sign. I let her. She'd never been to the family factorage before. Then we walked up the low stairs and in through the doors.

Khethila immediately stood as she saw us enter. She didn't run down from the desk on the rear dais, but she didn't dawdle, either.

"Rhenn! Seliora." She gave me a quick hug and Seliora a slightly longer one. "You're so kind to come."

"Have you heard anything else?" I doubted that, because it was more than two days to Kherseilles by ironway, even by urgent express.

She shook her head. "I won't hear anything until Lundi at the earliest, I expect."

"Do you know how badly Rousel was hurt?" asked Seliora.

"The message from Remaya said that he had broken ribs and crushed legs."

"Was there anything about how it happened?"

"No. Just that it was an accident."

"Can I do anything to help?" Seliora's words were both warm and supportive.

"Not right now. I can't think of anything." Khethila glanced around the factorage. "We're selling a bit more than we did last year at this time, and I've been writing up the bid for another Navy order. All I can do is make sure that Father doesn't have to worry about the business here."

We talked for almost another glass before Seliora and I took our leave and let Khethila and Eilthyr begin to close up the factorage.

As we stood outside at the edge of West River Road, waiting for a hack, I half turned to Seliora. "Do you have the evening planned, lady?"

"We could join Father and Mother at home and then go with them to Chaelya's. . . ."

I couldn't help smiling. "What did you tell them? That you'd ask me, and to expect us?"

Seliora blushed.

"I thought as much." I leaned forward and kissed her cheek.

We waited for less than a quint before a hack, even bound northward, stopped for us.

Once we were inside, I asked, "Do you think we could take a ride tomorrow, early in the afternoon?"

"How early?"

"Right after brunch?"

"Only if you come to brunch."

"I can manage that." That would even let me sleep late and still have a good meal.

"You'd like to head north?"

"How did you guess?"

She smiled knowingly.

I sensed a sadness, and I said, "The more this goes on, the more it seems that I don't have much choice."

"I know. Sometimes, we don't."

That was always going to be the hard part, I was coming to understand. "How do you know which choice is right?"

"When only one choice will save those you love," replied Seliora.

I didn't know that I could have put it that succinctly.

When we reached NordEste Design, Bhenyt was waiting outside. As we emerged from the coach, he ran over and called up to the driver. "Half silver if you wait a quint!"

"Done, young fellow!" agreed the bearded coachman. "Done!"

"Two coppers now," added Bhenyt, "and the rest on the fare."

I couldn't help grinning at Bhenyt. He grinned back.

Seliora and I walked quickly up the outer steps, then through the doors and up the stairs. Betara and Shelim were sitting on one of the settees, but both rose as we entered the main second-level entry hall.

"I thought we might be seeing you about now." Betara's eyes went to me. "How are you doing, Rhenn?"

"I'm fine. My brother Rousel's been seriously injured in an accident in Kherseilles. My parents are there."

"Do you know how accidental the accident was?" Betara asked.

"No. Given the difficulties Rousel has faced recently, I have my doubts as to how accidental this was."

Seliora and Betara exchanged glances.

Shelim nodded, then said, "Whatever we can do."

"We're going riding tomorrow," Seliora said. "Rhenn will need to borrow the mare from time to time."

"Is that all?" asked Betara.

"I hope so. You have already done much more than I ever could have asked for, and I appreciate not having to worry about people shooting at me every time I come to see Seliora." I offered what I hoped was both a thankful and a knowing smile.

"There are those who should not be trusted with rifles," Betara said lightly.

"That is true, but I'm still grateful." I paused. "By the way, you and Grandmama Diestra might like to know that Lieutenant Mardoyt suffered an accident earlier this week. On Lundi night an oak limb fell on him. He's expected to live, but he'll likely be stipended off because he won't walk well and can't use one arm."

"That will please Mama," Betara said. "He is an evil man." Her words were delivered evenly and factually. Then she smiled. "We should go. Staelia is expecting us." She adjusted a red woolen cloak trimmed in black.

Shelim escorted her down the steps and out to the waiting hack. Seliora and I followed.

Once the hack was headed southeast on Nordroad, I addressed Betara. "The other thing I didn't tell you was that one of the taudischefs was an imager. That was Youdh. He attacked me and another patroller on rounds on Meredi. We captured him. He was tried by the Collegium and executed on Vendrei."

Betara nodded. "We heard that he had been taken by the Patrol, but no one knew much more than that." She paused, then added, "Except that the Temple priests are very displeased."

"Do you know what they'll do?"

She shook her head. "Whatever it is, they'll get someone else to do it, and it will seem like the sansespoirs or the poor workers in the taudis are to blame."

To me, that translated into a riot when the conscription teams arrived, if not worse. "I'll watch for that, although I don't know if I can do much."

When we reached Chaelya's, I was the first out of the coach, and offered my hand and arm to Seliora, and then to Betara. I didn't know what Shelim paid the hacker, except that his response was definitely grateful.

"Thank you, sir!"

No sooner had we stepped in through the brick-framed doorway than Staelia bustled up to us. "Shelim, Betara . . . and Seliora and Rhenn . . . I'm so glad all of you are here. It's chill tonight, for this time of year, and we aren't that crowded. This way. You have the corner table."

Several diners looked up as we passed, and one, a younger man attired in a royal green jacket, swallowed. I looked at him and smiled. He paled. I wondered exactly what he'd done.

Staelia seated us at the rear table that was set off slightly from the others. Taelia immediately appeared with two carafes of wine—one a pale amber and the other a claret-red. "The white is Simota, the red Endaluz."

I hadn't had either, but opted for the white, as did Betara. Seliora and her father chose the Endaluz.

"Has the war had any effect on your business?" I asked Betara and Shelim once Taelia had half filled all four goblets.

Betara sipped her wine, then said, "No. Unless things get worse, I don't think it will. Most of our clients aren't likely to be affected. The only factors who come to us, except for a special side chair or armchair, are those like Glendyl or Diogayn who are possibly as wealthy as some of the lesser High Holders."

"Have you done a commission for Glendyl?" I tried the Simota; it was somehow slightly buttery, without being cloying.

"Not quite two years ago. He wanted a dining set for his estate here in L'Excelsis."

"How was he to work for?"

"Very demanding until he was satisfied with the design, and very easy after that."

"He wanted things his way, but trusted your abilities," I suggested.

"That's how it should be," Betara replied. "We won't do anything for Diogayn again."

Seliora winced.

"Oh?" I looked to her.

"He tried to insist that I should show great gratitude, if you know what I mean, for the commission, and became very upset when I declined. Then he insisted on changes after we'd already ordered fabric."

"Then he demanded that we change the back design of the chair frame," added Shelim.

"What happened?" I asked.

"We delivered what he requested, at a price set according to the agreement. He wasn't happy."

"Change escalation clause?" I asked.

"He didn't read it closely," Betara said. "We brought our advocate with the delivery. His advocate called him an idiot. Not quite in those terms."

"He said that Diogayn should not have signed an agreement with unfamiliar phrasing," added Shelim, "without consulting his advocate and that given the documentation we had produced he could pay us, or he could pay us and the advocate even more."

"He thought that his wealth and power would suffice," I suggested.

"Oh, he tried that, too. We had to deal with several incidents . . . until the body of one of his 'agents' was found inside his guarded compound inside his locked carriage house, garroted in the driver's seat of his favorite coach."

"He hasn't even said unkind things about us," Betara added. "Not anywhere in public, and the dining set we delivered was exquisite and without any flaws. We even used a new fabric design with the chair frames he rejected for High Holder Asathyn, and made a higher profit."

I could see the incident as another example of what Seliora had said about NordEste Design's ability to outcheat cheaters. I was also very glad that I did truly love Seliora.

One of the dinner specials was game hen stuffed with plums and hazelnuts, with a plum sauce, and I had that. Seliora chose a mushroom, fowl, and rice casserole in a cream sauce. I had a taste of hers, and she of mine. We agreed, in a fashion. She thought hers was better for her, and mine for me. So did I.

A hack was waiting outside Chaelia's when we left, doubtless arranged by Staelia, which was very good because the wind had picked up even more, although the sky was cloudless. Both Artiema and Erion showed half discs distinctly in the clear night air, the larger moon golden white, and the hunter moon reddish beige.

Again, I held the coach door and helped the ladies up, then followed.

When the hacker turned into Hagahl Lane, I cleared my throat. "I suppose I should go . . ." I didn't want to, but I also didn't want to intrude.

"Don't run off," Betara said.

"Please come in," added Seliora.

It didn't take any more persuasion for me to accompany them inside.

Only two lamps were lit in the main-level hallway, and the large space was hushed.

"It's early for you young people, but we need quiet time," Betara said. "Good night."

"Good night, Mama, Papa," Seliora said. "We won't stay up too late. Remember, we're going riding tomorrow after brunch."

"Better you than us. Good night."

As they turned and headed up the side staircase to the third level, Seliora said, "It's too cold on the upper terraces, but this late there won't be anyone in the plaques room. It does have a small settee that's not too uncomfortable. . . ."

Again, I wasn't about to argue . . . and I followed her to a door I hadn't noticed before, set almost in the northwest corner of the hall, but on the north wall. It was ajar, and Seliora eased it open and stepped inside the narrow room that ran across much of the north side of the building. In the dim light from the single pair of lamps still burning in the main hallway, I could see two boxes resting on the dark blue felt of the nearer plaques table, obviously holding plaques. Several other boxes rested on a cabinet against the far wall. The other two tables had nothing on them. Pharsis were known for being avid plaques players, but generally the gambling games, while the High Holders preferred whist.

Seliora didn't light one of the wall lamps, and I didn't suggest it. She did leave the door ajar. "This is the only time someone's not here on the weekends. Well . . . except before breakfast."

"Do you play?"

"Some. That's because Shomyr insisted I had to learn. I'd rather do other things." She turned and lifted her lips.

Thankfully, the settee was on the south wall and not visible from the doorway, unless someone actually stepped into the room.

43

On Samedi night, once more, despite the pleasant dinner with Betara and Shelim—and the even more enjoyable time with Seliora in the plaques room—I didn't sleep well. I woke not that long after dawn on Solayi feeling like my intestines were strangled and my legs had been under an iron weight. I was so sore and stiff that I had to do some exercises before I headed downstairs for a cold shower and a colder shave. I knew that every muscle in my body would have contracted into spasms if that water had hit me without my loosening up.

Because I'd get a filling meal at Seliora's, I didn't have to eat breakfast at the dining hall. That way I could avoid Heisbyl, who was the duty master. It wasn't that I disliked him, or even that I even disagreed with what he said. It was the condescending attitude. While he was older and more experienced, we were of the same rank, and I had been moderately successful both as a portraiturist and as an imager, facts that his attitude ignored.

I set out across the Bridge of Desires after eighth glass under a gray sky. Occasional fine flakes of snow drifted down, but melted as soon as they touched the stone of the pavement. In the sky to the west, I could see patches of pale blue. With some luck, the sun might be out before we started out on our ride. I had to wait more than a quint on the west side of the river before I could catch a hack to take me to NordEste Design and Seliora, and I wasn't all that certain the driver wanted the fare, but was afraid to turn down an imager. Because it was cold, when I got out of the coach at Seliora's, I gave him an extra pair of coppers beyond the normal one or two for a gratuity.

He didn't quite smile, but he looked to be the type who seldom did. He did incline his head and say, "Much obliged, sir."

"My thanks for the ride." I did smile before turning and hurrying up the steps.

The twins—Hanahra and Hestya—opened the door, even before I lifted the knocker.

"Good morning, Master Rhennthyl," offered one.

"Aunt Seliora," the other called up the entry staircase, "he's here!"

The twin at the door closed and bolted it, while the other scurried up before me.

Seliora was waiting at the edge of the carpeted part of the main entry hall. She wore long black riding skirts, with a pale pink shirt and a deep crimson vest.

She gave me an embrace and a kiss on the cheek, while the twins stood there and giggled, then said, "Mother and Aunt Odelia have fixed far too much. I hope you're hungry."

"I'm very hungry," I admitted. "I didn't have breakfast."

"Good. You might even eat as much as Shomyr." She took my arm, gently possessive. We walked toward the archway at the back of the entry hall that opened into the dining chamber.

Betara and Shelim turned as Seliora led me toward our places near the head of the table.

"Seliora told Mama Diestra about your brother. She is as sorry as we are." The concern faded from Betara's face, followed by a hardening expression as she added, "She also believes that we must give you anything we can to help. Anything."

Shelim nodded.

From where she stood just across the table from Betara, Diestra nodded as well.

"Thank you." I couldn't help but be touched . . . and a bit fearfully awed.

All three smiled.

Whether it was because of Rousel's accident, or informality, I actually ended up at the table beside Seliora, with Odelia and Bhenyt across from us, and Betara to my right.

Shelim cleared his throat as everyone continued to stand, then said, "For the grace that we all owe to each other, for the bounty of the earth of which we are about to partake, for good faith among all, and mercies great and small. For all these we offer thanks and gratitude, both now and ever more, in the spirit of that which cannot be named or imaged. . . ."

"In peace and harmony," we replied.

I reached out and squeezed Seliora's hand, and got a warm but gentle squeeze in return, and there was a scuffing of chairs as everyone sat down. Then platters of food appeared, along with a large teapot and carafes of heated mulled wine. One platter held the thinnest of fried cakes, rolled around a mixture of what looked to be sautéed mushrooms, cheese, and chopped sausage. I took several.

"They're better with the berry syrup," suggested Bhenyt.

"Thank you." I took his suggestion and dosed mine with the syrup, then ate one. Bhenyt was definitely correct about the syrup.

"You're going riding, aren't you?" asked Odelia. "Seliora says that you finally look like you've seen a horse before."

"Once or twice, if I don't have to ride one that doesn't care for me."

"The horses all like you," Bhenyt said.

I laughed gently, but I wondered where he'd gotten that idea.

"You're Pharsi at heart," Betara explained, "maybe more than at heart, and Pharsis have a way with horses."

I didn't think I'd pass that compliment along to my mother, not the way she felt about Pharsis. Yet I felt very much at home with Grandmama Diestra's clan.

"I heard indirectly from Horazt that you've been kind and helpful to his nephew," Diestra said from across the table.

"Shault's a good boy, and I'd like him to succeed as an imager."

"He also said that you got rid of Youdh before he could make any more trouble."

I shrugged. "He attacked me and another patroller. I did what had to be done." I really didn't want to discuss the details surrounding Youdh's hearing and death.

"You understand that one must act before too many suffer," Grandmama Diestra said carefully. "So often, the good innocents always believe that there is another way. They are convinced that there must be a way that hurts no one, or only the most evil of the evil. While they try in vain to find such a way, more suffer and more die."

"They believe," added Betara, "that there is always a way where few suffer. That belief is an illusion, and it is deadly. We Pharsi have learned that deadliness through too many years of too many deaths."

What could I say to that, especially since Ryel was proving that very point to me?

"Horazt has suggested you'd make a good Patrol captain for the taudis area. That's not likely, is it?" Diestra covered her mouth, blocking what sounded like a racking cough.

I waited until she finished. "There's nothing prohibiting it, but the Collegium—not to mention the Council—might well be opposed to an imager serving officially in the Civic Patrol."

"Is it that impossible?" asked Seliora, her voice guileless, yet teasing.

"It's not impossible, merely exceedingly improbable."

Betara and Shelim laughed.

After a very filling brunch, complete with another glass of cheerful conversation, Seliora and I walked through the back hall and down the back stairs into the courtyard and across to the stables. We stepped inside, and at the south end of the stable I saw a trap, covered with a canvas tarpaulin. I walked toward it.

"Rhenn . . . I thought we were riding," Seliora said. "Traps like that are more dangerous than the way you ride. That hasn't been used in years, anyway."

"Thank you, dear lady." I half turned and inclined my head. "We are riding, but I need to look over the trap first."

Seliora joined me, watching as I squatted and studied the wheel and axle assembly. When I'd first come to the Collegium, I'd had to learn about various axle assemblies and even how the drive train of an ironway locomotive was constructed and operated. The trap's wheels and bearings didn't look that different from those I'd studied.

"Do you know if all traps have wheels and axles like this?"

"I don't, not for sure."

I'd have to work from that. I rose and smiled. "Let's see if I can still saddle the mare." I was certain I could, not because I was that good at it, but because the mare was. Even so, it was close to two quints later before we were mounted and headed northeast on the Boulevard D'Este under a sky that had finally begun to clear, even if the sun had not quite broken through the thin clouds. The wind was light, if chill, but by the time we reached the Plaza D'Nord, I was glad that I'd worn my heavy winter cloak and gloves.

"Are you warm enough?" I asked, turning in the saddle to glance at Seliora, riding beside me and wearing a black leather riding jacket over her vest. Her gloves were also black.

She was entirely in black, and I was in gray, except for black belt and boots. Black and gray . . . If I were a poet or a philosopher, I could have made something out of it.

"I'm comfortable. I'm wearing silks under the riding skirts. How about you?"

"I'm more than warm enough."

There were almost no riders on the road, except for a private messenger who passed us heading into L'Excelsis at a good clip, not at a gallop, but at something less than a canter.

Another three quints or so brought us to the crest of the hill south of Ryel's estate, and as we descended into the small depression or valley through which the stream ran, I studied his lands again, especially the walls around the stream, and the small turnout on the west side of the road about halfway up—or down if one happened to be headed south.

Then, as I rode up the hill, keeping the mare on the right side of the road, as close to the estate wall as I could, I attempted to image a small stone into being near the tower off the south terrace. I could just barely do that. That confirmed that for any serious imaging, I'd have to be closer and on the estate grounds. That could subject me to Ryel's low justice, were I discovered, and that was something I'd need to avoid at all costs.

"Be careful. The mare won't keep you on the road if you're guiding her off it," Seliora warned me.

"I'm sorry. I was trying something."

She just nodded.

All the way uphill to the turnaround, I kept studying every aspect of the grounds that I could see, as well as the road itself, particularly on the steeper downslope below the gates to the estate. Then, while we ostensibly let the horses rest, I studied the chateau proper.

On the way back, I concentrated on the road, at least until we reached the crest of the rise south of the one on which the estate stood.

"Can you talk now?" asked Seliora.

"Now? Yes? Was I that intent?"

"More than that," she said with a smile. "Did you find what you were looking for?"

"I think so, but time will tell." Time and the effectiveness of what I planned.

When we finally returned to the courtyard at NordEste and unsaddled and groomed the horses, I was more than ready for the hot tea and cakes and cheeses that Betara had waiting for us in the breakfast room off the kitchen, a breakfast room larger than some formal dining rooms I'd been in. But then, I reminded myself, close to a triple quint of Seliora's family and relatives might fill the room for breakfast.

Once we were settled at one end of the long table, I said, "Thank you."

"You're more than welcome."

"If it's all right, could I borrow the mare on Mardi, possibly on Meredi, or even Jeudi? Is that possible?"

"Whenever you need her. You're not hard on her. You actually ride fairly well for someone with no experience before now."

"I won't be able to get here until close to half past eighth glass on Mardi."

"Just come to the family entrance. Someone will find me."

"Thank you."

In the end, I didn't return to Imagisle until close to time for Solayi services. I missed dinner, but that mattered little. I'd eaten more than enough having afternoon tea with Seliora.

Once an imager was a master, the anomen services weren't mandatory, but most masters went. I didn't mind going, because Chorister Isola's homilies were usually thought-provoking. Unfortunately, this Solayi was one of the few times I wasn't exactly enthralled by her homily.

I could tell that from almost the first few words after the offertory, when Chorister Isola stepped to the pulpit. "Good evening."

"Good evening," came the reply.

"And it is a good evening, for under the Nameless, all evenings are good." She paused as she always did. "All of you here are imagers or those close to imagers. Being an imager carries a special burden. You have all been told that. It is a special burden, but there is a tendency for all of us to hear what we want to hear. Too seldom do we concentrate on the important word of those two. The important word is 'burden,' not 'special.' Yes, we can do what others cannot, but thinking that because we have an ability, a talent, that we are in some way special . . . that is no more than another case of Naming. We name ourselves as 'special,' without understanding that this talent, like all great abilities of all those who possess them, demands equally great responsibility. . . ."

I didn't mind great responsibility, but it seemed to me that as a result of my special and great talent, I had been put in a situation where if I failed in the slightest, I'd be before a Collegium hearing and shortly thereafter rather thoroughly and specially dead. If I did nothing, my entire family would be slowly and specially ruined and many of them equally specially dead.

I was Namer-well aware that I had a special burden, and it had been dumped on me by Master Dichartyn and Maitre Poincaryt. My greatest problem would not even have existed if either of them had had the guts to deal directly with Lord Ryel's excessively spoiled son. But no, I had to do that, and ever so inexorably, events were pressing in on me, and as a result, one way or another, people would die, and one way or another, I would be responsible.

After the final prayer, I was still angry when I left with the others. Instead of heading back to my quarters, I slipped off to the walk along the west side of Imagisle and followed it to the Bridge of Stones, which I crossed. I kept walking southward along West River Road for almost a mille to the abandoned and burned-out shell of an old mill that I'd noticed earlier.

As I neared the shadowed and soot-blackened walls, I heard murmurs.

"Someone headed here . . ."

". . . go on by . . . patrollers never come here . . ."

". . . could be a demon . . . spawn of the Namer . . ."

". . . no such thing as demons . . ."

I really didn't want anyone to see what I was doing, nor did I wish them hurt. Enough people were going to suffer anyway. I raised concealment shields and moved closer, thinking about what I could do.

"Gone . . . whoever it was . . ."

". . . don't disappear like that . . . still say demons . . ."

Abruptly I smiled, thinking about how Youdh had imaged a cloud of dust to mark my position. In the chill air, something else might be better, scarier. I concentrated, imaging water from the river into a misty figure some three yards high, looming next to the tall south wall in the dim light of a fading Artiema.

A man yelled, and a woman uttered a cry between a scream and an imprecation.

". . . told you there were demons!"

I waited until the last of the five had scrambled southward before dropping my concealment shields and stepping forward to the ruins. The remaining sections of the mill walls were thick and constructed of heavy stones. In the dimness I couldn't see what kind of stone it might be, but I doubted it would matter that much. While I wasn't trying to image gold or aluminum out of the stone, heavy was still heavy.

Even though I had no idea exactly how I would do what I had in mind, I looked at the top stone on the low section of the wall to my right and tried to concentrate on image-removing the mortar. A puff of dust billowed from beneath the stone, and it rocked forward and backward, before settling back into place. I took several steps forward and pushed the stone. It wobbled.

I would have laughed if I hadn't been panting. My imaging had been successful enough. The mortar was gone, but the building stone had been fitted so well to its place that it had merely dropped the width of the missing mortar onto the stone below.

I just stood there, breathing heavily. There had to be a better way. There just had to be.

". . . imaging takes energy from all around you . . ." Who had said that? Master Dichartyn? I tried to remember what he had said, but I was fairly certain he hadn't said much more than that. But why not? Because it was dangerous, obviously, but dangerous to whom? All the lead and leaded glass in the Collegium . . . for whom did they provide protection?

I glanced at the scrubby bush by my feet. Could I?

I looked at a smaller stone set in the second course of stone below the topmost remaining, then at the bush, and concentrated on a tie between the bush and the stone. I took a deep breath and tried to image the stone out of the wall—but away from me and nearer the taller south wall.

Craackkk ... Stone chips sprayed everywhere, some striking my shields with such force that I took two steps backward in order to keep my balance.

A thump . . . thump echoed through the ruined walls, followed by a dull thud.

Where the stone had been, an oblong opening remained, with a powdery, dusty mist slowly settling and sifting down toward the uneven ground next to the wall. The stones around the gap in the wall had not moved.

I looked back to the scrubby bush. It wasn't there. Or rather, where it had been was an ash-outlined and flattened image of a bush that shifted on the hard ground in the light night breeze, then vanished as if it had not been as the air currents swirled it away.

I looked at the south wall of the mill, rising two stories. I found myself trying to moisten my lips, dry as my mouth suddenly was.

"Take it a step at a time," I murmured, trying to steady myself.

Abruptly I almost laughed, recalling what Alsoran had said about steps. My eyes took in a forlorn-appearing tree that had grown up in the sheltered corner where the west and south walls of the mill joined. Slowly I walked around to the outside of the south wall and studied it, trying to determine where its weakest points might be.

I shook my head. That wasn't what I needed. Where would removing stones cause the greatest damage? Finally, I stepped back from the wall. I didn't want to think too hard about what I was about to try, yet what else could I do? I had to know if what I had in mind worked.

This time I tried to create a link between the straggly misshapen tree and the southwest corner of the wall. Then, I focused on imaging out a section of that corner of the wall at ground level.

Craaack. . . .

Stones seemed to fly everywhere, or maybe I was, because I felt myself being flung backward. For a moment—it might have been a great deal longer—there was blackness over and around me. Then I was looking up at the sky. Artiema was still about where she had been . . . or maybe somewhat farther westward and lower in the sky. Slowly . . . very slowly, I sat up. My right buttock was sore, very sore, and my shoulder twinged as I struggled to my feet. My head ached, and my vision was blurry.

I looked toward the old mill, squinting through the blurriness to make things out. The entire south wall had slumped into a pile of rock and stone, as had the southern half of the west wall. There was no sign of the tree. In fact, I realized, there were no bushes or trees anywhere close to the building. All the undergrowth was gone, and a thick coating of frost was everywhere. The air was icy.

As far as I had moved back from the ruins, I definitely should have retreated farther, much farther. I'd proved that what I'd had in mind worked, but my technique, as Maitre Dyana would have said, definitely needed much more refinement.

As I walked—more accurately, limped—back toward the Bridge of Stones, the wind rose slightly, coming off the water with a bitter chill. I glanced down at the gray water, where I could see the shimmering of shards of rime ice breaking up even as I watched.

I swallowed, but kept walking.

At that moment, something flashed before my eyes—an oblong building that trembled and shook, and then exploded, with flames shooting in all directions, and then dust and smoke rising even as chunks of masonry and timbers began falling on the street and a low wall. I stopped, frozen in place, as the image vanished from my eyes or mind. I knew the building. It was the Temple of Puryon . . . but it couldn't have just exploded, because it was night, and the explosion had occurred in the light. Was I imagining it? Or had it happened? Would it happen?

How could I tell?

I resumed walking, cold inside and out, and realized that I was going to be very sore.

As I walked off the bridge and toward the quadrangle and my quarters, more like an old man than a young imager, an errant thought struck me—I'd probably convinced five vagrants that demons did exist and that the old mill was indeed haunted.

Demons indeed.

But the flash vision of the explosion seemed all too real.

44

Not only were my buttocks and shoulder sore and painful when I staggered out of bed on Lundi morning, but my legs were sore, and I still had a trace of the headache I'd gone to bed with. I could see, however, and I could raise shields. I couldn't help but frown at that. Did that mean that I'd handled the imaging part as I should have, but I was suffering the consequences of not physically protecting myself as well as I should have? Wonderful! My technique was better than I thought, but I still came close to killing myself . . . again. And then there was that vision of the Temple of Puryon exploding. I'd just have to see . . . and be very careful around the Temple.

Clovyl's stretching exercises did help, but my running left so much to be desired that I was in the group bringing up the rear. Fortunately, no one seemed to care. The cold shower that followed my return to quarters numbed the aches, but also stiffened me up some, and I was slow in shaving and getting dressed. I still made it to the dining hall without being terribly late.

"You're limping," Ferlyn observed as I sat down at the masters' table.

Chassendri slipped into the chair to my left before I replied. "That's what comes of all those exercises and running on wet stone."

I managed to look sheepish. "I do have a large bruise from falling." That was true. I just didn't say when or where.

"He's sitting lopsided," Chassendri affirmed.

"I wouldn't be in security for anything." Ferlyn poured some tea and handed me the pot. "Bad things happen to all of you, and there's never any rest from problems."

I filled Chassendri's mug, and then mine. "Is there any rest from problems for any imager? Isn't it just a choice of which problems we prefer and are suited to handle?"

Chassendri smiled, but only for a moment. "That may be true for us, but what about imagers whose talents don't match what they prefer?"

"I don't know that I have that much sympathy." My words came out more sardonically than I'd intended.

"Oh?" asked Ferlyn.

"I could have been a master portaiturist," I pointed out. "I didn't exactly get that choice. We sometimes don't. We only get to choose among some alternatives."

Chassendri tilted her head. "That's true . . . in a way."

"In what way?" asked Ferlyn.

"Some choices no one gets. We don't choose where and to whom we're born. We don't choose our physical characteristics. But that's true of everyone. We do get to choose what we do with what we have. Didn't you have to choose to work with Master Dichartyn, Rhenn?"

"Yes. I've already admitted that, but what does that have to do with sympathy?"

"Would you really prefer to work, say, imaging machine parts?"

"No." That was an easy and obvious admission.

"You had the choice. What about someone like Shannyr, or Sannifyr? They don't have your abilities and choices."

I inclined my head. "Your point is well taken and gently made." At least, she hadn't out-and-out called me spoiled because I had the ability to be good in two fields and was complaining I hadn't had much choice when others had none.

"Gently?" Ferlyn raised his eyebrows. "I'd hate to see what she'd do roughly, if that happened to be gentle."

I laughed softly. "We'd best keep that in mind, then, hadn't we?" I grinned at Chassendri.

She did smile back.

As I finished breakfast, I couldn't help asking myself if I were becoming too much like Master Dichartyn, or at least in those characteristics I disliked. Yet . . . there was so much I could tell no one—except Seliora—and I probably wasn't supposed to tell her. But she and her family could keep secrets. In my family, Khethila was the only one who could, and I didn't want to burden her.

I had to hurry to the duty coach, but the streets were relatively clear, and I arrived outside the station as the bells were chiming seventh glass. When I stepped inside, both Lyonyt and a fresh-faced patroller who looked to be a good five years younger than I was walked toward me immediately. I didn't see either Harraf or Warydt. I wasn't about to go looking for them.

"Good morning, Master Rhennthyl," offered Lyonyt. "This is Fuast."

"I'm pleased to meet you, Fuast." I inclined my head politely.

"I'm happy to meet you, sir." His voice was young and enthusiastic. I found that bothered me, and at the same time, it disturbed me that it did.

"I'm sorry I'm late," I offered. "We probably need to be headed out."

"We should." Lyonyt's head bobbed up and down, even as his eyes flicked toward the doors and then back to me.

I ended up leading the way, at least until we were headed east on South Middle, when I dropped back and let Lyonyt explain.

"Best thing to do is circle the round before you start going up and down the cross streets . . . gives you a feel for what might be happening. If there's trouble, you want to know about it before you get too deep in the taudis, goes for any round you do, but it's worse here if you don't know . . ."

When we neared the Temple, unchanged from when we had passed it last on Vendrei, I took a long and careful look. One of the priests was standing on the front steps, and he looked toward us and then away. Had I just imagined the explosion? Except . . . the last flash vision had been the fire at the factorage. We were nearly to the Avenue D'Artisans before Lyonyt stopped to take a breather from his nonstop briefing.

"They said that Third District's one of the toughest." Fuast looked sideways to Lyonyt.

"Has some of the tougher rounds, those going through the taudis, anyway. Every district's got tough rounds, even Fifth District. Just doesn't have so many."

I didn't know, but I suspected that Lyonyt had that correct.

"How many imagers accompany patrollers, Master Rhennthyl?" Fuast asked as we turned southwest on the avenue.

"Not many," I replied. "At the moment, I'm the only one. I'm the imager liaison to the Civic Patrol, and this is part of my getting to know how the Patrol operates. I've spent time in headquarters and watching justice hearings."

"Ah . . . sir . . ."

I had a good idea what he was thinking. "I've had duties like a patroller as an imager, and I've been trained in handling weapons and in taking them away from other people."

Fuast looked to Lyonyt.

"He's already taken down a taudischef and something like five toughs in less than a month, most of 'em with his bare hands."

"Oh . . . I'm . . ."

"People think imagers just image. We don't. There are imagers who are bookkeepers and sailors and machinists and advocates and justices . . . all sorts of jobs. We just do them on Imagisle. I also paint. I was a portraiturist before I was an imager."

"I didn't know that, sir," said Lyonyt.

"I don't believe I mentioned it."

Before long, Lyonyt was back to explaining about the round, and where to watch carefully, and about sewer grates and refuse and a hundred odd details. I just listened. Some of it was new to me, probably because Alsoran hadn't wanted to say much.

The rest of the day was uneventful, too quiet, really.

On the last section of the round as we headed back along South Middle, Lyonyt's eyes kept surveying the wall on the left as we crossed Mando, then the Temple of Puryon up ahead. He frowned. "Something . . ."

I studied the Temple as well. Then it struck me. "All the shutters are closed. Every last one. They weren't earlier."

"I've never seen that before . . . except once. Wager that means the scripties are coming. Frig!" Lyonyt shook his head.

"Scripties?" asked Fuast.

"The Navy conscription teams," I said. "They're not popular in the taudis."

"But they go everywhere," Fuast said.

"There are exemptions for youngsters and young men who are apprentices, or journeymen, or in school," I replied. "A far greater proportion of the young men in the taudis are day laborers or don't qualify for exemptions."

"Most of them don't," added Lyonyt. "They don't like working hard, either. The scripties get pissed when they do a taudis because there's always trouble. After they leave, there's more trouble, and a year or two later, when things get settled down, the scripties do it all over again."

"That's . . . do they really do that?"

Lyonyt nodded. He didn't say anything for a block, and that was the longest time he'd gone without speaking on any of the rounds I'd patrolled with him. After we'd passed the Temple, he glanced back, once, then twice. Finally, he shook his head. "Today's been the quietest I've seen it."

Captain Harraf was nowhere around when we returned to the station. Since he wasn't, I stepped partway into the lieutenant's small study. "Lieutenant? Have you heard anything about the conscription teams?"

He looked up from his desk, then smiled warmly. "I can't say as I have."

The smile and the pause told me that he knew.

"Well, sir, no one has told me, but we did notice one interesting thing today. The Temple of Puryon was shuttered up tight, and I've never seen it that way, and neither has Lyonyt. It could be that they know something we don't. I just thought I'd pass that along, sir."

"I do appreciate that, Master Rhennthyl. I will let the captain know. Thank you."

I nodded and slipped out.

As I rode the hack back to the Collegium, I wondered how the Tiempran priests had discovered the conscription schedule—if they had. If they hadn't, why was the Temple so closed up? Hostilities with Tiempre? Some operation Master Dichartyn had planned or undertaken?

As soon as I crossed the Bridge of Hopes and returned to the Collegium, I went looking for Master Dichartyn. For once, as he didn't seem to have been much lately, he was in his study.

"What is it, Rhennthyl?"

"Just one thing, sir. When I was patrolling South Middle, the Tiempran Temple was totally shuttered. Lyonyt said the only time he'd seen it shuttered was the last time the conscription team came through."

Master Dichartyn just nodded.

"I mentioned it to Lieutenant Warydt, and I could tell that he hadn't heard about the Temple, but that he felt the conscription team was about to begin. I thought you should know."

Dichartyn shook his head. "You could tell? That's hardly proof of anything."

"You're absolutely right, sir . . . except if they begin in the next few days, it would indicate both the priests and the lieutenant had advance knowledge. That's all I wanted to pass on, sir."

"Thank you, Rhennthyl."

"Have a good evening, sir." I made my way to the dining hall, stopping outside where Reynol and Kahlasa were talking.

"Good evening. You two look to be up to no good. . . ."

They both turned.

"Is any imager?" asked Kahlasa with a smile. "What about you?"

"I've definitely been up to nothing that pleases anyone."

"Except that lovely woman you've been seen with," suggested Kahlasa. "Some of the seconds and primes were almost drooling when they talk about you two."

Talk about us two? "Why would they do that?"

"Rhenn . . ." Kahlasa shook her head. "You're the only imager that any-one knows has actually *done* anything recently. Everyone else has managed to keep their accomplishments quiet. The younger imagers want to aspire to something . . . and what better than a tall and powerful imager who attracts a beautiful woman?"

I did groan at that.

"Even some of the girls are gossiping."

"Like Mayra?" She was one of the few I knew, besides the older imagers, such as Dyana, Chassendri, and Kahlasa.

"It doesn't matter." Kahlasa grinned at me. "You'll just have to live with it. Besides, it keeps people's attention on you and away from other matters, and that's not all bad."

The bells rang at that moment, and Reynol spoke. "I need to eat early because I'm meeting Meynard and a friend later."

They headed for the table for seconds and thirds, and I found myself moving toward the masters' table, empty except for Quaelyn and Ferlyn.

After greetings, I just ate and mainly listened to their conversation, partly because I was interested and partly because I was sore all over. At least, I was stiff and sore in so many places that it seemed like all over.

"... the yields on the eastern plains show a relation to the height of the rivers flowing through Cloisonyt and Montagne in Maris and Avryl ..."

"... but there's not enough water for irrigation ..."

As I got up to leave the dining hall, I couldn't help but think about Kahlasa's comments. In effect, because the woman I loved was beautiful, I'd become almost an internal lure for the Collegium ... and that was in addition to being an external lure. Just how had all that happened?

On my way out of the dining hall, I picked up copies of both *Tableta* and *Veritum* and brought them back to my quarters, where I read them, stretched out on the bed on my stomach, which was the most comfortable position. Neither newsheet had any stories that concerned either Caenen or Tiempre, but there was one about the battles west of the Jariolan coal mines. The sudden winter storm had been followed by a thaw and a rainstorm, and that had trapped another hundred Ferran landcruisers in mud, and cost them several thousand troops. Another story mentioned negotiations between a Council representative and a representative of the Oligarchy concerning a "supply base." That sounded like the coaling station on the isle of Harvik Master Rholyn had mentioned several weeks ago.

After what had happened the night before, I wasn't about to try anything else in the way of imaging—only to get a good night's sleep ... if I could, and if I could keep from thinking about Rousel.

45

By the time I dragged myself out of bed on Mardi morning, I was more than ready to get on with the day, especially after a dream about a memorial service in an anomen, where I'd kept trying to ask who was being memorialized, and no one would answer me. They just looked away. I didn't dream about the Temple of Puryon, exploding or otherwise, and the fact that I hadn't bothered me.

I ate breakfast quickly and finished just as Ferlyn and Chassendri arrived. I stood and smiled. "I'm off."

"Aren't you the fortunate one," said Chassendri cheerfully.

"Always," I answered with a smile, heading out of the dining hall.

The second duty coach was waiting, the driver wearing a heavy gray jacket against the wind, although I wouldn't have called it chill, merely brisk enough that I'd had to put on my imager's visored cap a bit more firmly than usual. On the way to the station, I thought through how I'd need to approach the day. I wasn't about to tell the captain anything.

Captain Harraf was standing outside his study when I entered the building, talking to Slausyl. Melyor was standing back and listening. I could only catch a few words.

"... come, and you stay clear ... cordon area ... no point ... they shoot anyone ..."

Both Slausyl and Melyor nodded.

I had no doubts that Harraf was warning them to avoid the conscription team. I half expected him to beckon to me or to Lyonyt after he dismissed the other pair of patrollers, but he pointedly avoided me and stepped back into his study without looking in our direction.

I turned to Lyonyt. "Did Captain Harraf mention anything about the conscription teams before I got here?"

"No, sir," replied Lyonyt.

Fuast just looked puzzled.

"Let's head out. I'll go over it while we start the round."

I actually waited until we were almost up to South Middle before I began to explain. "When the conscription teams come into an area, they don't want anyone else around. All we can do is patrol the area of our round outside their cordon." I was guessing a bit, but I thought I was fairly close to what Harraf had said to Melyor and Slausyl. "They come armed, and they will shoot. I've heard that some of them don't much care who they shoot."

Fuast swallowed audibly.

Lyonyt just nodded. He'd heard it before, and he didn't look like I'd missed anything. I hoped not. Harraf's "oversight" was anything but accidental.

During the first half round, the one where we did the perimeter of the round, we saw only women with children and a handful of men all roughly dressed, walking toward the avenue, most likely to where it and Quierca intersected. That was where builders and anyone who wanted a laborer could find one. When we reached the Avenue D'Artisans, on the return, close to two quints before eighth glass, I stepped up beside Lyonyt.

"If the conscription teams were hitting the taudis, they'd already be here. There's some imager business that's come up. I'll be leaving you for a bit, but I should be back and rejoin you around second glass. It's possible I may have to do this tomorrow as well."

"Yes, sir." Lyonyt didn't even look puzzled, although his eyes never stopped moving.

I wasn't sure they ever would, not until he was ashes.

I crossed the avenue and waited until they were a good block away before I hailed a hack to take me to NordEste Design. It was early enough that the direct route there wasn't that crowded, with the only slowness occurring around the Guild Square, and the hack pulled up on Hagahl Lane just as the last bells of eighth glass were dying away.

For the first time since I had met Seliora, when I knocked, I had to wait for a time before someone came to the door—and that someone was Methyr. He was wearing faded and ragged trousers and a woolen shirt that had seen far better days.

"I'm sorry, Master Rhennthyl. I was cleaning the tiles on the terrace."

"Up on the third level?"

"Yes, sir. It's my turn." He stepped back and let me enter, then shot the bolt. "If you'd come this way." He walked up the stairs and through the second-level entry hall, leading me through the indirect corridors that led to the back stairs leading down to the courtyard.

Once we were in the courtyard, he said, "Seliora had to go with Mother and Father this morning. She said she hoped you wouldn't mind. She should be here when you return, but if she isn't, she asked if you'd mind grooming the mare and stalling her."

"I can do that."

We crossed the courtyard to where the mare was actually saddled and waiting, tied to a post in the rear courtyard outside the stable.

"Who saddled her? Seliora?"

"Yes, sir."

"She didn't have to do that," I protested.

"She said it would be easier on you, and she wouldn't worry as much." Methyr looked away.

"If she's not here . . ." I shook my head. I'd have to express my appreciation personally. I didn't even dare write a note about it. "I do appreciate it, and I'll tell her when I return."

With that, I mounted and set out. Methyr watched until I was out of the courtyard and headed toward the Boulevard D'Este. I'd seen some mounted patrollers over the course of making patrol rounds, and Gulyart and the others had mentioned that there were mounted patrollers, used especially in riot situations. So I doubted that many people would take much notice of a Patrol rider headed along the Boulevard D'Este.

Once I reached the Plaza D'Nord, I added a concealment shield, the kind that blurred people's vision. They'd see a rider and a mount, but the details would be fuzzy. But along the ride out toward Ryel's estate, I passed only two wagons coming the other direction.

At the top of the rise south of the one that held the Ryel estate, I slowed the mare and studied the road and the estate itself. The road was empty, and the gates were closed. There was a flatter space, a semiswale next to the wall about a hundred yards up from the place where the stream flowed out from between the walls and into the large stone culvert under the road.

We started down toward the stream, and I could hear the rumble of a heavy wagon. It didn't sound like a trap, but I wasn't certain. I eased the mare to the right edge of the road and continued downhill. We'd almost reached the low ground between the two rises when I caught sight of a black wagon pulled by four drays coming slowly downhill, headed southward toward L'Excelsis.

Since the wagon wasn't what I was seeking, I kept riding, if slowly, then eased the mare off to the side on the upslope, if a good hundred yards below where I really wanted to be in order not to get close to the wagon. The teamster frowned as he passed, probably because he couldn't make us out too clearly. On the side of the wagon was a legend—"Kaenfyl & Sons, Fine Spirits."

Would anyone in the spirits business claim that their wares were anything but fine?

Once the wagon passed out of sight beyond the rise to the south, I rode the mare uphill to the swale, then dismounted and tied to a stubby but sturdy short scrubby plant that looked to be half tree and half bush. Then I leaned against the wall to wait.

A quint passed before I heard something and raised full concealment shields.

Before long a private messenger, with the red and white sash, rode down the hill and toward L'Excelsis. Only a few moments passed before a coach followed, ornate in blue with gold-painted trim—some High Holder whose colors I didn't know. But then, I really only knew Ryel's colors, although I thought Councilor Suyrien's were crimson and silver.

All in all, I waited for Alynat for more than two glasses, strengthening the concealment shields every time I heard the sounds of wagons or riders. More than a half score of wagons passed within a few yards of me and the mare, but no one even so much looked in our direction, and the mare didn't so much as snort or whinny, for which I was grateful.

By the time I reached NordEste Design, it was two quints to second glass. There was no one in the courtyard, and I rode the mare right up to the stables and dismounted, then led her in and unsaddled her and groomed her. I just hoped I'd gotten the saddle on the right rack.

I was leaving the stable, crossing the courtyard when Shelim and Seliora drove into the courtyard with a panel wagon I hadn't seen before. Both sides were painted with an identical design, an intertwined "N" and "E."

Seliora jumped off the wagon as soon as Shelim brought it to a halt. "Rhenn!" Her face was filled with concern.

"At the moment, nothing's happened, except I need to hurry to get back to Third District." I paused. "Would it be all right to borrow the mare tomorrow?"

"As often as you need to."

"Thank you." I put my arms around her. "I appreciated your saddling the mare. You didn't have to, but I do appreciate it."

"You need all the help I can give." Her arms went around me for a moment. Then she looked up and kissed me briefly. "You also need to wash up a bit. You smell too much like horse. Come along."

I did feel cleaner and fresher after that—and after the slices of bread and cheese I wolfed down before I headed out to catch a hack back to the Third

District. I had the hack drop me on the east side of the Plaza Sudeste. It was nearly two quints past two.

Guessing that Lyonyt was on Quierca, coming back toward the avenue, I headed south, but I'd only gone a block when an older woman, one who often had a cart with coal in it, called to me.

"Officer . . . you looking for Lyonyt, he just passed here heading for South Middle."

"Thank you."

I reversed directions and actually caught up with the two of them just short of Saelio.

"I was beginning to worry, sir," offered Lyonyt.

I shook my head. "Everything, every little thing, takes longer than you think."

The older patroller laughed.

"Any problems?" I asked.

"Not a one. Did see a few of Jadhyl's fellows in the green. They looked worried."

"They probably know something we don't—like when the conscription team is arriving." Everyone seemed to know, at least in general terms, except the Collegium and the Civic Patrol. I thought for a moment. Both the commander and Maitre Poincaryt had to know. They just chose not to tell anyone so that they could claim to the Navy that they hadn't let anyone know. So the Tiempran priests knew more than we did, as did the taudischefs, and Captain Harraf, who could not say much besides telling some patrollers to be careful because he wasn't supposed to know, either. Whether I cared much for him or not, there was definitely something wrong about that.

We walked down Saelio, but it was quiet, and so were each of the succeeding streets. A good glass and a half later, when we were headed back to the station, passing Dugalle on Quierca, I turned to Lyonyt. "The Tiempran Temple was still shuttered this morning. What about on the last round?"

"Locked up tighter than a High Holder's daughter, sir. When do you think the scripties will be here?"

"I don't know. Sometime in the next week, but whether that's tomorrow or Jeudi or Vendrei, I don't know. Probably not Solayi, but other than that?" All I could do was shrug.

When we returned to the station, I could see that the door to Captain Harraf's study was closed, but whether he was meeting with someone or had left for the day, I couldn't have said. I certainly wasn't about to ask.

We signed the round sheet, and then I left. The wind had gotten warmer, springlike, even though it was late afternoon, and the hack ride back to Imagisle was uncomfortably warm. When I returned to my quarters, another note was under my door, asking me to see Master Dichartyn.

I hurried back across the quadrangle to the administration building, half hoping that he'd left for the day. I wasn't that fortunate. His study door was open, and he was standing by the open window, almost as if he had been waiting for me.

"Rhennthyl, come in and close the door."

I did.

"Maitre Dyana told me that you handled questions about the Autumn Ball with a surprising amount of finesse. Master Rholyn also remarked on your comments about the taudischef's hearing. He said that he even baited you, but you were quite self-possessed." He paused and looked directly at me. "Maitre Poincaryt and I would appreciate it if you would continue that practice."

"I'm working on that, sir, and trying to follow the example that you both have set. Master Poincaryt made it clear that I should do so, and that I should not saddle you with anything that was not absolutely vital." I paused, then asked, "Are you aware of any inquiries being made by High Holder Ryel about Johanyr's health? Have any ever been made?"

"Don't you think that's an odd question, now?"

"No, sir. After my troubles with him, I asked how he was doing, but the way his sister dismissed him at the Ball brought that question to mind."

Master Dichartyn frowned. "So far as I am aware, Ryel disinherited Johanyr once he became an imager and has had no contact with his son since. Other members of the family may have."

And yet Ryel had declared me his enemy?

There was a moment of silence.

"Has anything vital come up today?" Master Dichartyn raised his eyebrows.

"Not vital, sir. Captain Harraf warned the patrollers who do the round in Youdh's territory that if the conscription teams arrived, they were not to interfere or even patrol the area. He avoided giving us the same information. In fact, he ignored me altogether."

"He's being a very wise man in the stupidest way possible." Dichartyn's voice was dry.

"Sir?" I doubted he'd say more, but it was worth the attempt.

"He knows you know all about him. He also knows that people have bad things happen when they cross you, but it's stupid to call attention to it by ignoring you and putting two more junior patrollers in possible danger because you're with them. Some of the patrollers will notice. They're not as dense as arrogant officers think. By the way, that goes for master imagers, too."

The last was clearly directed at me. I just said, "Yes, sir. I ask the patrollers, and I listen."

"I would hope so." He smiled politely. "Is there anything else?"

"No, sir. Not that I know."

"That's all I had, Rhennthyl." He paused. "Your young lady is quite beautiful. I hope you appreciate all she has to offer."

"I feel that I do, sir." More than I was about to admit to anyone.

He raised his eyebrows. "You don't. I didn't. No one as talented as you and as young as you does. You only think you do. Try to remember that."

Strangely, his words were delivered kindly, not cuttingly, and with a hint of something I couldn't identify. I also wondered when he'd seen Seliora. Or had he slipped into the studio and looked at the portrait? Then, we had walked through Imagisle several times.

"Yes, sir." What else could I say?

He turned back toward the window, and I left. I was more than a little hungry, given that all I'd eaten since breakfast had been a few slices of bread and cheese.

Meredi morning found me slightly less tired, and far less stiff, although I found it was still uncomfortable to sit still on the hard chairs in the dining hall by the time I finished breakfast, but I did manage to banter some with Ferlyn and Master Ghaend. Ghaend told me that Shault's reading had improved greatly, and that Shault seemed to show a definite aptitude for the mechanical side of science.

"That might be for the best," I replied.

"His background, you mean?"

I nodded.

"You never know with imagers." He gave me a quizzical look. "Do you think anyone would have picked a former portraiturist to be one of Maitre Dichartyn's covert types?"

I managed to laugh. "I'd better not judge too soon."

Ghaend did smile, if faintly.

I did get to Third District station a good quint before seventh glass. Both Lieutenant Warydt and the captain were there, because as I entered the station, Warydt stepped into the captain's study and closed the door. Had he seen me and wanted to avoid me? Or was I just suspecting the worst of everyone, or of the captain and lieutenant?

Fuast moved up to me. "Sir?"

"Yes? Is Lyonyt here?"

"No, sir. I was going to ask if you'd seen him."

"Not yet."

We didn't need to worry, because a few moments later, the older patroller hurried through the doors.

"Vierstyn was having trouble with an elver they picked up. I gave them a hand getting him off the wagon. Never know when you'll need a hand."

We exchanged glances and then, without a word, headed out of the station, up Fuosta, and then right on South Middle. The day was cooler, and thick gray clouds hovered in the west, suggesting cold and rain. Once we passed Dugalle, and as soon as I could get a clear view of the Temple of Puryon, I studied it, taking in the still closed shutters and doors. I felt better once we were well past it.

"Locked up tight," observed Lyonyt. "Wager it stays that way until after the scripties come and go."

"That's a wager I won't take," I replied.

"A wise man you are, sir."

"Wise enough not to wager against an experienced patroller," I bantered back.

As on Mardi, I left Lyonyt and Fuast near eighth glass and caught a hack to take me from the Plaza Sudeste to NordEste Design. When I rapped the knocker on the private entrance door, once more Methyr was the one to open the door and to lead the way to the courtyard. Unlike on Mardi, Seliora was there, helping load some heavily wrapped chairs into the two wagons—one the panel wagon and the other the canvas-topped wagon from which I'd made my first sketches of Ryel's estate.

She handed a chair wrapped in cloth—old blankets—to Shomyr and hurried over to me. "I did saddle the mare for you. Please be careful."

"Thank you . . . and I will." I knew I had to be. Then I wrapped my arms around her, and we held each other for several long moments.

Only then did we walk toward the stable and the mare—tied outside and waiting for me. I mounted quickly. Seliora looked up at me. She smiled faintly, but she might as well have asked me to be careful yet one more time.

I guided the mare out of the courtyard, waited for two coaches to pass on Nordroad, and then followed them out and down to the Boulevard D'Este, where I turned left. Before that long I was leaving the Plaza D'Nord and riding along the road flanked by the small estates of those High Holders who wished to have a presence in L'Excelsis.

The road wasn't that traveled in midmorning, doubtless because any farm wagons had gone into L'Excelsis early, as had those with business in the city. A few wagons and three or four coaches passed me heading into the city, but with my light concealment shields, no one paid me much attention.

From the top of the rise south of the Ryel estate, I could see gardeners in the garden, someone sweeping or washing the south terrace between the end of the chateau and the tower that would feature prominently in Ryel's so-called Foliage Festival, and several workers picking late apples from the small orchard to the east of the formal gardens. When I reached the depression between the two rises and was shielded by the wall from the sight of anyone in the chateau or grounds, I created full concealment shields. Absently, as I rode past the culvert, I noted that the water level in the stream was lower.

Then, some hundred yards uphill, I dismounted and again tied the mare to the trunk of one of the tree bushes and settled in to wait.

I'd only been in position along the side of the wall for less than half a glass, and three wagons and a post rider had passed, when, from the north, I heard a rumbling and rattling suggestive of a lighter vehicle being driven at high speeds. I turned and watched the road. For a time, only the sound increased, but I saw nothing. Then a black horse appeared, cresting the hill and pulling a trap bearing the black and silver of Ryel House.

I anchored my shields to the wall behind me, and prepared to do what was necessary, waiting as the black trap hurtled downhill, southward toward L'Excelsis. The single black horse was larger than a riding horse, but smaller than a dray, and was already heavily lathered.

I waited until I could see Alynat's face, hard and intent, and focused on the road and the horse. His eyes didn't even flicker in my direction, as if it wouldn't have mattered even if I had not been hidden behind concealment shields.

Then I imaged steel fragments into the wheel bearings, and what amounted to a shield directly in front of the wheels, if but for an instant or so, anchored to the wall. Everything seemed to freeze. For that moment, I was shaken and jolted, thrown back against the rough-smooth stone of the wall, not that hard, but as though I'd been shoved, indifferently.

The trap's wheels froze, but the body of the trap lurched forward with a terrible creaking and splintering sound, pivoting forward over the wheels. The traces and harness snapped, or partly so. Alynat flew from the driver's seat over the now-screaming and lathered horse and slammed headfirst into the stone pavement, then skidded along the stones. One arm was twisted back into an unnatural angle, the reins still wrapped around that wrist.

Still behind concealment shields, I eased forward, looking at the limp and now-frail body. His left temple was horribly smashed in, and his form was silent.

The trap horse struggled and kept screaming. I wanted to put it out of its misery, but I didn't dare, because that would leave too much evidence that someone had been there. I hurried back to the mare. She snorted and stepped sideways, but I managed to gentle her. Then I untied her and walked her back downhill on the edge of the road. Near the culvert I mounted and rode slowly southward, up the next rise and then back toward L'Excelsis.

Behind me, I could hear the screams of the trap horse. Those screams echoed in my head all the way back to NordEste Design. For a moment, I wondered why I felt more about the horse than Alynat. When I thought about that, though, I understood. Ryel's family had hardly shown that much concern about Johanyr, except as a symbol of the High Holder. That had certainly been true of Iryela. And Alynat, as shown by his attitude and words at the Autumn Ball, was merely an extension of all that placed me in an impossible situation. Effectively, Ryel, Dulyk, and Alynat were the same. Because they were all Ryel House, in effect, they had all set the fire that had killed the watchman at Alusine Wool. They had all arranged for the difficulties that faced my father, and they all had been part of causing Rousel's terrible "accident." The trap horse, on the other hand, had been truly innocent and without choice in the matter.

Methyr came running to meet me as I rode into the courtyard. "Master Rhennthyl."

"Yes?"

"Oh . . . they've all gone, but you're not to groom the mare. Seliora said to stall her, and they'll be back soon. She said it was important for you to get back to the Patrol."

"You're certain?"

"Yes, sir."

Given Methyr's seriousness, I dismounted and led the mare into the stable. After I settled her in the stall and closed the stall door, I turned to him. "You're certain?"

"Yes, sir."

"Give her my thanks." I hurried back out of the stable and across the courtyard, taking the south entrance onto Nordroad.

I did have to wait for a bit, but less than a quint before getting a hack, one of the older and more dilapidated coaches, but I wasn't feeling that choosy at the moment. After I got out of the hack at the Plaza Sudeste, I wasn't as fortunate at finding Lyonyt and Fuast as I had been on Mardi, and it was two quints before second glass when I finally caught up with them as they were coming up Saelio.

"Little earlier today, sir," offered Lyonyt.

"It is, and I won't have to be ducking out for the rest of the week. I finally finished what was required." Before he could comment, although I doubted he would, I asked, "Is it still quiet on the rounds?"

"Except for a grab-and-run on the avenue, sir, it's been real quiet."

"That's good for us."

"You still think the scripties are coming?"

"Yes. I just don't know when."

"Won't be long," murmured Fuast.

He was doubtless right about that.

We finished two more rounds through quiet streets of the taudis, streets that were never that quiet. Even the odor of elveweed was less pervasive, and that suggested that those who sold it didn't want to lose any of it to the conscription teams.

When we walked back into the station just after fourth glass, Lieutenant Warydt beckoned to me from outside his study. I walked back to join him.

"We haven't seen any conscription teams yet, Master Rhennthyl," said the lieutenant. "Have you heard anything?"

"Nothing more than before, that they've been operating in the west of L'Excelsis."

Warydt smiled warmly and nodded. "If you do hear . . ."

"I'll certainly let you know, sir."

"That would be helpful."

As I left the Third District station, I had the feeling that the entire conversation was really to point out how little I knew that was really helpful to the Civic Patrol.

It might have been my imagination, but it seemed as though there were fewer hacks on South Middle near the taudis. I walked all the way to the Midroad before I could hail one, and the ride down the Midroad, around the Guild Square, and along the Boulevard D'Imagers seemed interminable.

When I finally left the hack and crossed the Bridge of Hopes to Imagisle, carrying the blue-gray patroller's cloak because the afternoon had gotten uncomfortably warm, even though the gray clouds loomed closer in the west, I kept looking to see if some junior prime might be looking for me, but no one was. I reached my quarters and hung up the cloak, then went down to the main level and washed up. While it was still a good half glass before the time for dinner, I decided to walk over to the dining hall and see if I had any letters or messages. I didn't want to, because, sooner or later, I feared, there would be one.

As I walked into the dining hall, I made the point of looking up at the plaques that held the names of past imagers who had died serving the Collegium. There was a new plaque, one for Thenard, right below the one for Claustyn. Getting shot by Ferran assassins was serving the Collegium, even if the Collegium did frown upon my doing in one of the envoys who'd authorized those assassinations.

In that respect, I didn't agree with Collegium policies. I still thought that those who created evil should pay, even if it happened to be politically "inconvenient." I did agree that any action taken should not be traceable to the Collegium, at least not through proof. People would still speculate. Then . . . there might be times when others would know, but could prove and do nothing. That was dangerous, but I could see that there would be times when that was unavoidable.

I walked toward the letter boxes, opened mine . . . and froze. A red-striped letter sat there, as deadly as if I were looking at the barrel of a pistol. As I drew it out, I recognized Khethila's writing. I knew what was in the letter, but I still had to open and read it.

> Dear Rhenn,
> I have the feeling that this will come as no surprise to you. Rousel died late on Samedi. He never really woke up, Mother wrote.
>
> Father is closing the factorage there, for now, and they will be returning with Remaya and Rheityr. They plan to arrive back here on Solayi afternoon. I will be arranging a memorial service for Rousel with Chorister Aknotyn for some time next week . . .

For all that I had feared Rousel's death, even worried about it and half anticipated it, I felt encased in chill and as though I were being squeezed on all sides by massive unseen weights.

Numbly, I slipped the envelope and note into my waistcoat and hurried out of the dining hall and across the quadrangle toward the Bridge of Hopes. Hopes?

I had to wait almost a quint in the fading twilight before I could catch a hack to take me out to Khethila. Then as I sat on the hard seat of the coach, I couldn't help but think, yet again, about how everything had come about, how the seemingly smallest of actions created ever greater losses. Because I'd half blinded the arrogant son of an even more arrogant High Holder in self-defense, my brother was dead, his wife a widow, and his son fatherless. Alynat was dead because he would have carried on with what Ryel had begun, as would Dulyk, given half a chance. And Ryel thought he was in the right.

I couldn't help but reflect on Grandmama Diestra's words about how those who were good but naïve always believed that there was a way out where no one was hurt, and where all ended well. All too often, I was learning, such didn't exist.

Yet . . . what I had done—and would do—was not right. It was necessary to prevent a chain of further wrongs . . . and I intended that the example I set would do just that, hopefully so that other imagers would not be faced with what I had encountered.

Was that a vain hope? I could only trust in my feeling that it was not, but that required my success, and that was not at all certain. I only knew that I had to try.

The ride out the Midroad seemed to take glasses, but it was less than half a glass when the hacker pulled up in front of the gate before my parents' house. I gave him an extra few coppers over the fare and hurried up the walk to the door. I rapped loudly.

Khethila opened the door. Her face and cheeks were dry, but her eyes were red. "I thought you'd come."

"I'm here." I stepped inside and hugged her, then closed the door, one-handed, before putting both arms around her.

We just held to each other for a time.

Finally, I stepped back. "I've spent all week fearing it would come to this. Most people don't live through those kinds of injuries . . . but I still hoped."

"So did I."

"The service . . . can I . . . ?"

"I closed the factorage early and had Charlsyn take me to see Chorister Aknotyn. He won't set the day firmly until Mother and Father are back, but we're planning on Jeudi. I thought you'd speak for the family. Can you be there?"

"I'll arrange it." We didn't speak of it, but we both knew Rousel had been cremated in Kherseilles and his ashes scattered there, probably to the sea, because he had loved to sail.

We walked slowly back to the family parlor. Khethila dropped heavily onto the settee. I took the armchair across from Father's and waited for Khethila to say what she would.

"I never felt good about Rousel going to Kherseilles," she finally said.

"I worried about it." I had, but not for the same reasons, I suspected.

"Rousel . . . he trusted people too much. He couldn't believe that . . . that people could be so selfish . . . so uncaring."

That was true enough. Even though he'd annoyed me at times with his carelessness and gibes, what she said was true. Part of Rousel's carelessness came from his belief that things and people couldn't go that wrong. But his carelessness and overly optimistic attitude, the arrogance of the Ryels, and my imaging abilities . . . and even my own willfulness in not wanting to bow down to Johanyr . . . all those had combined to kill my brother.

And I could not say anything to my own family. What good would it do, except create greater bitterness and anger, both against me and against the High Holders and the Collegium?

That was another price of being an imager, I was learning. I wondered how many more I would discover in the days, months, and years ahead.

47

Needless to say, I stayed late with Khethila, but did get a ride back to the Collegium with Charlsyn, only to sleep fitfully and wake up early on Jeudi. Because of the nightmares, most of which I didn't remember, about all sorts of mayhem and violence being perpetrated on Khethila, one of the first things I did, after lighting the desk lamp, was to write a brief note to Seliora. I did take care to make it seem as harmless as possible.

> *Dearest,*
>
> *Since I won't see you until Samedi at the sitting for the portrait, I thought you should know that Rousel died over the weekend. Given the circumstances and the severity of his injuries, I had feared this might happen. There will be a memorial service here in L'Excelsis next week, but I do not know when yet.*
>
> *I know that this might be an imposition for Grandmama Diestra, but Khethila will be all alone at the house until my parents return on Solayi, and you understand that, as an imager, I cannot stay there at night. If there is anything that can be done to see that she is not disturbed, I cannot tell you how greatly I would appreciate it.*

I did sign it "With Love, Rhennthyl."

After I sealed the letter, I sat at the desk for a time, recalling what Martyl or Dartazn had said about Master Dichartyn—that he never seemed to sleep and that it was no wonder, with what he had done. I also recalled what Maitre Poincaryt had said about Master Dichartyn not having had as few problems or enemies as I did in more than ten years.

But why? Why did it have to be that way?

Couldn't the Collegium work matters out better with the Council and the factors and the guilds? Or had they, and what we lived under was the best they could do? That didn't seem like the most satisfactory of answers, not to me, but it had been brought home forcefully that at times the best of compromises exacted a great burden on those caught between the millwheels of the compromisers.

Finally, I got into exercise clothes and headed out.

Both Master Dichartyn and Master Schorzat were there for the morning exercises and run, and I thought about telling them about Rousel. First, I dismissed it because saying anything would just leave more traces back to me. Then I realized that I could certainly say that he'd died of injuries in a wagon accident and that I would need part of a day to be at the memorial service. Not mentioning it would suggest more than being straightforward.

After the exercise routines, where I got thrown more than I should have in sparring, and the run, I cleaned up and hurried through breakfast. I did force myself to eat because I knew I needed to, and then headed to the administration building to find Master Dichartyn. It was early enough that he was there, and no one else was, when I rapped on his study door.

"Come in." His voice was tired. "What is it, Rhennthyl?"

"Just one thing, sir. Last night I received word that my brother died of injuries he received in a wagon accident. I just wanted you to know that I'll need part of a day next week to go to the memorial service. I trust that won't be a problem."

Dichartyn looked at me intently. "I wondered. You seemed distracted this morning." He frowned. "You found out just last night? Last night?"

"Yes, sir. I got an urgent message from my sister. He died in Kherseilles over the weekend."

Master Dichartyn looked at me. "I imagine you're upset. Don't do anything foolish. Foolishness won't bring him back or help you."

"No, sir. I understand that. I won't do anything foolish." In time, I'd do what was necessary, but not until that time.

He kept looking at me. I met his gaze.

Then he nodded. "Please let me know when the service is. There won't be any problem."

"Thank you, sir."

I had the feeling Master Dichartyn knew about Alynat, and the timing puzzled him. That was fine with me.

After leaving Master Dichartyn and before leaving for Third District station, I did arrange with Beleart to send the letter to Seliora by private courier. That cost me a silver, but it was worth it. I hoped they could help . . . but Seliora and her family had offered.

I hurried off to the extra duty coach where, as the driver headed out over the Bridge of Hopes, I sat on the hard seat worrying about what Ryel might do next and hoping that Seliora's family could and would help—and that I could repay them without compromising my position at the Collegium. Yet . . . the Collegium's frigging unspoken and unbending rules and the frigging unbending customs of the High Holders were what had gotten me—and my family—into the position where I found myself. And . . . for all that I knew Alynat's death was necessary, the fact that it had been bothered me.

When the duty coach turned on Quierca and then on Fuosta, I thought I saw mounted riders ahead. The conscription team? That was all I needed.

I hurried into the station, where all the patrollers were drawn up, and joined Lyonyt and Fuast. "What's happening?"

"The lieutenant just said that he needed to talk to everyone before they headed out," replied Lyonyt.

"It has to be about the conscription teams."

"He didn't say."

It wasn't that long before the lieutenant walked from his study and stopped short of the assembled patrollers. He waited for the murmurings to die away before he spoke. "Some of you have already seen that the Navy conscription team has arrived. They've set up a cordon all along South Middle, up to Saelio and across to Quierca and back south to Goryn. . . ."

That mean the entire taudis was cordoned off.

". . . If past practice is any guide, all they'll do today is man their perimeter and grab anyone who's the right age without an approved job or schooling who tries to sneak by them. They'll start taking their teams door to door tomorrow. Just patrol the outside of your round and keep clear of their teams," the lieutenant said. "Don't try to cross the cordon lines, and don't argue with them. Is that clear?"

"Yes, sir," came a response, mostly in unison.

"That's all."

We let some of the other patrollers—those whose patrols did not include the South Middle taudis—leave the station first, then followed.

"Could be a long day." Lyonyt glanced up at the thin overcast that had turned the sky a bluish silver. "Good thing it's not too hot."

When we reached South Middle short of Dugalle, I could make out the pattern of the cordon. There were riders stationed every fifty yards or so and roughly three men armed with oak batons, longer than truncheons, set equidistant between the riders, who also carried batons. The riders had pistols, but the uniformed men in olive-green uniforms—I thought they were marines—did not. There was a larger group of marines opposite the Temple and another group, it appeared, farther up South Middle.

"Why do they do it this way?" asked Fuast.

I'd had the same question.

"They don't say, and they don't like us asking. If you ask me, I'd guess they figure that if they just hold their position for a while, everyone inside will calm down."

I had my doubts about that, particularly since the conscription teams cordoned the taudis areas of cities only before going house to house. It was almost as though they wanted to provoke resistance so that they could use force.

We kept back from the riders and marines, actually walking on the north side of East Middle until we passed Saelio where the cordon ended. Then we resumed our normal patrol round. After we patrolled the avenue and up to Saelio on Quierca, we crossed the street and walked past Dugalle to the end, before turning and retracing the same pattern.

We were nearing Mando on South Middle when a white-haired and bent old woman, accompanied by a boy, walked across South Middle. One of the riders was closest, and he yelled out, "You there! Halt!"

The woman either did not hear or did not understand, and while the boy tugged at her sleeve, she shifted the bundles in her arms and kept walking.

"Halt!" yelled the rider, turning his mount and lifting the long baton.

"Stay here," I hissed at Lyonyt, moving forward toward what I saw as an unnecessary use of force.

The mounted officer urged his mount into a quick trot toward the woman, bringing the baton into position for a vicious cut.

"Grandmere!" cried the youth, a boy not that much older than Shault.

I managed to throw a partial shield, at an angle, just as the officer struck, and the horse staggered sideways, nearly unhorsing the officer. I didn't know Navy rank insignia but the silver bars indicated an officer. His position suggested a junior one.

He wheeled the horse back toward the pair, raising the baton to strike again, even as the boy tried to help the old woman pick up her scattered parcels and groceries.

I stepped forward. "You don't ride down old women, Lieutenant, conscription team or no conscription team."

"What?" He reined up and turned in the saddle, looking down at me. He was older, probably a junior officer who'd come up through the ranks. His eyes narrowed as he caught sight of the grays and the insignia on my visor cap. "You don't tell a conscription team what to do. Not even an imager does. No one breaks a cordon, and no one carries in food for those taudis-types. No one, and don't tell us what to do."

"I'm just asking you not to ride down helpless old women," I said mildly.

"Get out of the way, or your Collegium will hear that you interfered."

I was getting very tired of arrogance, everywhere. Namer-tired, and there was no one close to us, not close enough to hear, not yet. "Do you prove your manhood by abusing women and boys? Are you that type?"

I could see him flush.

"Or do you just like abusing everyone? No . . . I can see it, you like women and boys . . . You're not really a man . . . just someone who pretends he is." While I'd kept my voice low, I'd tried to project total scorn and contempt toward him.

He lifted the long baton and urged the horse forward, toward me.

I imaged a barrier in front of the horse's knees and jumped aside. The mount stumbled and went to its knees. With a little imaging help from me, the lieutenant went from the saddle into the pavement, headfirst.

I could see he was still breathing. I tightened my lips and did another quick imaging into his brain, then yelled, "Officer down! Help!"

I gestured for the boy and woman to move. This time, they hurried away, leaving some of the groceries on the sidewalk. The old woman looked back at me, then scurried more quickly.

After they were beyond the taudis wall, I turned and waited as another rider trotted toward me, followed by several men on foot.

"What happened?" The Navy type who rode up wasn't an officer—no silver or braids—but he was even older than the lieutenant. "What happened here, patroller?"

"There was an old woman with a boy. She didn't listen to the lieutenant when he told her to halt. Maybe she was Tiempran or Caenen and didn't understand. I told him that. He didn't listen and rode over me—or he would have, if I hadn't jumped aside—and toward them. The horse stumbled, and he went right over."

One of the men on foot ran to the fallen officer and knelt down beside him, then looked up. "The lieutenant's dead, chief. He must have hit his head real hard."

"Frig! That's all we need." The chief turned back to me.

There were a few more questions, but no one had seen anything but the horse stumble and the officer pitch forward. In time I managed to slip back to where Lyonyt and Fuast were waiting. "We need to walk farther along the round."

"Be a good idea. Lieutenant said we weren't to get in their way." Lyonyt looked at me, then murmured, "Friggin' scripties . . . don't have to live with the mess they leave behind."

Fuast looked from Lyonyt to me and back again, opened his mouth, and then shut it.

Lyonyt looked to the junior patroller. "Really a shame those scripties can't ride as well as they think. If he hadn't been trying to hurt an old woman, nothing would have happened." He paused and looked at Fuast. "Would it?"

"Ah, no. No, sir."

"Terrible accident," Lyonyt went on. "Sometimes they happen, but like the lieutenant said, we leave 'em alone, and they make their own mistakes."

That might be, but I had to hope that no one took out the death on the taudis-dwellers, although it was clear that no one but me, and perhaps Lyonyt or Fuast, had seen anything of what had really happened, and even they hadn't seen much.

Dichartyn would have said that I shouldn't have interfered, but the way the lieutenant had been swinging that baton, the old woman would have been dead, or crippled for the rest of a short and miserable life. And for what? The old woman had been trying to get out of his way, and the boy was far too young to have been a conscription evader.

For the next two glasses, we just kept walking, circling one way around our section of the taudis and then back the other. Although a section of the Avenue D'Artisans was part of the round, it hadn't been cordoned off. Even so, word had gotten around, and there were far fewer people there, as well. Several of the shopkeepers and bistro owners couldn't be happy with fewer customers, either.

For a time, I dropped back behind the other two, scanning the taudis closely, trying to get a sense of what might be happening inside the cordon.

That was when I caught some of Lyonyt's low words to Fuast.

". . . good thing Master Rhennthyl was there . . . might help us later . . ."

"What did he do?"

". . . never ask . . . things happen to folks who cross imagers . . . all you need to know is that it was an accident . . . even if the captain asks . . .'sides, frigging scriptie deserved it . . . white-haired old Pharsi not that good, but never hurt anyone . . ."

At least Lyonyt felt I'd done the right thing. But had I? Probably not, in Master Dichartyn's eyes, were he to know. According to him, from what I'd seen and heard, I should have let the lieutenant beat and possibly kill an old woman, rather than involve an imager, because it might reflect badly on the Collegium. In Dichartyn's eyes, the old woman should have suffered, and I couldn't accept his arrogance or the dead lieutenant's. Yet that, too, was arrogance on my part . . . but I knew it, and the lieutenant hadn't cared that he'd been arrogant. Master Dichartyn? That was another question.

We kept walking, but everything was quiet, and I heard and saw nothing from the Temple of Puryon, even though I had the feeling that, locked up as it was, it was anything but empty. By the time we finished the last round, I was dreading returning to the station.

Fortunately, for the moment, anyway, neither Captain Haraff nor Lieutenant Warydt happened to be in sight. I didn't exactly rush in helping Lyonyt with the round report and signing off with him and Fuast, but I didn't dally either. I was out of Third District station in less than a quint after fourth glass.

Once I walked down Fuosta a block, I stopped to think. I wished I'd been able to think more quickly with the lieutenant, but there hadn't been time, not if I wanted to save the old woman. But I had very bad feelings about what would happen on Vendrei. Even if the scripties—and it was hard to think of them in other than derogatory terms after seeing their tactics and my encounter with the Navy lieutenant—didn't blame the taudis-dwellers for the lieutenant's death and saw it as an accident, they'd still be resentful and looking for targets. And I couldn't help shivering slightly as I recalled the flash image of the Temple exploding. Was that truly farsight . . . or just what I feared? How would I ever know?

Still . . . I had to do something.

I turned east at the next alley and stepped into the late-afternoon shadows, waiting, then raising concealment shields before walking slowly up the low rise of battered and cracked paving stones. Three blocks later, I reached the cordon. No one looked in my direction, not that they should have, as I walked as close to the midpoint between two marines as I could, some five yards from each, then continued up the alley and into the taudis, the west quarter. After a block I dropped the concealment shields. On top of regular full shields, holding them was an effort. Not a great one, but still an effort.

Coming as I was from the west, I took a little longer to find Chelya's house, and I didn't see any of Horazt's toughs along the way. Once I stood on the stone stoop, I drew back the patroller's blue cloak to reveal my grays, then rapped.

No one answered.

I rapped again.

Finally, the door opened. Through the narrow crack, I could see Chelya's eyes widen as she saw me.

"Shault's fine. I need to find Horazt. Now. There's going to be more trouble."

She looked at me. "He might be at the red house on Weigand near the corner of the crooked lane."

"If I don't find him there, I'll be back."

She kept looking at me, then offered a melancholy smile. "He will be there."

"Thank you."

The door closed before I could step back. I turned and began to walk the three or so blocks to Weigand, trying to ignore the growing soreness in my feet and lower back. I was glad the sun had not set, although it had dropped behind the roofs to the west, when I reached Weigand, because none of the row houses had numbers, all looked similar. The "red" house was more like faded burnt umber, but no other dwelling was painted any reddish color.

Once more I stood on a stone stoop and rapped, this time with a tarnished brass knocker that wobbled when I lifted it. There was a long silence before the peephole in the door opened. Then it closed. I was ready to rap again when the door opened and Horazt stepped out. He was barefoot, and his shirt was untucked.

"Master Rhennthyl . . . you friends with the scripties to get in the taudis?" His voice was sardonic.

"No. I had to use imager skills to get past them, but I needed to see you. The Tiempran priests are planning something, probably tomorrow. If . . . if they leave the Temple . . . or if you see them away from the Temple, and you can capture them and hold them for me, I'll give you five golds." I paused, then fumbled with my wallet, and handed him the gold I'd been carrying for days. "Here's what I owe you."

He took the gold, fingered it. Then it disappeared. "You don't want much, do you?"

I shrugged. "Something else. If there's anyone you like, keep them away from the Temple for the next few days. No matter who's there." I forced a grin. "But it wouldn't hurt if someone enticed Saelyhd to be there."

Horazt spat to one side. "Why are you telling me this?"

"Shault is one reason. He doesn't want anything to happen to you. When the Collegium tried and executed Youdh, he was terrified that someone might come after you."

That stopped his half-open mouth from uttering anything . . . for a moment, anyway.

"Another reason is that the Collegium and the Civic Patrol can probably work with you and Jadhyl, but not Saelyhd. A third reason is that I don't like the Tiempran priests using our taudis-dwellers as expendable weapons against the Council. I don't like the kind of toughs Youdh and Saelyhd use, and I don't want to see another riot between the taudis and the Patrol or the scripties. You'll get hurt, and the scripties will use it as an excuse."

"Like I said . . . you don't want much."

I shrugged again. "The golds are mine. I'd offer more, but I don't have it. I'll do what I can, but the next few days could be bloody. If you think it would help you, I'd suggest you pass on what I've said to Jadhyl and Deyalt." I stepped back. "That's all."

He was still watching as I moved down the steps and then toward the alley that would take me to and beyond the cordon. I thought he might be interested, but who could tell?

Again, most likely because of the presence of the conscription teams, I had to walk all the way out to the Midroad before I could find a hack to hail, and I felt as though the driver hit every hole and rough spot on Midroad and then the Boulevard D'Imagers on the way back to Imagisle.

My feet ached with every step I took across the Bridge of Hopes and the quadrangle. Thankfully, at least I thought I was thankful, there were no notes or messages in my letter box or under my door. But I wondered just how long that might last.

48

Dinner in the dining hall on Jeudi was quiet enough, but for all the effort I'd expended during the day, all I could do was drag myself back to my quarters after eating. Yet it was late before I drifted into an uneasy sleep. On Vendrei, I got up early, not that it was difficult, what with my uneasy sleep and worries about Khethila and what I was getting into with Seliora's family and what I'd done the day before with the Navy lieutenant. That didn't count my concerns about trying to use Horazt to capture the Tiempran priests or the fact that I was acting as though my flash vision of the Temple exploding represented true farsight.

After exercises and running, and showering and dressing, I rushed through breakfast and made it to the duty coach as fast as I could. In a way, there was no logical reason for that. If something happened, it was just as likely to happen whether I managed to be near the Temple or not. Yet . . . something impelled me to hurry.

When I stepped out of the coach outside the station, the sun shone white, and a gentle breeze, under a pale blue sky, offered a perfect late autumn day. That didn't cheer me much as I walked toward the station doors.

Even if I had wanted to escape the captain, I couldn't have, because he was clearly waiting for me to arrive. He signaled for me to join him, a gesture as close to a command as anything nonverbal could be, then turned and stepped into his study.

I did close the door behind me when I entered.

He stood by the corner of his desk. "Master Rhennthyl . . . the Navy is not happy with us. They're not too bright, but they have some questions as to why one of their horses spooked and threw a lieutenant and killed him. They know some patrollers were nearby, and it appears that you and Lyonyt were the ones. Lyonyt and Fuast have already told me what happened, and I'm certain it happened that way." The captain paused. "The lieutenant was a fool to ride after an old woman, and what occurred was his own fault. If something else like that happens, they won't see it that way."

"Yes, Captain."

"Let them frig this up their own way, without any help from us, or you. Do you understand?"

"Yes, sir." I smiled. "The Tiempran priests might have explosives in their Temple. I thought you'd like to know."

His face froze. "How do—don't bother. If you happen to be right . . . if . . . just what do you suggest? There's already a crowd gathered around the Temple. It looks like their priests rousted them out, but with that cordon, there's no way to tell. I've called up the mounted riot patrollers, but they only sent half a squad. They're just backup for us if things get out of hand."

"My only suggestion is to keep your patrollers well away from the Temple for now."

"You think that they'll blow up the Temple and their own worshippers?"

"No one can say that for certain, but the First Speaker of Tiempre sent a warning a month or so ago saying that because we gave favorable treatment to the evil Caenenans, they would strike at the heart of Solidar." I shrugged. "Those might be just words, but . . ."

"I think, Master Rhennthyl, that you and I will watch, from a moderate distance, how the conscription teams handle the crowd around the Temple. Lyonyt and Fuast can handle their reduced duties without your assistance. I've already informed them and sent them out."

"Yes, sir." I had more than mixed feelings about accompanying Harraf, but the very fact that he wanted to observe and be in a position to handle the patrollers indicated that he was far more worried than his even voice and small and intent black eyes revealed. So did the fact that he'd already dispatched Lyonyt and Fuast.

We walked up Fuosta and along the north side—the non-taudis side—of South Middle alone. Two other patrollers, whom I'd never seen before, followed us. When we reached Dugalle, the captain halted.

"For now, this should be satisfactory." He said nothing more, but looked eastward.

Ten mounted patrollers in riot gear were lined up the north side of South Middle, about fifty yards farther east. The mounted conscription forces and the naval marines occupied the south side, right up to the low wall that marked the beginning of the taudis. Unlike the scriptie horses, the patrol mounts all wore gray padded armor across their chests, necks, and forequarters. The patrollers wore similar padded armor of the same material as the mounts, except it was pale blue, and riot helmets. While the mounted patrollers carried revolvers, their first weapons were riot lances, effectively long hardened oak truncheons with padded grips.

Even from where we were, I could see some of the crowd around the Temple, and I could hear a low repetitive chant.

Town of Georgina (KESWICK) Public Library

"Equal coins for equal souls,
Equal golds for equal roles! ..."

That definitely had an equalifier tone to it, but I couldn't see if there were any Tiempran priests leading the chant or whether those leading the crowd were merely local converts. Given what I suspected, I would have wagered that the crowd leaders were locals.

"Chanting won't stop the marines," Harraf said. "All that will do is make them mad. They'll eat all those taudis-dwellers alive and come up hungry." He looked to me.

"Getting the marines angry might well be the point, Captain."

At that, Harraf frowned, then straightened as a rider neared. "Be polite, Rhennthyl," he murmured. "He's a marine colonel."

The colonel rode up, followed by two other mounted marines, and reined his mount to a halt. He looked down at Harraf. "I thought we might find some Patrol officers here."

"Captain Harraf, Third District, Colonel." Harraf's smile was cool.

"We're about to disperse that crowd, *Captain*." The slight emphasis on Harraf's rank contained a hint of contempt. "Unless you see another way to allow us to proceed."

Harraf smiled again, nodding toward me. "Why don't we ask Master Rhennthyl, here?"

The colonel looked at me. "Do you have any ideas, Master Imager? Good workable ideas?"

"Just one, Colonel." I smiled politely. "Unless they attack your men, leave them alone."

"They're in the way."

I didn't feel like arguing with a senior marine officer, but I knew what was likely to happen, and yet there was no way to explain it, because I didn't know when or how the priests had planned the explosion . . . or if, for certain, that they had. "Perhaps I'm mistaken, but I didn't see any crowds on Saelio or any of the other streets more than a block east of the Temple. It seems to me that you could start your conscription efforts there, and you'd have little trouble."

"Master Imager," replied the colonel, his voice holding the tone of a parent talking to a child who did not understand, "we cannot allow anyone to defy the will of the Council. If we do, before long, there would be chaos throughout Solidar."

"Colonel, sir," I replied, "I must be missing something. No one has thrown anything at you, or fired pistols, or even stood in the street blocking your way. They seem to be chanting something like a religious saying."

"That's against the law, and I don't see the honorable Civic Patrol doing anything about that, Master Imager, Captain."

Since Harraf chose not to answer, I did. "The last time any patrollers were allowed close enough to look by your men, there weren't any priests outside the Temple. As long as they don't preach on the streets, it's not illegal."

"You sound like an advocate, Master Imager, and advocacy belongs in the Halls of Justice, not on the streets." The colonel was getting angry. He just wanted to disperse the crowd, quickly, bash a few skulls and subdue the taudis, ransack the place for recruits, and leave the Patrol to clean up the mess.

"No, sir. The job of the Civic Patrol is to maintain order, not to destroy it."

"Enough. We have a job to do, and we're going to do it. You can help, or you can watch and be reported as obstructing the will of the Council."

"Colonel," Harraf said smoothly, "your men are admirably suited to the task. I would remind you that allowing you to do what you see as your duty is in no way obstructing you."

"We will do our duty, Captain, with or without your assistance. Good day."

After the colonel rode away, Harraf turned to me. "What will happen now, Master Rhennthyl?"

"Nothing good, sir."

"We'd best watch." Harraf turned to the two patrollers behind us. "Both of you keep your eyes open." He paused. "Kharyt . . . have the mounted squad move back west of us. They're too close to the Temple. We wouldn't want them to interfere with the colonel's men."

"Yes, sir." The taller patroller loped off eastward along South Middle.

Before that long, Kharyt was back, and the riot squad rode past us and drew up a block more toward the station. At the same time, the naval marine formation turned west and marched another hundred yards west, then turned to face the Temple. On the east flank of the formation, a squad of riders formed up.

"Company! Forward!" The order echoed toward us.

The marines marched forward, their batons ready.

My eyes shifted from them to the Temple . . . then back to the marines . . . back to the Temple . . . and stopped.

Just as I had seen in that momentary flash I could not forget, the Temple seemed to tremble, its walls shivering and bulging outward. Even as I expanded my shields to cover Harraf and the two patrollers behind us, light, a brilliant golden orange, was everywhere, followed by what sounded like thunder from all directions.

I was shaken within the shields, like a pea in a dried pod in a winter storm, and then . . . everything was quiet . . . for a moment.

All that remained in an area a good hundred fifty yards across was a low jumble of rubble, none of it more than knee-high, if that. South Middle was covered in bricks and fragments of bricks and timbers, and there was acrid smoke and dust everywhere.

Faint sounds of injured men were drowned out by the screams of several horses. I had no doubts that the sounds of the maimed and wounded were louder near the Temple—assuming that there were any still alive there.

Harraf turned to me. "What did you do?"

"I didn't do anything. The Tiempran priests blew up the Temple."

"No. We're untouched. We shouldn't be."

"Imager shields, Captain. I shielded you and the others close by. That was as much as I could do, and I won't always be able to do that."

Harraf swallowed, then moved forward. "Let's go! We need to see what we can do."

"You deal with the Patrol, sir. I need to handle something else."

The captain opened his mouth, then closed it and nodded.

"I hope to see you before too long, sir, with some answers." I didn't wait for a response. I just trotted across South Middle, dodging the bricks and other debris.

For a while, the marines would be preoccupied in dealing with the chaos and their wounded. Then they'd start thinking about retaliation. Before that happened, I needed to see if Horazt and Jadhyl, as I hoped, had decided to follow my advice.

No one even looked at me as I headed down Dugalle for a block, then turned east, striding toward the alleyway that would bring me out on Weigand and the "red" house. I just hoped Horazt was there, because I didn't want to track him all over the taudis.

I didn't even have to knock. He stepped out onto the front stoop. "One of my runners said the Tiemprans blew up the Temple."

"They did. They probably killed a hundred marines and a bunch of Youdh's people."

"Too bad for them."

"If we don't get Saelyhd and some of those priests, it's going to be too bad for everyone here in the taudis. Do you know where they are?"

"My boys followed them," Horazt said. "He's got a safe house on the other end of Bhaettyr, maybe a block off Quierca. All boarded up. No one thinks anyone's there."

"And the Tiempran priests are there?"

Horazt grinned. "Might be."

"If you don't want several thousand marines razing the taudis, we need to find them and hand them over to the Patrol."

Horazt frowned. "The Patrol . . . don't know as I like that . . . not for Sae-lyhd. That's too easy on him."

"If they don't go to the Patrol, the scripties will just kill them and then raze the taudis anyway. This way, Harraf gets to save his buttocks, and the scripties can't sweep everything into the nearest sewer. If someone isn't held to blame, all of you in the South Middle taudis will pay dearly. If the Patrol gets them, the Tiemprans and Saelyhd will all get executed, but the hearing will make it clear that the Tiemprans did it, not the taudis." I looked at him. "Them or you?"

"Then what?" he asked.

"I can't promise anything, but I'll do what I can to keep things calm and point out that you and Jadhyl and Deyalt kept your people out of it."

Horazt nodded slowly. "You don't offer much, Master Rhennthyl, but no one else is playing this game of plaques."

No, and if I'd had any sense, or followed Master Dichartyn's ways, I wouldn't be playing it, either. "Can you get enough of your men together to drag the Tiemprans to where I need them after I subdue them?"

"I've got men here. How are you going to get Saelyhd and his boys out of the building?"

"I have something in mind. Oh . . . we will need rope or cord to tie them up with."

"We've got that . . . other things, too."

"Then let's go."

Horazt whistled twice, and taudis-toughs began piling out the door. I stepped back to give them room.

Horazt waited until twelve men and youths gathered round. "Like I told Mynewyr, we're going to collect Saelyhd and the friggin' priests, help Master Rhennthyl deliver 'em to the Patrol so as the scripties don't burn us out."

Then he turned and nodded to me, and started walking.

I took two quick steps and matched his pace. Squat and muscular as he was, that was easy enough because my legs were considerably longer than his. We traveled four short blocks east, and one and a half long blocks south—without seeing anyone—before Horazt stopped and pointed. "That's it."

The "safe" house indeed looked like it was abandoned, a squat, brick-built, blockish thing of two stories. The windows on the lower level had been crudely bricked over. Those on the second level were boarded shut.

"Any rear doors?" I asked.

"Nah . . . they bricked that up, too," Horazt replied.

"I need a fire. Get as many things as you can that will burn and pile them in the middle of the street. I don't want to burn anything down. I just want to drive them out."

Horazt frowned.

"Just trust me."

Horazt shook his head, but raised his voice. "Stuff that'll burn! Find it. Pile it in the middle of the street! There."

The taudis-toughs spread out, and before long all manner of things had been piled in the middle of the street—old tree limbs, rotten boards and timbers, sections of broken shutters, dried brush and leaves.

Once the pile was big enough, I imaged flames into several places and waited until fire, ashes, and smoke were pouring upward. Then I went to work, imaging the hot air and smoke into the boarded-up building. A quint passed, and despite the coolness of the day, I was sweating profusely.

Then thumping and banging began to emanate from within, and finally the boards on one of the windows were pushed away, and a darker soot-stained face appeared, gasping. I imaged a shield across the open space. More thumping followed, but no window boards moved, or not much, and smoke began to seep out from between the boards.

Another half quint more passed, and then the front door burst open, and two men staggered out.

Horazt's men were ready and immediately grabbed and tied them up.

More figures staggered out, followed by gouts of smoke, only to be caught and trussed. I stopped imaging hot air and smoke and wiped my forehead.

Finally, no one else emerged, and I walked over to the figures lined up along the sidewalk.

"This one . . . he's the head priest," offered one of Horazt's men, pointing to a figure in blue and black.

I noted two others in the same garb.

"There's Saelyhd." Horazt gestured to a burly man who had recovered and was struggling against the ropes.

"You!" Saelyhd glared at the younger taudischef. "You have sold out to the trolies. . . ."

I stepped forward. "No. You sold out to the Tiemprans. You'll pay for it. Just like Youdh did."

His eyes turned to me. He started to speak, then looked again and fell silent.

"We need Saelyhd and the priests. We can leave the others." I looked to Horazt. "You know who they are?"

"Yes. Most of them."

"Are they safe to let go after we're away?"

He looked over the others. "All but Donmass, there." He pointed to a square-faced man in soiled gray. "He killed many."

"We'll turn him in with Saelyhd, then. Can we leave a few men here to let the others go in a bit?"

Horazt nodded. "Selyst, Boazt . . . you know how to cut them loose so they have to work themselves free."

The smallest tough grinned. "I can do that good."

"Just cut the ropes," Horazt said, then coughed and shook his head. "That's all."

Horazt's remaining nine men marched the three Tiempran priests, along with Saelyhd and Donmass, back the way we'd come, then up Weigand and across to Dugalle and then toward South Middle. About a half block short of South Middle, I gestured for a halt.

"I don't want anyone here shot," I told Horazt. "I need to arrange where we're going to take them. I'll be back as soon as I can."

"Figured something like that." He didn't look happy. I supposed I wouldn't have, either, but I hadn't been the one to create the mess.

Since I'd have to do it some fifty yards ahead, as I walked away I raised concealment shields.

". . . frig! . . ."

". . . do that?"

I thought that might provide some additional incentive for cooperation.

When I reached the wall at the end of the taudis, I saw a patroller on the far side of South Middle, but until I crossed the street, again dodging debris that had not been removed, I couldn't tell that it was Slausyl. Then I was within ten yards, and I dropped the shield just before I reached him. His mouth dropped open, but surprising him was the idea.

"Where's the captain?"

For a moment, his mouth didn't work. Then he finally said, "Over there . . . toward Mando . . . he's trying to keep the scripties from doin' something stupid."

"Thanks. I'll see if I can help him." I began to trot up along South Middle, avoiding more of the bricks and debris. I could smell the odor of smoke, and thin whitish gray plumes drifted up from the ruins of the Temple.

Harraf was talking to a mounted officer, who was glaring down at the captain and gesturing. Then, Captain Harraf caught sight of me, said something to the officer, and walked toward me.

I spoke first. "Captain . . . I think I can help stop this before it gets out of hand."

"How, Master Rhennthyl?"

"We can come up with the Tiempran priests and the taudischef who engineered the explosion. That will give the scripties someone to be angry at besides the taudis-dwellers. It will also prove that the Patrol knows better what's going on. Besides, the priests are the ones who blew up the Temple."

"The major there isn't likely to listen."

"Let me try, sir."

"Be my guest."

Harraf turned and walked back to the major. "You might want to listen to Master Rhennthyl here."

"About what?" The major kept looking toward the ruins of the Temple and the space along the sidewalk where marines had laid out the bodies of comrades they'd found.

No one had bothered with the bodies of the taudis-dwellers.

"About why it wouldn't be a good idea to use force on the taudis right now." I wasn't going to say more until I got his attention. He was half listening at best.

"We'll be going in before long. No one does that to us."

"The taudis-dwellers didn't do it to you," I pointed out.

"I don't care. We've lost more than a hundred men . . . and the colonel."

"Major!" I snapped. "That's exactly what the Tiemprans want. They're the ones who blew up the Temple. That's why it was set up that way. So the conscription teams would blame the taudis-dwellers and then go wild and slaughter hundreds. Now . . . do you want to call off this idiotic assault, or do you want to face a court-martial for playing into the Tiemprans' hands? It's your choice. I warned the colonel, but he didn't care to listen."

"Who are you?" For the first time, his eyes actually took me in, seeing the grays and the imager's visor cap, not that different from that of the Civic Patroller's, in form, but straight gray with the insignia of the Collegium rather than that of L'Excelsis above the bill.

"Rhennthyl D'Image, the Collegium's liaison to the Civic Patrol, and yes,

I am a master imager. And yes, I have served the Council directly. And no, you really don't want to send your men into the taudis—not when the Council is aware that the Tiemprans threatened to do what just happened. Do you really want to lose your career? Maybe even be shot?"

Fury fought with common sense within him. I could see that in his eyes and in the hardening of his jaw.

"If it will make you feel better, let this settle over the weekend, and I'll personally accompany your conscription teams through the taudis on Lundi. Maintain a cordon if you want, but don't let your men shoot anyone. That's what the Tiemprans are looking for. And I can guarantee it's not what the Council wants." I softened my voice. "And if you're not happy, you can blame me."

"You'll personally accompany my men?"

"Any one team at a time." I couldn't do more than one at once, but he might expect the impossible, rather than the merely incredibly difficult.

"I'll take that promise, imager. I don't like it. I don't have to like it."

"None of us like having men killed. But killing the taudis-dwellers won't get at those who did it." I nodded. "Thank you. Now . . . if you'll excuse me for a moment, I need to deliver the prisoners to Third District station for transport to the main gaol. Those are the Tiempran priests and some others who did it."

"You have them?"

I gestured toward the far side of the wall. "Back there. That's why I wasn't with the captain. I had to get them before they escaped."

"You did that alone?"

"No. I had some local help. They don't want to be blamed for something they didn't do." I smiled politely and turned to Harraf. "I've got five prisoners. If you could have some of the patrollers meet us at the wall just west of Dugalle . . . ?"

"We can manage that, Master Rhennthyl."

"Thank you. I'll see you and them there shortly."

Then I turned and half walked, half trotted back to where I'd left Horazt and the others. When he saw me returning, he offered an inquisitive look.

"The marines were about to attack. They won't. They'll probably cordon the taudis for the weekend, but they say they won't shoot. Don't tempt them. On Lundi, they'll start through the taudis, but I'll be with the lead team. That should keep them from getting out of hand." I hoped it would.

Horazt frowned. I was getting tired of that.

"Everyone faces a scriptie team," I said, more sharply than I should have.

"They came to my door growing up. More than once. I'm trying to keep people from getting shot and burned out."

"Like I said . . ."

"I know. I don't offer much. It's a lot better than the alternative. Now . . . I said we'd deliver the priests and Saelyhd and Donmass to the wall on the north side of Dugalle. We get them there, and then you leave. I really don't think you want to be that close to Captain Harraf. I can hold them for a while."

"Imaging stuff?" asked Harraf.

I nodded. I was getting more than a little tired, but I could handle that.

"You heard Master Rhennthyl. March 'em up to the wall."

Where we were headed was less than half a block away, if a long half block. That walk felt longer than all the others I'd made since I'd risen that morning, including the four-mille run after exercising.

When we reached the wall, I took a careful look around. No one was close, but I could see a group of patrollers gathering on the far side of South Middle, if more to the west.

"Master Rhennthyl?"

I turned.

Horazt stood there. The five prisoners had been seated against the wall, their feet roped together. Saelyhd glared at Horazt, then at me.

Horazt smiled at the other taudischef, then said to me, "We got some extra rope. We tied 'em together some. Make it a bit easier on the trolies that have to collect 'em. Might watch Donmass . . . nasty boar's ass."

"I appreciate it." Then I lowered my voice. "I owe you. But I don't carry that many golds around with me."

"Told you before. You're good for it." He offered a crooked smile. "Not like I could spend it this weekend."

"One other thing," I said. "Do you know if Chelya's all right? Shault will ask me."

"She wasn't near the Temple. I saw her before you came. She's fine. You can tell him that."

"He'll ask about you, too, but I could answer that."

That brought the trace of a smile. Then he nodded, and he and the others hurried away.

I kept a close eye on the prisoners. The Tiemprans wouldn't look at me, and Saelyhd kept squirming and glaring. Donmass wasn't saying anything, and I wondered why, until I saw that someone had stuffed a gag in his mouth.

Captain Harraf arrived in less than half a quint, accompanied by Slausyl,

Melyor, Lyonyt, Fuast, and the two tall patrollers I didn't know. He looked over the three in the rather dusty Tiempran robes, and then Saelyhd and Donmass.

He didn't even ask any questions. He just nodded. "Take them in." Then he inclined his head to me. "We need to talk." He shook his head. "We lost one—Shagnyr—and a couple more got banged up. It could have been worse."

I understood that was as much of an acknowledgment or thanks as I was about to get. That was fine.

We turned back down South Middle, ahead of the patrollers. From some of the sounds behind us, I could tell that they hadn't been too gentle in getting the five to their feet, but I couldn't say that I blamed them.

"Did you make any promises to get them?" Harraf asked.

"Just one . . . the same one I made to the major. I said I'd be with the scriptie team and try to keep everyone calm." Paying Horazt wasn't a promise.

"Nothing . . . else . . . ?"

"No, sir. I did suggest that no one tempt the scripties this weekend."

"Do I want to know how you did it?"

"Imaging and appealing to their self-preservation, sir. I also used some imaging to persuade them to leave their hiding place."

He nodded, but he didn't say more, and he didn't look at me all the way back to the station.

49

By the time I wrote up the reports and the preliminary charging slips and made sure that the five were on their way to the main gaol under heavy guard, it was almost second glass of the afternoon. I knocked on the captain's door. "I'll need to report on this to the Collegium, immediately, sir."

"You've finished all the reports, Master Rhennthyl?"

"Yes, sir, and the transfer wagon left about a quint ago."

"Then I'd say you'd best report. You'll be here early on Lundi?"

The last wasn't really a question. "Yes, sir. Very early."

"Good. We don't need to disappoint the major. Try to have a good weekend."

Although his voice was cheerful, the cheer was forced. I had the feeling that I'd upset the captain in some other fashion, and I'd have to be careful in the days ahead. "Thank you, sir." I nodded and smiled, then turned and headed out to find a hack.

Again, because South Middle was closed to coaches and wagons, I had to walk all the way to the Midroad. My feet hurt, and my stomach was growling, and I was light-headed. Once I did get a hack, it was a relief to sit down, even on the hard seat.

Much as I didn't look forward to it, once I left the hack and walked tiredly, very tiredly, across the Bridge of Hopes, I headed straight for Master Dichartyn's study. He wasn't there. So I went to the duty prime, who happened to be Jakhob.

"Master Dichartyn's not in his study."

"No, sir."

"Is he here at the Collegium?"

The prime squirmed.

"Don't tell me. He's with Master Poincaryt."

"Ah . . ."

"Yes or no?"

"Yes, sir."

"Thank you." I turned and walked to the back of the receiving hall and up the stone steps. My boots echoed in the silence.

Master Poincaryt's study was on the second level of the administration building in the southwest corner overlooking the quadrangle. I'd never been in his study, but I did know where it was. I shouldn't have been surprised to see Gherard sitting at the small desk outside the door . . . but I was.

"I assume that Master Dichartyn and Maitre Poincaryt are inside and not to be disturbed?"

"They didn't say that, sir. Not exactly."

"Good. Please tell them that the Tiempran priests exploded their Temple in the taudis late this morning, and I need to tell them what happened."

Gherard had been around. He didn't question me. He immediately rose and walked to the closed door, where he rapped. "Master Rhennthyl is here with some very urgent news, maitres."

I didn't hear the response, but Gherard opened the door and stepped back, nodding for me to enter.

"Thank you," I murmured as I passed.

He offered a faint smile in return.

I closed the door behind me. Windows dominated the south and west walls of the study. Maitre Poincaryt's desk was set at an angle to them so that the southwest corner of the room was directly behind his desk chair. The walls flanking the entry door were built-in bookcases running from floor to ceiling. In the middle of the north wall was a door, closed, which probably led to a conference room, and the wall on both sides of that door also held full-length bookcases. The bookcases and the paneling were all of the same dark wood, as were the desk and the two chairs before it and the one in which Maitre Poincaryt sat, behind the desk. Master Dichartyn sat in the chair opposite the front south corner of the desk.

Master Poincaryt appraised me in that way he had that seemed quick and casual and was not, then gestured to the empty chair opposite him and out from the other corner of the desk from where Master Dichartyn sat.

"Thank you, sir." I was happy to get off my feet.

"What disaster have you caused now, Rhenn?" asked Maitre Poincaryt, his tone genial.

"I had nothing to do with causing this one, sir. The Tiempran priests exploded their Temple in the South Middle taudis. They'd gathered some of their followers, and the people were chanting . . ." I went on to explain exactly what had happened step by step. The only thing I left out was my promise to pay Horazt five golds. ". . . and as soon as I finished writing up the reports and making sure the priests and the taudischef were on the way to the main gaol, I hailed a hack and came here."

"I'm not quite clear on one thing," Maitre Poincaryt said. "Why did you suggest that the Tiemprans might have explosives in the Temple? How did you know that?"

"I didn't know that, sir. That was the problem. But I remembered what the Tiempran First Speaker said, and when I saw all the taudis-dwellers chanting and the naval marines ready to charge them, I got a very bad feeling. The priests had already started one riot, and the Patrol had managed to contain it." I shrugged. "I can't explain more than that."

"Can't . . . or won't?"

"I can't. I knew, but I had no proof. I just knew."

"This has posed a problem before," Master Dichartyn said mildly.

"You've mentioned that." Maitre Poincaryt's voice was dry. He looked back to me. "Why did this Horazt agree to help you? Taudischefs don't usually help either imagers or patrollers."

"I know him. He brought in Shault when I had the duty. He claims young Shault is his cousin, but I'm fairly sure that Shault's his son. Has Master Dichartyn told you . . . ?"

"Yes. I know you've been acting as an unofficial second preceptor to him."

"I've also delivered messages from him to his mother, and I've run across Horazt several times. He's provided some information about the taudis. I just pointed out to him that if we didn't come up with the priests and Saelyhd that the marines were most likely to burn down the taudis and worse than that."

"You aren't very complimentary to the naval marines," said Maitre Poincaryt.

"After what I saw . . ." That meant I needed to explain about the lieutenant, but I gave the "official" explanation.

"That isn't quite what happened, I imagine, knowing you," said Master Dichartyn.

"That is what everyone saw, sir."

"And it's best left that way." Master Poincaryt leaned back slightly in his chair, then glanced at Master Dichartyn, then back at me. "It does appear that you have managed to mitigate a disaster. Tell me honestly. Do you think that the marines would have reacted less violently if nothing had happened to the lieutenant?"

"No, sir. I don't think the lieutenant's fate even crossed the mind of the colonel or the major. The major didn't even consider that more than a hundred taudis-dwellers were killed or injured or that they were as much victims as the marines."

"You will be questioned most rigorously at the hearings, you know," said Maitre Poincaryt.

"Yes, sir. I had thought as much."

"Why did you suggest accompanying one of the teams?"

"I thought it might reduce the risk of attacks by both sides."

"You're going to bring order to the taudis all by yourself?" Master Dichartyn's voice was gently sardonic.

"No, sir. I just wanted to reduce the chance of violence."

Once more, the two exchanged glances.

"Is there anything else we should know about this?" asked Maitre Poincaryt.

"I'd guess that Captain Harraf isn't happy about Saelyhd being captured, but I have no proof at all about that."

"There is that," offered Master Dichartyn. "We'll have to let the plaques fall where they may where he's concerned."

Abruptly Maitre Poincaryt smiled. "I think that will do for now. Oh . . . have you finished the portrait of Master Rholyn?"

"No, sir. I'm close. One more sitting, two at most."

"Good. If we need anything more from you, Master Dichartyn will let you know."

"Thank you, sir." I inclined my head to him, and then to Master Dichartyn, before turning and leaving the study.

I walked back down the steps and out into the quadrangle, where I looked to the northeast. There wasn't even a hint of a cloud of dust, or anything to mark what had occurred. Why had the colonel been so intent on ignoring not only me, but Captain Harraf? I already had learned that to preserve some lives, others had to be taken, and I'd done that. But how would riding down taudis-dwellers have solved anything? Removing a Youdh or a Saelyhd might reduce the violence or killing in the taudis, but I wasn't sure that removing Jadhyl or even Horazt would help matters. And beating up people who hadn't so much as picked up a stone would only make matters worse. I couldn't have been the only one to know that.

After a time, I made my way back to my quarters, where I tried to rest.

I didn't, not much, not when I kept thinking about Rousel, and how and why he'd died. Why did the Nameless—if the Nameless even existed—allow people like the colonel and the lieutenant and Ryel to kill so many just for the sake of transitory power? But then, the Nameless had given us free will. Did that mean that it was our responsibility to stop them? If so, if we killed to prevent killing, where did it all end?

I thought about that for a long time, but in the end, the basic questions remained. Were there any real answers?

Somewhat before sixth glass I left my quarters and walked slowly to the dining hall. I wanted to be there early because I didn't know where else to find Shault. I didn't see him, but while I was waiting, I checked my letter box and found a note from Khethila. It was very brief, just noting that Father and Mother and Remaya and Rheityr would be arriving on the Mantes Express at third glass on Solayi and that she would be sending Charlsyn to pick them up. That made sense because it would have been impossible to fit luggage and any more than four people in the coach. That meant I needed to be with Khethila sometime around third glass.

I slipped the envelope into my waistcoat and continued to wait for Shault.

He walked in with Lieryns and Cholsyr, an even more recent prime than Shault himself. When he looked up and saw me, he almost started to run, but then managed to hold himself to a quick walk.

"Sir, have you heard—"

"The Temple explosion wasn't near your mother or Horazt. They were both fine when I left the taudis this afternoon, and the scripties' commander promised they wouldn't go into the taudis until Lundi when I'm with them."

His eyes widened. "Sir?"

"It's a long story that you'll have to hear later."

"Mama is all right? And Horazt?"

I nodded.

"Thank you, sir." He inclined his head seriously, then turned and walked back to the others.

Once the three entered the dining hall, I waited for several moments, then made my own way in. Ferlyn, Chassendri, and Isola were already at the masters' table and must have come in by the south doors. I walked toward them.

Ferlyn looked at me as I sat down. "The word is that a Tiempran Temple exploded in the taudis, and hundreds were killed or wounded."

"That's right. About half marines and half taudis-dwellers and some patrollers. The priests planned it. Some of them and the taudis-leader who helped them are in gaol."

"And I suppose you managed to capture them?"

"With some help, yes." I smiled. "If you wouldn't mind passing the red wine. It's been a very long day."

On the far side of Ferlyn and Chassendri, Isola laughed. "You did ask, Ferlyn."

"You aren't going to say more, are you?" he asked.

"I'd rather not. I'm sure I'll be asked a lot of questions at the hearing. The wine, if you would?"

"I've told you this before, Rhenn, but you know how I hate the fact that you covert types keep everything so quiet."

I offered a deep and loud sigh. "Ferlyn, over two hundred people died this morning. Probably as many as that were injured. The Tiemprans put explosives in their Temple and gathered worshippers to chant for the conscription teams to leave, just to goad the marines into advancing on the Temple. I warned the colonel against it. I couldn't prove what would happen. He ignored me. The Temple exploded. I did my best to clean up what I could." I offered a very polite smile. "You'll pardon me if I don't feel like saying more." I paused. "Now . . . might I please have the wine?"

He passed the carafe to me.

After a long period of silence, Isola spoke. "Ferlyn, there are reasons why the covert imagers don't feel like talking about what they do. It might help if you respected those reasons."

That was as close to a reprimand as I'd ever heard from Chorister Isola. Chassendri winced.

Ferlyn turned to me. "I am sorry, Rhenn."

"I apologize for being short, Ferlyn. It really has been a very long day, and I'll have to work with the conscription teams next week as well."

Isola looked to me. "Shault?"

"His mother is all right. I found that out and told him before dinner."

"Thank you."

Ferlyn didn't quite look at me for the rest of the meal, but I wasn't certain I wanted to look at myself, either. For all that I'd told myself that I'd done what I could, couldn't I have done something more? Yet I couldn't have persuaded the colonel not to attack on the basis of a Pharsi farsight vision, and anything that would have persuaded him would have been an invention, if not an outright lie that would have come back to haunt me, the Patrol, and the Collegium—assuming I could have even thought up something like that quickly enough. Harraf had accepted my warning only because he knew something about me and because it fit in with his own plans.

50

I did sleep on Vendrei night. The gray drizzle that greeted me when I woke on Samedi morning and looked out my window wasn't cheering. On the other hand, when I stopped outside the dining hall and picked up the newsheets, I was gratified to see that while there were stories about the Temple explosion, the stories blamed the Tiempran priests and only noted that patrollers from the Third District had captured the priests and others involved in the explosion. That would change when I appeared at the hearing, as I suspected I would, but for now, few knew, and that was for the best.

Even more cheering was that no one was at the masters' table at breakfast except Isola when I arrived. I sat down beside her gratefully.

"Thank you for your words last night."

"You're welcome." She smiled warmly, and genuinely, not that she wasn't always genuine. "You were upset. I could tell."

"I was." I filled my mug with tea, then took a sip before saying more. "I knew that it would be wrong to attack the taudis-dwellers. I mean, that something terrible would happen, but I couldn't persuade the colonel. Even Harraf could see I knew. That's one of the few times he's listened, but the colonel wouldn't listen to either of us."

"That's one of the problems with being a military officer," she replied. "In combat, you can't hesitate. Many of them can't break that habit when they're not dealing with out-and-out warfare, not unless you can lay out absolute proof. Dealing with people, even mobs, takes a different set of skills." She shook her head. "I don't think anyone could have changed the colonel's mind."

"I can tell myself that, but . . . I still keep trying to come up with what I might have said."

"That's why there is a covert branch of the Collegium. That's also why it must be small."

I understood the first; I wasn't sure I understood the second.

"There's always the temptation to think we know better, that our way is better, that everyone else doesn't see what is obvious to us. Our way usually is better, but that doesn't matter if people fear and distrust us to the point where they would do anything to destroy us. With a small covert branch, things do happen, but they don't happen to many people, and the people to whom they happen usually deserve them. Even when people aren't sure about that, there's enough distrust of those who are well off and powerful that people are likely to think there must have been a reason. That works only so long as people don't think it could happen to them, and it can't with a few handfuls of covert imagers." She paused. "If they're careful."

That made sense.

"You pose another problem, though. Covert imagers have great individual powers. You have to have them to survive. We have to let you have them so that we can survive."

"I feel like everyone wants me to resolve things, but they don't like the way I do things, but can't suggest a better way, at least not until after I've acted."

"It's always that way when people have great abilities. You'll learn to live with that. You have a greater problem than that, Rhenn." Her voice turned sad, yet sympathetic. "What happens when an imager's powers are too great to conceal? Does he refuse to act, because it will make him and the Collegium a target? Does he limit his power, when that limit will assure that others die? Or does he act and endanger all that generations of imagers have striven to build?"

"You make it sound like I have that kind of power."

"I think you do, but if you don't, you will."

I wanted to ask how she knew, but decided against it. Instead, I said, "Do you have any suggestions for how to deal with that?"

"No matter what you do, when great power is applied, people get hurt. Even when you're right, people will get hurt. Sometimes, when you're wrong, fewer get hurt in the short run, but more over time. But"—she drew out the word—"most of the time, failing to use power at all ends up hurting people worse. That's something that some fail to understand. And that's all I want to say about it."

"Thank you, anyway." I laughed softly. "How are the fried cakes?"

"Quite good. They're not even soggy this morning."

Later, as I left the dining hall, hurrying through the drizzle, I considered what Isola had said. I thought I'd already known it, but it helped to have someone else say it. I wouldn't have been surprised if she had known I knew, but had said what she had to help me sort things out. It was also clear that she did not see quite eye-to-eye on the issues of power with either Master Dichartyn or Maitre Poincaryt.

I reached the studio a good two quints before eighth glass and immediately set to work on those sections of Rholyn's portrait that I could complete without him being present. He arrived promptly as the bells were chiming the glass.

"Good morning, Rhenn."

"Good morning, sir."

"How are you coming on the portrait?"

"I'll try to finish what I need from you today. If you wouldn't mind standing again?"

Master Rholyn put one foot on the crate and turned his head.

"A touch back to the left, if you would."

"Like this?"

"Good. Thank you."

I needed to sharpen his jawline, and his right ear, and that's where I started. I didn't say anything for a good quint, just painted.

"You can relax for a moment, sir." I had to change the tint of the skin next to his eye, and I didn't have the right umber.

Rholyn shook himself, loosening his shoulders. "I understand that the Temple explosion happened where you were patrolling."

"Not exactly. It was near the round I was helping with." I added a touch of umber to the palette.

"You know, Rhenn, too many strange things happen around you. That's not good for the Collegium. The Collegium has survived by being unobtrusive, by not flaunting power or suggesting mystery."

"I understand that, sir. What happened yesterday would have happened whether I had been there or not. Without my cautions, more would have died, and without my searching the taudis, no one would have any proof of what happened and how."

"All that is true. Is it all for the good? Doubtless the hearing will reveal the Tiempran presence in the taudis. That will require that we exact some penance or cost from the Tiemprans. To do so will result in the Caenenans feeling vindicated, and that will create greater friction and conflict in Otelyrn." He shrugged. "The Council may feel that matters would have been better had the Tiemprans not been implicated."

"If they were not, sir, the marines would have attacked the taudis, and even more taudis-dwellers would have been killed and injured."

"That is doubtless so. But how many more in Solidar will die because we must do something to demonstrate to the Tiemprans that they cannot foment disruption in L'Excelsis? And how many councilors will wish that you had not brought that aspect of matters to their attention? How will that affect the Collegium?"

All of what he said made sense, unhappily. It also suggested that there was no end to anything, because no matter what anyone did, someone somewhere would react adversely, leading to more violence and death somewhere else. "Less than positively, sir, I am certain. Yet I would have difficulty in not trying to protect those who would have been hurt or killed through no fault of their own, save that of being poor and with fewer abilities."

"There are powerless innocents who always die. That is not the question."

"What is, sir?"

"The real question is what is necessary to preserve the government that offers all citizens the greatest protections and opportunities. Unless one preserves the structure, all protections and opportunities will vanish, except for the powerful."

"I can see that, sir." I could also see that we did not agree totally on what constituted that structure, because, limited as they were, the taudis-dwellers were still part of L'Excelsis and Solidar, but I pushed away those thoughts for the moment and concentrated on the portrait. "If you wouldn't mind resuming that position . . ."

Rholyn did so silently.

I actually worked until a quint past ninth glass before I finally looked up. "Thank you."

"Is it finished?"

"It's not quite finished, but I won't need you to sit anymore. I would like you to come by next Samedi and see it before it's framed."

"Might I look?" For the first time, he sounded deferential.

"Of course." I stepped away from the easel.

Rholyn walked around and stood about two yards back from the canvas. He didn't say anything for a time, then turned. "It's accurate, if not so flattering as it might be, but far less severe than it could have been." He nodded. "I thank you."

Once Master Rholyn left, I went back to work on his waistcoat, touching up some details that had bothered me, and then on his trousers. All in all, it was less than a quint before noon when I finished cleaning up. I never liked to mix the pigments for one portrait for those used for another. It was too easy to slip into similar colorations.

Then I hurried to the dining hall, where I ate alone at the masters' table. I could see Shault, sitting with Lieryns and some other primes, and he didn't seem withdrawn. For that, I was grateful.

After eating, since the drizzle had stopped even if the clouds remained, I wandered toward the Bridge of Hopes, where I needed to meet Seliora, but I reached there well before first glass. I almost took a seat on one of the stone benches before realizing that it was so wet that my trousers would have been soaked through.

I couldn't help but think about what Master Rholyn had said. He and Master Dichartyn were saying the same thing, if in different ways. Master Dichartyn was basically saying that anything I did had to be invisible because visibility would hurt the Collegium. Master Rholyn was saying that innocents should be sacrificed for the good of Solidar. In both arguments, the implication was the same—the individual mattered far less than either Solidar or the Collegium. While that was certainly true, the corollary was that the individual mattered not at all, except in service to the larger group . . . and that I could not accept.

Just before first glass, a hack pulled up on the east side of the river, and three figures emerged—Seliora, Odelia, and Kolasyn. I stood and walked to the west end of the bridge.

After seeing me, Seliora hurried across the Bridge of Hopes, even though the drizzle had died away. Just before she reached me, she turned and waved to Odelia and Kolasyn. They reentered the coach, and the driver flicked the reins. She did not step toward me.

I moved to her and hugged her, but her response was almost perfunctory.

"What's the matter?" I asked.

She shook her head.

"Is it your family? Or me?"

"How can I say? I feel . . ." She shook her head again.

"Do you know what's happened this week?" I asked.

"With you, Rhenn . . ."

"How would you know? Is that it?" I wanted to laugh, and not happily, either.

She looked intently at me. "Will you tell me?"

"I will. I said I would."

"Do we have to do the portrait today?"

"No. I wouldn't want you to sit for it when you don't feel right about it." And it was clear she did not feel like sitting.

"Would you come home with me? This very moment?"

"Of course." I took her arm.

"What about the paints?"

"I didn't leave anything out that will harden or spoil. I can clean up the rest tomorrow morning."

"You're certain?"

I could sense the relief in her voice. "Very certain. Do you want to talk now?"

"No. At home."

Whatever it was, it had to be serious if the independent Seliora didn't wish to say anything except within the walls of NordEste Design. I wanted to ask what I'd done, but decided against that. Had she decided that I was not for her? Was it because she'd learned how I'd handled Alynat? Or the fact that I'd struck at Alynat first?

We walked back across the bridge. A long silent quint passed before we could get a hack, and the two quints before we reached Hagahl Lane were even quieter. Seliora refused to look at me. No one greeted us at the door, and Seliora unlocked it with a heavy brass key. After we stepped inside, she re-locked it, then started up the steps to the second level. I had to hurry to catch up to her.

Betara met us at the top of the steps, and Seliora slipped away from me and stood beside her mother.

"We're glad to see you're all right," Betara said. Her voice was even, neither pleasant nor unpleasant. "The newsheets said that only one patroller was killed when the Tiempran Temple exploded."

"That . . . it was fortunate."

"Was it mere fortune?" asked Betara, her voice still even.

"Not totally," I admitted. "I had another farsight flash on Solayi night. I couldn't tell when it would happen, only that it was in daylight. I let it be known the priests might have explosives. The captain wasn't certain, but he kept the patrollers away. We tried to dissuade the naval marines, but they wouldn't listen. The captain insisted that he and I observe. I had to use my shields to protect us." My laugh was rueful. "I didn't even want to save him."

Betara nodded. "That might frighten him more than anything." Her face turned somber. "You might like to know that so far there have been three people who our friends have had to vanish around your parents' home." Betara raised her eyebrows. "How did you know that they would attempt to attack your family? Was that farsight?"

I couldn't not explain, not when Betara was using her contacts to protect my family. "No. Alynat—that's Ryel's nephew—died on Meredi when the wheel bearings froze on his racing trap. After I'd done that, I had the feeling that something might happen to my sister. There weren't any flashes. I'm not in a position to protect her. I don't know if Seliora told you why I can't stay there at night . . ."

Betara nodded, reserving judgment.

I gave a ragged smile. "I've always wanted to ask for Seliora's hand. But I couldn't risk letting anyone know until I finish dealing with Ryel. For that to work out right, I had to start with Alynat, not Ryel or Dulyk." I knew Betara and Seliora would understand that, given the chain of inheritance for High Holders. "But I'm not done. I can't be."

I could see consternation and relief mixing in Seliora's eyes.

Betara smiled, warmly, actually. Then she nodded. "I thought that might be what you had in mind." She glanced to her daughter, then laughed softly. "He's Pharsi inside and out. By finding someone who didn't seem to have the blood, dear, you found one who was more so than any man in the family."

That chilled me, even as I had to accept what she was saying.

Betara's eyes went back to me. "When?"

I understood what she wanted. I shook my head. "The dangerous parts will be over before Year-Turn, one way or another, but no one except us— and Shelim—should know until Ryel's successor is confirmed." If what I had planned worked, if nothing else came to pass that might upset those plans . . . and if I survived my own plans.

"His successor?" asked Seliora.

"His holding will have a successor, one way or the other, according to law. I have to make certain that the successor is someone not bound to continue against me and my family."

"I understand." Betara nodded. "It might be best if our precautions continue for a time."

"I cannot thank you enough." And I couldn't. But in time, I'd end up repaying all that had been done for me. I knew that, and Betara knew I knew, and so did Seliora.

I also knew one other thing. "How is Grandmama Diestra?"

"She is weak . . . but she will see Seliora wed. She has seen that." Betara offered an expression somewhere between rue and apology. "She saw—before anyone—that you were to be trusted, that you would do what was necessary."

"Farsight?"

Betara smiled crookedly. "And intuition. She has always had faith in you."

"Even when I didn't deserve it, I expect."

Betara almost nodded. Almost.

"Since I met her, I have never looked at anyone but Seliora with love." I forced a grin. "Or even lust."

They did both smile.

"We need to see Grandmama," Seliora said.

"Where is she?"

"In the plaques room upstairs. The stairs are getting hard for her."

"She is expecting you," Betara said, adding after a pause, "Both of you."

I did reach out and take Seliora's hand. She let me, and we walked to the staircase leading to the upper level. Narrow as the steps were, we walked side by side.

Seliora stopped on the landing between floors and turned to face me. "Why didn't you tell me?" Her words were gentle.

"I thought you knew. I'd said that it wouldn't be over until there were no male heirs. You acted as though you knew. I didn't want to say more than I had to. I didn't want you any more involved than absolutely necessary. All that I ever asked for—in words—was to borrow the mare. I wanted to protect you as much as I could."

"Please . . . don't protect me out of your life. It is, and will be, my life, too."

"I'm sorry. I didn't mean . . ."

Then we were in each other's arms, just holding tight.

While we would have liked to stay there for longer than we did, we needed to see Grandmama Diestra. We made our way up the last steps and across the far smaller upper hall.

Diestra was the only one in the plaques room, sitting at the single table. She set down the deck of plaques, leaving a pattern of placques on the dark blue felt. "Join me, children."

I took the chair to her right, and Seliora sat down across from me.

Diestra's eyes took in Seliora.

"You were right," she said. "He was trying to protect me."

Diestra looked to me.

"It was my fault. I didn't tell her enough so that she understood."

"Life is always a balance, and the stronger two who are a couple each are, the more they must seek that balance, or they will destroy each other."

That was clearly an evenhanded reprimand. Accurate as it was, it didn't bother me nearly so much as had some of those delivered by Master Dichartyn.

"There is one other thing." She paused. "It matters as much *why* something is done as what is done. Mercy or forbearance in return for true evil is not virtue; it is disaster. Condemning the killing of those who have murdered and created great suffering and who would continue to do so is an exercise in empty righteousness. Yet there are always those who would judge without sullying their hands, and for that reason, much that is done must remain un-spoken and unacknowledged."

From what I'd seen, Grandmama Diestra was all too right, and too often the Collegium was too forbearing.

Diestra swept up the plaques from the table, then shuffled the deck, her short fingers still nimble. "Life is akin to many things. Sometimes, it is a melody, sometimes a year with seasons, but when people are involved, it is most like a game of plaques. Some are able to play, while others are merely played. Always be the player." She smiled. "Except with each other. Never play the other, and never suffer yourself to be played."

I didn't think I'd ever heard how a couple should treat each other put more succinctly.

Diestra looked at me once more. "Seliora is the only one you will ever be able to trust fully. Do not forget that." Then she turned to her granddaughter. "Rhenn is trustworthy, more so than anyone. Do not assume the worst be-cause he has not told you something. Just ask, gently. He will tell you."

The last words, although addressed to Seliora, were really meant for me, and the quick sidelong look Diestra gave me emphasized that.

After a moment, Grandmama Diestra shuffled the plaques and laid out a pattern on the dark blue felt. "You two have better things to do than to keep me company. Or you should have. I've said what I will."

I inclined my head. "Thank you."

Seliora reached out and took her grandmother's hands. She didn't say anything, just squeezed them, but her eyes were bright.

Shortly, we rose and left Diestra pondering over a form of solitaire I'd never seen before.

Once we stood in the upper hallway, I turned to Seliora. "What would you like to do with the rest of the afternoon?"

"Could we . . . just talk? Aunt Aegina has a special dinner planned."

"Planned in advance as either condolence or celebration?"

"Grandmama said it would be fine . . . she said everyone should celebrate and that they all worried too much."

"Not everyone else was that certain," I said teasingly.

"Bhenyt was. He said that no one who'd been shot at as many times as you had in coming to see me would ever hurt me. He also said that no one else ever looked at me the way you did."

Bhenyt? "I would never have guessed."

"He sees more than he lets on."

"Another Pharsi trait."

Seliora tilted her head, and a hint of that mischievous smile appeared. "By that token, you are more Pharsi than anyone here."

I shrugged helplessly, then laughed, knowing that I would enjoy the rest of the afternoon and evening. The worries and concerns would return, as they always would, but for the next few glasses, I would enjoy the moments.

51

Dinner with Seliora's family on Samedi was good, but what happened before, and especially afterward, was better. But all that did bring up another point— I needed to be more careful with my coins because, if I survived the weeks ahead, I'd need to arrange for a wedding ring for Seliora. I almost regretted my promise to Horazt, because that would take close to half of my meager savings—yet how else could I have persuaded him that I was serious? As a Maitre D'Aspect, I did make a gold a week, but I'd been putting away only three or four silvers a week, if that, since I'd been with the Civic Patrol.

I did manage to get some untroubled sleep, until shortly before dawn when I had a nightmare where my parents and Remaya were all looking at me as if I'd killed Rousel. I didn't sleep after that because, in a way, I had, although I'd had no idea at the time that my actions would have led to that. So I got up and washed and shaved and dressed and headed over to the dining hall.

Maitre Dyana was alone at the masters' table, and I joined her.

"I heard from Master Dichartyn about your brother. I am sorry to hear of it."

"Thank you." I poured my tea and helped myself to the ham strips and rubbery eggs.

"Do you think it was Ryel's doing?"

"I have absolutely no proof of High Holder Ryel being involved."

"No proof. That's often the case with High Holders. There is little proof on either side, not even after the matter is resolved."

"I've come to realize that, maitre."

"I also heard that you're the one responsible for capturing the Tiempran priests who exploded their Temple in the South Middle taudis. Maitre Rholyn felt that the capture and hearing . . . might complicate matters before the Council."

"He mentioned that yesterday." I paused and took a sip of tea. "I can understand his concerns, and his points are logically made."

"He is always logical," agreed Dyana.

"There are times when I feel logic misses the point."

"Such as?" She raised her eyebrows.

"Well . . . if one values not having to fight a war or a conflict with the Tiemprans to the point of allowing part of one of our cities to be razed or to permitting the conscription teams to vent their anger on our own people, that implies that at least some of our own people have less value than the merchants and sailors who might suffer from conflict. If the people come to believe that, then that will create more unrest and less support for the Council."

Maitre Dyana laughed. "You have made a very logical counterpoint, but you haven't said why or where Master Rholyn's logic misses the point. Are you sure you aren't just saying that Master Rholyn offers logical-sounding arguments that aren't really that logical when analyzed?"

I shrugged. "That could be. I still feel that you can't reduce every situation to logic."

"Of course you can't. People aren't logical. They just use logic as needed to justify what they already believe. In governing, you have to appeal to their beliefs . . . or minimize the impact of those beliefs when what you are or what you're doing stands against those beliefs."

"That's why you and Master Dichartyn emphasize that the Collegium must be as invisible as possible."

She nodded. "People in every society in every time in every land want to believe that small groups of powerful people rule them secretly, even that such groups play people as though they were plaques in some arcane and complex game. While such games are played, they usually involve a very few people at high levels, most all of whom know the rules of such games. The majority of the populace thinks such games are widespread because they cannot accept that bad things usually happen because of greed and stupidity, usually involving many people, if not the entire population of a land. So . . . if the Collegium is seen as powerful and influential, according to people's beliefs, we must be evil and out to rule them, or play them as if they were plaques."

Unhappily, I could see that.

After breakfast, I walked northward along the west side of the quadrangle through the intermittent fog that rose off the river and drifted in patches through the Collegium. I'd decided to try to finish what I had to do on Maitre Rholyn's portrait. That was something I could get done before I had to leave for my parents' house. Seliora and I had talked it over the night before after dinner and decided that it would be better if she did not join me while I waited with Khethila for my parents and Remaya and Rheityr. I had promised either to stop by or drop Seliora a note to let her know what day and time Khethila had arranged for the memorial service at the Anomen D'Este.

Once I was in my studio I set to work and kept at it for close to six glasses, with perhaps half a glass off for a quick lunch. Then I cleaned up the studio, and myself, and set out across the Bridge of Hopes. The fog had lifted, except for patches drifting across the river, but a thin overcast kept the day from being comfortable, and I was glad to be wearing my heavy gray wool imager's cloak.

The hack dropped me in front of the house at about two quints before three, and Khethila opened the door. She gave me a sad smile and then an embrace. I held her for a moment, then followed her into the family parlor, and we sat down. The hearth stove warmed the parlor, for which I was grateful after the chill ride in the hack.

"Charlsyn left just after two. That should be enough time, shouldn't it?" she asked.

"On a Solayi, I would think so. How are you feeling?"

"Running the factorage helps. I know I have to keep things going." She laughed nervously. "Everything is in perfect order, even the sample racks, and I went through all the past invoices and found several that hadn't been paid in full. So I sent out reminders. Some won't ever be paid, but some might."

"How are the finances here?"

"The fire damage didn't help, but it will still be a good year for the factorage here. Father is supposed to bring back the ledgers from Kherseilles." She shook her head. "I hope the losses there aren't too bad."

So did I.

"When is the service?" I finally asked.

"Oh . . . I should have told you. It's on Jeudi, the second glass of the afternoon." She went on to provide the details, including the fact that I would offer the family remembrance.

By a quint before fourth glass, every few moments Khethila would glance out the window that overlooked the drive leading to the side portico.

"The train could have been late, and we don't know how much luggage Remaya may have brought for her and Rheityr." I paused. "Will she be staying here?"

"I don't know. Mother will want her to, but . . . her parents may have their ideas."

At just after a quint past four the familiar brass-trimmed brown coach pulled up under the portico. Khethila hurried out, and I followed.

Father was the first out of the coach, then Culthyn and Mother. Remaya handed Rheityr, bundled and squirming, to Mother before stepping down herself. All of them looked tired.

I gave Mother a hug. She needed it.

"I'm glad you're here, dear."

"Good to be home," Father said, to no one in particular.

"I'm hungry," said Culthyn.

"Dinner will be ready at fifth glass. You can wait," replied Khethila.

Remaya held Rheityr tightly, then looked at me. "Thank you for coming. Rousel . . ." Her voice trembled. "He said you would always be here."

"How could I not?" I replied gently. "He was my brother, and I did introduce you." I offered a smile, trying somehow to inject some warmth into the chill that seemed to permeate everything. That was hard, because my acts had led to Rousel's death, and yet, how could I have known? I smiled at the squirming Rheityr. "He's beautiful. I'd heard he was."

"I need to change him," Remaya said.

"The guest chambers are all ready for you," Mother said.

Remaya hurried off, close to tears, I feared.

"It's cool out here," Mother said. "There's no reason to stand here in the wind."

Culthyn had already vanished, doubtless into the kitchen, but the rest of us followed Mother into the family parlor, where she stood before the stove in the hearth.

"The train was cold the entire way from Mantes," she said.

"And entirely too hot from Kherseilles to Mantes," Father rumbled.

"Cook says I can't have anything," Culthyn interjected, walking dejectedly from the kitchen.

"That's right," Khethila said. "We'll all eat together, and it won't be all that long from now."

"I'm hungry now."

I turned to Culthyn. "Not another word. Sit down and be quiet." I wanted to slap him silly. Mother was still shivering. Remaya was probably crying again. Khethila had been trying to hold everything in L'Excelsis together, and all Culthyn could think about was filling his stomach.

As I looked at Culthyn, he turned pale. "Yes, sir." He did sit down on the settee next to Khethila.

Father actually stepped up behind Mother and enfolded her with his arms, one of the few times I'd seen him be that demonstrative even just before family.

"How are matters with you, Rhenn?" he finally asked.

"Compared to what's happened here . . . I can't complain. The Tiempran priests blew up their Temple in the South Middle taudis and killed close to two hundred marines and taudis-dwellers. There were a lot of other injuries."

"You were there?" asked Khethila. "I read about that. What did you do?"

"What I had to. It comes with the assignment."

She gave me the oddest look, but didn't say more.

"Can't trust those Tiemprans," Father said. "Not any of those southerners, really, Caenenans aren't any better, maybe worse."

"I'm just about finished with another portrait. This is the one of the Collegium's councilor . . ." I explained a bit.

Then Father told us about the train trip to Kherseilles and the one back, but said nothing about Rousel, and that I understood.

In another quint, Remaya rejoined us with a quieter Rheityr. "I fed him, and that helped." Her eyes were slightly bloodshot, and while she'd removed any other physical traces, I had no doubt she'd shed more tears. How could she not, being in the home where her husband had grown up?

Just before five, Khethila slipped out to the kitchen, then returned to announce, "Dinner is ready." She glanced to Culthyn. "Even for you."

Culthyn looked to me before getting up, and he didn't bound toward the dining chamber in his usual fashion. I didn't care about that. As the youngest, he'd gotten away with far too much for too long.

Dinner was subdued, and no one talked much about anything except the food, the weather, and the dismal state of the world, but only in general terms where the world was concerned. I wasn't surprised that no one said much about Rousel. For all his faults, he'd been cheerful and lively, and even alluding to him would have been too painful.

I finally left the house sometime after seventh glass, and I had to walk all the way to the Plaza D'Este to find a hack. I hadn't been about to ask Charlsyn to stay on what was usually his day off. As I rode toward NordEste Design, I realized that I'd missed services at Imagisle, and I hoped that Seliora would be back from services, but then, hers were at sixth glass, not seventh as was the case at Imagisle.

When I finally walked up to the door and dropped the brass knocker, only a few moments passed before Seliora herself opened the door, dressed in a muted dark blue shirt and jacket, with a silver necklace and earrings.

"I hoped you'd come."

"I hoped you'd be here." I stepped inside and let her close and bolt the door. Then I put my arms around her. "I can't stay too long."

"I know."

We walked up the staircase to the main hall and then over to the settee midway back and near the west wall, where we sat down.

"It was hard, wasn't it?" she asked.

I nodded. "Rousel's dead, and I caused it, but it's not really my fault, and yet it is, and I don't dare say anything. What good would that do?"

"It wouldn't. Your parents and Remaya don't need to bear hate for you because of Ryel's actions."

"Still . . . it's hard. I'm glad you're here."

"I want to be here for you."

For that I was grateful, and I reached out and embraced her again. After a time I said, "The memorial service is at the second glass of the afternoon on Jeudi at the Anomen D'Este. You know where that is—just off the Plaza D'Este?"

"We go to the Nordroad Anomen, but I've seen it. I'll be there. Odelia might come with me."

"Thank you."

"You don't have to thank me." She leaned toward me and brushed my cheek with her lips, then leaned back. "Rhenn? How do you feel? Tell me."

I turned to her. "I feel guilty, even though I had no way of knowing that half blinding Johanyr would lead to Rousel's death, and I didn't even mean to hurt Johanyr that much. I'm angry, because Ryel's arrogance and pride have created so much turmoil and death, and because I've had to do things I'd rather not do to protect my family and stay alive. I've dragged your family into it, and they've supported me because you love me. I'm angry at that, too, because there doesn't seem any other way to resolve things. I'm angry at the Collegium because their frigging rules mean that no one will stand up directly to the High Holders and because it means I have to fight something all alone except for you and your family, and that's one family against everyone. That's the way it feels, anyway."

"And when you win, what then? Will you be able to put the anger aside?"

When I won?

"You will win." Seliora took my hands. "You must destroy those who would kill your family . . . and us . . . but no more."

Were her words based on Pharsi farsight . . . or faith? Or both? Whatever they were based on, there was no doubt of her absolute conviction, and that was more chilling than my own doubts about whether I'd be able to prevail.

For a time we clung to each other, although I was the one clinging, really. Then it was time for me to return to Imagisle.

When I returned to the Collegium, I found my steps lagging as I approached my quarters. Was it because I wasn't looking forward to anything in the week ahead? The corridor outside my quarters was empty, and so were they, but I could not shake a feeling of apprehension and dread as I laid out my garments for Lundi before preparing for bed.

52

Lundi was the coldest morning of autumn so far, with frost everywhere and a biting wind out of the northeast that rattled my windows and seeped into my quarters. Even so, I was in the duty coach before a quint past sixth glass, wearing the blue-gray patroller's cloak that wasn't as warm as my imager's cloak. I walked into Third District station just after half past the glass. Lieutenant Warydt was waiting.

"Major Trowyn has suggested that your presence would be appreciated on the conscription team that will begin at the northwest corner of Mando and South Middle at seventh glass." Warydt did not smile, for once, and for which I was grateful.

"I'll join them now."

Warydt nodded, saying nothing. I turned and headed for the station doors.

As I walked up Fuosta and then eastward on South Middle, I tried to remember what Maitre Jhulian had taught me about the laws concerning conscription. The five rights of citizens did not preclude searches of private property, but they did preclude seizure of property without cause. Conscription was not a seizure and was allowed for those older than fourteen who were not in school, not artisan apprentices or journeymen or higher, or otherwise engaged in trade or commerce as a proprietor or holder—or those who could show a worth of a hundred golds or more. In short, the Navy could conscript the jobless, day laborers, young idlers, and the like—and taudis-toughs . . . if they could find them. I doubted that many of the taudis-toughs would be found.

Three large stake wagons with bench seats were lined up on South Middle, opposite the ruins of the Temple. Did the marines expect to fill all those wagons with conscriptees? I certainly hadn't seen that many young men or men who weren't mindless elvers.

As I approached the marines gathered at the corner of Mando and South Middle, I did a quick count. Ten men—a chief, eight marines armed with truncheons of a length between a patroller's truncheon and a riot stick, but with pistols at their belts, and a ninth marine with a bound folder. Did they need that many?

The chief kept surveying South Middle in both directions, until he saw me. Then he just waited until I stepped up to the marines.

"You're the master imager working with the Civic Patrol?" he asked.

"Rhennthyl, Maitre D'Aspect, and liaison to the Civic Patrol."

"You're the one that captured those Tiempran friggers?"

"I worked with the Patrol and some of the local dwellers to bring them in. The locals didn't want to be blamed for something they had no part in."

The chief shook his head. "Smartest thing I ever saw in a taudis. Like as not, I'll never see it again." He looked to me. "You're coming with us?"

I nodded. "That was the agreement with the major."

"Then we'd better get started." The chief gestured. "We'll start on this side, go down as far as the alley, then come back and do the other side that far."

I walked beside the chief to the first house on the corner, half of a duplex, with soot-smeared bricks and the windows and front door boarded up. Two of the marines produced pry bars, and in moments had the boards away from the door.

Three other marines slipped into the house.

In what seemed like moments, they returned with a bearded man, perhaps thirty, clad in a tattered leather jacket and trousers with ragged ends. His shoes were held together with rags, and his mouth worked silently for a moment before he spoke.

"I work! Over on the avenue."

"Name the place and the owner."

"Gosmyn's. Hetyr owns it."

I thought for a moment. I hated to say anything, but the fellow would probably live longer as a conscript. "Gosmyn's place has been gone for two or three years."

"Friggin' trolie . . . frig you."

"Take him to the wagons." The chief's voice held the resigned boredom of a man who'd heard all too many stories.

Two of the marines marched him off, but he turned and looked in my direction and spat.

We waited on the sidewalk while one of the remaining marines used a hammer to replace the boards over the door. Then we walked the few yards to the next stoop, where the chief rapped loudly.

A graying woman opened the door to the adjoining duplex. She might have once been pretty, but the gray in her reddish hair was less than flattering, and her eyes were a flat brown, not quite uncaring.

"Navy conscription team," the chief announced.

She said nothing.

"Did you live here in the year 750?"

"Yes." The resignation in the single word and the lines worn into the woman's face suggested she was too tired to have moved anywhere in the past six years.

"The last enumeration states that eight people lived here, and two were boys aged eight and eleven," the chief stated. "Where are they?"

"Doylen's thirteen. He's at the grammaire. Smart boy, he is." The momentary smile removed the sullen dullness from her face.

"Which grammaire?"

"Number thirty-one. That's the one at the corner of Weigand and Alseyo. You want to go there, he'll be there."

"What about his brother?"

She shrugged. "Left here last Juyn. Said he wouldn't be staying till the scripties came back."

"You mind if we look?"

With a resigned expression, she stepped back.

The chief nodded. "We won't need to. Thank you very much."

The woman moved forward, but waited to close the door until the chief and the two marines and I stepped off the stoop.

"You decided not to look because she agreed?" I asked.

"Not just because she agreed, but the way she did. No hesitation."

At the next three houses, there were children, but they were either too young or had left, except for the one who was at work as a tile setters' apprentice, which exempted him from conscription. The marines on the cordon would have let him pass so long as he showed his apprentice's card. The fourth house was boarded up, but no one was there. Absently, I noted that all were in what had been Youdh's territory. I had no idea who, if anyone, had succeeded Saelyhd.

When we reached the fifth house, the door opened but a crack.

"Navy conscription team," the chief declared.

"Don't need nothing from no one." The voice was that of a woman.

"You are required to open your door for the purpose of allowing us to determine whether anyone of conscription age is present."

"Don't have to."

"I will warn you that if you do not open the door we are required to force it open." The chief paused, then said, "Open up, or we'll break in."

The door slammed.

In moments, the marines with the pry bars had the door open, the bolts ripped out of the casement and wall and the edges of the door splintered. Then five marines charged inside as a woman screamed.

Close to half a quint passed before the five returned. They had two young men, one about fifteen and the other eighteen. The woman, presumably the one who had slammed the door, stood impassively at the back of the tiny front foyer. She was stout and black-haired.

"Does either of you work?" asked the chief.

The younger one shook his head, his eyes darting from one marine to another to the chief.

"Work's for fools," offered the elder contemptuously.

"You're about to become a greater fool," replied the chief. "Take them both to the wagons. Put the younger one in for boot training."

As we walked away from the house, he added in a lower voice to me, "The older one will end up as coal loader or some such. The other's young enough he might be able to make something of his life."

The next dwelling held an older couple, and an even older bedridden woman.

Then we retraced our steps back to South Middle and crossed to the east side of Mando where we started with the corner dwelling.

The woman there had three children. The oldest was something like seven.

When we came to the second dwelling, the chief made his announcement once more.

The door opened, and a woman stood there. Her skirt and blouse were grayish and close to shapeless, but clean, and her light brown hair was pulled back into a bun. Her face was narrow.

"Is there any man or boy living here who is over age fourteen?"

"I got two."

The marine with the folder murmured to the chief.

"Those are Aillyn and Dhewn? What do they do?"

"Aillyn just made journeyman roofer. Dhewn's an apprentice at the foundry."

"Are you sure they're the only ones here?"

I stood back, but the woman looked past them to me. "Master Rhennthyl . . . I got no other sons, but you want to look, they can."

The chief's eyes flickered, but he only nodded. "Thank you."

The next two houses produced neither resistance nor conscripts.

At the fourth house, the white-haired man with the wooden peg leg looked past the chief, even before the chief could say anything. "Master Rhennthyl, Alsoran told you my son's already in the Navy. All's here is my daughters . . ."

That was the way the next glass or so went, when we finished almost four complete blocks on both sides of Mando.

We were at the second house on the fifth block, in Youdh's old territory, when, after someone opened the door, a bearded man charged the marines.

"Friggin' scripties, worthless scum . . . !"

The marines had him down and trussed in moments. The odor of elve-weed was overpowering.

The chief looked down on him. "He's young enough. We'll take him, but like as not, he'll end up dead or on a road gang."

When we went back to the east side of Mando, the first woman to open the door, again, looked past the chief to me. "My oldest is just twelve. Please, Master Rhennthyl, don't let them take him."

"He'll be thirteen in Ianus," the chief said, "but we don't take them that young. If he doesn't want to be conscripted, have him get a job . . . or an apprenticeship." He nodded and added, "Thank you."

Once the door closed, the chief glanced back at me. "You know all of them, imager?"

"No, chief. I only know a handful, but I've been patrolling the taudis for a month, and they watch patrollers very closely."

That was the pattern of the day, but I did understand why they needed so many marines on a team, because some were always escorting conscriptees back to the wagons, and there were some who were violent. One good thing was that I didn't have to use any imaging, but I didn't get back to the Collegium until almost fifth glass.

There was a note waiting for me, asking me to report to Master Dichartyn. So I turned around, went back down the stairs and across the quadrangle to his study.

He was waiting, his door open, standing by the window.

"Come in, Rhenn. How was your day with the conscription team?"

"Uneventful, sir, as those things go. They didn't get any of the taudis-toughs, but I didn't expect they would. They did sweep up a bunch of idlers and able-bodied elvers—that was on the team I accompanied, anyway."

"You sound as cynical as you think I am. What I wanted to tell you was that the hearing for the Tiempran priests is on Meredi. They pushed it ahead of some other hearings to get it over and done with. It begins at eighth glass. We had thought about sending Master Jhulian with you, but that would have given the wrong impression." He paused. "Now . . . is there any aspect of imaging that might come up?"

"I didn't use much imaging, except to shield Captain Harraf and me from the blast, and some concealment shields in the taudis after the explosion, but there was only one patroller who saw them, and they already know I have shields."

"That might not even come up. Please don't bring it up yourself, unless it's in answer to a question."

"Yes, sir."

"How did you know where to find the priests?"

"I didn't. I asked Horazt."

"The west quarter taudischef? You didn't use any imaging otherwise?"

"I imaged smoke into their hiding place until they came out. The priests wouldn't know that, only that they were smoked out. I can just say that I had help in smoking them out. That's true enough."

Dichartyn turned and looked out the window. Finally, he turned back.

"Rhenn . . . no matter what you do, you seem to end up making the Collegium more visible. Why do you think that's so?"

I'd thought about that, and I had a very good idea why. All the alternatives that would make the Collegium less visible or not call attention to the Collegium happened to be ones that would have resulted in my death or even greater numbers of deaths for others. I wasn't interested in being a martyr, and I didn't like the idea of making others involuntary martyrs, either. I wasn't about to tell Dichartyn that. "I don't think that it's necessarily so. The newsheets didn't even mention me."

"They will after the hearing on Meredi."

"What will they mention? That I was worried about explosives because of what the Tiempran First Speaker said and that I helped the Civic Patrol capture the priests? Those aren't things that will get people upset about the Collegium."

"What about the Harvest Ball? You think that was low visibility?"

"Sir . . . there was an explosion, and Ferran spies were revealed. No one even mentioned the Collegium. Even when Dartazn and Martyl managed to deflect another wagon filled with explosives near the Council Chateau, very little appeared in the newsheets, and none of it mentioned the Collegium."

"More influential people know," he countered.

"Haven't they always known? Mistress Alynkya D'Ramsael-Alte had no trouble discovering who I was by name even though I never told her who I was. So did Madame D'Shendael."

Master Dichartyn laughed humorlessly. "Someday, you won't have such easy answers. I'd also like to point out that master imagers have no private lives to speak of, even if their names never appear in the newsheets. Someone always knows what you've done, even if there's no evidence and no proof. Part of the success in being covert is handling matters in a way in which it is to everyone's advantage for them not to become public."

I didn't care for that at all.

"You're young, and you are still somewhat idealistic, less than you should be, I fear, and you don't like my words. I'm not saying that all actions should be covert in that way, but most should be, and there should be a great and compelling reason for undertaking acts that cannot help but become public knowledge. In that light, I sincerely hope you don't get yourself and the rest of us into great difficulties."

"Sir, I would be the first to say that I am well aware that I cannot keep doing what I have been doing, and I am working very hard so that I will not have to." If I couldn't deal with Ryel, and soon, I'd end up with no family and far too exposed in dealing with the High Holder, and then indeed, publicly every finger would point at me. "When I rounded up the priests, I was careful to work through the Civic Patrol, and they were not captured by imaging, but by taudis-dwellers with ropes."

"You didn't make any under-the-table deals with that taudischef?"

"No, sir." Even if I had, I wouldn't have told Dichartyn. "Well, except for the promise to keep an eye on Shault and try to keep him out of trouble."

He laughed. "Master Ghaend has discovered a powerful tool in dealing with young Shault."

"Oh?"

"He just asks Shault, 'Do you want me to tell Master Rhennthyll you haven't studied hard enough?' That's more than enough." He paused. "What exactly did you do?"

I shrugged helplessly. "You know everything that I've done."

"He acts as though you were the taudischef and not this Horazt."

"I don't know why. The only thing I've done out of the ordinary is carry a letter of his to his mother because there was no other way."

"That's dangerous. How could you know—"

I laughed. "The letter had all the silvers he'd earned in his first month here, and I had to read it to his mother because she can't read."

For a moment he was silent. "Shault must have known that."

"I'm sure he did, but he wanted his mother to get the coins, and I'm certain he felt someone would read it to her."

Master Dichartyn didn't look entirely convinced, but he only said, "That's all I have. The duty coach will be ready for you on Meredi at half past seven. Try not to stir up anything else controversial."

"There is one thing, sir. I'll be going to my brother's memorial service on Jeudi."

"I thought he died over a week ago."

"He did, but that was in Kherseilles. My parents returned yesterday."

"I'm sorry. Take whatever time you need on Jeudi."

"Thank you." I nodded and left.

There were no messages in my letter box, for which I was grateful, because anything there wouldn't have been the best of news. I just hoped dinner was good.

53

After a quiet dinner in the hall on Lundi night, with Chassendri, Isola, and Ferlyn, none of whom pressed me, I walked back to my room. I was ready to sit down and relax when I realized that I had to work out what I was going to say at Rousel's memorial service. I couldn't count on having much time for the rest of the week, because I'd said I'd stop by the house on Mardi after my Patrol duties, and I had no idea how long the hearing might take. While it began on Meredi, it could easily drag into Jeudi morning.

So I sat down at my writing desk and began to struggle to put words on paper. When I finally gave up close to ninth glass, I had perhaps a sheet and a half of disjointed comments. How could I say what I felt? I loved Rousel, and yet, all through my life, he'd subtly and not-so-subtly belittled me. I'd found the woman he'd loved and who had loved him, and while she had thanked me often for that, I wasn't sure he ever had. Father had accepted Rousel's faults and trumpeted mine, and yet, in the end, Rousel was dead because of my acts, no matter that I'd never ever meant for it to come to that—and it shouldn't have. But it had. All that I really could do was to praise his good points and the fact that he had brightened the lives of many.

Was that enough? It would have to be, I suspected.

With that on my mind, I didn't sleep all that well, and I wondered, when I pulled myself from bed in the darkness on Mardi morning, if that would be the case more and more in the years ahead. I'd seen the dark circles under Master Dichartyn's eyes all too often. Was that inevitably part of being a master imager?

Once more, there was a thick frost on the grass and stone walks as I made my way to morning exercises. The exercises and run did help clear my mind, and after I showered and shaved, I dressed and made it to breakfast early enough that only Chassendri was at the masters' table. I joined her.

"You're here even earlier than usual," she offered.

"Another day with the Navy conscription team."

"Are they as brutal as people claim?"

"They're tough, and they don't hesitate to use force. I haven't seen any permanent injuries so far, and I haven't seen force used except against elvers and resisters, but nothing severe." I paused to pour my tea. "On that first day, though, the colonel would have ridden down people who weren't resisting, just chanting slogans. I have the feeling that they can get nasty when their authority is challenged."

"So you're keeping them in line."

"I wouldn't say that."

"I would. By being there as a representative of the Collegium who can bring matters directly before the Council, you've cooled matters off. No one will tell you that, but I'd wager that's the way it is."

"I'm the most junior master in the Collegium," I protested.

"I hate to tell you this, Rhenn, but you don't look like or act like the most junior master, except maybe around Maitre Dichartyn and Maitre Dyana."

I didn't know how to answer that. So I served myself the egg toast and poured berry syrup over it.

"I notice you're not saying anything to that." She grinned.

"What could I say? I don't know how my appearance or acts look to others."

"Trust me. When you think you're right, you project an assurance that's overpowering. Tell me. Do you have trouble with women? I shouldn't think that you would, and the rumor is that the young lady you've been escorting is gorgeous."

That question left me speechless.

Chassendri laughed. "It's good to see you blush. You're not so formidable that way. Are you going to answer me?"

"I don't know. I've only been interested, really interested, in two women. The first married my brother, and Seliora is the second." As I spoke Seliora's name, I realized that I'd never mentioned it to any of the other masters.

"Seliora . . . that's an old Pharsi name, isn't it?"

"She's Pharsi."

Chassendri nodded. "That would figure."

"Why?"

"She'd be one of the few to stand up to you, and you've been wise enough without knowing it to pick women like that. Was the first Pharsi?"

"Yes." I shook my head.

She smiled again. "I'm too old for you, but even if I weren't, the only way I'd have you would be as a friend."

"You think you know me?"

She laughed. "You're unpredictable, and no one really knows you, except maybe your Seliora. That's what worries the senior maitres. I'd wager that all of them will heave large sighs of relief if you marry her, or someone like her."

"I'm unpredictable?" I found that hard to believe.

She shook her head. "I'm certain that you believe that everything you do is perfectly predictable. It probably is, to you, or to someone who thinks like you do. But for the rest of the Collegium . . ."

I didn't say anything.

"It's not what you feel," she finally said. "It's what you do about what you feel. That's what has Maitre Dichartyn and Maitre Poincaryt concerned."

I still wasn't sure what to say. So I shrugged.

Chassendri didn't pursue it. She just asked, "Do you think we'll have an early winter?"

"I'm beginning to think so. We've had more and colder frosts this year. . . ."

After breakfast, on my way across the quadrangle to the duty coach, I couldn't help thinking about what Chassendri had said. Was she right? Was I that unpredictable? I didn't think I was at all unpredictable. I just tried to re- solve the problems I faced as well as I could.

Was that the problem, that often the Collegium really didn't want any real resolution, or not one that upset the established ways? Even though I pon- dered those questions on the ride across L'Excelsis, I still had no real answers by the time the coach came to a halt outside Third District station.

When I walked inside, I saw Captain Harraf standing by his study door. A quick gesture made it clear that he'd been waiting for me. I walked into his study, but didn't close the door.

Nor did he ask me to, instead inquiring sardonically, "Might I ask exactly how you managed all this? I've never seen a conscription team so well be- haved. They're even letting the patrollers do their rounds."

"I doubt I had much to do with that, sir. They lost something like a hun- dred marines. It could be that someone in charge decided that it might work better if they were polite."

"And your Collegium had nothing to do with it?"

"No, sir. Not in the slightest. Except for my presence." I wasn't about to mention that the Collegium wasn't exactly pleased with my actions.

"Or could it be that the taudis-dwellers are being more cooperative? How did you manage that?"

"The only thing we did was capture Saelyhd—"

"That's something else, Master Rhennthyl. You knew he was Youdh's suc- cessor before anyone."

I shrugged. "When I persuaded Horazt to help me, he told me that Sae- lyhd had taken over."

"I can understand that, but no one has ever been able to get anyone in the taudis to cooperate before, let alone a taudischef."

I smiled wryly, although I had my doubts, since Harraf had had some sort of arrangement with Youdh. "No one else has had the favorite nephew of a taudischef as a junior imager on Imagisle."

"Those taudischefs have been known to kill nephews and cousins." Harraf imbued the words with great skepticism.

"He says the boy is his nephew. I suspect the boy is his son. Either way, he had to talk to me, and that allowed me to persuade him to help."

"You're going with the team today?"

"Yes, sir. I can't tomorrow because I have to be a witness at the hearing for the Tiempran priests and Saelyhd. But I only promised the major yesterday. And I won't be here on Jeudi because I'll be at the memorial service for my brother. He died in a wagon accident in Kherseilles last week."

"I'm sorry to hear about your brother, but going to his service shouldn't be a problem. The marines should be finished by Meredi . . . in Third District, that is."

I hoped so. "I'd better find the team chief. They're starting on Dugalle."

Harraf nodded.

I inclined my head in return and headed out.

Mardi wasn't an exact repeat of Lundi because the area the conscription team covered took in some of Youdh's old area and all of Horazt's, and there were more elvers and vagrants along Youdh's streets, but the procedures and results were similar.

The team finished at half past fourth glass. Once I left the chief, I didn't return to the station, but walked out to the Midroad and hailed a hack to my parents'. I wasn't exactly looking forward to seeing Remaya.

I was still wrestling with "what ifs" when the hacker pulled up before the front walk to the house. I paid him, then started up the walk. My breath steamed in the air that had gotten progressively colder as the day had passed, and I wondered if we might get snow, although the sky remained clear.

Nellica had already left for the day, and Remaya opened the door, then stepped back to let me in. "Rhenn . . . Khethila said you'd be here this afternoon. Will you be staying for dinner?"

"Tonight, I can do that. Tomorrow, probably not. I have to be a witness at a justice hearing, the one involving the Tiempran priests who blew up their Temple in the South Middle taudis."

We walked into the family parlor where Mother was rocking Rheityr. She looked up. "I thought that might be you. We're having roasted lamb."

"That's something I miss."

"We thought so."

I looked down at the dozing infant. Already, he looked more like his father than his mother. I swallowed, and I found my eyes burning. If I had said anything at that moment, I would have choked on the words. So I turned and sat in the armchair across from Father's.

"It shouldn't be that long before your father and Khethila are home," Mother said.

"Culthyn?" I asked.

"He's upstairs doing schoolwork. He had much to catch up on. He's less than pleased."

That sounded like Culthyn.

"How was your day, Rhenn?" asked Remaya.

"I had to spend it with one of the conscription teams. They didn't have too many problems, except for vagrants and elvers, and one or two resisters."

"If I were facing conscription," Remaya said, "I might resist."

"You only have to have a job, or be an apprentice, not to be conscripted."

"That's what the law says. Do you really think the teams that don't have an imager with them are that scrupulous?"

"I don't know. I'd hope so."

"More than a few Pharsi boys with jobs ended up on ships," Remaya said. "I knew some of them."

I couldn't argue with that and didn't have to because I saw Charlsyn driving the coach under the side portico. "They're home." I stood and walked to the side door.

In moments, Khethila burst into the parlor and gave me a hug, which felt good. "I'm glad you could come."

"I'm glad you're here." And I was, but I did step back.

"I'll need to get the wine," she murmured as she moved toward the kitchen.

Father stepped into the parlor and asked, "How is my grandson?"

"He's sleeping," Mother replied, "and he won't be for long if you keep bellowing."

A faint smile crossed Remaya's lips.

Father dropped into his armchair with a heavy sigh.

No one said anything for a time, until Khethila carried a tray into the parlor, with a goblet of Dhuensa for Father, tea for Remaya, and hot mulled wine for me, Mother, and Khethila herself. Mother nodded to Remaya, then eased Rheityr out of her own arms and back to Remaya, who settled onto the settee. Rheityr remained sleeping, which was a wonder to me.

"Dinner won't be long," Mother said in a quiet voice, slipping off to the kitchen.

As long as I didn't look at Rheityr too often, I thought I could get through dinner without revealing all the Namer-demons that plagued me. Before all that long we were gathered around the table, where Father said grace, and then we all sat down to crisp roasted lamb and rice.

At one point, Khethila glanced over and said, "You're quiet tonight, Rhenn."

"The last weeks have been hard for everyone. I have to appear at the hearing tomorrow about the explosion of the Temple. With what happened to Rousel . . . and everything else . . ." I just shook my head.

Remaya nodded, and I wondered how much she knew—or guessed. She didn't quite finish dinner with us because she had to leave to change Rheityr, and I begged off staying longer, pleading the press of the day ahead.

Mother did have Charlsyn stay late so that he could drive me back to Imagisle. I didn't protest. When I opened my door there was an envelope slipped under it. Inside was a single note card with one line hastily written.

See me in morning right after breakfast.

Under that line was the initial D.

What other problems had surfaced? Had Master Dichartyn discovered Alynat's death? Or did he just have last-moment instructions or information about the hearing. I hoped it was the latter, but feared it was the former. Sooner or later, Alynat's death would come to his attention, but I preferred it be later, when everything was completed. Then, either I'd be successful . . . or dead.

54

Again on Meredi, I rose early and hurried through the next glass or so, until I finished breakfast and made my way to Master Dichartyn's study. As always, he looked unflustered and calm, for all that he'd done the same exercises and run as I had—and he'd finished several hundred yards behind me. But then, he was a good fifteen years older than I was, and I wondered if I'd be doing that well in fifteen years.

"There is one bit of information that has come to my attention," he began. "At this point, we don't know exactly what has occurred, but Baratyn reported that High Holder Suyrien was requested to meet with Ryel later today. Do you have any knowledge of this meeting, or the possible reasons why it might be taking place?"

"Sir, any thoughts I have would be very speculative." Accurate, in all probability, but speculative.

"I'd appreciate some speculation."

"I cannot believe that my brother's death was strictly an accident, sir, but that is speculation. There have been other events that do not seem coincidental, but I would rather not say anything at the moment. I would like to get through the next few days with as few distractions as possible."

For a moment he seemed as though he wanted to press. Then he nodded. "That is a reasonable request. When you feel it is appropriate, I would appreciate more information."

"Yes, sir."

"If I don't see you before tomorrow, convey my condolences to your family." He did sound sincere, as if he understood.

I thought he very well might. "Thank you."

As I walked from the administration building, I considered the short meeting. In effect, Master Dichartyn had warned me that matters had gotten more serious. He'd also backed off, and that definitely signaled that I was on my own. I only hoped that Grandmama Diestra's "measures" and my abilities would be adequate to protect my family, because that was clearly Ryel's focus.

The duty coach was waiting, as always. Because the Square of Justice was only about half as far from the Collegium as Third District station, it pulled up outside the Hall of Justice just as the single bell of the half glass echoed from the nearby Anomen D'Council.

I walked up the main front steps and then along the center hall toward the main hearing room in the Hall of Justice. Outside the open double doors stood the bailiff with his heavy oak staff, topped with the bronze sheaf of grain.

"Master Rhennthyl, I presume?"

"Yes, sir?"

"You'll likely be the second witness. Just go into the hall. Turn right and take a seat in the first room. That's for witnesses. You are not to speak of the subject of the hearing to the other witnesses, you understand?"

"I do, thank you."

He nodded, and I stepped into the justicing chamber, a good thirty yards from the back to the black dais at the north end with its wide and featureless black desk, and close to fifteen yards from side to side. Already, more than half the low-backed benches that faced the dais were filled, although there seemed to be more people on the side to the right of the center aisle. The shorter rows of benches on each side of the open space before the dais were empty.

When I entered the witness chamber, I saw that Captain Harraf was already there, as were the two patrollers who had stood behind us when the Temple exploded.

"Good morning, Captain," I said as I took a seat on the other end of the bench on which he sat.

"Good morning, Master Rhennthyl." Harraf's voice was pleasant, and he actually smiled as if he meant it.

I wondered if he'd been wanting to strike a blow at the scripties for years.

A few moments later Major Trowyn stepped into the room and sat down on the other bench. He did not address us, nor did he look in our direction.

No one else entered the witness chamber.

Somewhat later, outside the closed door, I heard the bailiff. "All rise!"

A time of silence was followed by the bailiff's next words, somewhat muffled. "You may be seated. Bring forth the accused."

We sat there for some time before the bailiff opened the door to the witness chamber, and a voice, presumably that of the prosecuting advocate, announced, "Naval Marine Major Trowyn to the bar."

The major rose and, without looking at the rest of us, left the witness chamber. The bailiff closed the door.

Close to a glass and a half passed before the door opened, but the major did not return. The bailiff left the door open, and the prosecuting advocate announced, "Maitre D'Aspect Rhennthyl to the bar."

I stepped out and walked down the center aisle until I was standing below the dais. I inclined my head politely to the justice, whom I had never seen before.

"Master Rhennthyl," began the justice, "do you understand that you are required to tell the whole truth, and that your words must not deceive, either by elaboration or omission?"

"Yes, sir."

"Proceed."

The prosecutor turned to me. "Please recount what occurred on the morning of Vendrei, sixth Finitas, after you reported to the Third District station, with particular attention as to how those occurrences relate to the Temple of Puryon and the naval conscription efforts scheduled to begin nearby."

"Yes, sir. When I reached Third District station, Captain Harraf explained to me that the Navy was concerned about what might happen in the taudis because there was already a group of taudis-dwellers gathered around the Temple of Puryon. He had already requested that a squad of mounted riot patrollers be dispatched to the area, but only half a squad had arrived. I told him that I had concerns about what the Tiempran priests might be planning because of the reports about what the First Speaker of Tiempre had said earlier. . . ." I went on to explain what had occurred once Harraf and I had arrived to observe, emphasizing that both the captain and I had suggested that the chanting taudis-dwellers did not pose a threat and that the colonel had ignored our warning. Then I just detailed what had happened and what I had done after that, all the way through to the capture, preliminary charging, and transport of the three priests, Saelyhd, and Donmass.

"Thank you, Master Rhennthyl," the prosecutor said. "Can you explain in more detail how you managed to come into possession, as it were, of the three Tiempran priests and the so-called taudischef Saelyhd?"

"Yes, sir. I knew from questions I'd asked of various people in the taudis that Saelyhd's predecessor—that was Youdh—had been working with the Tiemprans. I thought it was likely that Saelyhd was as well. After the explosion, I went into the taudis to see if I could find them. I was fortunate enough to find one of the other taudischefs. He was deeply concerned that he and his people would be blamed for the explosion. They had nothing to do with it, but he realized that unless some of the priests could be found and brought to justice, the entire taudis would suffer . . ." That and what followed was oversimplified, but essentially true. ". . . because of the justifiable anger of the marines, I managed to sneak the priests and Saelyhd into Third District station."

"They did not give you any trouble?"

"The men with the taudischef helped tie them up. Saelyhd did object, and it took several men to march him to where the patrollers could bring him in."

"Master Rhennthyl . . . we understand that you advised Captain Harraf not to aid the marines. Why not?"

"First, I believed that attacking those who were chanting was not justified unless they blocked the marines from doing their duty, or resisted in some way, and at that time, the taudis-dwellers were not. Second, as I mentioned earlier and told the captain, there were rumors that the Tiemprans had placed explosives in the Temple. While I could not verify that, it seemed unwise to attack people who were not an immediate threat, especially that close to the Temple."

"Master Rhennthyl . . . do you have any experience in conducting conscription?"

"No, sir."

"Then why did you see fit to recommend what you did?"

"Sir . . . the colonel wanted to make an example of people. I had learned earlier that the First Speaker of Tiempre had vowed to strike at the heart of Solidar. There had already been one riot in the taudis, over a month ago, and it was caused when the Civic Patrol tried to put down another demonstration by force incited by the Tiempran priests. This looked to be uglier than the last one because the taudis-dwellers hate the conscription teams."

"Master Rhennthyl . . . what happened with the conscription efforts on Lundi and Mardi?"

"I accompanied the first teams through the taudis. There was no violence."

"And how did this marvelous change come to pass?"

"I told some of the local leaders that any more violence would likely result in the marines leveling the entire South Middle taudis, that peaceful cooperation was their last chance."

"Why would they believe you?"

"I can't explain that, sir, except that I have been accompanying the local patrollers through part of the taudis for nearly a month. I wasn't going to question why they cooperated, not after what had already happened."

The questions seemed to go on forever.

When the prosecuting advocate finished, the advocate for the defense stepped forward.

"Master Rhennthyl, as an imager for the Collegium, you are known to be able to protect yourself from weapons. Why did you not employ your abilities to contain the damage and protect the marines?"

"Sir, contrary to stories and popular belief, the abilities that we as imagers have are often overestimated. I did attempt to use those abilities. Even at the distance we were from the Temple, when it exploded, I was only able to offer limited protection to Captain Harraf and the patrollers close by. Had we been closer, I would not have been that successful."

"How did you come to the remarkable conclusion that this explosion was caused by those accused?"

"First, as I mentioned earlier, there were public statements by the First Speaker of Tiempre. Second, in accompanying patrollers past the Temple in the days previous to the explosion, we had noted that the Temple had been closed and shuttered, as if the priests had advance knowledge of the arrival of the conscription teams. Third, I had heard the statements of those involved in the earlier riots that they had been incited by the priests. At the very least, the priests had to have some knowledge of what was in their Temple, and I thought that by capturing them, the Patrol would have a chance to determine how much they knew and how involved they were . . ."

After another half glass of questions, the advocate for the defense stepped back and turned to the justice. "I have no more questions for this witness, Your Honor."

The justice looked to me. "You are excused, Master Rhennthyl. You may leave the hall, but you may be recalled at a later date. If so, you will be notified."

"Yes, sir."

I had the feeling that wouldn't happen, that no one really wanted to see my face there again anytime soon, but I was more than relieved to be able to walk out of the hearing chamber and then out into a sunny, if chill, afternoon.

By that time, it was well past second glass, and I hadn't eaten since breakfast. Thankfully, there were always hacks around the Square of Justice, and I caught one almost immediately. I had the hacker drop me off on the Boulevard D'Council, just short of the Bridge of Desires, because there were several patisseries there.

I chose Jhesepa's and took my time over a rolled lamb flatbread and some hot tea. Then I walked back over the bridge and made my way to my quarters.

Once there, I forced myself to sit down at the writing desk and take out the two sheets of paper that held what I had written about Rousel. Over the next two glasses, I rewrote everything twice, but only ended up with another half page of thoughts and comments, but I felt better about what I had. Then I slipped them into a folder and left to make my way to dinner.

The quadrangle was windy, but not quite so chill as earlier, or so it seemed. When I entered the dining-hall building, I saw a group gathered in the corridor outside the hall proper. In the center was Kahlasa, surrounded by Reynol, Meynard, Engmyr, Martyl, and Dartazn. The conversation was animated, and I eased my way toward them.

"Kahlasa's been made Maitre D'Aspect," announced Reynol, turning to me as I approached. "Now you'll have to listen to her again at meals."

"When he's here, and that's not often anymore," Kahlasa replied.

"Talk about not being here," I countered. "Congratulations."

"Thank you."

"She had to have done something special, but she won't talk about it," added Meynard.

"You wouldn't want her to," replied Engmyr, who was close to finishing his training as a field operative.

As the bells chimed six, I walked to the masters' table with Kahlasa. She sat between Ferlyn and me.

"When did you find out?" I asked.

"This morning, but Master Schorzat had hinted it might be coming."

"You already held it as a concealed rank, didn't you?"

"For a while."

"Does that mean you'll do more planning and less fieldwork?"

She nodded. "It's the right time. Besides, it's hard to do fieldwork when you're expecting."

I almost choked on the wine that I'd begun to sip. "I . . . I didn't know."

"Claustyn and I were married just before we were sent out on our last tours." Her tone was matter-of-fact, but it had to conceal pain.

"That has to be a true mixed blessing," I said. "I'm glad for you, but . . . it can't be easy, either." I'd liked Claustyn, and that he had a legacy seemed only right, but that Kahlasa would be without him seemed so wrong. Maybe I felt that way because of what had happened to Rousel, but I would have liked to have thought it wouldn't have mattered.

"We'll manage." Her smile was slightly forced. "The word is that you've upset the Collegium, the Civic Patrol, and the Navy all at once."

"Something like that," I admitted. "I warned the naval marines not to ride down unarmed taudis-dwellers outside a Tiempran Temple. They did, and the Tiemprans exploded the Temple and killed something like two hundred people, half of them marines. I persuaded one of the local taudischefs to help me capture the priests and the collaborating taudischef and also persuaded the major left in command not to raze the taudis, and then I accompanied one of the conscription teams after things settled down."

Kahlasa shook her head. "The Collegium will look good when it's over, and everyone else will hate us for making them look bad, including the Council. Master Dichartyn is doubtless already ruing the day he decided to recruit you for security. For an imager who's supposed to be covert, you're not exactly invisible."

I tried another sip of wine before replying. "Enough people had already been killed, but it's been pointed out to me that more will die because pinning the blame on the Tiemprans will lead to more violent acts on their part at a time when we can't spare the ships to retaliate quickly to put an end to such a response." Master Rholyn hadn't quite said that, but he might as well have done so.

"The joys of security and operations, Rhenn. No matter what you do, someone's unhappy, and the better you do it, the more who are displeased. That's why it helps to remain out of sight. That way, there's no direct target for blame."

That bothered me, but I couldn't argue against her point. "Let's talk about something more cheerful. Do you think you'll have a boy or girl?"

She smiled. "It doesn't matter. He or she will likely be an imager, anyway."

"How do you know that?"

"If the mother is an imager, and so is the father, the child is almost certain to be one."

"I didn't know that."

"If the mother isn't an imager, even if the father is, there's less than one chance in a hundred that the child will be, and that's only if there are imagers in her background somewhere. Or a strong Pharsi background, for some reason."

"Is there . . . pressure . . . ?" I didn't know whether I wanted to know.

"No. Not as such. I was told early what the odds were. I wanted those talents to continue. Some women imagers don't."

Just as I thought I'd gotten close to understanding the Collegium, something like this came up. "Then I'm glad for you."

"Thank you." She sipped her tea. "Have you heard that another blizzard struck the Jariolan hills, and the Oligarch's troops are pushing the Ferrans back and inflicting heavy losses?"

"I hadn't heard, but Quaelyn speculated that might be the case some time back. His patterns suggested that . . ."

Our conversation for the rest of dinner dealt with the war in Cloisera and all the implications for the Council.

55

After breakfast on Jeudi, since I didn't have to report to Third District station, I returned to my quarters to go over what I'd written about Rousel . . . and to study my drawings and notes about Ryel's estate. Then, at ninth glass I walked across the Bridge of Hopes and then slowly up the Boulevard D'Imagers until I found a hack to drive me to my parents' house.

Khethila, dressed in a gray jacket, a green shirt, and flowing gray trousers, was the one to open the door. "Rhenn, we didn't expect you so early."

"I took the day off. You're doing door duty?"

"Nellica's helping cook."

With all the people who might well drop by after the memorial service, that was certainly understandable. I followed her back to the family parlor, where Father sat in his chair, wearing a gray jacket he'd last donned, I thought, at his older brother's memorial service close to ten years ago. It still fit. So did the green shirt.

Father gestured toward the trays set on the side tables. "No lunch. Eat what you need."

Culthyn was sitting on the edge of the settee closest to the tray that held an assortment of sweet rolls.

"Culthyn . . ." Khethila's voice was low, but warning. "Leave the rest of the rolls for Rhenn and the others."

"All right. . . ."

Mother hurried from the kitchen. Like Father and Khethila, she wore gray and green. "Rhenn, you're early."

"Sometimes, I can manage that. Can I do anything?"

She glanced toward Culthyn. "Keep your brother from eating all the rolls."

"Mother . . ." Culthyn's voice was almost plaintive.

I looked at him.

"Don't do that, Rhenn. Please . . . I won't eat any more."

"How's Remaya?" I asked.

"She's feeding Rheityr. Nellica will take care of him while we're at the service."

No one said anything profound or disturbing, and after a while Remaya joined us, holding Rheityr, who was awake and smiling. At his age, I wondered if he even knew what he was smiling about, but his bright face, showing so much of Rousel, cheered the others. Knowing what I knew, every time I looked at him, I wondered what else I could have done . . . and yet, given Johanyr and the institutionalized arrogance of the High Holders, I felt that what had happened would have been fated no matter what I'd done—unless I'd allowed myself to become Johanyr's sycophant.

That didn't help the way I felt.

Finally, it was time to leave for the anomen. I took my place next to Charlsyn on the driver's seat so that the others wouldn't be that crowded inside the coach. Given the comparative warmth of the day, with the slight overcast, I was doubtless more comfortable beside Charlsyn than I would have been inside the coach.

The ride to the Anomen D'Este wasn't that long, only about a quint, and we arrived early enough that Charlsyn had no trouble drawing the brass-trimmed brown coach along the east side of the building, on Elsyor. Once I helped Mother and Remaya out of the coach, I took a few moments to see if Seliora happened to be in any of the coaches that had just stopped to leave those coming to the service. She wasn't. So I hurried up the steps into the anomen.

There were already close to fifty people there, gathered near the front below the chorister's pulpit. I caught sight of Culthyn, Khethila, and Father in the east side corridor, set off by columns, that flanked the main hall. Khethila's dark green mourning scarf had slipped off her hair and lay across her shoulders.

"Mother? Remaya?"

"They'll be back in a moment," Khethila replied. "They're fine."

I nodded. "I'm going back near the doors to wait for Seliora."

"You didn't say she was coming," Culthyn said.

I hadn't, I realized. I just thought it would have been obvious. "I'm sorry. She wanted to come."

"I'm glad she is," Khethila said.

Even Father nodded to that.

I walked back toward the entrance, then waited several yards inside the open brass-bound double doors of the anomen, back far enough that people would not immediately walk up to me.

Donalt, a distant cousin of Father's I'd met only a few times, hobbled up the stone steps, accompanied by a younger woman who might have been his daughter. Neither even glanced at me as they walked toward the front of the anomen. A handful of others, some of whose faces I recognized vaguely, followed.

Then I could see a coach pull up, and Seliora alighted, by herself, and hurried up the steps. As she neared, I could see she wore gray, with but the faintest touch of green piping on the jacket sleeves and lapels, and a dark green mourning scarf.

I stepped forward and down the steps to meet her. "I was watching for you. I thought Odelia . . ."

"It's better this way." She glanced back over her shoulder. "We'd better go inside."

I didn't question her, but I did make sure that my shields covered her as we walked back up the steps and toward the front of the anomen. Remaya, Mother, Father, Khethila, and Culthyn were standing at the front of those waiting for the service to begin.

Mother glanced back at us, then nodded to Seliora. So did Khethila. Remaya did not turn, nor did Father.

Shortly, Chorister Aknotyn stepped up to the pulpit. "We are gathered here together this afternoon in the spirit of the Nameless, in affirmation of the quest for goodness and mercy in all that we do, and in celebration of the life of Rousel D'Factorius."

The opening hymn was "The Glory of the Nameless." I sang, but as quietly as possible. I noticed that Seliora wasn't singing any louder, although she sounded more in tune than I did.

Then came the confession, for without confession there could be no understanding and no healing. At least, that was what I'd always been taught. In a way, I agreed, although I couldn't have said why, especially since I wasn't even certain I believed in the Nameless.

"We do not name You, for naming is a presumption, and we would not presume upon the creator of all that was, is, and will be. We do not pray to You, nor ask favors or recognition from You, for requesting such asks You to favor us over others who are also Your creations. Rather we confess that we always risk the sins of pride and presumption and that the very names we bear symbolize those sins, for we too often strive to arrogate our names and ourselves above others, to insist that our petty plans and arid achievements have meaning beyond those whom we love or over whom we have influence and power. Let us never forget that we are less than nothing against Your nameless magnificence and that all that we are is a gift to be cherished and treasured, and that we must also respect and cherish the gifts of others, in celebration of You who cannot be named or known, only respected and worshipped."

"In peace and harmony," came the response.

After that came the charge from Aknotyn. "Life is a gift from the Nameless, for from the glory of the Nameless do we come; through the glory of the Nameless do we live, and to that glory do we return. Our lives can only reflect and enhance that glory, as did that of Rousel, whom we honor, whom we remember, and who will live forever in our hearts and in the glory of the Nameless."

Another hymn followed—"In the Footsteps of the Nameless."

> *"When we walk the narrow way of what is always right,*
> *when we follow all the precepts that foil the Namer's blight . . ."*

I'd never been certain that following the footsteps of the Nameless led to anything, let alone to glory, or even if the Nameless had feet, let alone footsteps, but then, I'd never been convinced of the validity of theological metaphors, either. But . . . I sang, if only because the service was for Rousel.

Then Aknotyn said, "Now we will hear from Master Rhennthyl D'Image, speaking for the family."

Seliora reached out and squeezed my hand. I didn't realize how cold my own hands were until the warmth of hers touched mine.

I did not take the pulpit, but walked to the topmost step of the sacristy dais, where I turned and faced the less than hundred people who had come to pay their respects to the family and to Rousel. I had to clear my throat several times before I could say anything.

"Rousel was my brother. For twenty-three years he was my brother. Over the past few years he was a wool factor, and he expanded the family business by seeking new opportunities in Kherseilles. So often that is what people remember—what others did for a living. But that was only a small part of what made Rousel special. Rousel loved life. Sometimes, when we were young, he loved it so much that chores didn't always get done. But Rousel always understood that there would always be chores, while the joy of the moment is always fleeting and soon lost. . . ."

I went on to talk about his joys in Remaya, and in factoring, and in his son Rheityr. Somehow, I got through what I had to say and then stepped down.

Remaya was weeping, and so was Mother. I just hoped that their tears were because I'd created an image of Rousel that touched them.

Chorister Aknotyn stepped forward to the pulpit once again. "At this time, we wear gray and green, gray for the uncertainties of life, and green for its triumph, manifested every year in the coming of spring. So is it that, like nature, we come from the grayness of winter and uncertainty into life which unfolds in uncertainty, alternating between gray and green, and in the end return to the life and glory of the Nameless. In that spirit, let us offer thanks for the spirit and the life of Rousel," intoned Chorister Aknotyn, "and let us remember him as a child, a youth, a man, a husband, and a father, not merely as a name, but as a living breathing person whose spirit touched many . . ."

At that moment, an image flashed before me—clear, instant, and then gone—of an angular figure with a rifle looking at the main doors of the Anomen D'Este.

". . . let us set aside the gloom of mourning, and from this day forth, recall the glory of Rousel's life and the warmth and joy he has left with us . . ."

With those words, all the women let the mourning scarves slip from their hair.

Then came the traditional closing hymn—"For the Glory."

> "For the glory, for the life,
> for the beauty and the strife,
> for all that is and ever shall be,
> all together, through forever,
> in eternal Nameless glory . . ."

As the last words of the closing hymn echoed through the anomen, I squeezed Seliora's hand, then eased away toward the side of the chamber, hurrying toward the open doors. I stopped just inside them and surveyed the buildings across the street, especially along the roof lines, where a sniper might well be concealed. I saw no one that looked out of the ordinary.

Then, people began to depart. Some of those at the back left immediately, hurrying past me as if they had fulfilled some obligation. One of them was Ferdinand, the masonry factor. Another was his brother, Tomaz, the produce factor.

For a bit, then, no one departed. I judged that was because many of them wanted to offer condolences to Remaya and my parents, some of them at the anomen, so that they would not feel obligated to call at the house later.

After a short time, a trickle of mourners began to file out, but I didn't see Veblynt or others I would have expected.

Before long, I could hear Culthyn's voice. "There he is, by the doors."

I glanced back, but didn't see Seliora, and that bothered me, but I had the feeling that she wouldn't be a target of an assassin. I hoped not, but I waited as my parents approached.

"Go ahead," I said, "I'll be right behind you."

I looked back again, and Seliora stepped out of one of the alcoves and moved up beside me. We walked down the steps just behind my parents, Khethila, Remaya, and Culthyn. I extended shields, trying to make sure that they protected Father and Culthyn.

Something slammed into me—my shields, rather—and I barely managed not to stumble, even when a second bullet struck.

Almost without thinking, I imaged a line of caustic back along what I felt was the path of the bullets, even as I kept walking and shielding my family. Remaya never looked up, or looked in my direction.

Khethila looked back at me with a puzzled expression. "Rhenn."

"I stumbled." That was all I said.

"What did you do?" Seliora leaned toward me and murmured the words.

"Another assassin," I murmured back.

Seliora looked at me. "There shouldn't have been . . ."

I understood what she meant. "Maybe there were too many." This time, I had no doubts who was behind the attempt, because none of the shots had been at me. All had been aimed at members of my family. The attack also confirmed that I had no choice but to carry out what I planned, because Ryel would not stop until he was stopped. Nor would Dulyk.

For that moment, though, either I'd been successful or the shooter had fled, because there were no more shots all the way to the coach. Father helped Remaya inside. She was trying to hold herself together, I could tell, so much so that she had not looked back or in any direction during the service or on the walk back to the coach.

After the others were all in the coach, except Father, I said to him quietly, "We'll just take a hack."

He nodded and climbed into the coach.

Seliora and I left the family coach and walked back down Elsyor for less than thirty yards to the two hackers remaining. They knew when there were memorials. We took the first coach.

Once we were inside and on our way, Seliora studied me. "You knew, didn't you?"

"I had a flash during the service. That's why I hurried off."

"Grandmama thought someone might be shooting after the memorial service, but she arranged for people to be watching."

"I'm sure they were, but there might have been another. She'll get a report, won't she?"

Seliora nodded, then reached out and squeezed my hand. "You spoke well and lovingly."

"I loved Rousel. Sometimes I could have strangled him, but I still loved him, and I didn't want anything like this to happen to him."

"You're worried about what someone might say at the house, aren't you?" she asked.

"I don't want anyone to suspect what really happened. Everyone's suffered enough."

She nodded.

Charlsyn was just pulling the brown coach past the portico toward the rear stable at the house when Seliora and I alighted from the hack and began to walk through the front gate and up the walk.

Remaya was standing under the portico, holding Rheityr against her shoulder and rocking him gently. She didn't see us until we neared the front door. Then she stared, and even from yards away, I could see that she paled.

"Salari Seliora ind puitre d'esprit vengael . . ."   ϸ

I couldn't believe I heard the words, because Remaya hadn't spoken that loudly, but more in an involuntary murmured exclamation, but I did. The only word I knew was Seliora, and that meant "daughter of the moon" in old Pharsi, something I hadn't known until Seliora had told my parents months before.

Remaya's words halted Seliora as well. We looked at each other, then back toward Remaya, but she had turned away and fled, almost, into the house.

"What did she say?" I asked.

"That's an old Pharsi expression." Seliora hesitated, then went on. "It doesn't translate directly, but it means something like 'Protect us from the daughter of the moon and the spear of vengeance.' The other part's not really in the words, but the spear of vengeance traditionally refers to Erion, the lesser moon, and the coupling of the daughter of the greater moon with the lesser moon creates the terror of combining truth and power."

"The terror of combining truth and power," I repeated. "Why would she say that?"

"You said she had farsight."

"Not so much as you, but she said she'd had flashes. One was that she'd marry Rousel."

Seliora shivered. It wasn't that cold out.

"You two," called Khethila from the door. "Are you just going to stand there, or are you coming inside?"

"We're coming," I replied.

One of the first people I saw when we stepped into the formal parlor was Factor Veblynt. I hadn't seen him at the anomen, but he might have been there.

He immediately came toward us. "Master Rhennthyl, I am so sorry for you and your family. Such a tragedy for you all, especially when matters like this happen to those who are innocent." His eyes did not quite meet mine.

"Often the worst happens to the innocent," Seliora replied. "They don't realize how unpredictable life can be, and they're not prepared."

"That is true, Mistress Seliora." Veblynt nodded to her, then looked to me. "Did anyone ever discover the cause of the . . . accident?"

"For everyone concerned, it was a terrible accident," I replied. "Terrible."

"Did you know that a similar sort of incident occurred last week here in L'Excelsis?"

"I would not be surprised," I replied. "There are far more wagons and horses here than in Kherseilles."

"Alynat D'Ryel died racing his trap on the road last week. Rather sudden, it was. Apparently, the wheel bearings froze suddenly."

"Alynat?" I frowned. "Wasn't he the nephew or some such of High Holder Ryel?"

"He was. Apparently, Ryel took his death rather hard, although, interestingly enough, he has not canceled his Fall Foliage Festival on Samedi. I thought you might find that interesting." His eyes glittered.

What I found interesting was that Veblynt had brought it up. I managed to smile. "He has a foliage festival this late in the year?"

"A whim of his," Veblynt said with a smile that was anything but sincere. "Oh . . . I see your mother. If you would excuse me?"

Seliora looked at me. "He's very afraid of you. He also hates Ryel. He would not have spoken so otherwise."

"His wife must be a very close relation to Madame D'Ryel," I said dryly.

Seliora's eyes followed Veblynt.

After that people began to arrive, including Donalt and other relations I had not seen in years, if at all. We did not see Remaya anywhere, and I assumed she had retreated to her quarters, overwhelmed by people and grief.

Despite the close to thirty people who descended upon the house, by sixth glass everyone who was not family had left, and Charlsyn was more than ready to take Seliora back to NordEste Design and me to the Collegium. The way things were going, I wanted Seliora home safely.

"Tomorrow?" she asked.

"I could see you for dinner."

"At home . . . that's better until . . . for now."

"When will you be done with work?"

"Whenever you get there." Her smile lit up the interior of the coach.

"Between fourth and fifth glass?"

We held tightly to each other for the rest of the way to NordEste Design, and I walked her to the door, making certain my shields protected her. No one shot, not that I felt, in any case. Then I hurried back to the coach, and Charlsyn drove me to the Bridge of Hopes.

Comparatively late as it was, when I returned to the Collegium, there was a prime waiting for me at the Collegium end of the bridge.

"Master Rhennthyl?"

"Maitre Dichartyn wishes to see me?"

"Yes, sir. He's still in his study."

"Thank you." I didn't hurry, but I didn't dawdle, either, in making my way into and through the administration building to the study with which I was all too familiar.

Dichartyn was actually sitting behind his writing desk, working on something when I stepped inside the study and closed the door. I took the chair across the desk from him.

"How were the services, Rhenn?"

"As I would have expected, sir, mainly family and close friends. Many came to my parents' house afterward."

He nodded. "I wanted to talk to you tonight."

That suggested something was not well.

"I had a report on your testimony yesterday."

There was nothing to say to that. So I didn't.

"Actually . . ."—Master Dichartyn drew out the silence—"you handled it very well. By bringing up the Tiempran problem and bringing in the priests, you got everyone off the hook. The conscription team can't be blamed for not knowing there were explosives there. The taudis-dwellers can't be blamed for being pawns of the evil Tiemprans. And the marine major can't be blamed because his superior failed to heed your warnings. Captain Harraf and his observers were quite clear that you were not trying to tell the marines what to do, but only to point out that they had not been resisted. The justice found that your account was true in all particulars. That didn't hurt the Collegium . . . too much." He leaned back and sighed. "That brings up what seems to be the eternal question. What exactly are we going to do with you?"

"Let me keep being a liaison," I suggested.

"After this? You're powerful and dangerous, and too visible to discipline publicly. Not a single officer in the Patrol would dare to order you around after all this—or even suggest that you do anything. Like it or not, the word is out that sometimes strange things happen to people who cross you. The newsheets already have a story about how you stood up against a power-hungry scriptie officer for the poor downtrodden taudis-dwellers." He snorted.

I didn't say anything. I wasn't about to suggest a solution because it was clear I wasn't suited to quiet covert work, and that Master Dichartyn knew it. I also wasn't suited to merely observing, and he knew that as well. And I didn't want to end up imaging machine parts, either.

"Rhennthyl, you've just lost a brother and survived a harrowing week in Third District. Just spend some time with your family and the young lady for the next few days. Try not to get into trouble. I've already sent a note to Commander Artois saying that you'll be tied up with the Collegium for a few days. Maitre Poincaryt and I need to consider your situation."

"Yes, sir." I wasn't about to argue with that.

As I walked across the quadrangle to my quarters, I kept thinking about Veblynt's comments. Why he hated Ryel, I had no idea, but he as much as suggested that I act during the Foliage Festival. What bothered me was that was when I'd already planned to do just that.

Were Veblynt's words a lure? Or a suggestion?

In the end, it didn't matter. I was running out of time, and some opportunities occurred only once . . . and it was more than clear that waiting would only result in more attempts on my family—and eventually, if I did not act, more deaths.

56

Somehow, I didn't think that taking off the next few days meant skipping exercises and running. So I got up and subjected myself to Clovyl's tortures, then cleaned up and headed to breakfast.

Kahlasa, Ferlyn, Chassendri, and Maitre Dyana were all at the masters' table. Maitre Dyana was on the right and beckoned for me to sit by her. There was no reason not to, and I might learn something.

Dyana let me pour my tea and take a sip before she spoke. "The events of the past week cannot strengthen your position in certain matters."

"That's likely." I wanted to see what she might say.

"Have you decided what to do?" Dyana might have been asking about the weather.

"My brother's memorial service was yesterday. What I decide does not matter. Only what I do and how I do it matters."

"That is true." She sipped her tea. "It also matters who knows what."

"Or who does not," I pointed out.

"Someone always knows, even if there is no proof."

"Master Dichartyn always wants proof."

"Does he? Or does he merely want proof when you wish the Collegium to act?"

I smiled. "There is a difference."

"Exactly."

I knew what she had conveyed, but I appreciated the confirmation. "What do you think about the Jariolan-Ferran war?"

"The Ferrans will attempt to hold on until spring so that they can then attack with their superior equipment. They will likely lose before then. Even if they win, they will lose."

"Because they will lose so many men?"

"Because they will lose so much expensive equipment and so many highly trained men while the Jariolans will lose men that they can easily replace. We have already destroyed the best vessels in the Ferran fleet."

"Why didn't they see that would happen?"

"Technically advanced equipment is only effective when it is used where it was designed to be used and when its use embodies superior tactics. You have among the strongest shields of anyone in the Collegium, but you know enough not to use them against a heavy cannon. That is a question of usage. . . ."

Mostly, I just listened.

Then, after breakfast, I went to the studio and worked for close to two glasses on the final touches to Master Rholyn's portrait, then made arrangements with Grandison for framing it, after Rholyn saw the final version when I showed it to him on Samedi morning.

I cleaned up the studio to some degree, then washed myself up again, before heading out across the Bridge of Hopes to find a hack to take me out to my parents'. I walked more than a block up the boulevard before finding one. Once in the hack on the way out the Boulevard D'Imagers and then the Midroad, I went over what I'd planned for Samedi and decided on one change—if I could make it work.

I arrived at the house at a quint before noon.

Mother opened the door. "Rhenn! What a pleasant surprise. Are you here for lunch?"

"I'd thought so . . . if it's possible." I stepped inside and closed the door, then followed her back through the parlor toward the kitchen.

"Remaya will be pleased. Just the two of us are here . . . and Rheityr, of course, but he's napping right now."

Remaya looked up from where she was sitting at the table in the breakfast room. "Rhenn . . . I'm glad you came. I wasn't at my best yesterday."

"I cannot imagine why," I said lightly. "Are you feeling better today?"

"There are days, and there are days that are not quite so bad."

"Rhenn . . . just sit down," Mother insisted. "I'll be out with lunch in a bit."

I sat down across from Remaya.

"Thank you for what you said about Rousel. It was so like him. He was so alive. You should have seen him with Rheityr." Her eyes brightened with moisture that did not quite turn into tears. "You never did."

"No. I've not been allowed to travel much."

"He did have that," she said. "He loved Rheityr so much."

"He loved you," I pointed out.

"Rhenn . . . I know you were once interested in me." She smiled sadly. "I loved Rousel. I still do. I always will. Besides that . . . your Seliora is far better suited to you than I ever would have been."

I had to agree. "I know. I just didn't know it back then."

"I did."

"Yes, you did." I paused. "Why did you say that yesterday, those old Pharsi words about the daughter of the moon? You looked so stunned when you saw us."

"I couldn't help it. There's an old book in my parents' house. Father said it was very rare. It was written in Pharsi, but he let me read it—look at the drawings, really. I had to promise to be careful. My favorite drawing was the daughter of the moon. Seliora looks just like that drawing, and that's her name, and you looked so powerful and severe, like Erion. I . . . I never saw anything like it."

"Farsight . . . or real sight?"

"Both . . . I think." She paused. "Rhenn . . . please don't take this the wrong way, but . . . I've always known there was something different about you, besides being an imager. Rousel didn't always do things right, and sometimes he said things that could be hurtful. I know. I saw it with you, but he didn't mean to. He never did. You seldom say thoughtless or cruel things, yet . . . I think I'd be truly terrified if you ever became my enemy. Not that you would, but do you understand?"

I was afraid I did. I nodded.

"Seliora is like you in that, too."

"Like him in what?" asked Mother, carrying in a teapot and mugs. "Who is?"

"She was saying that Seliora and I were more alike that we might have realized." I looked to Remaya. "That was what you said, wasn't it?"

"They're both very determined," Remaya confirmed.

"It's good Seliora is," Mother replied. "If a woman doesn't have a mind of her own with Rhenn, she won't have any at all."

Those words surprised me. "Mother . . ."

"You know that, dear. That's why Khethila's so strong. She had to be to argue with you." She smiled and returned to the kitchen.

"She knows you, Rhenn," Remaya said.

Moments later, Mother came back with a large platter filled with warmed items left over from the afternoon before—pastry crescents filled with spiced ground lamb or cheese, cheese and sausage slices, grape leaves stuffed with rice and lamb, and beef baolas. There was enough on the platter before us to feed the entire family and then some.

"I think that's more than enough," I suggested.

Remaya smiled.

Still, I was hungry, and I didn't talk much while I removed a fair share of what was on the platter.

"This being with the Civic Patrol," Mother said, "it sounds dangerous. How long will you be doing this?"

"Usually, an assignment there is for a year, sometimes longer. But the conscription teams only visit an area every two to three years. It's likely that the worst is over for now."

"I can't say as I like it."

"Sometimes, it's just fate," Remaya interjected. "Rousel wasn't . . . he wasn't doing anything dangerous." She shook her head, her eyes bright, again. "It doesn't make sense . . ."

"You mean that I can be standing close to an explosion," I said, "and escape, while Rousel dies in a freak accident?"

Remaya nodded.

"Life's never what we expect," Mother said. "You'll send yourself to the madhouse if you think it's always going to work out or make sense. Chenkyr thought Rhenn here would be a factor. Rhenn thought he'd be a portraiturist. They were both wrong."

"I think he's better off as an imager," Remaya said, sniffing slightly.

I stood. "I think I ate too much. I'd just like to walk around in the garden for a bit. I need to stretch my legs and think." That wasn't quite true. I needed to see if I could approach Ryel's chateau in the way I'd planned.

"It's a bit chill out there," Mother said.

"I'll be fine." I made my way out onto the rear terrace, beyond which lay the garden, more to the north than directly back, a modest wall garden no more than twenty yards by ten, with a stone path making its winding oval way around the bushes and the flower beds, although the annuals had succumbed to the recent frosts.

When I reached the northwest corner, I studied the small lily pond. It was partly dry, but that wouldn't hinder my attempt. Where I stood also wasn't visible from the kitchen or the parlor. I looked at the corner of the pond, then concentrated on imaging a narrow bridge along one side. I stepped on the imaged bridge, and it cracked, and I had to jump back. Clearly, I needed a stronger structure.

It took me three tries before I managed to image what I required. In time, I made my way back to the parlor, where Remaya and Mother had gone from the breakfast room. Remaya was nursing Rheityr.

"I see my nephew is awake."

"Awake and hungry," Remaya replied dryly. "Very hungry."

"I'll need to go."

"It was nice of you to come, dear. Will you be able to come for dinner to-morrow?" Mother asked.

"I'm afraid not. I can't make any plans until I find out what the Collegium has planned for me. They're concerned that I was too visible because of the problems with the Temple."

"The newsheets were very complimentary," Remaya said.

"The Collegium tries to avoid being public, even in a positive way," I replied.

"Will we see you at all tomorrow?"

"Like Father, we often work on Samedis. There are things I have to finish," I pointed out, "and I'm the duty master on Solayi."

"It sounds so much like the Navy," Remaya said.

"In some ways, it's much easier. In others, it's much harder." I inclined my head to her, and then to Mother, before she accompanied me to the front door.

"You do take care, dear," were her parting words.

"I'll certainly try."

I did have to walk out to Saenhelyn Road before I could find a hack, since Charlsyn wasn't around. By the time I stepped out of the coach on Hagahl Lane it was two quints past fourth glass.

Bhenyt was the one who opened the door. He grinned and called upstairs, "You were right, Aunt Seliora. It's him!" He locked the door and raced up the stairs.

I followed, more sedately, at least in comparison.

Seliora was waiting, wearing what looked to be her working garb—the dark blue split skirts and a matching jacket over a beige blouse. She still looked wonderful.

She felt wonderful, too, when I put my arms around her and kissed her.

When we disengaged, she said, "It's a good glass until dinner."

"We can talk, can't we?"

"Is that all you had in mind?" She raised her eyebrows.

"No, but that's all that will happen."

"It's too cold to sit out on the terraces, and Father has some friends in the lower plaques room," Seliora said.

We ended up sitting on the settee in the main entry hall.

"There were more assassins than the one yesterday," Seliora said carefully.

"That's what you hinted," I replied.

"Mama and Grandmama are still looking into it."

"We should talk about it," I said, "but can it wait? I'd rather not until after tomorrow."

"Tomorrow? What will you do?" Seliora asked, her voice calm enough that I knew she knew that I intended to act.

I forced a smile. "First, there's something I won't be able to do. That's the sitting for your portrait tomorrow."

"I thought as much after what Factor Veblynt said."

"I'd also like to borrow the mare tomorrow afternoon, say around second glass." I paused. "It's an imposition, but I hope it's the last one."

Seliora raised her eyebrows.

"Not in the same way," I amended my statement. "I'll probably always be imposing."

She did offer that mischievous grin, the one I hadn't seen in a while, and had missed. I tried to concentrate on that and not what Samedi might bring.

57

After completing my normal early-morning schedule on Samedi, I put on my heavier winter grays and headed along the quadrangle to the dining hall and breakfast. The few masters who did eat at the dining hall must have slept in or gone somewhere for the weekend because Chassendri was the only one at the masters' table.

"You're dressed for winter," she said cheerfully.

"I was cold after my shower."

She laughed. "That's right. You covert types practice masochism." She shook her head. "No, thank you. I'll take my smelly laboratory any day."

"What do you do besides give grief to primes and seconds?" I could still recall my earlier sessions with her.

"I try to work out chemical formulations that can be imaged into being."

"If they can be imaged . . ."

"Think about it, Rhenn. Would any imagers be able to image metals or the like if they didn't know what they were imaging? And for some things, like gun cotton, the manufacturing process is very dangerous, but the end product is less dangerous. So it makes sense."

She was telling me yet another aspect of imaging I hadn't even considered. So I listened carefully.

After finishing breakfast, I hurried to my studio. Once there, I checked over Master Rholyn's portrait carefully, both in shadow and in half-light, and in full light, trying to make sure that there wasn't anything that appeared untoward in differing lighting. So far as I could tell, there wasn't. I set it up on the easel, angled so that it was in good light from the north windows, and then went to work on Seliora's portrait. I couldn't do much else, anyway, and I did want to finish it before too long.

Rholyn arrived a few moments after the last bell of eighth glass, wearing the imager's standard heavy gray winter cloak, and shaking himself as he stepped into the studio. His face was red. "It's too much like winter out there."

"It is cold," I agreed, refraining from pointing out that he hadn't had to take a cold shower after running four milles in the chill.

"Is it finished?"

"I'd like to think so, sir, but I'd appreciate your looking it over." I pointed toward the easel.

Rholyn stepped toward the portrait, warily, seemingly as if he expected some unpleasant surprise. Then he stood and studied it. Finally, he looked to me. "It will do." Then he grinned, the first time I'd ever seen him do so, so far as I could recall. "I have to admit, Rhenn, it's very good. Not as flattering as I might like, but Mharrie will be very pleased when she sees it." He paused. "What happens next?"

"I've made arrangements for it to be framed, and Maitre Poincaryt will determine where it will be hung. I'd judge that might be either in the receiving hall or possibly in the public corridor outside the dining hall. He has not told me, however."

Rholyn turned away from the portrait. "Master Dichartyn told me about your accomplishments with the Civic Patrol. You were fortunate in finding the Tiempran priests."

"Yes, sir."

"Except it wasn't fortune at all, was it? You had someone watching for them for days, I'd wager."

"I asked someone. I didn't know if they would."

"You know, Rhenn, you're the kind of imager that every maitre of the Collegium wishes for . . . and then regrets wishing for when he arrives."

"I'm going to have to request a little clarification of that, if you wouldn't mind, sir."

"Often, I'm requested to clarify. I will, for you, but I'm not certain it will be at all helpful." Rholyn chuckled. "You have powerful shields and untapped abilities. You're intelligent, moderately good-looking, but not excessively so, and generally deferential. You continue to work and learn. You quietly, and sometimes not so quietly, question why the Collegium and the Council operate in the fashion that they do. I imagine you do the same with the Civic Patrol. You're always seeking a better way to do something. The problem is that you are already sometimes correct, and you're likely to become more so as you learn more. Very few people really want better ways to do things. They want easier ways, and seldom is better easier. Better also means change, and no matter what they say, people resist change. You have the power to change things. When someone has that power, it disturbs people. When someone actually forces change, it disturbs them even more. You'll have to determine where you go from here, but I would suggest that you limit your suggestions and acts to those that are most valuable to the Collegium." He smiled. "But I do appreciate the artistry in the portrait. Thank you."

He was still smiling, as if at a private jest, when he left.

I couldn't give the portrait to Grandison until Lundi. So I set it where it wouldn't be disturbed and went back to work on Seliora's portrait until slightly before noon, when I headed back to the dining hall. Since I was the only master at lunch, I ate quickly and then returned to my quarters.

After cleaning up and making a few preparations, I left my rooms and crossed the quadrangle on my way to the Bridge of Hopes and East River Road. From what I'd garnered from Iryela and Veblynt, Ryel's foliage event was a late-afternoon and early-evening celebration. It might even last into evening, but to see the trees from the tower required daylight.

With the blustery afternoon wind, there were fewer hacks about, and it was slightly after first glass when I arrived at NordEste Design. Seliora was the one who let me in, and since no one else was in the lower foyer, we did enjoy a few moments with each other before walking up to the main entry hall.

"I've already saddled the mare." She paused. "How long . . . ?"

"I don't know. I might not be back until after dark."

She nodded.

I appreciated her not asking for details. "I'll tell you everything when I return."

She squeezed my hand. "We'd better get you on your way."

We walked to the back of the hall and then through the maze of narrow passageways that led to the staircase down to the rear courtyard. The courtyard was empty, and the wind swirled dust this way and that.

"It's going to be a cold ride," Seliora said.

"I'm wearing my heaviest woolens, and I brought my gloves."

"Good. I left the mare in the stable."

We crossed the courtyard, and I slid open the stable doors.

"You will be careful?" she said.

"As careful as I can be."

I unlatched the stall half door and swung it back, and she untied the mare and led her out. I walked beside Seliora out to the courtyard.

As I was about to mount the mare, Seliora handed me a long leather case. "Take this. It might help."

I eased off the hardened leather cap at one end. Inside was a polished brass spyglass. I closed the case and looked at her. "Thank you. It will."

"I know." She paused, then embraced me, murmuring as she did, "Please be as careful as you can."

"I will." I let go of her and climbed into the saddle, if not gracefully, at least not so awkwardly as had been the case weeks earlier. Then I flicked the reins, gently, and the mare began what could be a long journey, a very long journey, and one I hoped I survived.

The Boulevard D'Este wasn't that heavily traveled, and before long I'd ridden around the Plaza D'Nord and was headed north toward destiny, whatever it might be. Once I was away from the plaza, I set up the blurring shields, the ones that didn't hide me, but made me look less distinct, so that passersby would see a rider but not recall details.

I was less than a mille from Ryel's estate when a stylish bronze and silver coach, drawn by a matched pair of grays, swept past me. Then, when I neared the top of the rise south of the Ryel estate, I could see another coach, decorated in blue and bronze, slow before turning and passing through the estate gates.

I kept riding downhill, but once I had ridden into the depression short of where the stream left the estate and where I could not be seen directly, I extended full concealment shields. Then I rode the mare along the road over the culvert and into the brushy space between the wall and the road. I dismounted and tied the mare to the base of a bushy tree, or a treelike bush, where she was largely out of sight from the road, although I did "tie" a blurring screen to her.

Then I slipped the spyglass inside my waistcoat and walked downhill until I stood next to the stone walls that channeled the rushing stream toward the stone culvert under the road. I concentrated on imaging a narrow stone bridge affixed to the wall on the north side. A dark, ledgelike structure appeared.

I swallowed, then put one boot on the ledge. It seemed firm. I put my full weight on the structure, then moved forward, staying close to the wall. Once I was past the extension of the stone walls and off my imaged ledge bridge, I imaged it out of existence, because I didn't need anyone to see it.

Standing where I was, at the bottom of a gradual slope that ended with the stream to my right, Ryel's chateau, and especially the tower off the low-walled terrace beyond the south wing, loomed into the pale blue sky. The edge of the stream was marked with perfect pale white gravel that ended at a stone coping at the top of the stream bank. Neatly cropped grass covered the three yards between the coping and the waist-high boxwood hedge that bordered the stream. Uphill from the hedge was another swathe of grass with curving stone walks winding around flower beds already mulched and banked for the winter, topiary representing various animals, and perfectly trimmed trees of all sorts, both deciduous and evergreens. Varying patterns of grass and walks and trimmed vegetation filled the entire space between the stream and the gray stone wall that formed the base of the south wing of the chateau, the terrace, and the lower part of the tower. Earlier, I had judged the square tower to be five yards on a side, but it seemed smaller, perhaps because the chateau and terrace base seemed larger from below. From the middle of the terrace, a wide stone staircase descended to a landing halfway down the wall, and from each end of the landing, staircases circled back to rejoin and descend to the gardens.

A low howl issued from somewhere uphill, and I immediately glanced to the north, my eyes trying to pick out the kennels that held the guard dogs. I thought I could see the grayish tile roof of the kennel building over the garden foliage, but I wasn't completely certain. Another low howl followed. I waited, but there were no more howls, not for the moment.

I returned my attention to the terrace. It appeared empty.

Because I needed to get closer to the chateau and especially to the tower, behind my concealment shields I edged along the stone walkway leading toward the northeast. Some hundred yards farther into the gardens, I stationed myself beside a narrow evergreen, on the downhill side, but where I had an angle to see who was on the terrace or tower, at least near the southern side of each. After slipping the spyglass case out I used the telescope to study the open top of the tower. No one was there.

From what I could see, everyone was inside, and only two guards stood on the terrace.

Had Ryel called off his festival? How could he have, when I'd seen two coaches, obviously belonging to High Holders, headed toward his estates, and seen one of them actually pass through the gates?

Had I been set up as a target? By Iryela? By Veblynt? Or was everyone inside because it was too cold to celebrate in the chill wind? Would that make my plan totally useless?

Slowly, I used the spyglass to survey the deciduous trees that looked to have leaves and were visible from the tower. The tightness in my chest eased slightly when I saw a placard on the third tree I checked, an oak. Then I saw another placard on a maple.

I took a deep breath. Surely, Ryel would at least have to come out on the terrace.

He might have to, but the faint bells of fourth glass chimed from somewhere, and no one had yet appeared outside.

Even in my heavy woolens, and shielded from the wind, I had a hard time keeping from shivering as I waited . . . and waited. Every so often, a low howl issued from the kennels, and the two guards I could see on the edge of the terrace changed their positions.

In time, the five bells from that distant anomen chimed the glass.

Then, without warning, there were four guards on the terrace, and ten appeared on the wide stone staircase, walking down toward the gardens in which I waited. At the base of the stone stairs, they spread out into five pairs, all with drawn pistols, although they also had what appeared to be sabers at their belts. All wore black jackets and trousers with silver piping. One pair looked to be walking directly toward me. As I stepped back closer to the evergreen, a fir of a type unfamiliar to me, I could only hope that my concealment shields would indeed keep me from being discovered.

The two guards passed within several yards, but barely looked in my direction.

". . . never had to check the grounds this much . . . third time today . . ."

". . . you want to question Armsmaster Gwillam?"

". . . nonsense . . . who'd want to get in here? Besides, what could they do down here?"

I scarcely dared to breathe as they passed because while they might not see me, they certainly could hear any sound I might make.

After close to a quint, the guards patrolling the gardens returned to the staircase, but four remained at the base, while four stationed themselves at the landing midway up toward the terrace, and the remaining two joined the four guards who had stayed at the top.

Because I was still a good fifty yards from the base of the tower, I moved slowly across the grass until I reached another vantage point behind a low and bushy fir, only about thirty yards from the southwest corner of the tower and directly below the stone staircase leading down to the gardens.

Finally, I could hear voices. They all sounded as if they were male. Several heads bobbed up and down, moving toward the tower. One figure stopped at the top of the staircase to gaze down in my general direction. I used the spyglass to look at him closely. Although he was resplendent in a green and gold jacket and black trousers, I did not recognize him, except as a likely High Holder and guest of Ryel's.

The voices diminished, and I trusted that was because they were ascending the tower through an internal staircase. Through the spyglass, I began to study the top of the tower. For a time, I saw no one at all.

Finally, Ryel appeared, standing against the crenellated southern wall of the tower. He gestured expansively, pointing toward one of the placarded trees. I eased the telescope farther left, catching sight of a face I did not know, then another.

Where was Dulyk? I kept scanning the tower, but I still could not see the younger Ryel as the other four High Holders clustered around Ryel and gestured in slightly varying directions, presumably toward different trees.

Abruptly Dulyk appeared beside his sire, holding what looked to be a small golden tree of some sort. That meant there were at least six people on the top of the tower, all High Holders.

Did I dare go ahead?

I lowered the telescope. Did I really have any choice? My opportunities were few, my resources fewer, especially if I did not want overt signs pointing back to me and my family. As Master Dichartyn had pointed out, unless there was proof, people could surmise, but they could not act against or through the Collegium, Council, or Civic Patrol.

Based on my experiments with the walls of the old mill, I'd decided against even trying to image out the mortar. That wouldn't collapse the tower, and it would warn people. I needed to do what was necessary quickly—and all at once. Unfortunately, I hadn't practiced my technique extensively, not the way Maitre Dyana would have wished, but how did one really practice destroying entire buildings in a city where one's duty was to protect the people and their dwellings?

As I concentrated on imaging out whole sections of the base of the tower, I focused on drawing energy from everywhere around me, but especially from the gardens and the stream. My mouth was dry, and I was all too conscious of a strange stillness that had descended upon the estate as if time had slowed to a stop, even every sound frozen as if part of a portrait that held not only colors and shapes, but sounds, energies, textures—everything that comprised the world.

Rising into the pale blue sky to the north, seemingly all too close, was the tower. While the tower seemed to shudder, it did not move. I forged more links, some to the stream, some to the trees, others to whatever might take those thin unseen image-wires.

The base of the tower exploded, with huge chunks of stone spinning outward. The sound was so great that there was no sound at all, only a tremendous sense of pressure that enfolded me and my shields. Fragments of stone crashed into my shields.

I could feel myself being hurled backward, then rolling downhill.

Blackness surrounded me . . . but not for all that long. Then I was looking upward, if at an angle from the base of a oak, toward where the tower had been. Dust had settled out of the sky onto a pile of rubble. Absently, I noted that all the damage to the tower and terrace appeared to have been to the south. There were a few gashes on the stonework of the south wing of the chateau, but little more. The terrace walls and the lower section of the stair-case had partly collapsed as well.

My back and legs felt numb, but they seemed to work as I worked my way into a sitting, and then a standing position. As I half expected, my entire skull throbbed, and my vision blurred, with whitish stars flashing before my eyes intermittently.

Suddenly I was chilled to the bone, and my entire body began to shiver. I forced myself to put one foot in front of the other as I started back toward the wall and the western part of the stream where I'd entered the estate.

One step, then another, and a third.

Abruptly hard rain began to fall, except that it wasn't rain, but tiny droplets of frozen water, an ice rain, and I realized that I was still holding the telescope. I fumbled it inside my cloak and inside my waistcoat, not wanting to leave it behind. At that thought I almost laughed.

I'd just imaged a disaster, a certain indication of an imager, and I was worried about leaving a telescope behind?

As I tried to move faster, I began to hear again, and the loudest sound was that of the guard dogs howling, but it wasn't the baying of dogs seeking a quarry. It was a different howl, one almost of fear. I could but hope that they remained in their kennel and fearful for a time longer.

By now the sun had dropped behind the hill to the south, and I could hear cries and voices from the terrace, women's cries mostly. I hurried on-ward, my boots crunching on what seemed to be icy sand, and I realized that I was fully exposed to anyone who looked my way, because I had no shields, and there were no trees and no bushes near me, just a form of icy dust that did not quite swirl under my unsteady boots. From what I could tell, no one had looked my way, or if they had, they hadn't raised an alarm.

As I neared the gap in the walls where the stream left the grounds, I knew I could not reimage the bridge I'd used to enter. I'd just have to take my chances with the stream. I was having enough difficulty walking and could not even raise minimal shields as I staggered down toward the pair of walls flanking the stream. When I got there, I realized I didn't have to worry about a bridge. The stream was frozen solid.

I did have to worry about the ice, though. I slipped and fell twice—hard—before I struggled to my feet outside the wall. Walking uphill toward the mare was hard, but the ground underfoot outside the wall was not icy or slippery.

Even so, it took much of my remaining strength to clamber up into the saddle, and my entire body continued to shake as the mare began to walk back uphill, southward through the twilight toward L'Excelsis. The ride back to NordEste Design was precarious, not because the mare was fractious, but because I could barely manage to stay in the saddle.

How long it took, I didn't know, only that it was late twilight when I turned the mare into the open courtyard gate of NordEste Design. I must have taken half a quint to cover the last fifty yards to the stable. That was the way it felt.

Seliora had appeared from somewhere and was standing beside the mare. She helped me down. Her face seemed to move nearer and then away.

"Done . . ." I managed.

Then darkness, not that of twilight or night, but another kind, dropped over me like instant sunset.

I woke up stretched out in a bed in an unfamiliar chamber. Seliora was sitting beside me, her face pinched in worry. That I could see even though she appeared blurred.

Seliora bent forward. She held a tall glass of amber liquid. "It's lager. I know you like wine better, but Mother says the lager will help you regain your strength sooner."

Weak as I was, I wasn't about to argue as she helped me sit up and I began to drink. Some of the fuzziness in my sight diminished by the time I'd finished the lager, and I didn't feel as though I'd topple over if pushed by the slightest of breezes. I also recognized the chamber. It was the room where I'd changed into exercise clothes when I'd first gone in the wagon to study the Ryel estate.

Seliora tendered something like a sweet cake. "Eat this."

Whatever it was, it also helped within moments, and I began to think I might actually recover.

"I was so worried," she finally said. "It got later and later, and darker and darker."

"It's over." I didn't have anything that Master Dichartyn would have called proof, only a solid inner certainty.

"Can you tell me what happened?" she finally asked.

"I can, and I will, but would you mind if we included your mother and grandmother? I'd rather not go through it twice, and they should know."

Seliora smiled, then leaned forward and kissed my cheek. "Thank you for asking." She studied me. "You have some color. You were shivering and shuddering. You were as pale as ice."

"I felt like ice."

"Can you walk? Grandmama is waiting in the plaques room across the hall. I'll get Mama."

"I'm tired, but I'll be all right."

Still, Seliora stood right beside me as I got up, but I wasn't nearly as unsteady as I'd been on the endless walk from beneath the fallen tower to the mare. She didn't have to summon her mother. Betara was already in the plaques room, quietly talking to Diestra. Both stopped and watched as we entered.

"You're feeling better?" asked Betara.

"He couldn't have felt much worse," Seliora said dryly. "The lager helped a great deal."

The four of us sat around the plaques table. I waited.

"We have been worried," Grandmama Diestra said, absently shuffling the plaques with a dexterity I envied, and that bespoke long familiarity with plaques. "Seliora and Betara should have told you that we . . . arranged for friends to watch your family and Seliora at all times. What they have not told you is that there were three assassins waiting outside the anomen after the services for your brother. They disposed of two, but did not know about the third because he was concealed atop a water tower on a nearby building. They saw him fire, then topple over. When they reached his body, his face was swollen and disfigured. He had a look of horror frozen there." She looked to me. "That was your doing?"

"Yes. I had shields around Seliora, and my father, mother, sister, and brother. When the bullets struck, I tried to image caustic back at the shooter. The shots stopped, but I didn't know whether the shooter had run off or whether I'd been successful."

"Now . . . you know," Diestra said. "Our friends took care of the bodies. That makes some nine in all this week. Since all were bravos for hire, that is likely to make your duties with the Patrol somewhat less risky. Or the duties of some patrollers less dangerous, and the innocents of L'Excelsis subject to less killing."

"How much longer will this go on?" asked Betara.

"It should be over, although there might be a bravo or two who doesn't get the word for a day or so. Ryel, his son, and his nephew are all dead. I brought down his tower around him. Several other High Holders perished as well. I hope none were your clients."

"Even if they were, we'll survive." Betara's voice was sardonic.

"Those who celebrate with the Namer fall with him," added Diestra.

I had to admit that I had little sympathy or remorse for any High Holders who had fawned over Ryel, especially when all knew just how cruel and ruthless he was. Claiming innocence while courting evil was false righteousness.

"The only possible heir is Ryel's daughter," I concluded, "and since there are no males left, that means that we have prevailed, at least, according to tradition."

" 'We'?" asked Diestra.

"I'm an imager, ladies, but I have limits, and without your help, I would not have prevailed. Without Seliora, I would have died the first time I was shot. Without you and your friends, I would have no family at all left." I paused. "We. Not me."

Both Betara and Diestra nodded.

In the silence, I turned to Seliora. "By the way, how did you know I'd need a spyglass?"

"She didn't," replied Grandmama Diestra. "I did. I saw you in the middle of a swirl of ice with a spyglass."

I couldn't help but wonder what else she had seen.

"Did you plan all this?" I asked her. "Did you know from the beginning?"

"Only that you would be the king of stags, so to speak, and meant for the daughter of the moon. Beyond that?" She shook her head. "No. Even the best plaques player does not control how the plaques fall, only how to play them." She paused. "And there is always the chance that others may play better or unpredictably."

King of stags? If I'd thought of myself in terms of plaques, I'd have imagined myself more as the knight of crowns, because knights always served others. That triggered another thought. "It is amusing," I found myself saying quietly, "that both the heirs out of this are women."

No one said anything.

"I'm an imager, and the only thing I can pass on is whatever I've made as an imager. I cannot inherit anything from my parents. Once Seliora and I are married, if she and you will still have me, she can pass anything to our children." I smiled. "But then, isn't the Pharsi tradition to pass everything through the daughters?"

Betara and Diestra exchanged glances, then laughed.

In the end, I didn't remain long, much as I would have preferred to, but my eyes kept closing, and Seliora sent me off in a hack that Bhenyt had hailed for me.

Getting out of my clothes in my own quarters was a chore, and I collapsed into bed.

58

Exhausted as I was, I didn't dream on Samedi night, but on Solayi morning I still had to get up early as duty master. The numbness in my back and legs had passed, replaced by bruises and soreness. I could raise shields, but before long my head began to ache. So I went shieldless to the shower, so to speak, then returned to don another set of warm grays.

After breakfast, eaten early and alone, I made my way to the administrative building where, after telling the duty prime where I'd be, I settled into the conference room off the receiving hall, trying to gather a greater sense of how I should handle the repercussions from Samedi and hoping for a quiet day, while knowing that it was not likely to be so.

The one chilling thing that struck me as I sat there was that I felt no remorse or sadness for the deaths of Ryel, Dulyk, and Alynat. Had I become just like Master Dichartyn? Or was it that they had caused so many—not just me and my family, but countless others—so much loss and pain that any remorse would have been hypocritical? Or was any remorse I might have felt outweighed by my anger at having been forced into a situation where I had been left no choice at all if I and my family wanted to survive? Or was I still numb from all that had happened?

I wasn't certain that I knew. Maybe I never would.

Sometime just after ninth glass, Master Dichartyn peered in. His face was stern. "You'll be here for the next glass?"

"Yes, sir."

"Good." Then he was gone, striding down the corridor.

Less than a quint later, he returned, striding into the conference room, closing the door, and dropping into the chair nearest me.

"You know why I'm here."

"I prefer not to guess, if you don't mind."

"Let me begin another way." He sighed. "Chassendri mentioned to me that you looked absolutely shocked when she suggested that you were unpredictable. Why were you so surprised? It cannot have escaped your attention that we have often had to deal with unforeseen situations involving you."

"I don't see why any of them should have been unforeseen. I don't believe in avoiding problems when they can be resolved. You instructed me that resolution was desirable in ways not calling public attention to the Collegium. That is what I have attempted to do."

Dichartyn shook his head. "Maitre Poincaryt and I, as well as Maitre Schorzat, all understand that facet of your character. What was most unpredictable was not your desire to resolve matters, but the way in which you have repeatedly done so. High Councilor Suyrien sent an urgent messenger requesting that Maitre Poincaryt join him for dinner on Lundi night . . . I imagine you can guess the subject."

"As I said before, sir, I'd rather not. I've had to guess at far too many things recently."

"Then I will tell you. The terrace tower on High Holder Ryel's estate collapsed suddenly yesterday during his annual fall foliage celebration. Besides his son, four other High Holders were killed. Interestingly enough, at about that same time half of Ryel's gardens were destroyed by an unseasonable frost that struck only his estate and no other, and a sudden chill froze the stream beneath the gardens solid. The chill was so intense that it turned all the gardens to dust, and ice droplets rained from a cloudless sky."

"That does seem strange."

"Strange indeed," Dichartyn said dryly. "Might I point out that in less than a year, the single greatest internal threat to the Collegium, in the presence of the late High Holder Ryel's son, has been removed, that the head of the deadliest spy and foreign assassination conspiracy in centuries suffered a fatal fall, that an explosion destroyed all traces of the remaining conspirators, that the two most corrupt officers in the Civic Patrol have been stipended off, that disaster in the South Middle taudis was averted and the Tiemprans responsible apprehended, that the taudischefs who facilitated the Tiempran plot were both brought to hearings and executed, that the feared conscription team was given a warning that has resulted in the reduction in abusive behavior, that the most arrogant, dangerous, and powerful High Holder died in a tower collapse that was totally unforeseen, and that those High Holders most slavish in their support of that High Holder also perished." Dichartyn paused, then added dryly, "It is a rather remarkable set of 'coincidences,' wouldn't you say?"

"Yes, sir."

"Do you honestly think that any right-minded master imager could possibly have predicted all those events, especially the collapse of a stone tower built to last centuries?"

"Sir, you made it absolutely clear on repeated occasions that you neither wished to hear of my personal difficulties with the late High Holder Ryel nor to have the Collegium involved in any fashion. I acceded to those wishes. High Holder Ryel also made it perfectly clear—after instances of arson in my family's factorage, legal actions based on irrefutable but fraudulent records, numerous accidents and damages to equipment, and finally the death of my brother—that no accommodation was possible. Since none was possible, and since it was also made clear to me that any male heir would have to continue Ryel's actions, the only course of action, assuming I wanted to save myself and my family, was to invoke the Nameless on my behalf. Obviously, the Nameless listened, because Ryel's nephew was foolish enough to go racing on the highway with a defective trap, and Ryel and his son were unfortunate enough to stand on a tower hit by lightning or some such." I shrugged. "Sometimes, fortune does favor those who are less powerful and wronged by the arrogantly powerful."

Master Dichartyn laughed. "Your explanation is better than many I've heard, and publicly, the less said the better. I have absolutely no doubt that the other High Holders will become remarkably less strident in the days ahead. Maitre Poincaryt has stated that he will point out to the High Councilor that Ryel's actions were excessive, and resulted in excessive repayment. You should be hearing what results from that repayment in time. However, right now, we need to walk down the hall and meet with Maitre Poincaryt."

I rose, trying not to show my stiffness and soreness, and walked to the staircase with Master Dichartyn and then up and to the southwest corner and straight into the maitre's private study.

Maitre Poincaryt was wearing grays that were frayed and stained in places, doubtless those he wore around wherever he lived when he did not expect visitors. He offered a wry smile and gestured to the chairs across the desk from him.

We seated ourselves, and I waited.

"You realize, Master Rhennthyl, that neither Dichartyn nor I would prefer to be here on a Solayi."

"I can understand that, sir. I'd prefer not to be here." And that was absolutely true.

"You will come to understand that even more in years to come, provided you survive the current year. Some more unrealistic and impractical than I might suggest that you be put on trial. That will not occur."

I was half relieved to know that I wasn't about to be hauled up before the Collegium on charges . . . or not on serious ones.

"Nonetheless, you will be punished in another and more lasting fashion, as are all imagers who must work outside the formal structures of the Collegium and the Council." Master Poincaryt smiled wanly.

I waited, not knowing what was to come.

"There is always a price, Rhennthyl. Always. Those who do not understand Solidar and the Collegium have no idea. From this day forward, you will never be able to leave Imagisle without carrying the heaviest possible shields. Even if you choose to marry, you will always sleep alone and wake alone in a lead-lined room, because your power is so great that a nightmare could kill all those you love. Everyone, save a handful who know you well, will shy away from you. So, in time, will your children. If you have any perception at all, you will have to weigh every request, every word that is addressed to you. If you do not, you will come to regret any such lapses more and more with each passing day."

I swallowed. Some of that I had considered, but not the totality.

"Now, in regard to High Holder Ryel, unlike Dichartyn, I will not be indirect. Only a powerful master imager could have accomplished what happened at Ryel's estates yesterday. Since I did not do it, nor did Dichartyn, you had to be the one. Given the situation facing you, and the strictures we placed on you, you had no choice but to confront Ryel. I would have preferred a more . . . indirect method, but you did not involve the Collegium, nor is there anything remotely resembling proof. In fact, there's Namer-little of anything left within an arc of three hundred yards south of the tower ruins. When I meet with High Councilor Suyrien, I will make certain that he understands the dangers involved in placing any imager in a situation where his family is threatened and he has nothing to lose. I will also point out that, at the moment, High Holders are held in even lower esteem than the Collegium, in part due to your efforts in dealing with the South Middle taudis. This has created other problems, which I will address in a moment." He smiled ruefully before continuing.

"There is also the matter of the four other High Holders who perished in the frost-storm. Their families will doubtless grieve, at least in public, but I will suggest that the Nameless repaid them in kind for consorting with a High Holder who was so ruthless that he could not foresee the inevitable consequences of seeking absolute power over anyone and anything that displeased him. Even High Councilor Suyrien will find that an appropriate message, and he will convey it to all High Holders . . . for his own reasons."

The absolute certainty held in Maitre Poincaryt's words was far more chilling than any reprimand could have been. He was telling me what would happen and how the Council would handle it—and that there would be no questions whatsoever. What was more chilling than that was the total lack of surprise in and behind his words.

"That brings us to your future. Commander Artois has made a request of the Collegium." Master Poincaryt looked to Master Dichartyn and then to me.

That scarcely surprised me. If I hadn't made every senior Patrol officer wary or unhappy, I'd doubtless come close, and I didn't want to think how the Navy and naval marines felt.

Master Poincaryt offered a smile that looked ironic, but I wasn't at all certain. "His letter and his subsequent conversation with me have left no doubt that certain aspects of the . . . situation with the South Middle taudis were not precisely to his liking. This has left him in a position where he feels, with some justification, I might agree, that the Collegium is obligated to assist him in resolving the situation. And since you were instrumental in creating this situation, Master Rhennthyl, it only seems fitting that you be part of the resolution."

"Exactly how, sir? I can't imagine that the commander would ever wish to see me again." Except at my early funeral.

"I would agree. He does not wish to see you again, and certainly not soon. That is not the question. All of us with responsibility and power have to deal with situations and people we would rather not, and it is true that the commander does not particularly like you. It is equally true that he respects your abilities and your courage. More important than that is the fact that the majority of the taudischefs also respect you. Add to that the fact that they do not respect any other senior Patrol officer, and you can see the difficulty facing Commander Artois. Then there is the fact that Captain Harraf has requested that he be granted a full retirement stipend immediately. His wife has suffered ill health, and retiring on a stipend would allow them to move to Extela, which would benefit her health greatly. Given your actions, he may well feel that it will benefit his as well."

Why would Captain Harraf do that? Was it my statement on the day of the Temple explosion about not always being able to protect him, and the implication that such lack of protection might be fatal?

"Rather unusually, but fittingly, he has indicated privately that Third District station might benefit from a new captain and perhaps one less traditional. We have consulted with the Council . . . so that there would be no misunderstanding, and the councilors were virtually unanimous in approving the solution reached by the Patrol and the Collegium."

I waited for the ax to fall, or the gallows trap to spring.

"Effective immediately, you are now a Civic Patrol captain. You will take over command of Third District exactly one week from tomorrow. You are not to appear anywhere in Civic Patrol buildings until then. That will allow for an orderly transition. The term of appointment is for three years, renewable twice, if necessary. Oh . . . and in recognition of your considerable skills as an imager, you are also advanced to Maitre D'Structure. You will be paid by the Collegium, and of course, as a Maitre D'Structure, you are entitled to one of the larger family quarters at the north end of the isle, should you ever require such. I do suspect, given your . . . informal arrangements, that you will be needing it in the near future." He stopped and looked at me.

I just sat there for a moment. "Surely . . . I don't have enough experience . . ."

"You—and the family of your young lady friend—can certainly discover some trustworthy and experienced first patrollers and lieutenants and request them to assist you. I suspect some would even wish to do so. You have, like it or not, one quality that no one else in the Patrol can offer—a reputation for honesty and strength in dealing with the taudis-dwellers and taudischefs."

Master Dichartyn was smiling, but the expression was sad and sympathetic before he added, "In addition, this will provide you with another form of valuable experience, Rhennthyl. This time, you will have to find the means to clean up the mess and consternation that you have created. Even with the aegis of the Collegium behind you, you will run into the problems of being short of patrollers or supplies, of having corrupt patrollers, and there will always be those, and you won't be able to remove very many through 'accidents' or the entire district will fall apart under you." Dichartyn's smile turned almost gleeful. "I'm very much looking forward to watching how you handle this. Oh, and while you can occasionally skip the morning runs and exercises, it is strongly recommended that you keep such absences to a minimum."

"Yes, sir."

I already had some ideas about how to improve matters with the Civic Patrol, but now . . . ?

"If you're thinking about a wedding . . . you only get a week's leave, but you can take it whenever you want. I did insist on that. I know enough about women, families, and Pharsi traditions to understand it's a rather significant event, involving more than merely running the most demanding Patrol district in L'Excelsis."

"I will have to wait to make that public and formal, sir. Until High Holder Ryel's heir has been determined."

"Given the exigencies of the situation facing others, Rhennthyl, you may not have to wait that long at all. You have forced many hands in ways few foresaw." Maitre Poincaryt took a deep breath, then stood. "Now . . . if you don't mind, I'd like to spend some time with my granddaughter, and I'm certain Dichartyn has better things to do with what is left of his day off."

"Yes, sir."

In less than half a quint, I was back in the conference room, trying to puzzle out what lay behind what had just occurred. I still had a long and, hopefully, boring day as duty master.

59

After the remainder of Solayi that was indeed quietly and comfortingly long and boring, I had managed to determine, at least in my mind, much of what must have occurred, although it would likely be weeks before the events that would confirm, or disprove, what I thought I had worked out. I was still exhausted when I finally went to bed, and my sleep was thankfully dreamless.

For all that, when I woke, my thoughts were of Rousel. Matters seemed to be working out for me—or I had managed to work them out. Yet in a way, Rousel had been the one to pay for them. Because of his death, so had my parents, and Khethila, and even Culthyn. I'd always feel that loss . . . and the lesson that came with it, one that Dichartyn had hammered at me from the beginning, but which I hadn't felt. Everyone around a powerful imager paid when the imager failed to see or to anticipate what he should have. The costs fell, I was beginning to see, most heavily on those closest and those who could not protect themselves. That was why there were security and covert imagers, not so much to resolve problems, but to stop them before they became too large and the consequences too great.

Inadvertently, I had just provided an object lesson to High Holders, one that I had no doubts Maitre Poincaryt would ensure that they understood. Yet, few except High Holders would ever know of that lesson, and that was because of something else that had become apparent to me, but well understood by Maitre Poincaryt and Maitre Dichartyn. Given human nature, every large catastrophe or event with adverse consequences that could be attributed to someone or some human creation would be, and that attribution would provoke a reaction, and the reaction would provoke yet another. Sometimes, if rarely, public attribution was salutary. Sometimes it was necessary. Usually, it just led to demands for action and revenge, which led to more demands and actions.

I noted those thoughts as I dressed to head out for exercise and running. The cold shower didn't feel all that bad when I returned, and I was feeling less depressed after I dressed and walked across the quadrangle to the dining hall.

"Rhenn, how was your weekend?" asked Ferlyn as I settled down to eat.

"Long. I was duty master yesterday. Oh, I did finish the portrait of Master

Rholyn, and it's being framed. I don't know where Maitre Poincaryt will hang it, though."

"How do you think things will go with the Civic Patrol after that Temple explosion?"

"I imagine they'll settle down. Most people just want to get on with their lives." I helped myself to two of the fried flatcakes and dowsed them with berry syrup.

"What will they do with you?"

"Whatever Maitre Poincaryt and the Civic Patrol decide, they'll let me know in a few days. It just could be that they'll want me to stay with the Patrol and be more circumspect. We'll have to see."

"You don't seem that worried."

"It won't do any good. Not now." I laughed. "I should have worried when Master Dichartyn asked if I wanted to be a covert imager."

From beside Ferlyn, Maitre Dyana offered a slight nod and a smile.

After breakfast, given all that had happened, I did use a duty coach to take me out to NordEste Design for one last important action, something that I felt had been assumed, but never formalized, and in some matters, formality was absolutely necessary. So I stood outside the private door at just past seventh glass. I clearly wasn't expected, because I had to bang the brass knocker several times.

Finally, the door eased open, and Seliora stood there. She looked less than pleased, although some of the irritation faded as she recognized me. "Rhenn! What are you doing here? Aren't you working?"

"You might say that my duties have been temporarily suspended. A few more things have happened, and we do need to talk." I tried to keep my face formal.

"How bad . . ." She stopped. "It can't be that bad if you're here."

"That depends on how one defines 'bad.' Might I come in?"

"Oh . . . yes." She paused, then stepped back. "This is a working day, you know?"

"I know. That's why I'm here early." I stepped into the foyer, closing the door and turning to her.

"What is it?"

I thought I caught a trace of humor behind the question, but I wasn't quite certain. "To begin with, Madame D'Rhennthyl-to-be, assuming you agree, you see before you a Civic Patrol captain and Maitre D'Structure."

For a moment, Seliora looked absolutely stunned. "A Patrol captain and a Maitre D'Structure?"

"Apparently, I've made it impossible for anyone else to be Patrol captain in Third District, and my imager abilities merit an advancement, and that advancement entitles me—if I am married—to one of the larger quarters for families on Imagisle."

She still kept looking at me.

"So I would like to ask you, and your parents, formally, for your hand. I haven't actually done that." I paused. "We can't announce it to anyone else until Ryel's successor is confirmed, but I've been told that will occur within the next month or two. That will allow quiet planning for a suitable and proper Pharsi wedding."

At that, her arms did go around me.

This time, we held on to each other for a very long time.

EPILOGUE

In the fading twilight, I glanced out the coach window at the snow and ice alongside the road. It was cold enough and the paving stones clear enough that the hoofs of the two chestnuts were throwing little or no mud against the polished body of the coach. Mother had insisted that Charlsyn drive us, and that the coach be spotless, winter or no winter.

My eyes went to the hand-calligraphed invitation I held again. Seliora looked over at it from where she sat beside me, attired in another formal outfit of shimmering black and red, and I turned it for her to see, not that we both hadn't perused it more than a few times.

YOUR PRESENCE IS REQUESTED
AT THE WEDDING OF
IRYELA D'ALTE
AND RYEL [KANDRYL D'SUYRIEN-ALTE] D'ALTE
RYEL ESTATE, L'EXCELSIS,
THE TWENTY-FIRST OF IANUS
AT HALF PAST SIXTH GLASS.

"I still say that's a rather odd way of describing her husband-to-be," said Seliora.

"It's the only possible way. She cannot keep the holding without marrying another High Holder, and whoever she weds must take the holding name."

"So he can't be Suyrien's heir?"

"He could be, if he were the oldest, but he's the younger son. But it does resolve any inheritance problems for the High Councilor. In fact, his younger son may end up with more than his own heir—and sooner."

"Rhenn . . . was this all Ryel's doing?"

I shook my head. "No. Much of it was Iryela's. She played her father, her brothers, and me in order to gain the freedom and power she felt she should have had through her abilities. I wouldn't be surprised if she wasn't looking for a possible tool when she asked me to dance with her back at the Harvest Ball."

For a long moment, there was silence. Finally, she looked into my eyes. "How long have you known?"

"I had wondered, but when the invitation arrived, I knew."

Seliora waited for me to explain.

"At the Autumn Ball, she had just danced with Kandryl when I asked her to dance. She revealed more than she should have about Ryel's, Dulyk's, and Alynat's activities, but that could have been resentment and knowing that I was someone who could never really tell anyone in a way that could hurt her—except what she said about Kandryl. She said that he was very sweet and had a very redeeming quality. I asked her if that quality was being willing to accede to her wishes and desires, and she replied by saying that he was sweet."

"She plotted it all out, then, possibly even pushing her father to seek revenge on you for blinding Johanyr and knowing that you would destroy Alynat, Ryel, and Dulyk."

"I doubt she had to push her father too much." Not with the arrogance I'd seen in Ryel.

"And you . . . how can you? After everything?" Seliora shook her head, even her whole body. "I cannot imagine . . ."

"I disagree. You can imagine. She is smarter, more beautiful, more talented, and, despite her horrible plotting, more evenhanded than any of the men in the family. I met them all, if in passing in some instances, and not a one of them had a single redeeming quality. She did not wish to be married off and minimalized . . . or suffer a fatal accident if she could not be married off. Exactly what were her options, given her position?"

"And we're going to her wedding? You're going to her wedding?"

"What are our options if we wish to end the game?" And it had been a game, a deadly game. I could have claimed I'd been a player, but I'd been played, as had Master Dichartyn and the Collegium. The only two real players had been Grandmama Diestra and Iryela, and in a sense, both had won, although Iryela had lost far, far more than she realized. I had the feeling that Maitre Poincaryt might have understood some of it, at the end. He had certainly taken the opportunity to play me against the High Holders.

Seliora nodded, as I knew she would. "I can't say that I like it."

"Nor do I, but we don't deal the plaques. At best, we can but play what we have."

Charlsyn slowed the coach, then guided it through the massive ironwork gates, calling out, "Master Imager Rennthyl and Mistress Seliora D'Shelim."

He eased the coach up the well-swept stones of the driveway and under the portico. There, a footman in black and silver stepped forward to open the coach door and to extend a hand to Seliora.

When I stepped out in my black formal wear with poison testing strips inside my jacket and joined Seliora, I saw a black and silver coach stationed on the far side of the circle. At that moment, I recalled where I had seen that coach before—when I had first come to Imagisle and had watched an imager met coolly by a blond beauty. That had been Iryela meeting Johanyr, and now I understood the coolness I had seen.

We had taken but three or four steps into the entry when an older man, wearing a black velvet jacket with silver piping over a silver shirt and black trousers, stepped forward, inclining his head deeply. "Master Rhennthyl, Mistress Seliora, if you please, Mistress Iryela would like a word with you both before the ceremony."

We nodded, and followed him down a side corridor. I did continue to maintain full shields over both of us. Nothing was settled until it was settled.

He stopped at the door at the end of the side corridor. "Master Rhennthyl and Mistress Seliora."

"Have them enter."

The functionary opened the door and gestured for us to go in.

The chamber was a sitting room, decorated in pale blues and silvers. Iryela turned from where she stood before a full-length mirror. She wore a silver gown, but one trimmed at the hem in thin lines of blue and green, and her bride's vest was a silvered green.

For a moment, I was most conscious of standing between two beauties—one dark and one fair—and both dangerous, if in differing ways.

Iryela stepped forward, and then inclined her head first, a complete breach of High Holder etiquette. "Master Rhennthyl, I am pleased that you are here, and I trust that your acceptance of the invitation signifies what I hope will be a long and close relationship between our families. I would not wish ever for my family to incur your displeasure."

I inclined my head to her, then looked directly into the hard depths of those blue eyes. "My lady Ryel—and you merit that honor on your own, regardless of custom—we will treasure that friendship, and I would that it had not cost all so very dearly. Even so, or especially so, you have my greatest respect, as well as my friendship."

Her smile was unforced, yet gentle, so much like the sun struggling from behind clouds after a spring shower. Even so, I sensed the cold steel behind that unfamiliar warmth. "You have acted with restraint and honor, and you are always welcome." There was the faintest emphasis to the word "always."

Iryela's eyes turned to Seliora. "You also played a part in this, I know, equally honorable, and you and your family also have my respect, and I would wish you for a friend and a sister."

The last words did surprise me, yet they did not seem to surprise Seliora.

Seliora returned the smile. "I would be honored to be either, or both, as you wish."

"I would like both . . . very, very much." Her smile actually appeared nervous. "Thank you both so much for being here."

"We're pleased to be here."

"Fahyl will escort you to your place in the family anomen."

Seliora and I both inclined our heads, then turned and left.

Back in the corridor, Fahyl bowed again, then said, "If you would . . ."

We followed him to the family anomen—at the end of the north wing of the chateau on the main level—a space larger than some public ones used by worshippers of the Nameless. While the anomen was without ornamentation, as were they all, the stonework of the walls was precise and perfect, and the joins in the polished floor tiles were nearly indistinguishable.

Fahyl led us to the front of the anomen, just a few yards back from the low stone dais, and had us stand on the left side, exactly in line with High Councilor Suyrien and his wife, who stood on the right. "Once the ceremony is over," Fahyl said, "the guests leave in order and process to the grand salon, where they are announced. You will be the last to leave, and the last to be introduced in the grand salon, before the bride and groom."

I didn't say anything, nor did Seliora, but I was more than a little surprised. Iryela was definitely making a statement, not only to me, but to every High Holder present.

As we stood there, waiting, Seliora murmured, "She has no one to trust, does she?"

"Not now, certainly among the High Holders, and possibly not ever." I paused. "Except us."

"She's not quite like I thought," Seliora said in a low voice.

"No," I replied gently. In many ways, Seliora and Iryela were indeed alike, but there was no need to say that, none at all.

We stood in the stillness of the anomen, while others filed in behind us, and I held full shields. In time, the organ at the back of the anomen shifted from the quiet background to what sounded more like a cross between a waltz and a march, and a pair of viols joined in.

Kandryl appeared first, accompanied by his brother, but while Kandryl wore the black and silver of Ryel, with a green vest of the same silvered sheen as Iryela's, his brother wore the crimson and silver of Suyrien. They stopped short of the low dais where the silver-haired chorister in his green vestments waited behind the arched canopy of flowers. In Ianus, the fresh flowers were a statement of wealth and power.

Then came Iryela, unaccompanied. She stepped up beside Kandryl.

The chorister smiled at the couple, then began to speak. "We are gathered here today in celebration of the decision of a man and a woman to join their lives as one. The name of a union between a man and a woman is not important, nor should anyone claim such, for the name should never overshadow the union itself. Iryela and Kandryl have chosen each other as partners in life and in love, and we are here to witness the affirmation of that choice. . . ."

From there the ceremony went exactly as any other I'd witnessed, down to the final charge.

"From two have come one, and yet that unity shall enable each of you to live more joyfully, more fully, and more in harmony with that which was, is, and ever shall be."

The chorister stepped back, and Iryela and Kandryl exchanged a chaste kiss under the flowered canopy, before turning and facing those in the anomen. From Kandryl's side, a small girl, possibly the daughter of his brother, stepped forward and handed the small green basket of flower petals to Kandryl, who held it while Iryela scooped out a handful and cast them forward and skyward. Then she took the basket, and he scattered his handful.

They both smiled and walked, arm in arm, from the anomen.

As instructed, we were the last to leave, just behind High Councilor Suyrien and Madame D'Suyrien, and we followed them at a stately pace, along the main corridor of the north wing and back along the main corridor of the south wing, until we came to a halt a good ten yards from a set of double doors that presumably opened into the grand salon.

Ten other couples stood before us, and I could hear each set of guests being announced.

Finally, after the High Councilor, we stepped up to the archway.

Fahyl cleared his throat and then announced, "Rhennthyl D'Imagisle, Maitre D'Structure and captain of the Civic Patrol, and Mistress Seliora D'Shelim."

A footman escorted us into the long chamber with the high vaulted ceiling, and I could sense more than a few eyes turning in our direction as we entered the grand salon, filled with close to twenty circular tables, each seating six.

According to protocol, we should have been at one of the tables far from the bride's table. We weren't. We were seated at her table, across from High

Town of Georgina (KESWICK) Public Library

Councilor Suyrien and his wife, and the empty two places showed that I was seated immediately to Iryela's left.

None of Iryela's family was present, although her mother and the half-blind Johanyr were the only survivors of her immediate family. Their absence, and that of any other relations, underscored just how much Iryela's determination had cost her. Yet I recalled, too, the morning I had been required to execute the wife of a High Holder because she had been unable to escape and had murdered her abusive husband, and I could understand how far desperation could take one. Understand . . . and accept. In time, I might forgive.

As soon as we were seated, Councilor Suyrien smiled, pleasantly, almost warmly. "Master Rhennthyl, a pleasure to see you here . . . and you, too, Mistress Seliora. I must say that you two made a powerful and impressive entrance . . . and I'm sure we'll be seeing more of you both, as I know Kandryl—he may be Ryel now, but to us, he'll always be Kandryl—and Iryela will be."

Fahyl's voice silenced the murmurs. "Iryela D'Ryel and Ryel D'Alte."

Everyone watched, but there was not a single sound as the couple moved sedately toward the table. After they were seated, Iryela turned, looked directly at Seliora, and smiled, an expression just slightly tentative, yet warm.

I smiled politely at Kandryl, and he nodded politely in return.

Seliora reached out under the table and squeezed my hand, and that warmth reaffirmed what lay ahead for us.

When I had first crossed the Bridge of Hopes, I had thought that my life could not have gotten much more complicated. How little I had known, and how much I still had to learn. Life was far more complex than a game of plaques, yet in life, as in plaques, there were those who played and who were played. I had learned something from it all, though, that in the game of life, you had to know when you were the player and when you were the plaque, because each role demanded a different response, and anyone who thought he or she would always be the player was a fool.